T0150675

AWAKENING OF SPIES

Also by Brian Landers

Empires Apart: The Story of the American and Russian Empires

The Dylan Series:

Families of Spies

AWAKENING OF SPIES

BRIAN LANDERS

Red Door

Published by RedDoor

www.reddoorpress.co.uk

© 2020 Brian Landers

The right of Brian Landers to be identified as the author of this Work
has been asserted by him in accordance with sections 77 and 78 of the
Copyright, Designs and Patents Act 1988.

ISBN 978-1-913062-33-0

All rights reserved. No part of this publication may be reproduced, stored
in a retrieval system, copied in any form or by any means, electronic,
mechanical, photocopying, recording or otherwise transmitted without
written permission from the author.

This is a work of fiction. Names, characters, businesses, places, events and
incidents are either the products of the author's imagination or used in a
fictitious manner. Any resemblance to actual persons, living or dead, or
actual events is purely coincidental.

A CIP catalogue record for this book is available from the British Library.

Cover design: Rawshock Design

Typesetting: Tutis Innovative E-Solutions Pte Ltd

Printed and bound in Denmark by Nørhaven

Sir Harold Maguire, Director-General of Intelligence,
Ministry of Defence, 1968-72

PROLOGUE

Buenos Aires, 1973

The Englishman couldn't understand why the Swedes had sent Kirsten here in the first place. He was never at the Embassy and when you did get hold of him he did nothing but complain. The maid had stolen a few pesos. The phones never work. The drivers are all mad. And Kirsten had never heard of Hector Bunge, so inviting him to lunch had been a complete waste of time.

Then at that moment everything seemed a waste of time. Another month to waste before going home. He'd fly directly home, the Englishman decided. It was nice of Pedro to suggest stopping in Rio, but he wanted to get away from it all. A couple of days debriefing in London, perhaps a little dinner party. A few kind words from the Director General and then out. A cottage in Suffolk.

Strange that a year ago he had been planning to retire here. No, he corrected himself, 'we' had been planning. A house in Cordoba, near Martha's brother.

It was Martha's family, he realised, that had tied him here. Nothing more. Argentina had changed too much to have any other attractions. Without Martha the Hurlingham Club and the Royal British Legion had lost their appeal. The English community was dying. The young spoke Spanish. The old lived in a private, Victorian world slowly fading away. The Deaths column in the *Buenos Aires Herald* always seemed to be longer and to contain more British names than the Births or Marriages. He didn't want to see his own name there, Andrew Howard Williams.

The old retirement plans seemed totally unreal, they belonged to someone else. Was it really just a year ago that Martha's doctor had pronounced, 'Cancer'?

'Woman of her age,' Lawley had said, 'I'd say a year, eighteen months. Might even be sooner.'

And it was sooner. Three weeks after they'd returned home from the West Indies.

'Perhaps it's for the best,' Lawley consoled him, in a tone halfway between doctor and old friend. 'Better than lying in hospital wasting away. And she had that holiday, she went happily.'

That at least was true. When the assignment came up it seemed a golden opportunity. Just a routine observation job.

'Can I bring my wife?' he'd asked.

And back had come the telex, from the DG himself, 'Of course.'

The mission had not been a success but Martha had been able to have her last drop of Caribbean sun.

He turned into Calle Florida: a small, bowed man pushing through the crowds.

The electric sign above the Banco de la Ciudad de Buenos Aires stopped showing the time, 15.02, and flashed the temperature, 20°C. Warm. Officially the first day of spring was 21 September but it felt like spring already.

The crowds made it seem hotter. Brazilians, he thought disparagingly, as a group of tourists pushed past. They reminded him of the trip home. Perhaps he should stop in Rio and see Pedro, brief him on the situation here. The sheer stupidity of it all! When he'd arrived in Argentina, after the war, Naval Intelligence alone had two people here in the capital and another in Bahia Blanca, although he'd never understood that. Since then there had been cut after cut culminating nine years ago when the Defence Intelligence Staff had been created bringing Military, Naval and RAF Intelligence together. Suddenly he was supposed to become an expert on tanks and jet planes and to look after not only the whole of Argentina, but Uruguay and Paraguay as well.

And when he left? Nobody would replace him. That really showed what London thought of his job. The day would come when the whole of Latin America would be the responsibility of some Whitehall tea-boy. So very stupid. Perón was sure to win the election in a month's time and then anything could happen.

He had told London how close the military junta had come to doing something reckless in the Falklands but they never believed him. He was, after all, just an old sailor, not a real spy. The real spies were the smooth public-school boys in Six with their double agents and triple crosses. They had the 'tradecraft'. More importantly they had the ears of the policymakers back home and their view was that the return of civilian rule meant an end to any worries about the generals. But one day the military would be back. Perón could not last, he was old and frail. Just like me, Williams thought.

The shop opposite the Richmond belched out a syrupy male voice singing in English. As always, he imagined it was his namesake.

He wondered what this Bunge person would look like.

'I'll recognise you,' the Swede had said.

It had been a strange phone call, but then the whole business was a bit odd. It began with London asking him to look into rumours that the Argentine Air Force was considering replacing their French Mirage fighters with the new Swedish Saab Viggen. He could have told Watkins, who had sent the request, that the idea was nonsense. Instead he had dutifully started asking questions here and there, when, out of the blue, Bunge phoned.

A voice speaking English but with a peculiar accent, northern European probably. He had a funny way of pronouncing Calle Florida. The intonation had been just right, very Spanish, but the double 'l' was wrong: neither the 'j' of Argentina nor the 'ly' of Spain, nearer the hard 'l' of Portuguese.

'My name is Hector Bunge,' he had started. 'I am a Swedish national and have information that may be of some value to you concerning the procurement plans of the Argentine Air Force.'

His voice sounded flat, as if he was reading a prepared text, an impression strengthened by his choice of words. Did anybody really call themselves a 'Swedish national' or talk about things being 'of some value' in everyday conversation?

'I will meet you,' he continued, 'at the Richmond tea bar in Calle Florida tomorrow at three o'clock. I will recognise you.'

And that was it. Very peculiar… Why give his name and nationality? And why such a public meeting place? It was probably a wild goose chase but it had to be investigated.

'That's what I am here for,' he thought as the glass door closed behind him, 'chasing wild geese.'

A blond-haired, heavily built man in his late forties waved invitingly from a chair near the door. The Englishman sat opposite Bunge, sinking into the red simulated leather chair.

'Tea with milk,' Bunge said, more as a statement than a question. His face creased in a smile that seemed forced.

The Englishman nodded. He always drank tea with milk, clever of him to guess.

'Anything to eat?'

'No, thank you.'

An ageing waiter brought the pot of tea and the milk, placing them on the low table beside Bunge's black coffee and half-eaten toasted ham and cheese sandwich.

Bunge poured out the tea as he spoke. 'I have some information for you. It's something I believe you require.'

'How did you know that?'

Bunge paused as if trying to remember a line from a script.

'That is unimportant I think. You have been asking questions. I heard about them. That is all. What we must do now is decide how much this information is worth.'

The other said nothing, slowly sipping his tea.

'I have the details here,' continued Bunge, taking two folded sheets of paper from his pocket.

The Englishman nodded. He could see nothing but a bundle of typing as Bunge opened the papers. He tried to focus but couldn't. 'Upside down,' he thought. He moved his gaze to the paper serviette. The blue stylised lion seemed to move. Bunge started talking. His thin lips opened and closed but his face was going red, his nose ballooning and merging with the red of the chairs. An image of a red lollipop appeared, the sort the Englishman had bought in his childhood.

'Martha,' he whispered, 'Martha.'

Bunge watched him closely and then rose.

Nobody looked at him, or at his tubby little friend still seated at the table, eyes now closed. No eyes followed his exit or his swift, strangely arrogant, strides along Florida to the corner of Avenida Corrientes. No ears but the taxi driver heard him ask for the international airport at Ezeiza. And no post-mortem was held so nobody knew that there was poison in the body or in the milk left standing on the table beside the half-eaten toasted sandwich.

I

The first time somebody tried to kill me was in Holland in 1974. It seems such a very long time ago.

I had only been with the Defence Intelligence Staff for a few months and still wasn't sure I had made the right career choice. I didn't see myself as a lifelong Ministry of Defence civil servant.

Joining the DIS had not been the result of any well-thought-out-plan. My tutor at Durham had taken me aside and asked if I would be interested in a role serving my country. There was someone in London, he said, who was looking for linguists. I duly arrived at an anonymous office in Carlton Terrace to take tea with a smartly dressed man who introduced himself simply as Mr Smith. We did not warm to each other.

This was just a preliminary chat, he told me, to see what sort of chap I was.

I suspect he had determined that the moment he heard my accent and confirmed it when I had the temerity to suggest that the Prime Minister, Harold Wilson, was unlikely to be a Communist. I was not the easiest person to like in those days, cocky was probably the most charitable description.

'Why,' he asked, 'did you as a Cornishman decide to go to Durham University at the other end of the country?'

My reply was simple, 'St Andrews didn't accept me.'

Mr Smith clearly did not consider that as clever a response as I did, and looking back on it now he was right.

'Frankly, Mr Dylan,' he concluded after half an hour of small talk, 'now that Heath has taken us into the Common Market people seem to think we should all be learning foreign languages. But the truth is everyone in Europe speaks English. Now if you had

Russian or Arabic that might be useful but languages like Italian and Portuguese, not really. But I do have an idea. You joined the Officers' Training Corps at Durham. That's very good. If I may I will pass your details to a colleague.'

As I later discovered, what Smith meant was that I wasn't good enough for the Secret Intelligence Service, more popularly known as MI6, but somebody else in Whitehall might have lower expectations.

I didn't tell him that I had joined the OTC largely to annoy my father. As it turned out, I discovered I had what was probably an unhealthy interest in guns and shooting and had half seriously considered a career in the Army. I was therefore intrigued when two days later I received a phone call offering me a first-class train ticket down to London, a night at a rather nice hotel and a nine o'clock appointment at the Ministry of Defence. There, after a whole day of interviews and tests, I was ushered into the office of the DG, the Director General of Defence Intelligence, a peer of the realm with considerably more of the common touch than Mr Smith.

Well over an hour of meandering conversation followed, ranging from the political situation in what was then called Rhodesia to a book the DG told me his niece had just made him read, Germaine Greer's *The Female Eunuch*. Then, without warning, the DG decided the conversation was over. He had made up his mind.

'We need an analyst,' he announced. 'A linguist with an independent mind. The job is desk-bound and the pay is miserable but it's important and it's yours if you want it.'

I had decided before coming down to London that if I was offered a job I would take time to think it through and then probably decline. I still don't know why I accepted immediately.

Intelligence in those days was still recognisable to anyone brought up on films about wartime spies. Cipher pads and secret messages in newspapers remained part of my very brief induction. I soon discovered that I wouldn't be needing them. In the secret world of British Intelligence the DIS in which I had enrolled was second division. All the exciting work abroad was done by MI6, attached to the Foreign Office, and at home by MI5, attached to the Home Office. DIS was the poor relation, our job was to analyse what others collected. Six and Five, as we referred to them, were independent services with their own traditions and peculiarities, only loosely linked to their sponsoring departments. The DIS on the other hand was an integral part of the Whitehall and military establishment which is why our official title was Defence Intelligence Staff not Defence Intelligence Service.

The oddest part of my induction was a day listed as 'An Introduction to the Security Landscape'. Along with a dozen others I arrived at the Home Office in King Charles Street for what I had been warned was to be a 'First Names Only' event. We had also been warned not to discuss the organisations we worked for, which made introductory conversations difficult.

During the day various speakers described the activities of their part of the Intelligence 'landscape' in terms so vague that a journalist managing to sneak in would have learned nothing new. My own boss, who arrived in RAF uniform, made the role of the DIS seem so fundamentally important that I caught the GCHQ representative behind him shaking his head in disbelief.

Most of the participants were recent graduates like me, predominantly male, and on their best behaviour. Over lunch we amused each other with tales of the irrelevant trivia unearthed during the prolonged positive vetting we had all gone through. I tried to guess where the others were working. One slightly older man with a broad Midlands accent made that easy by showing me a photo of his new baby and inadvertently revealing a pass marked Atomic Energy Authority Constabulary. I knew I was the only one there from the DIS.

I suspected most of those attending were from MI5 or MI6. They laughed knowingly at anecdotes about their secret lives: the message left in a dead-letter drop in Regent's Park only to be eaten by a fox, the officer bumping into his next-door neighbour while staking out a 'house of ill repute' in Paddington, the implausible cover stories used by colleagues to hide their true occupations from inquisitive relations. The organisers of the day clearly wanted us to come away proud to be members of a secret and exclusive club. I'm not sure that worked for me. I had not been invited to join a club whose members had to pretend to be something they were not. I could happily tell friends quite truthfully that I was a civil servant at the Ministry of Defence. The world of spies and spying was enticing but I wasn't truly part of it – yet.

The Defence Intelligence Staff in those days was an organisation where inter-service rivalries were still strong, civilians like me were tolerated rather than accepted and rank was all-important. Ministry of Defence civil servants and military officers were rotated through the DIS as part of their progression to jobs elsewhere. Very few dedicated their careers to Intelligence.

The Director General who had offered me the job was an admiral in his last post before retirement. I liked him very much but never really understood what he actually did. Below him were the four men, known as the 4Ds, who effectively ran the place.

Adam Joseff was the DDG, Deputy Director General. Joseff had been invalided out of the Army minus his left foot towards the end of the war. After a couple of years as a pen pusher in one of the more obscure parts of what was then called the War Office he had moved to the DIS and unusually stayed there. For many outside the DIS Joseff was the DIS. He was part of the Intelligence Establishment and knew everyone who mattered. He had a phenomenal memory for names reinforced by a Rolodex card file that was locked away in his safe each night. He was a detail man with a passion for precision even when it was completely unnecessary. At a meeting to discuss Russian intentions in the Arctic Joseff insisted on referring to Norwegian military intelligence as the *Etterretningstjenesten*, despite everyone else simply saying the NIS. In others it might have been showing off but not in Joseff's case, he had no interest in what others thought of him. He was simply using the correct term. I wasn't surprised to learn that he devoted all his time outside the office to his stamp collection.

The head of my section was the DAP: Director Analysis and Production. Group Captain Christopher Watkins always appeared to be in a hurry. He had been with the DIS for four years and,

I presumed, would soon be returning to the RAF. It was a prospect he didn't seem to find attractive.

'Come on!' he would tell me, as we set off at breakneck speed for a meeting elsewhere in Whitehall. 'I'll be back freezing my arse on some windswept stretch of East Anglia by the time you get into second gear.'

Watkins could best be described as medium: medium height, medium build, medium brown hair thinning on top compensated for by a wispy moustache. And medium intellect, although he would certainly not have agreed with that. He was, he often said, a thinker not a theoretician – a phrase he had picked up somewhere but which I suspect nobody really understood. I remember the look of utter bemusement on the face of the interpreter accompanying a South Korean delegation when Watkins explained that the role of our Directorate was to be the organisation's thinkers not theoreticians. Whatever the interpreter said the delegation smiled and nodded at this pearl of Western wisdom.

Watkins was not an easy man to like as he seemed to have a permanent chip on his shoulder, but he clearly liked me. He would drag me along to numerous presentations at which he outlined the latest threats to national security identified by our Directorate. He wanted me to take extensive notes and I became expert at producing bland minutes of meetings at which his more outlandish conspiracy theories had been shot down.

The other two of the 4Ds I rarely came across.

The then DE, Director Establishment, went off to work on the Multi Role Combat Aircraft project soon after I joined and Richard Mendale, Director Operations, seemed to spend most of his time elsewhere 'liaising'.

Mendale had been with the DIS for ten years or so and, like Adam Joseff, now seemed to be a permanent fixture. Watkins described him as 'laconic' which I suspect he did not mean as a compliment.

When I did eventually meet Mendale he introduced himself with the words 'I'm the DO, I do.'

It was his only known joke.

The DIS in those days was not a happy ship. There had been a series of unfortunate incidents: an operation in Warsaw that had gone wrong, a serious misunderstanding with the Americans here in London, a colleague drowning while on a mission in the Caribbean. We had apparently upset Six and they were now pressing for our wings to be trimmed. For reasons I did not understand Watkins held Mendale responsible for Six's antagonism. Watkins, as Director Analysis and Production, was in constant turf wars with Mendale, as Director Operations. Because Mendale never seemed to be in the office Watkins was winning.

My new colleagues spent most of their time analysing and 'planning'. We produced meticulously detailed plans for dealing with Soviet threats that remained frustratingly vague.

The commitment to planning did not extend to our own organisation. The DG had told me the role would be desk-bound but fortunately that proved to be untrue. My first overseas jaunt came with only a week's warning when I was sent on a CIA psychological warfare course in Langley, Virginia. A place had been booked months ago for an army captain who had since left the DIS. Someone else would have to go and I was deemed the person most easily spared.

For me the course was an eye-opener, not because of the subject but simply because of where I was and who I was with. This was real intelligence. The lecturers were not describing wartime cases from thirty years ago but operations last year in Vietnam. There was an immediacy and excitement and an almost frightening sense of purpose. These people were not there for 'Analysis and Production', like my Directorate in London, they were there to change the world.

Their enthusiasm was infectious although, at times, the certainty of their convictions was unsettling. One afternoon I was with a CIA agent named Gary Stover coming out to Langley along Dolley Madison Boulevard, Route 123 South. Gary was driving, very quickly but in full control. We were arguing.

'The problem with England,' he told me, 'is that unless you do something about it the country is "going Commie". Half your politicians are socialists and half your economy's controlled by the government.'

'Oh come on. The free world's largest socialist enterprise is the Tennessee Valley Authority. Does that mean the US is "going Commie" too?'

Gary was outraged. Just for a second his concentration slipped and we drove right past the Immanuel Presbyterian Church where he should have turned down through the trees to the CIA headquarters. He realised his mistake immediately and we turned round at the Route 193 fork to Langley and Dranesville. It took no time at all to go back but Gary was furious with himself. He kept on about the importance of concentration and the ability to split one's attention. It was more than dedication or indoctrination; he had a craftsman's pride in the profession he had chosen. It was something I hadn't seen in the DIS, except perhaps in the Deputy Director General Adam Joseff.

Joseff asked me how the course had gone when I returned and I casually mentioned that I might like to move into a more operational role at some stage. A month later I was sent for ten days of operational training in the Brecon Beacons. That was very enjoyable, if only when it was over, and I was grateful to Joseff for setting it up. But I had to admit it didn't help at all with the job I had been hired to do: analysis.

At that particular time the Portuguese military dictatorship was on its last legs and because I spoke Portuguese I had become the Department's resident expert, spending hours studying Portuguese troop movements, trying to make sense of intercepts, reading between the lines of Portuguese newspaper reports and wading through diplomatic cables cluttered with administrative trivia. As Portuguese forces were busy fighting bitter guerrilla wars in three of their African colonies the volume of material was at times overwhelming. When I noticed a group of military officers based in Lisbon suddenly being posted off to the Azores in the Atlantic I insisted to Watkins and Joseff that something significant was happening. We should flag it up to our lords and masters. Sure enough two weeks later, on 25 April 1974, a military coup toppled the dictatorship. The coup organisers had clearly been strong enough to survive a few of their suspected leaders being shipped out to the mid-Atlantic. For a few days I became the hero of the hour. The Director General personally congratulated me on being 'way ahead of Six' who had been caught completely unawares when what became known as the Carnation Revolution started Portugal on the road to democracy.

I was really enjoying the work but, as I told my parents on a weekend back in Cornwall, it involved hour upon hour in a stuffy Whitehall basement.

'Poor dear,' said my mother sympathetically. 'Make sure you get plenty of fresh air.'

Her wish was soon granted when I was plucked from my desk again and told to look out my passport. Group Captain Watkins briefed me.

'The BVD have arrested a local couple living near the NATO base at Brunssum on suspicion of espionage.'

Watkins assumed that by now I knew that the BVD was one of the Dutch intelligence services.

'The husband immediately confessed, blamed everything on his wife and agreed to tell all. He told us his Russian handler used the code name Samovar which is a name Five have come across before over here.'

'Did this man give us a description of Samovar?'

'Nothing that wouldn't fit half the male population.'

Although the BVD had reported all this to us, we had not been so open in return. If, as MI5 suspected, Samovar was running agents in the UK we didn't want a foreign agency getting in the way of our finding them. For that reason nobody had told the Dutch that a Russian diplomat in The Hague, Pyotr Leonov, was not only KGB but was more or less in our pocket. Six had discovered that he was what would now be described as gay but in those days was simply regarded by every Intelligence agency as an appalling security risk. Fortunately, a risk for the other side meant an opportunity for us. We were hoping he would lead us to Samovar. Watkins and I were to be on the early morning flight to Amsterdam.

'Our mission is simple,' the Group Captain told me. 'Find Samovar and keep him under observation. If possible we will follow him back to England where Five will take over surveillance. I am in charge of this operation but Six have insisted that they be involved. Their man in The Hague, Ronald Jacobs, has been running Leonov for some time. Moscow have instructed Leonov to contact Samovar by using dead-letter drops in Zandvoort. As an added security measure identical messages will be left in two different drops.' Watkins always seemed to speak as if each sentence was an order to be barked out. 'Jacobs will familiarise us with Zandvoort when we arrive. Leonov will be travelling by train from Amsterdam to Zandvoort via Haarlem and you and I board the train in Haarlem. Under no circumstances will we approach him. We are just there to ascertain that he is not being followed. When we reach Zandvoort Jacobs will be waiting for us, having kept the station under observation to ensure the other side aren't playing silly buggers. Leonov leaves the messages and then you and I split up and watch the two drops until Samovar turns up.'

I was excited, my first taste of real espionage had arrived.

Watkins made it sound like the sort of operation he handled every day. Clearly in the absence of the Director Operations he was determined to grab any glory going, although I already knew enough about the DIS to know that this was certainly not what the Analysis and Production Directorate had been set up to do. In fact, I didn't think anyone in the DIS got involved in this sort of mission.

'What happens if we find Samovar and he doesn't go back to England?' I asked.

'In that case I will use my judgement. We must try to ascertain his travel plans. Only if we have reason to believe Samovar is not planning to return to the United Kingdom will I call off the operation and authorise Jacobs to contact the BVD. At that point the Dutch can have him.'

Watkins explained that when Leonov had told his handler about an urgent message from Moscow, Jacobs had immediately relayed it to London. Most unusually Six had copied it on to us.

'Leonov to contact Samovar immediately: Operatsiya Ann Arbor.'

The reaction in London, said Watkins, had been electric. The DG had rushed upstairs to see our minister and then disappeared to Century House, in those days the MI6 headquarters in Westminster Bridge Road. The next thing we knew primary operational responsibility had been transferred from Six to the DIS, an unheard-of event. At the last minute Watkins himself was ordered to go to Holland.

'There was a humdinger of a row between the Foreign Office and the Ministry of Defence about the whole operation,' Watkins told me. 'The FO wanted Six to handle everything while the MoD naturally wanted us involved. This is after all a military matter.'

'What is?'

'Ann Arbor.'

I waited for him to explain but he didn't. 'I'm afraid I am not authorised to tell you any more. Let me just say Ann Arbor is not a matter for Six. We are the ones with the required expertise.'

I had no idea what expertise he was talking about. It seemed logical to me that Six would be in charge; after all, up until now this had clearly been their operation. And they would be able to put a team of real professionals in place. Six, I guessed, were still suffering the backlash from some unfortunate press coverage they had received when one of their agents in Berlin, a man named Koenig, had been caught. Or perhaps they wanted to ensure that if anything else went wrong on the Continent someone else would take the blame.

Watkins bustled around, issuing superfluous orders, the most important of which seemed to be that Jacobs should have a car waiting for him at Schiphol airport and it should be at least a Jaguar or Mercedes. Only Adam Joseff carried on as if nothing had happened; quietly making sure that we had all we needed, such as three midget cameras, variously camouflaged, in case any of us actually caught sight of the mysterious Samovar.

I remember going home that evening wishing I could tell my flatmates about the adventure I was about to embark on. I still had difficulty believing that just a few months out of university this could really be happening, I had joined the secret club.

'No doubt the Director Operations would have preferred I take along someone from his Directorate,' Watkins told me, 'but as I explained to the DG we have all the required capability in Analysis and Production.'

I was excited and apprehensive but also bemused. I don't know how I had imagined the world of espionage functioned but it certainly involved more than an RAF officer on temporary secondment and someone like me chasing the KGB around the Netherlands. I suppose I felt flattered at the responsibility entrusted to me.

It was only much later that I realised that in fact I had been trusted with absolutely nothing. I was just intended to be part of the scenery.

II

'*De trein van veertien uur vijf naar Amsterdam heft acht minute vertraging.*'

The station loudspeaker made the woman's words mingle into a metallic monotone.

'What's that about?' Watkins asked. 'Does that affect us?'

'The train's eight minutes late,' I told him. Dutch is not one of my languages but I'm always surprised when anyone hears something in a language so close to English but can't work out what is being said.

'Well we've plenty of time.'

Watkins started another of the rambles along the tiled platform that he'd been making since we arrived in Haarlem from Zandvoort fifteen minutes earlier, gazing up at the white wooden roof with its metal struts. Despite a barrage of telephone booths and slot machines selling everything from drinks and snacks to cigarettes and the *Woning Journaal*, the wide platform seemed empty. It was curiously lifeless. Grey, except for a multitude of small picture signs indicating the waiting room, restaurant, WC and so on. Typical of the Dutch, it was spotlessly clean.

The Group Captain seemed unsettled by the unusual experience of running an operation in the field.

'God are they all poofs over here?' he asked, pointing at a sign starting '*DAMES TOILETTEN*' over what was clearly a male silhouette.

It amazes me to recall how casually prejudiced so many of us were in those days. It was impossible to imagine that one day gay men would be welcomed into our world in the name of diversity. The irony of course is that the then Head of MI6, Sir Maurice Oldfield, was himself a regular user of male prostitutes, something kept carefully hidden from the lower ranks.

'I think "*DAMES TOILETTEN ANDERE ZIJDE VAN DIT GEBOUW*" probably means that the Ladies is on the other side of the building.'

Watkins marched away without comment. When he returned he glanced up at the clock above us, emblazoned with a rabbit advertising 'Haas Azijn'.

'Well I don't need that translated. A gin might be just what we need after this is over.'

I was pretty sure the rabbit was advertising vinegar but said nothing.

We split up. Watkins stood looking at the ornate wood and stained-glass building housing the station restaurant and waiting rooms on the opposite platform. A mosaic of two steam trains proclaimed '*Wachtkamer Eerst Klass*', the old first-class waiting room. I sat down opposite what had been the old '*Wachtkamer Derde Klass*' and waited for the Zandvoort train.

Four more minutes and then the train pulled into the cavern-like station, an electric wraith of blue and yellow.

'When you spot Leonov for heaven's sake don't stare,' Watkins had warned unnecessarily. 'Just keep an eye open and see if anybody's following him.'

Fortunately, I spotted Leonov near the front of the train and was able to board well away from him. There was someone with him. I settled back for the short journey to Zandvoort. To my surprise Watkins joined me.

'Let's run through things one more time.'

We had been through everything with Jacobs in Zandvoort that morning, surely we didn't need to repeat everything now. I looked around anxiously.

'Don't worry,' Watkins insisted. 'The train's almost empty, nobody's going to hear us. I want to make sure there are no foul-ups. The other side are being extremely cautious, they've chosen to use two drops. We must act the same way. I'll take the drop at the station, the one behind the postbox. Jacobs will take the one he showed us earlier, behind a litter bin in the car park at the nature reserve. You go with him. If Samovar appears at the station drop I'll try to get a picture of him and then get on his tail. I'll call for Jacobs to join me. It should be easy if Samovar's heading for Haarlem and Amsterdam. If he goes north it might be more difficult. Meanwhile you wait where you are and watch that litter bin, in case they're making two drops because there are two collectors. If nobody comes in an hour or so, collect the message yourself. It will be in an empty cigarette packet remember, Caballero. Take it to the nearest phone and call London. You've got the special number?'

'Yes I have.'

'Good. If Samovar turns up at the nature reserve instead we just do things the other way round.'

I nodded, he was telling me nothing new. Nevertheless he carried on talking.

'In that case you get a picture of him, and Jacobs gets on his tail. Call me on the radio right away and I'll join in. The target for both Jacobs and I is Samovar. Your role is to get hold of the message. Once you've seen Samovar take one message go to the other drop and see what's there.'

It all sounded very simple. Watkins had finished his explanation before we reached Overveen, just three minutes from Haarlem. Then the train moved off on the eight-kilometre run to Zandvoort.

The line travelled through a wood of deciduous trees which, as we crossed a small canal or 'sloot', gave way to fir trees. Haarlem had been bathed in bright, wintry sunshine, but as we approached our destination we moved through sand dunes half hidden in a mist rolling in from the North Sea. In less than five minutes the train passed the golf course, barely distinguishable under its white blanket, and drew into Zandvoort aan Zee.

Jacobs was standing discreetly near the exit.

'Welcome to Sandcastle-on-Sea.'

We had emerged from the station ahead of Leonov. 'Come on,' said Watkins when he saw Jacobs, 'we need to move where we can't be seen. We have a problem: Leonov's not alone. There is someone with him.'

'Of course he has someone with him', replied Jacobs in a surprised tone. 'That's standard procedure for the opposition. Nobody's allowed out alone. Does it make any difference?'

'Possibly not,' Watkins conceded. 'It's not what we were expecting.'

Jacobs simply looked at him as if to say, 'Well it's what I was expecting.'

I wondered what Jacobs had thought when he learned that the amateurs from the DIS were being allowed to take over what should have been his operation.

Group Captain Christopher Watkins and Ronald Jacobs could not have been more different. Where Watkins talked with the authority that derived from his position as head of the Analysis and Production Directorate, Jacobs had that quietly authoritative manner that comes from superior knowledge and ability. Watkins, I suspect, had blustered his way up the ranks. Although I was at times disparaging about his medium intellect he had finished *The Times* crossword on the flight over, although his technique seemed to be to enter whatever he first thought of and then repeatedly change it so the crossword ended up looking like a child had spilled his printing set over it. Jacobs was quietly methodical; Watkins wasn't quietly anything. Whatever subject was raised, Watkins would be able to find a memorandum he'd written about it. He had an opinion on everything, from Albanian weapons training to the tactics of nuclear warfare. And he never hesitated to voice his opinions. Jacobs, on the other hand, was the sort of man who spoke when he was spoken to. And when he did, people listened. He had been the Six Station chief in the Netherlands for nearly fifteen years and his name was a byword for quiet efficiency.

When we arrived we found radio-equipped cars waiting, a Mercedes for Watkins, an Opel Kapitan for me. Jacobs also had a radio in his Marina Coupé. We had tried them out on the drive to Zandvoort earlier in the day. There was a lot of static on mine, but otherwise there were no problems. Watkins insisted on using code names on the radio for no obvious reason. He became Alpha One, Jacobs Alpha Two and I was tagged Alpha Three.

Jacobs seemed to have thought of everything. In addition to the radios, the cars each contained a pair of powerful binoculars, a bag of 25 cent pieces for the phone, a large scale road map of the

Netherlands, street maps of every town between Amsterdam and The Hague and even a couple of postcards of Amsterdam, already stamped, which I could drop into the postbox at Zandvoort station if I needed a reason to approach the drop there.

'This bloody mist could mess things up,' said Watkins. 'I'd hoped it would have cleared up. If it's still as thick as it was this morning out by the nature reserve, we could be in trouble.'

Jacobs merely responded, 'I'll be off,' and disappeared.

I followed him into the small square in front of the station, leaving Watkins standing beside a bookstall.

Watkins and I had passed most of the morning in Zandvoort with Jacobs, who had spent two holidays at the Hotel Sonnewende near the nature reserve. 'The geography of Zandvoort is easy,' he had insisted and then simplified it madly. 'The beach runs directly north–south. Leonov makes two drops. One is behind the postbox at the station at the north end of the town. The other is in a litter bin in the big car park on the south side of the town. The only other feature to bear in mind is the road to Haarlem and Amsterdam which goes directly east, at right angles to the coast from the town centre.'

In fact, the set-up was more complicated than that because of the maze of one-way streets spreading out in all directions. However, it was true that the two dead-letter drops were easy to find, which was presumably why they had been chosen.

I had parked opposite the station near the Smickelbar. The mist was thicker than it had been in the morning. Looking across the Stationplein, I couldn't see the Berliner Kindl sign which had been visible when we left Zandvoort little more than an hour before. As I reached my car I saw the Russians standing by the red postbox. They had their backs to me but one of them, I was sure, would be pushing a Caballero pack into the space between the back of the box and its metal supports.

I looked away and started the engine.

Visibility was less than thirty-five feet. I kept the windscreen wipers on as I drove off towards the other deadletter drop, edging out of the Stationplein past the Hotel van Houten into Zeestraat and then left into Burger Zeestraat and left again into Burgermeister-Engelbertstraat. The road curved round past a Chevron garage and rows of red-roofed houses that appeared as faint blurs in the mist. I kept on south past the watchtower where we'd had lunch. From there it was only a short distance to a series of roundabouts and the Friedhoffplein where Ronald Jacobs appeared out of the mist.

'I've parked my car over there,' he said, pointing vaguely through the gloom with his cigar and pulling open the passenger door. 'Let's put this one in the car park where we can watch the drop.'

I drove past the BP station into the huge car park. A sign I'd noticed earlier at the other entrance had announced that there was room for 1 000 cars. As we nosed through the mist it seemed that the car park was now completely empty except for an old Volkswagen which I nearly ran into. There were sand dunes on the southern and eastern flanks of the car park, part of the nature reserve that stretched away to the south. Surrounding the car park was a string of blue and yellow litter bins. Samovar's dead-letter drop was in one of these, a blue one, the fourth to the west from the south-east corner.

I parked so that we could just make out the bin. Anybody standing there would find it impossible to see if the car was occupied, unless we moved sharply.

'This is fine,' said Jacobs. 'Let's leave the car until Leonov and his friend have put in an appearance. I wouldn't want them spotting us.' There didn't seem to be much chance of that in the mist.

We wandered off towards the sea. 'If you take all the seaside towns in Britain together,' Jacobs commented, 'you'll find fewer really beautiful houses than the Dutch cram into one square mile of somewhere like Zandvoort.'

As I couldn't see any of them through the enveloping white shroud I just nodded.

We clambered down a steep path to the beach and stepped on to the clinging, cold sand. The sound of the sea reached us long before we saw the surf pounding firmly and monotonously on to the vast expanse of sand. The white breakers appeared suddenly out of the grey-white blur that eddied in above the sea, only to shatter themselves and fall back again into the mist's clammy embrace. The beach was deserted. We strolled along deep in shallow conversation.

'Perhaps you can tell me who Ann Arbor is,' Jacobs said. 'I'd never heard of the woman until Leonov mentioned Operatsiya Ann Arbor. The name certainly seemed to change everything; I hadn't realised the DIS had any interest in Samovar. Russian agents over here are not the sort of thing you chaps normally get involved in.'

I shook my head. 'I've no idea who Ann Arbor is. Like you, I don't need to know.'

He looked at me with justified scepticism. I now knew more about our mission. That morning Watkins' driver had picked me up from my apartment before collecting Watkins from what he called his 'quarters' in Chiswick. By then Watkins had decided that he could after all let me know why the inclusion of 'Operatsiya Ann Arbor' in Leonov's instructions had aroused such interest. But if Jacobs still didn't know I should obviously keep my mouth shut.

I couldn't even tell him that Ann Arbor was a place not a person, the seat of the University of Michigan. I didn't know much about it myself. All Watkins had revealed is that an Irish-born American scientist named Donnell had walked out of a research laboratory with a highly secret piece of equipment called a Griffin Interrogator. The gadget probably had something to do with ships because the DG had apparently said that his fellow admirals were 'Flapping all over the place like nuns in a Playboy Club.'

The only link between the events in the US Midwest and those taking place in Holland was the one phrase used by the Russians to describe the new mission for their agent Samovar, 'Operatsiya Ann Arbor'. It was a very tenuous connection but it was apparently enough to justify giving the DIS a leading role in finding Samovar.

Jacobs was still feeling talkative. 'Did you know your predecessor, Roger Black?' he asked.

'Not at all.'

'I gather he drowned. Sad business. His father was in Holland during the war, had a hell of a reputation with the old Resistance people, married a DP later.'

He tried another tack. 'What's the DIS view on Koenig, the chap we lost in Berlin?'

As Koenig's name had been all over the newspapers the affair was not secret any more but it struck me as an odd question.

'I'm not sure the DIS has a view. It doesn't directly concern us.'

Watkins had made a sarcastic comment which I certainly wasn't going to repeat to Jacobs. 'At least,' he'd said, 'Six can't accuse us of leaking Koenig's name. None of us knew Six had someone inside the opposition's Berlin station.'

Jacobs nodded and then asked why Watkins was running this operation rather than the Director Operations, Richard Mendale. I suspect that was what Jacobs really wanted to talk about but I didn't have an answer for that either.

It struck me that MI6's station chief in Holland seemed surprisingly well informed about the goings on in the DIS. But then I suppose the whole point of his job was to be well informed.

When we returned to the car I turned on the two-way radio in case Watkins was trying to get in touch with us. He wasn't. We settled down in silence. The car was soon full of smoke from Jacobs' perpetual cigars. Smoky tendrils drifted out through the partly opened windows to merge into the mist.

For more than an hour nothing happened.

'If he's coming I suspect he'll be here soon,' said Jacobs. 'As dead-letter drops go these two are not very good. Bit too obvious. Not the sort of places you would want to leave a message for days.' We sat staring at the blue litter bin, mesmerised as the mist swirled around it. Sometimes it would momentarily disappear, leaving its image still imprinted on the mind.

'I'm going to look around,' Jacobs proclaimed. He left the car and was swallowed up by the white cloud around us.

Five minutes later Samovar arrived. The weather suited him perfectly. My eyes were focussed steadily on the bin but I almost missed him. Suddenly there was a grey blur behind the bin that took on the shape of a man. He had climbed the steep slope that lay immediately behind the row of bins and stretched up from the fence that surrounded the nature reserve. Before I had time to raise my camera, disguised as a copy of Günter Grass' *Die Blechtrommel*, he was gone again. Lost. I couldn't even begin to describe him.

I threw open the car door and ran silently towards the slope. I could hardly see the fence at the bottom. There was certainly no sign of the Russian. He could have turned left towards the dunes, which seemed unlikely, or right in the direction of the nearest road. I ran towards the road and before I reached it a man emerged, running, from the mist. It was Jacobs.

'He's back there,' he shouted, waving his cigar over his shoulder and pulling me towards the car.

'I missed him,' I said, but Jacobs ignored me.

'I found a Mercedes just outside, white with a blue top. Licence 57 LB 91. Got that?'

'Yes.'

'Good. Radio it to Watkins. I'll get after Samovar. Here, I got a snap of him.'

He tossed me his camera, disguised like mine as a book, this time Carol Burns' *The Narcissist*.

'Did he see you?' I asked.

'He may have done. I don't know. There's no reason why he should be suspicious of me. I wasn't staring into the Mercedes or at him. Just lighting a cigar when he came bounding along and jumped into his car.'

We reached the Opel. 'Remember that number,' Jacobs shouted, '57 LB 91. White and blue Mercedes.' Then he was gone.

I grabbed the radio microphone and pressed the transmit button. Nothing seemed to happen. The small red light on the set that should have come on stayed off. 'Alpha Three to Alpha One,' I shouted into the mouthpiece. 'Alpha Three to Alpha One!'

There was only silence. I tried once again. 'Alpha One, come in please.' Nothing. Just the faint buzz of static from the receiver.

III

I couldn't tell whether the whole radio had failed or just the transmitter. It didn't seem to matter. Our well-made plans had gone astray. The only thing to do was to drive to the station and talk to Watkins directly. There was no point trying to follow Jacobs if I couldn't contact him. I had no idea which way Samovar had gone.

I started the car and drove carefully through the mist. As I left the car park and entered the Friedhoffplein a car went past, heading east towards Haarlem and Amsterdam. It might have been Jacobs' Marina but in the swirling mist I couldn't be sure.

I crawled towards the station behind a Volkswagen laundry van; the inscription '*Peeperkorn, Heemstede*' on its rear door and the bundles of washing inside were barely visible. There was no sound from the radio until I was approaching the station. Then the voice of Christopher Watkins boomed into the car. At least the radio receiver was working.

'Alpha One to Alpha Two and Alpha Three. Is anything happening? Out.'

After a few seconds Jacobs replied. 'Alpha Two. I'm right on his tail. Just leaving Zandvoort on the main road to Amsterdam. Where are you?'

Watkins responded instantly. 'Whose tail? What's happening?' The irritation in his voice plainly audible through the heavy static.

Jacobs responded patiently. 'Alpha Two. I'm following the suspect we saw at the nature reserve.'

Watkins interrupted him. 'What suspect? Why didn't you call me Alpha Two?' The last syllable was missing because he'd snapped off the microphone too quickly.

'A man collected the message,' said Jacobs. 'I'm now following him. Didn't Thomas tell you? It's a white Mercedes, blue roof, licence 57 LB 91.'

'Alpha One. Stay on air, I'll be right with you.' Then Watkins turned his attention to me. 'Come in Alpha Three. Where are you?'

Instinctively I tried the transmitter again but it was still out of action. I could only stare at the receiver as it sounded once more, 'Alpha One to Alpha Three. Come in.'

There was a moment's silence and then Watkins returned to Jacobs. 'Where the hell's Alpha Three?' he barked.

'His radio may be broken,' Jacobs responded.

There was another brief silence. Perhaps Watkins was starting his engine or else simply deciding what to do. Then he spoke again. 'Alpha One to Alpha Three. If you can hear me make your way to the station and collect the other message. Then phone London.'

I was almost at the station as Watkins clicked off. Two minutes later I turned into Zeestraat. Leaving the Stationplein was a grey Mercedes similar to the one Watkins was driving. It turned left towards Amsterdam. I drew up at the side of the station near the postbox.

Standing beside the box was a man wearing a grey suit. As I got out of the car I saw him reach behind the box for the cigarette packet that Leonov had left. Taking the camera in one hand and a postcard in the other, I walked towards him. He turned as I approached, slipping something into his pocket. A startled look crossed his face, almost as if he recognised me. The camera was operated simply by pressing the base of the book's spine, and I took what I hoped were two good pictures.

The man stepped towards a green Ford Capri and climbed into the passenger seat. I could see nothing of the driver except for his hands which were encased in black leather driving gloves perforated at the knuckles. I made a mental note of the Capri's number.

Obviously Leonov had made two drops not as a security precaution but because there were two collectors. What should I do now: phone Adam Joseff in London or follow the Capri? Unless they had been unbelievably lucky in timing their arrival to coincide with Watkins' departure the two men had obviously been waiting for him to leave. Therefore they were on to us, or at least on to Watkins. In that case London should know about it at once, so they could take action before the Russians decided to abandon ship. On the other hand, phoning London seemed tantamount to doing nothing and passing the buck. I didn't know what was in the message or who the men who had collected it were: by following them I at least might be able to answer the second query. Probably at the back of my mind there was the thought that I might even return a hero.

The Capri came past. I could see the driver clearly: thin face, pinched cheeks, sharp nose, short, black hair stopping above unusually small ears, and wearing a blue jacket. All I could see of the other man was the radio in his hand.

I started the Opel and moved after them. Due to the mist they had their lights on and it was easy to follow the twin red rear lights as they turned out of the Stationplein into Zeestraat and then into Engelbertsstraat. They were headed back the way I had just come, south towards the nature reserve. I expected them to turn east, towards Haarlem, but they kept on parallel to the sea. They seemed to be driving to the other drop.

Sure enough, the Capri eventually turned off the coast road towards the dunes and entered the car park. Switching off my lights, I cruised slowly after them. I wanted to make sure they were here just to check the other drop. Leaving the Opel near the entrance I ran through the mist towards the blue bin on the other side. The Capri was parked almost exactly where Jacobs and I had spent an hour waiting for Samovar. I crouched on the ground, confident that I would not be seen by the occupants of the car whom I could vaguely make out still seated inside. After a few minutes both doors opened and the two men got out. To my surprise they made no attempt to approach the bin but instead walked quickly to the road where Jacobs had found the Mercedes, and then turned left towards the nature reserve.

I moved slowly in the same direction.

A large sign announced that this was both nature reserve and *DUINWATERWINPLAATS*, one of Amsterdam's municipal water supplies. The notice also warned that anybody found in the reserve without a ticket would be fined. Unsurprisingly the two men had ignored this. They were standing inside the gates looking at a large map. I could barely make them out through the cloying mist, and as I approached they walked off eastwards towards the dunes. Neither of them looked behind and it didn't occur to me to wonder why not. I ran quickly to the map.

The enclosed area swept south in a broad band away from Zandvoort, flanked on one side by a narrow stretch of dunes and beach and then the North Sea. The reserve consisted mainly of rolling sand dunes and narrow canals used to collect water. On the map the canals looked like thin blue sausages. Presumably at each end there were pipes linking them together into a grid.

On the bottom of the map was a red sign warning 'reeën gejaagd', deer hunted. I could only pray that there were no idiots wandering round in the dense mist with loaded rifles just waiting for some sign of movement.

The two men had disappeared.

I should have stopped then. It would have been better to wait for the men to return to their car rather than risk losing them in the reserve. And I should have found a phone and called London to let them know what was happening. But I didn't.

Instead I struck out eastward along the path, hoping that the two men hadn't branched off into the dunes. The path had once been tarmacked but the ravages of time and weather had left it liberally bedecked with sand and tufts of grass. It led gently up through the dunes. The only sign of life was a small rabbit hopping across the track. The mist was getting heavier, grey and clammy. I could feel droplets of water on my hair. Occasionally I came across part of a clearly defined footprint in the wet sand speckled along the path.

I heard a noise ahead, muffled by the mist. It could have been the sound of falling water from the canal that I knew was not far away or it could have been voices. My eyes strained through the grey-white shroud. I edged slowly forward and heard the sound again, people talking.

Vaguely I made out the silhouette of two men, but I couldn't be sure that my eyes weren't playing tricks. Wish-fulfilment: I wanted to see two men and therefore I saw two men. Then I was sure, because the two clinging silhouettes split apart for a second and then moved off.

They had been standing by a squat distance marker on the intersection between our path and a broader one, wide enough for motor traffic, running at right angles. The signpost showed that I had come 0.8 kilometres from Zandvoort, while by turning left I would reach the Natuurpad in 1.7 kilometres. It gave no indication of what I would find by turning right as the two men had done.

I turned right.

The track was now made of large concrete rectangles, perhaps fourteen feet by seven feet, laid two by two. Between each block were a few inches of sand covered with grass and rabbit droppings. To my right, bushes and dunes disappeared into the mist, while on my left there was just a white blanket. Unknown to me at that time, the ground to the east dropped away almost vertically twenty feet to a canal. Twice there were sounds of pumps coming from that direction, but I could see nothing. Occasionally I caught a glimpse of the two men ahead of me. They were moving quickly now and I had to stretch to keep up.

Eventually they stopped in the middle of the path. I stood stock still hoping that neither would spot me if they turned round. They didn't turn. One of them seemed to be pointing towards the east. They couldn't be lost. Even in the dense mist the path we had followed was the simplest possible. I could only imagine that they didn't know where they wanted to go, which seemed unlikely.

It was a sign of my total lack of field experience that it never occurred to me to wonder why the men I was following had headed off into the dunes with no more idea of where they were going than I had.

They turned eastwards. I followed, dropping back further so that they couldn't see me if they looked over their shoulders. It also meant of course that I couldn't see them. I heard water and realised we must have crossed a canal on a bridge or dyke but I couldn't see anything through the increasingly thick blanket of mist. I sensed, rather than saw, the men turn left again. A track sloped downward.

I advanced cautiously, trying desperately to muffle each step. I was starting to curse myself for not having phoned London rather than blundering around as I was doing.

The ground underfoot was sand sprinkled with shells and here and there patches of grass. Almost subconsciously I noticed the wide, deep tread of a tractor tyre.

Suddenly a building loomed up in front, black and oddly menacing. There was no sign of habitation. I could see no more than four or five feet in front of me. Slowly I edged forward and found a door painted white and padlocked. The solitary window was covered by a white metal shutter and, like the door, securely locked. Turning to the right I groped my way around the corner of the building. The windows there had been bricked up. My foot kicked a fragment of brick and it hit against the wall with a hollow thud. I stood as still as a statue, petrified in the eerie silence.

Then I heard a movement behind me.

For a reason I'll never understand, I dropped to one knee and, as I did so, a bullet thudded into the wall, ricocheting away into the dank, grey clouds. I ran.

There was another plop and a bullet whistled past, missing me by a yard or so. I kept running.

There were no more shots and no sound of pursuit. Glancing over my shoulder into the enveloping white behind me, I lost my footing and tripped over a log, falling forward on to the sand. I reached back, found the log and picked it up. It was about four inches in diameter and two feet long. I don't know what sort of tree it came from but balancing it in my hand it seemed incredibly light. As a club it wouldn't do much damage, but it was all I had.

Picking myself up I ran on again, straight into a horizontal metal pole. The pole was painted bright yellow, presumably so that people wouldn't run into it!

The pole formed the bar of a gate, hinged at one end on to an upright brown metal post. I felt my way to the other end of the pole, which was about twelve feet long, and discovered that it rested on a small yellow post. The gate was obviously meant to be swung across the path that ran beside the canal. It was now open but presumably somewhere on the other side of the track there would be another yellow support for the gate pole to rest on when it was closed.

There was a canal on my left but there was also the sound of falling water coming from the right. That must be water from a subsidiary canal falling into a pipe under the path and into the canal by which I was standing.

I moved around the gate, stepping carefully so that I didn't fall into the water that I could just make out beside my shoes. The gate was now between me and the path. I stood stock still and, as I did so, there came the sound of two men walking slowly down the path towards the canals, and towards me. I felt calmer now. I was getting used to the mist, confident the men wouldn't see me unless I moved. I had only been able to distinguish their dark and blurred silhouettes because they kept moving. But I had to do something. The mist wouldn't last for ever.

As the men came parallel with the closed gate, perhaps six feet away, I lifted the pole off its support and swung it across the path with all my strength. It caught both of them in the small of their backs and sent them sprawling forward.

I jumped on to the nearest of the two men. It happened to be the one in the blue jacket, the driver of the Capri. My swinging club crashed against his head and the wood disintegrated. The man staggered and fell sideways on to the grass that ran beside the canal.

I turned towards the other man, the one with the gun, and almost tumbled into his arms. I tried desperately to remember the tricks I had been taught in the Brecon Beacons but Sergeant Dominic hadn't spent much time lecturing on what to do when struggling on a narrow path between two canals in a thick mist. My opponent was strong but not supple. We grappled helplessly as I reached for his gun hand while he alternately squeezed me in a semi-bear hug and then tried to turn his gun on me. Suddenly he stepped back, lost his footing and fell into the canal that lay at right angles to the path, pulling me in with him.

The shock of the ice-cold water jarred through every inch of my body. The man underneath me was splashing around as if he was drowning, although the water in the canal wasn't deep. He struck me a glancing blow on the cheek. I felt a ring on one of his fingers but there was no power in his flailing arms. Reaching out a hand I felt a wooden stake sticking up out of the water. With my other hand I grabbed the man's head and smashed it against the stake. Once. Twice. Three times. His arms fell back into the water and his whole body seemed to soften.

Next to me was a large pipe leading under the footpath into the main canal. I felt the water surging into it, pulling at my legs. I still held the man's head in one hand like a ball and I pushed it roughly into the pipe. It was no time for hesitation. He had been trying to kill me.

There was no sign of the other man but he must be close, my makeshift club wouldn't have done much damage. It seemed to me that I'd been making an enormous noise, splashing around, but the mist had muffled it. The man I'd fought had dropped his gun when he fell into the canal. I groped around on the canal bed but couldn't find it and quickly gave up the search. There were more important things to do. Who were these men? I reached into the pockets of his expensive grey suit. His wallet must have fallen out but I found something else, an empty cigarette packet. As I drew it out I saw the brand name, Caballero.

Suddenly I heard a sound on the path above me.

A voice shouted into the mist behind me. I thought it was a name, 'Nikki.'

Silence followed, tomb-like in its intensity.

I decided not to stick around and, clambering up the opposite bank, I grabbed at a post bearing a notice, '*VERBODEN TOEGANG*'. Desperate not to make any more noise I turned eastwards. The only sound came from a small weir. Turning off the bare track into the dunes I walked aimlessly for four or five minutes before stopping to listen for the noise of pursuit. Nobody came. I was shaking.

People don't carry guns in peacetime. Nobody had suggested we should arm ourselves.

'It's just a routine dead-letter collection,' Watkins had said. 'Think of it as a training exercise.'

After fifteen minutes I crossed back over the canal and, shivering with the wet and cold, cut back through the dunes towards the sea. I reached a barbed wire fence at the edge of the nature reserve. From that it was a short hike to a path that led between two more rows of barbed wire down on to the beach. Then I walked back to Zandvoort beside the cold and grey North Sea.

When I reached the car park the Capri had gone. The mist was still clinging on. I walked over to my Opel, warily, half expecting another bullet to appear from nowhere. But nothing happened. The car was as I had left it. I tried the radio but still without success. Watkins and Jacobs were evidently either not transmitting or out of range. I drove slowly along the few hundred yards to the Hotel Sonnewende.

The receptionist seemed not at all surprised to see a complete stranger, still wet from the canal, wanting to make a phone call to Britain. He led me to a fairly large cubicle containing a phone, wrote down the number I wanted and explained in faultless English that he would go and connect me.

'You can pay me at reception when you are finished,' he added, almost as an afterthought.

Within seconds I was through to London. To my surprise I was put straight through to Adam Joseff.

'How are things?' he asked.

'Awful. This line is clear, right?'

It was a silly question. If anybody was listening in they would almost certainly be listening at my end which Joseff would know nothing about. Nerves were getting to me.

Joseff told me to go ahead.

'The other two are chasing someone, but I've lost radio contact and I think I've just killed a man who jumped me.'

There was a momentary silence. 'I see. Are you injured?'

'No.'

'Right, Thomas, no more on the phone. Go straight to Schiphol. We'll have a ticket waiting for you at the British Airways desk. And you'll be met at Heathrow. Leave everything to us. Just get out of Holland as quickly as possible. You can leave the car wherever it suits you.'

IV

A few weeks earlier the cabin crew had been wearing the uniform of British European Airways. Now they were part of the brave new world of the recently formed British Airways. I hoped they were facing a brighter future than I was. My first mission had been a complete disaster.

I was met at Heathrow by an unsmiling man who led me to a windowless room, pointed to a telephone and told me I was to 'phone the office'.

I was put through to Adam Joseff who quizzed me for five minutes before suddenly breaking off. 'Sorry, Christopher Watkins is on the other line. Come on in Thomas. There should be a pool driver waiting for you.'

I did as I was told. The pool driver had been listening to the latest Eurovision winner, ABBA singing about Napoleon's defeat at Waterloo. Not entirely inappropriate. He switched the radio off when I emerged and said nothing the whole way in from the airport.

Joseff's enormous office, rather than the DG's, was the effective nerve centre of the organisation. Although Joseff always seemed to be organised and methodical in his actions the room itself was invariably chaotic, with metal chairs scattered around and usually a flip chart propped against a wall.

His office could have been designed by a machine. Everything appeared to be numbered: the heavy metal door inscribed 'Mark IV Manifoil C127732 M4' beneath its combination lock; 01 66 533 stencilled on the metal desk. Even his pencils were marked 'Government Property 48-75'. It was a cold room, the walls a faded green, the ceiling too high. The green carpet failed to reach the walls. Watkins had found a similar carpet in his office when he arrived and had fought for three months to have it changed. He had been successful, as he had been in his campaign for a wooden desk. Joseff remained content with things as they were. As well as his metal desk there was a metal table, both invariably covered in papers that he scrupulously put away in his safe every night. On the desk sat a leather jar containing pens and pencils, a letter opener and a box full of paper clips and treasury tags. Four briar pipes stood in their rack beside a gold table lighter inscribed 'To Adam J. Joseff from his friends at GCHQ.' It bore no date.

The only other sign of individuality was a single framed poster of a nineteenth-century Portuguese postage stamp.

Joseff was on the phone. He waved a neatly manicured hand in the direction of the window where Richard Mendale was standing.

'The DO will fill you in.'

Mendale turned towards me. He was a big man, tall and straight-backed with a big, red round face who had spent his service career in the Royal Marines. I knew that the previous year the Director Operations had been seconded to Six for an operation in Warsaw involving a Russian general who was supposedly planning to defect. The operation had been an embarrassing failure.

'Nothing much to tell,' Mendale said, the rain pattering on the window behind him. 'Jacobs and Watkins followed their suspect east to Nijmegen, near the German border. He went into an apartment above an antique shop. That's all we know. Watkins says he has him cornered.'

'He was wrong,' interrupted Joseff, holding his hand over the phone's mouthpiece. 'I've got Watkins on the line. Our bird has flown.'

He removed his hand from the mouthpiece. 'You'd better leave Ronald Jacobs to handle the police and come on home, Christopher.' Joseff was the only person, with the exception of the DG himself, who ever called Watkins by his first name. 'Perhaps you'd come right into the office when you land. I'll have you met at the airport.'

There was a moment's silence. Presumably Watkins replied because Joseff continued, 'No, that won't be necessary. Come back through Amsterdam.'

He put the phone down. 'Watkins wants to drive over to Munster and let the RAF fly him back. Can't stand the idea of having anything happen without his presence. Anyway, Samovar's gone. Slipped out the back while Watkins was phoning us earlier. When the Dutch police arrived to put the place under observation, somebody noticed a peculiar light in one of the windows. Our friend had set the place afire. When the police broke in, the apartment was gutted.'

'What a cock-up,' said Mendale. 'Amateur hour. Back to square one.'

It was the first time I had heard the American expression 'amateur hour' and it struck me as highly appropriate. Joseff ignored it. 'We'll get some of the small fry and the ring is broken. It's just that the lynchpin has escaped. Watkins reckons he'll be back inside Russia within a few hours. Let's hope he's wrong.'

'Fat chance of that,' put in Mendale, voicing all our thoughts. We were all wrong.

Once more I went over the events in Holland. Mendale was particularly interested in the men who jumped me.

'The descriptions could fit half the Dutch population,' he commented. 'Let's hope the photos come out. What about the gun, you didn't find it?'

'No, and I didn't see it too clearly. But it was a revolver.'

'Ah,' said Mendale quickly, 'so there won't be any cartridge cases lying around.' He flashed a look at Joseff, who said nothing. It was as if Mendale was saying, 'Look, my suspicions are confirmed.' But it was a long time before I discovered what those suspicions were. And why nobody told me.

'The DG will be in later,' Joseff said. 'He may want to see you. Perhaps you could sleep in the dormitory downstairs.'

It was his dismissal. Back in my office somebody brought up some sandwiches while I carefully wrote down my version of the day's events. After that I tried to clear my mind by switching my thoughts to the mundane. I had attended a Middle East review meeting at the US Embassy two days before, one of those meetings where nobody wanted to give anything useful away. Now I settled down to write the required Ministerial brief: the meeting, I lied, had been a fruitful example of inter-agency cooperation.

There was still no word from the DG when I finished so I went down to the dormitory and watched television until midnight. I had plenty to think about.

I was surprised by my own reaction to the events in Zandvoort. I had almost certainly killed someone and someone had nearly killed me. I should have been in shock. What today would be labelled post-traumatic stress. And yet I felt something altogether different, something that I didn't want to think of as pride. I had held my own. Somebody had tried to kill me but I had been the one to emerge victorious. When the shots came my autonomic nervous system would have released a barrage of hormones racing through my body. They could have triggered fight or flight. My first reaction had been to run but I had turned and fought. And I had won.

The mission had been disastrous but I slept soundly.

The first person I saw when I went up to my office the next morning was Watkins' secretary, Judy Brown.

'Mr Watkins is on the warpath,' she warned me. 'He wants to know why you haven't written your report yet.'

I explained that I had written and submitted it as soon as I returned.

'Not that report. The one on the American Embassy meeting.'

'It's on my desk.'

With that Watkins appeared. 'Ah, Thomas, you're here. We're to go up to Adam's office right away. I understand the DO's in the office, no doubt he'll be finding fault with everything we've done. No need to fill me in on what happened to you in Zandvoort, I've read your report.'

Joseff put down the phone as we entered. Nobody would guess from his immaculate appearance that he had been there for twenty-four hours without a break.

We sat around his desk. Watkins upright, as straight as the chair back, clipboard on his knee. Mendale pushing his chair on to two legs and leaning back against a filing cabinet, while he stared out of the window. And finally myself, wedged between a filing cabinet and the door. Joseff tapped his desk with the stem of his pipe as he spoke.

'At last we've got a name for Samovar: Kardosov. Dick found him in the records, recognised him from Jacobs' photo.'

Mendale drew his eyes away from the window where the first light of dawn was awakening the building opposite. He glanced towards the desk. 'It was pure luck really. The photo we had is nine years old.' He pointed at a black and white snapshot on Joseff's desk.

Watkins picked it up. 'That's the man. No doubt about it, that's Samovar.'

He passed the photo to me. A man in his mid-thirties was climbing stone steps past an inscription. He looked thoroughly ordinary, short hair, hat, raincoat just below his knees.

'Where was it taken?' Watkins asked.

'New York,' I said before Mendale could reply, 'the steps going up to East 43rd Street, opposite the UN building.'

'Good man,' Joseff commented.

Mendale nodded. 'Kardosov was there for a year on the Byelorussian delegation. As I said, nine years ago. Absolutely nothing else on him. The Americans have fingerprints which they've sent to the Dutch authorities. I'm sure they'll just confirm the picture.'

'Just a name,' said Watkins, 'it doesn't get us very far.'

'No,' agreed Joseff, 'but we do have more. The message that Leonov left behind the postbox at Zandvoort station. The boys at Cheltenham have cracked it. Just a simple transformation cipher, five-digit duplication and a few dummies. Their standard B system tarted up a bit.'

Joseff loved technicalities. He was probably sorry that because of the urgency the message had been sent to Cheltenham rather than left for him to play with on the computer terminal in the second basement. He picked up a computer printout from the desk in front of him. 'I'll read it out. The first bit's not too explicit but at the moment that's not the important part:

```
"Thunder urgent crashdive mermaid stop remain
active
Operation Ann Arbor stop use Swedish identity
stop
Collect orders Copenhagen two stop danger
code impossible
Stop victor stop"'.
```

'They're mad,' Mendale said when Joseff had finished. 'They're going to use him again immediately. No debriefing. No analysis. No post-mortem. Nothing.'

'Cost-effective,' Joseff interrupted. 'They've got a man in the field on our side of the curtain with a Swedish cover all ready and waiting to be used. My guess is that the man who stole this naval gadget at Ann Arbor, Paul Donnell, just saw an opportunity and grabbed it, then he somehow contacted the Russians and offered an immediate exchange. He wouldn't want to hang around. The reds have simply gone for whoever is available. And if Donnell's still in the US, Kardosov's experience there will be an added reason for keeping him operational.'

'Perhaps Donnell and Kardosov knew each other,' Watkins suggested. 'Donnell was over here last year. Perhaps Kardosov got on to him then.'

'Perhaps,' said Joseff. 'Right now the priority is action.'

'Send someone to Copenhagen,' suggested Watkins. 'Thomas here could go.'

'We've done that already,' Joseff said. 'John Burton took a couple of chaps from Operations over last night, courtesy of the RAF. We were lucky. Burton has just spotted Kardosov at the civilian airport, Kastrup, checking in for a flight to Canada. Toronto. He's using the name Nils Olssen.'

'The Swedish identity,' Watkins murmured, remembering the deciphered message.

'That's right. Thomas will follow Kardosov to Canada.'

Neither Watkins nor Mendale looked happy at that.

'Don't we need someone more senior?' Watkins asked. 'Perhaps I should go.'

'This should be handled by Operations,' interjected Mendale.

Joseff was not about to get involved in turf wars between the DO and the DAP. 'The Director General has made his decision. He's talked to the RCMP. They will take over the operation now and track Kardosov from the airport.'

Mendale nodded at that. 'The Mounties know what they're doing.'

The Canadian 'Security Landscape' was even more byzantine than the UK's. At the summit was the Royal Canadian Mounted Police Security Service. We had worked closely with them in the past.

In October 1970 separatist violence in Quebec had culminated in the bombing of the Montreal Stock Exchange and the kidnapping of the British Trade Commissioner James Cross and a government minister, Pierre Laporte. Cross survived but the minister was murdered by his captors. The Mounties had tracked down and captured Laporte's killers in an operation that paid no attention to legal niceties. Nobody in London was surprised a few years later when the RCMP Security Service was abolished following revelations about the tactics they had employed in Quebec. But at the time Joseff was briefing me they were still top dog in the security world and a law unto themselves.

'The DG has arranged for one of our people over there, by the name of French, to work with the Mounties,' Joseff continued. 'The plan is that if Kardosov ends up in their hands the Security Service will let French and the RAF bring him back here without waiting for all the rigmarole of an extradition.'

Joseff turned to me. 'You needn't get involved in that. If the man who stole the Interrogator, Donnell, turns up in Toronto to meet Kardosov we want the Griffin Interrogator. That's your objective. Bring it back here.'

'If it's been stolen from the Americans won't the Canadians want to give it back to them?' I asked. 'Rather than letting me walk away with it.'

Mendale laughed. 'Not after last year's furore. There's no love lost between the Canadians and the Americans at the moment.'

I must have looked blank because Joseff explained. 'The Americans declassified a lot of historical files last year without apparently realising that they included details of War Plan Red.'

I still looked blank.

'War Plan Red was a proposal developed by the US Army in 1927 to invade Canada, the plans included bombing Canadian cities. It was approved at the highest level and new airfields were specially built. Of course it never came to anything but it upset the apple cart when the files were declassified. Even after nearly half a century the Mounties don't like the idea that American spies were carrying out reconnaissance missions in Canada without being detected.'

'What happens if Kardosov doesn't stay in Toronto?' I asked. 'Suppose he intends meeting Donnell in the US.'

'That would be unfortunate. You and French might try to follow him. The DG has spoken to Ottawa to see if they would be willing to do anything more. But the reality is that if we think Kardosov is heading for the US we may need to let the Canadians grab him before he can cross the border and forget about the Griffin Interrogator. Six have people on the ground in Washington who might be persuaded to help but operating in the US is not easy for any of us, logistically or, more important, politically.'

'We don't need Six involved,' said Mendale. 'They're too close to the Americans. Brasenose would be happy to sacrifice Griffin to score a few points in Langley.'

I had no idea who Brasenose was but Watkins agreed. 'Six has to be a last resort.'

Joseff handed me a batch of files. 'Read these, you leave here in fifty minutes. There are some logistics to fix first.'

'Any sign of the men who attacked Thomas in Zandvoort?' Watkins asked.

'None.'

'Has there been a search?'

'No. As far as the Dutch are concerned Kardosov was followed over the border from Germany and never went anywhere near Zandvoort. We don't want them thinking we're poaching on their territory. And the photo Thomas took at Zandvoort station didn't come out – too dark.'

So I was off again. Joseff must have been pleased with my performance in Zandvoort after all. Or alternatively I was being given a chance to redeem myself.

Back in my office I opened the Griffin file. Although marked 'Office of Naval Intelligence', it was written in the computer jargon language peculiar to the CIA's analysts at Langley, starting with the title: 'GRIFFIN. Garble-Recognition Interrogation-Friend-or-Foe Inboard Nautics – Master Control Unit'.

Most of the report was devoted to Griffin's history from 'Initial Program-Parameter Formulation' to 'Pre-production Prototype'. There was practically nothing on the actual mechanics other than obscure references to quartz chip technology, electrostatic units, microelectric circuitry and so on. The approximate dimensions of the stolen prototype were given as: cylindrical, length five inches, diameter two inches, both ends 'multi-point socketed'. There was a sketch but no photographs.

The report bore another CIA hallmark; it said only what they wanted us to know: no details of Griffin's functions or indications of what would happen if the Russians got hold of it. The CIA case officer who had sent us the report, Richard Newell, had suggested that if we needed further information we should contact him and had provided his number. I was sure that if I did so he would, in a phrase recently used in reference to a government minister, provide every form of assistance short of actual help. The Royal Navy had tried to provide more background but after reading their appendix twice I was little wiser.

The Griffin undersea interrogator was developed from the now obsolete British airborne PTR446. The appendix started with excerpts by W. Mitchell AMITPP from an old *Electrical Engineering* magazine, hardly top-secret, dealing with the PTR446.

The article was full of references to subjects like defruiting, garble recognition and real-time coding that left me cold.

I was always amazed when one group of experts tried to clarify the works of another group of experts by simply replacing one set of jargon terms by their own.

If I understood what the Navy's appendix was trying to say it seemed that the PTR446 had been a miniaturised transponder that allowed aircraft to be interrogated using specific interrogation modes, presumably to see which side they were on, friend or foe.

In Britain the same technology was now being developed by the Navy for ground-to-ship interrogators. However the US Navy were clearly much further ahead.

The appendix continued with a brief explanation of how the interrogator had been adapted at the laboratories in Ann Arbor, Michigan for undersea operations. In addition the weight had been considerably reduced. It concluded: 'The Griffin Interrogator, of which the master control unit stolen by Donnell is the "brain", represents a breakthrough in undersea surveillance techniques. It enables US submarines to definitively identify vessels as friendly, hostile or neutral and attack or evade when appropriate. The efficiency of US killer submarines could be increased by up to 60 per cent. More important than these gains are the losses that would be incurred if the Russians obtained Griffin. Not only is Griffin Interrogator's technology at least six years ahead of its Soviet equivalent, but Russian knowledge of US interrogation modes would nullify the entire Griffin programme and leave Allied submarines dangerously exposed in the event of hostilities. Submarine-based first strike nuclear capacity could not be guaranteed.'

What the Navy meant was that if the Russians got Griffin they could win the next war because they would be able to launch their submarine-based missiles but we wouldn't. It was sombre reading, even allowing for our naval colleagues' obsessive exaggeration of the Communist menace and their belief that all wars are settled at sea.

The other two files I read quickly. The dossier on Donnell I had seen before, a photocopy of an FBI clearance we'd received when he attended a Cambridge physics symposium. Born Dublin, 1935, parents emigrated to Pittsburgh, Pennsylvania, 1939. Bachelor's and Master's UCLA. Naval Service Bethesda, Maryland, and Naval Telecommunications Command, Washington DC. Access to unspecified secret material. Doctorate MIT. Currently deputy co-ordinator Griffin program, University of Michigan. Unmarried. Five feet ten inches. One hundred and ninety-five pounds.

The photograph was four years old and the fingerprints blurred in transit.

The file on Kardosov contained the photo Mendale had shown us and just three paragraphs. The first gave details from his passport, if they were correct he would now be forty-seven. The second was an unilluminating summary of his UN activities concluding: 'subject's primary role remains uncertain'. The third listed a confirmed sighting in Moscow six years ago in the company of known KGB executives and an unconfirmed sighting in Ankara six months later.

I had just returned the files when Watkins appeared clutching a new briefcase. 'Follow me,' he barked in my direction.

In his office the walls caught people's attention. One was devoted to aviation: prints of hot air balloons and Da Vinci's parachute; a graduation certificate from the Senior Flying Training School in Manitoba, covered with the autographs of fellow graduates; photos of the young Watkins in a Harvard trainer and beside a Mosquito, bullet holes clearly visible in the rear fuselage.

The other walls were covered with posters showing the opposition: serried rows of photos and organisational charts with titles like 'CPSU Politburo and Secretariat', 'Czechoslovakian Socialist Republic Government Structure', 'USSR Council of Ministers' and 'Military Organisation of the People's Republic of China'. They were produced by an American agency and sent to us by the dozen. Only Watkins displayed them. They served no purpose and the organogram headed 'Government and Party Structure of the Democratic Republic of Vietnam' was long out of date, a souvenir perhaps of Watkins' plan to create an Indochina network. As usual, his scheme had been far too elaborate, full of impossible to recruit sleeper cells with impossible to understand cut-outs. The DG had finally vetoed it and if he hadn't Six certainly would have.

He flipped through a batch of pink FBIS daily reports to show that he was busy. The reports from the American Foreign Broadcast Intelligence Service were summaries of the previous day's Russian news broadcasts which I had soon stopped reading. When he had finished he started talking at me through his moustache.

'Have you read the files?'

'Yes.'

'Good. Langley sent us the Griffin report on Monday. Apparently it was supposed to be as secret from us as from the Russians. No wonder the Navy's so excited.'

He opened the briefcase lying on his desk. Inside was a compartment about six inches long by three inches deep and the same wide and full of cotton wool.

'Operations have produced this to transport Griffin, just to make sure you don't break it. As the Americans know you we've arranged a cover. You're Rupert Ashton, travel agent. There's a profile here. Read it on the way to the airport, then give it to your driver Morgans. Don't take it with you.'

'Of course.'

He handed me my new passport. I wondered how anyone had been able to produce a passport with my details in so quickly but then I remembered that Watkins had wanted us to use false papers in Zandvoort. The idea had been vetoed but not before he had set the wheels in motion. Watkins also passed over the airline ticket, a roll of US and Canadian dollars and an American Express card, and pushed some travel leaflets into the briefcase.

'French will contact you at the airport. If Donnell's got any sense he'll have got out of the US as fast as possible but in case he hasn't, and you have to follow Kardosov from Toronto, there's an American multiple-entry visa in the passport. I hardly need tell you to be cautious in the US, we can't afford another Lechlade.'

Robert Lechlade was a CIA analyst who had offered to sell us material we wouldn't normally see. Although the special relationship with the US meant that any intelligence we acquired

41

was automatically shared with the Americans it didn't always work the other way round. We bought reports from Lechlade for eighteen months until, somehow, he was blown. All hell broke loose. Vitriolic recriminations flew across the Atlantic and only assurances from Downing Street that it wouldn't happen again maintained the surface cooperation of the two services. It would be unwise to tread on American toes and this operation was blatantly poaching on their territory. We should have told the FBI about Kardosov and kept our noses out of it. Just as we should have told the Dutch BVD about Leonov and let them monitor the Zandvoort drops.

'Remember,' Watkins concluded. 'Your target is the Interrogator. Bring that back and there will be champagne all round. If the Canadians are as good as everybody says they are it should be easy. Let French look after Kardosov.'

'Have you met French?' I asked.

'No, someone from Washington or Ottawa I suppose. Probably an old crony of the DG. As you heard I offered to go myself but clearly I'm needed here.'

I collected my standby suitcase and went to find Morgans, one of the pool drivers. I was surprised to find Mendale waiting with him.

The Director Operations took me aside. 'Let the Canadians handle things,' he said. 'You were lucky in Zandvoort, don't try to be a hero again. Your role this time is delivery boy, just bring Griffin back.'

At least, I thought, Watkins and Mendale agreed on something.

Once in the car I opened the personality profile. Rupert Stanley Ashton. Home: Watford. Wife: Maureen. Children: John and Sandra. Occupation: travel agency manager, Leadenhall. Hobbies: golf, travelling, music. They'd made me two years older.

Morgans weaved expertly through the traffic, not hesitating to put his foot down when there was the smallest gap ahead.

'Why do we pay for police driving courses,' I asked, 'when you could teach us?'

'I couldn't do that,' Morgans replied. 'That's professional grade, I'm a mechanic.'

I sat back after that masterpiece of Civil Service logic. What grade was I? The thought still nagged away at the back of my mind: I was just a delivery boy but even so Operations must have had a host of people better qualified than me. Why had I been chosen?

V

Canada was having another of its airline disputes and we were delayed in Montreal for what seemed ages. When the plane reached Toronto I just wanted terra firma under my feet. It was not to be.

A typical Foreign Office type approached; no chin, receding hair shorn rather than cut, late twenties, squeaky voice and unrecognised old school tie.

'Rupert Ashton? I'm Jeremy Atholl. Welcome to Canada. 'Fraid you won't be here for long. I'm to tell you your man is in Chicago. I've a ticket here, Air Canada flight leaving now from Gate 91.'

He handed me the ticket and stepped back to make way for a neoteric surrey: a trailer with a fringe on top pulled by an electric tractor, the driver expertly weaving her dozen passengers across the blue carpet.

Suddenly the mission looked very different. I had asked Joseff what would happen if we discovered Kardosov was planning to meet Donnell in the US. 'That would be unfortunate,' he had replied. 'You and French might try to follow him.' It looked like that was happening. So much for the idea of letting the Canadians grab Kardosov and forgetting about the Griffin Interrogator. Perhaps after all it had been agreed that Six would send some of their Washington team to Chicago.

Atholl stood making conversation until my flight was called. I left him to write home to mummy that he'd been helping one of our spies. 'Funny sort,' he would write, 'bit stand-offish you know.'

There was no Jeremy Atholl at O'Hare Field Chicago. Just a message. 'You are booked into The Drake, Lakeshore Drive and Michigan Avenue. French.'

'Nice hotel,' the taxi driver told me, 'the best.'

I could believe him; I had been told that the Russians always travel first class.

'You a Limey?'

'British, yes.'

'Thought so. You can always tell.'

That exhausted his conversation until we reached the hotel which was opposite the Playboy Tower. Pity Kardosov wasn't staying there.

I had been to the US before as a tourist and on the Psychological Warfare course as a guest of the US government. The position now was quite different. I was here to bring back something that actually belonged to the Americans themselves, our closest ally. Joseff had said that our operating in the US was not easy 'politically' and I had already been in the DIS long enough to know what he meant. Relations between US and British Intelligence had not always been easy. During and after the war the deep-seated anti-British prejudice of America's new spymaster, Allen Dulles, had collided with the patronising arrogance of the old hands at MI5 and MI6. Much of the Whitehall Intelligence establishment considered the ascendancy of the CIA an insult to the natural order. They were still proud of the MI6 disinformation campaign in 1956 which had prevented the Americans gaining even an inkling that Israel, France and Britain were about to invade Egypt. But that had infuriated both the CIA and the White House and since then MI6 had been making desperate attempts to build bridges. The Lechlade business had not helped. Was the DG really going to risk another transatlantic bust-up? The Americans might well have agreed to share the Griffin Interrogator if we had simply told them about Kardosov and let them get on with it.

The taxi driver's assessment of The Drake was correct. Brown-liveried doormen. Red velvet covered handrails. Marble lobby. The registration desk an impressive mass of dark wood, mirrors and glistening metal. Dignified opulence.

'I believe you have a room for me. Rupert Ashton.'

'Certainly sir. Please check that your address is correct on here and sign.' I signed and registration was complete.

'Front,' the clerk shouted. 'Room three sixty-four for Mr Ashton, and there is a message. I hope you have a pleasant stay at The Drake sir.'

'I'm sure I will.'

My third-floor room was large, I hoped the Department budget would cope. Twin beds, easy chairs, marble-topped coffee table, walk-in wardrobe, spacious bathroom and small bar in the lobby. European prints hung on the wall; French airships, reminiscent of Watkins' office, and German buildings with Latin inscriptions. Above the desk sat a large but unostentatious mirror. The lights were plentiful but not glaring. Altogether an elegant room.

The bellhop, replete in black blazer and gold crest, left my case on a folding rack by the bed. I opened the message he'd given me. It was right to the point. 'Phone Julia French, room 541. If no reply wait in your room.'

Julia French it said. Julia. That was the first surprise of the day. I hadn't been expecting a woman. Why? Not just because of the Department's inveterate male chauvinism. No, it was because nobody in London had suggested the possibility. I couldn't remember anyone referring to French as either he or she. 'Probably an old crony of the DG,' Watkins had said, but nobody had mentioned her gender.

Five and Six had a few female agents but to the best of my knowledge the DIS had no women in operational roles. Where, after all, would they recruit them from? The Women's Royal Army Corps and its Naval and RAF equivalents provided typists and drivers but certainly not combat personnel who might be able to take on the sort of role we needed in Chicago. Perhaps Julia French had been recruited during the war and now, thirty years later, was still attached to an Embassy somewhere.

I punched 541 on the push button phone: no reply. But as I put the phone down there was a knock on the door.

'Who is it?'

'Julia French.'

The second surprise of the day. I was expecting someone who would take over the operation. Julia French was not that person. She was far too young, probably no older than me. She was beautiful: dark, almost black hair, brown eyes, Roman nose, full mouth and strikingly curved figure. Not the 'swallow' type some Intelligence agencies use to entrap unwary men, but certainly beautiful. In other circumstances her arrival in my room would have been very welcome.

'Do I meet your requirements?'

I hadn't realised that I was staring at her. 'You're not what I expected,' was all I could murmur in embarrassment.

Her question had been gently posed, not angry or sarcastic or even mocking. But not flirtatious either. Her voice was warm without being soft. Her accent upper crust but not pretentious. When she spoke there were no pleasant introductions. It was as if she was trying to demonstrate, or prove, her professionalism.

'You've gathered that things didn't go as expected in Toronto. I'd better explain.' She sat down in one of the easy chairs.

'The Mounties identified Kardosov at the airport and followed him to his hotel. He had a reservation for one night. There was a message waiting for him which he picked up before it could be intercepted. He was only in his room for ten or fifteen minutes and then he vanished.'

'What do you mean he vanished?'

'Exactly that. While the Canadians were setting up their surveillance Kardosov slipped out of the hotel through the kitchens and disappeared. Apparently something similar happened in Holland. Group Captain Watkins thought he had Samovar cornered in Nijmegen.'

'That's right. We supposedly had him under observation when he vanished and popped up in Copenhagen.'

'Well this time we're expecting him to pop up in Chicago. He seems to be travelling here by road. He may have had help, which is something the Mounties would like to talk to him about.'

'So how did you find that out?' I asked.

'The hotel receptionist in Toronto told the police that the message he had received was a phone number, not local. When they checked the phone records they discovered that as soon as he

47

reached his room Kardosov had dialled a number in Chicago. He was on the phone for exactly four minutes. He then dialled another Chicago number and spoke for about the same length of time. The first call was to a Holiday Inn. There was no way to determine who he spoke to or what was said. He doesn't seem to have made a booking so it's assumed he spoke to a guest. The second call was to another hotel, this one, The Drake. The Canadians managed to establish that a Mr Nils Olssen had phoned and booked a room for two days starting tomorrow. And that's not all, at the same time he booked a room for the same period in the name of Walter Henning.'

'You think he phoned Donnell at the Holiday Inn and then booked them both rooms here?'

'I did think that. But why would Donnell want Kardosov to book his room? He could do that himself.'

'To cover his tracks?'

'Perhaps, but if you were Donnell would you risk meeting in a hotel room where Kardosov could pull a gun?'

'No, I wouldn't.'

French was right, Donnell would want Kardosov to come to him. I remembered what Ronald Jacobs had said in Zandvoort about the other side not liking to operate on their own. 'Kardosov must be expecting backup.'

'That's right. London have just called. They think they've found Walter Henning. Someone with that name is about to take off from Helsinki bound for New York. It would be too much of a coincidence for there to be two Walter Hennings. Moscow is sending a backup.'

I nodded. 'So when Kardosov booked a room in Chicago you decided to come here.'

'That's right. I was in Winnipeg just about to get on a plane for Toronto so I rerouted to Chicago. Luckily Kardosov must have stopped somewhere between here and Toronto. I managed to get to Chicago ahead of him.'

'But now what do we do? You and I can't do much on our own.'

'We're not on our own. The RCMP Security Service agreed to send a team down here.'

'The Mounties are still involved?'

'Yes they are but it's an enormous risk for them; fortunately their Security Service seems to like taking risks. The DG refers to them as The Cowboys. I don't think they've told their political masters what they are doing. We've helped them in the past and they're returning the favour. We couldn't mount anything on our own and because Six won't help the DG had to ask the Canadians. If they get caught here there will be hell to pay. That's exactly why Six wouldn't countenance operating inside the US. It does mean that the whole operation is very, very sensitive. Any sign that the Americans are on to us and we all get out immediately. Abort everything. The DG hasn't told Brasenose that Kardosov is now in Chicago.'

'Who's Brasenose?'

'Justin Brasenose from Six. He handles liaison between Six and the CIA.'

Watkins and Mendale had mentioned his name, I remembered. Mendale had complained that Brasenose was too close to the Americans.

'You think the DG has told our minister what we're doing?'

French seemed surprised by the question. 'Of course he has.'

The Defence Secretary, Roy Mason, was a former Yorkshire miner with a particular passion for the SAS and Special Operations so perhaps we did have political cover. Relations between the Labour government and the Americans had long been prickly. When the Labour Party conference had demanded that Prime Minister Wilson condemn US intervention in Vietnam he had refused only because Lyndon Johnson had threatened financial retaliation. As Wilson told one of his more left-wing ministers: 'We can't kick our creditors in the balls.' Perhaps, though, we could tickle them.

'I'm sure the DG has thought this through,' French continued. 'Mendale and Watkins both recommended we go ahead.'

French stood up and walked over to the window. There was something about the way she stood that made me think she belonged in uniform, not something I ever fantasised about. She just looked military. It would be entirely normal for the DIS to second in someone from the Army for an operation like this but not someone like Julia French, she was far from normal. She was far too young.

And she wasn't a DIS type. The one characteristic of everyone I had met in the Intelligence world is that they took themselves extremely seriously. French didn't have that gravitas. It was almost as if she was acting out a role. She was certainly confident, but it was the effortless self-confidence that gets poured out with the cornflakes at the more expensive private schools. It wasn't the confidence that comes from hard-edged experience.

On top of that nobody in London seemed to know anything about her, Watkins didn't even know French was a woman, but she certainly knew everything about them. It wasn't surprising that she knew the names of the Director Analysis and Production and the Director Operations but how on earth did she know what course of action they had been recommending to the DG? Come to that, how did she know who Justin Brasenose was and what the DG had or had not told him? She could hardly be any more senior than me and yet she seemed to have been briefed in remarkable detail. Did she really need to be told about Nijmegen or that we had originally code-named Kardosov Samovar?

'The Canadian team is led by Inspector Nick Broadbent,' French continued. 'He's here now. The rest of his team are on their way. They will all be in place before Kardosov and Henning arrive. Nick will have someone at O'Hare to pick up Henning when he lands. Kardosov won't be able to disappear again.'

'Assuming he shows up in the first place. I don't understand why Kardosov rushes to phone Donnell as soon as he arrives in Toronto but they then wait two days before actually meeting up. Why would Donnell wait for Kardosov to receive reinforcements?'

'Because Henning will presumably be bringing the money to pay him. Kardosov seems to be travelling very light, he just had a flight bag in Toronto.'

'That's a hell of a presumption,' I said. 'Kardosov could have collected funds on his way here, you said he may have had help in Canada. And why would Donnell want cash? If the Griffin Interrogator really is worth as much as the DG seems to think it is there would be an awful lot of cash to carry around. Why wouldn't he demand funds paid into a Swiss account?'

French had no real answer. 'London are confident nothing will happen before Henning arrives.'

I wasn't so confident. Donnell had Griffin and so he had the whip hand. In his position I wouldn't hang around until the Russians had sorted themselves out.

'If Donnell is clever enough to have stolen the gadget in the first place and remain out of sight ever since, I'm surprised he hasn't got out of the country. I would have left the US as soon as possible, jetted off to the Cayman Islands and demanded the Russians meet me there.'

French had been thinking along the same lines. 'You could be right, although the Americans did say they thought the theft of the Interrogator was entirely opportunistic. Donnell just saw a chance and took it. But let's think this through. Donnell isn't our concern. Once he's passed Griffin to the Russians we can forget about him. We want Kardosov and we want Griffin. It doesn't matter when Donnell passes the Interrogator over. Once he does the team just needs to grab Kardosov before he can get out of Chicago. It's really quite straightforward. There's no reason for Kardosov to think he's under observation.'

'But he's a professional, he's bound to check for surveillance. He's already got away from us twice.'

'Well if worst comes to worst we forget about trying to grab Kardosov. We just bop him on the head and take the Griffin Interrogator.'

I shook my head in disbelief. Kardosov had been operating under cover for years, how could she imagine he wouldn't be looking out for surveillance? And the expression 'bop him on the head' was more Secret Seven children's book than Secret Service training manual. How long had French been with the DIS?

'You make it sound easy. The Canadian team's not even here yet. What's going to happen when they do get here? And when do I get to meet Broadbent?'

French turned and looked me straight in the face. 'You don't. You don't need to know anything about that side of things. London has been very clear. I'm to handle all liaison with the Canadians. If we can grab the Griffin Interrogator you take it home. Nick's team are professionals, we leave everything to them. Like I said, this is very sensitive, the less either of us knows about the Canadians' plans the less risk there is that we'll give something away. Don't worry about them. Your job is to take the Griffin Interrogator back to London.'

She must have realised how sharp she sounded. 'I don't mean to snap but you're a civilian. I promise you Nick Broadbent knows what he's doing. The best thing you can do is get some rest. If you want to eat, the Cape Cod room on the ground floor is pretty good. I'm meeting Nick first thing tomorrow. Why don't you and I meet after that?'

I could only nod. 'Coffee downstairs at, say, nine-thirty?'

She shook her head. 'That wouldn't be very secure, would it? I'll come to your room.'

French walked towards the door. 'I shall call you Ashton by the way, as Rupert is a pet hate of mine, and obviously we can't use Thomas in public.'

'And what do I call you? Are French and Broadbent cover names as well?'

'We don't need covers.'

She left still smiling and I was left still bemused. Julia French knew far too much, including, it seemed, my real name. Another breach of the need-to-know principle. Something didn't feel right about her. She seemed to have no more understanding of 'tradecraft' than I did but she was clearly trusted far more than I was. I was feeling out of my depth and wanted to talk to someone. Watkins had insisted I should call him if anything went wrong but I wasn't sure he was the right person to call about something as nebulous as a vague disquiet. In any case it was the middle of the night in London and I didn't want to talk to the night duty staff. I decided that if I still felt uneasy in the morning I would phone Adam Joseff. The Deputy DG was the one person with both the knowledge and the experience to understand my concerns.

In the event London phoned me at six o'clock in the morning Central Time.

'How's it going?' asked Watkins. I couldn't decide whether he didn't know he had woken me up or simply didn't care.

'I'm not sure how it's going. I haven't been allowed to meet the Canadians. They clearly want to handle everything themselves. And French seems to have no more experience of this sort of thing than I do.'

'I don't know French,' Watkins replied. 'I wasn't aware that Operations had a permanent presence in North America outside the Embassies. We must rely on the Director Operation's judgement about French.'

I had not appreciated that French was Mendale's responsibility. It sounded as if Watkins was lining up his excuses in case things went wrong.

'The Director General is confident that adequate DIS resources are being devoted to this assignment. You must concentrate on retrieving the equipment that has been lost. Leave everything else to the others; I gather French has an extraction plan for his target.'

'His target?'

'Yes. You know who that target is. We should be cautious with names on an open line.'

'I know who the target is, but you said *his* target. French is a woman.'

There was a moment's hesitation. 'Well, Thomas, we must move with the times. Even the RAF Officers' College has started admitting women. I can see now why you might think you need more support from here but that would mean calling upon another Service. The Director General has decided against such a course of action. Quite rightly in my judgement.'

If French was right the DG had not decided against calling upon another Service, Six had decided not to risk stepping on American toes. Watkins wasn't waiting for me to respond. He continued in the stilted terms he considered appropriate for an open line.

'I was phoning to ensure you were aware that the target may be about to receive support from Finland.'

'Yes, I had heard.'

'This is of course an unwelcome complication. There may be more support which we don't yet know about. But as I said the DG has decided that you and French constitute a sufficient resource commitment. I offered to come over myself, as you know, but the DG values my presence here.'

Watkins must have realised he was hardly sounding reassuring. 'Listen, Thomas, I understand your concerns, of course I do. The news from Finland is unsettling. Make sure you keep me fully informed of all developments. My advice to you now is to observe the Canadians, if they don't succeed in their own mission then there will be nothing for you to bring home, but don't be distracted from your own objective. Our Directorate's priority is the item you were sent to retrieve, anything else can be left to French. You will have my full support in that.'

He rang off, leaving me no wiser than I was before he called. And it was clear that I was going to learn nothing more from French and the Canadians.

I understood why the Canadians wouldn't want someone as inexperienced as me getting involved with their operation but I hadn't been happy with French effectively telling me to go to bed and leave everything to the grown-ups.

If Broadbent was intending to follow Kardosov and Henning to their meeting with Donnell he would need to have transport immediately available. There would be no time to recover cars from the hotel's own parking. I had already checked that the hotel had two entrances: the main entrance on Walton and another on Lakeshore Drive. Both could be reached either from the lobby level or from the basement arcade. There was nowhere to park on Walton. Broadbent would have to rely on leaving his vehicles on meters opposite the rear entrance.

However professional French judged the Canadian team to be, it seemed to me that there was no realistic chance of them getting away with kidnapping two trained Russian agents on the streets of Chicago. Their only practical plan was to wait until the Russians had the Interrogator in their possession and had returned to the hotel. Even then jumping somebody like Kardosov in his room would not be straightforward.

I put that to Julia French next morning when she came to my room. I expected another lecture on leaving everything to the Canadians but she had clearly been mulling the situation over, either that or she had talked to someone in London who was more forthcoming than Watkins.

'This isn't what we wanted,' French started. 'Everything would have been much easier in Canada but we had no choice. Nobody would choose to mount an operation like this inside the US. Six didn't want to help not just because of the political risk, Brasenose doesn't believe the mission can succeed. And he may be right. Nick Broadbent is pretty realistic about our prospects, that's why he's so obsessive about secrecy. If things don't work out he doesn't want to leave the slightest trace behind. But on the other hand the Canadians like the idea of twitching the tail of the elephant next door. And in London Mendale and Watkins seem to be saying we've come this far so we might as well go on.'

Again I was surprised that French seemed so well informed about the thinking of the DIS Directors. But she was right. Ministry of Defence projects never seemed to be abandoned until they were so far over budget or so far behind schedule that even the *Daily Telegraph* had stopped enthusing over them. Watkins had taken me to a meeting at the Treasury where a junior civil servant had condescendingly explained the principle of sunk costs: when you are evaluating a project you must only look at future costs, what you've already spent is irrelevant, it's gone. Watkins simply did not understand.

'We've spent a fortune on this project,' I remember him saying angrily, 'we can't stop now and just write it all off.'

'That's exactly what you can do,' he was told. 'It doesn't matter how much you've spent, it's not worth spending a penny more.'

The Treasury, of course, had won on that occasion but I could well believe that the momentum of the current mission was proving unstoppable. If we had suddenly discovered that there was a Russian

55

agent inside the US trying to buy a piece of stolen American kit we would have told the Americans right away. But that wasn't what happened. We had identified Kardosov in Zandvoort, lost him and then found him again in Copenhagen, tracked him to Toronto and then discovered he was off to Chicago to meet Donnell and acquire the Griffin Interrogator. We couldn't stop there. After everything we had already done it had to be worth one more throw of the dice.

'So what's the plan?' I asked French. 'You met Broadbent earlier. What did he tell you?'

'He didn't say much. He's keeping his cards very close to his chest. Some of his team are already here but they're waiting for something to arrive from Canada.'

'What?'

'I don't know, something to do with what he calls the extraction plan. If the Mounties can grab Kardosov they still have to smuggle him back across the border. Nick's set a kick-off point of noon today. Everything will be in place by then.'

'And if Kardosov turns up before then?'

'He won't. Henning can't get here before three-thirty at the earliest.'

'So what do we do?'

'Nothing.'

'Neither of us?'

'Neither of us. Nick obviously thinks we will get in the way. We're to be in our rooms at noon and stay there until we're called. Once Kardosov has checked in he'll be kept under surveillance and if he goes out they will try to follow. But the important thing is to spot him when he returns. If Nick thinks Kardosov's picked up the Interrogator the Canadians will grab him in his room. They seem confident about that. If when they grab him they find he doesn't have the Interrogator you'll have to go home empty-handed. Nick's set up what he calls a control room in room 544. There will always be someone there if we need to get in touch, but he clearly doesn't expect that to happen.'

I had no right to expect more but after being shot at in Zandvoort and turning the tables on my attacker it was disappointing, to put it mildly, to be expected to sit in a hotel room while all the action happened elsewhere. I had assumed I would be present when we moved in on Kardosov. I sensed that Julia French was feeling the same.

The previous evening I might have described Julia French as condescending, even smug, but that would have been a misjudgement. London had evidently told her that she was in charge of the operation and she had been determined to act appropriately. Now I suspected Broadbent had made clear that this was a Canadian operation and French was here merely as decoration. The days when decisions on Intelligence matters were made in London and simply relayed to Ottawa were long gone. She was discovering that the RCMP Security Service might be doing us a favour but they would do it their way.

'How long have you been with the DIS?' I asked.

'Not long.'

'You're Army?'

'RAF.'

'I didn't know we had people stationed in Canada.'

'There was training I had to complete in Manitoba.'

'What sort of training?'

She looked straight at me and I noticed her eyes were a warm greeny-brown. The warmth didn't extend to her voice.

'Am I being interrogated?'

'Of course not.'

'Good. If there is nothing more to say about the operation let's keep the conversation to the weather and what we did on our holidays shall we?'

'OK. What did you do on your holidays?'

She had the grace to smile. 'You first.'

'Well I spent four summers in a row with a Portuguese pen pal named Luis jumping on trams in Lisbon and cycling around Cornwall. What about you?'

'I was in Cornwall too. All my Long Leaves and holidays were spent with my cousin Susan near Port Gaverne.'

'Long Leaves?'

'That's what we called half-terms at Wycombe Abbey. Susan and I were inseparable. My uncle bought us two of those new Australian

57

fibreglass surfboards and we spent one summer trying to stand up on those without making complete fools of ourselves.'

'Did you ever surf at Polzeath?' I asked. 'Luis and I spent a whole afternoon watching a couple of gorgeous girls surfing there, although I'm sure if you'd been one of them I would have remembered you.'

Her theatrically raised eyebrow seemed to say: 'You'll have to do a lot better than that!'

'Let's go for a walk,' she suggested. 'But I need to phone London first.'

The lobby was crowded. I sat waiting for her near the massive open fireplace and people-watched. A group of Japanese businessmen bowed to each other. Behind them a very large woman and even larger man were in a heated discussion with each other. A man who had just collected what looked like a laundry parcel from reception tried to get past them. Julia appeared and crossed towards me as the man with the package strode past the carved wooden table with its silver vase of chrysanthemums which greeted guests entering the hotel. It was Kardosov.

He wore a fawn raincoat although it had stopped raining thirty minutes earlier. There was an airline bag over one shoulder with the familiar blue and white logo of Pan Am.

I grabbed Julia's arm. 'That's him. Kardosov.'

'Are you sure?'

'Positive.'

We both ran outside in time to see the Russian climb into a taxi. Julia waved at the next in line.

Nick Broadbent and our plans were completely forgotten.

'Follow that cab,' she said, pointing at Kardosov's taxi.

VI

'Follow that cab,' the driver repeated the cliché. 'Man you gotta be joking. I ain't never followed no cab. Where you wanna go?'

'Come on, just follow that yellow taxi.'

'But where you goin' man? You gotta know where you wanna go.'

'Look, just follow the man in that cab, he's stolen money from my wife.' It was the first thing that came into my mind. Julia French looked startled.

The driver didn't reply but we moved off. It looked as though Kardosov had decided not to wait for backup. Or more likely Donnell had decided not to wait for the Russians to fly in reinforcements. The other taxi was now in Michigan Avenue. We followed, the driver gunning the engine and the taxi skidding on the wet surface. He had obviously got the message that people do follow other people in taxis.

Kardosov's taxi turned right into Wacker, past the circular towers of Marina City across the river and then left down La Salle.

'Man, perhaps he's going to put the money he stole in the bank,' the driver suggested. 'There's a whole lot of banks down this way.'

We passed under The Loop. A green and white train trundling overhead. La Salle is one of the few Chicago streets that is not dead straight. At Jackson Boulevard it kinks around the Chicago Board of Trade building. It was there that Kardosov's taxi stopped.

I gave our driver a generous tip.

'That cabby will remember us,' Julia commented.

'True, but nobody will question him unless the mission's already gone wrong.'

The lobby of the Board of Trade was enormous. To the left stood the 'Visitors' Centre', at the back a row of lifts. A sign indicated Bollings Restaurant in the basement.

We reached the revolving doors as Kardosov disappeared down a staircase.

'Stay here,' I shouted, running after him. But he'd gone. And when I found him four minutes later I almost failed to recognise him. Now I knew what his parcel had contained: a faded red jacket emblazoned 'Chicago Board Options Exchange' and a badge with the same inscription and, in large letters, 'RVB' above the name Robert Burens.

I was walking towards the stairs when he emerged from the men's room. I strode past him, reasonably confident that he hadn't seen me at the hotel or in Zandvoort. He didn't look at me.

I found Julia's arm and guided her towards the lifts. 'He's going to the Options Exchange.'

'Did he see you?'

'I don't think he really noticed me. Still I'll try to keep out of his sight. He's wearing a red jacket and a badge with the initials RVB.'

'Are you sure he's on the floor of the Exchange?'

'No, but why else would Donnell send him the jacket? An exchange at the Exchange. It's a good idea. Crowded so Kardosov shouldn't be tempted to any funny business. A distinctive badge so Donnell can recognise him. And a place Donnell presumably knows well and therefore with a well-planned escape route. There's only one problem: how do we get in?'

'We just walk. Look as if we know exactly what we're doing and nobody will interfere.'

There was a desk at the entrance but the attendant was surrounded by people. We walked quickly past.

The overwhelming impression was of a mass of people scurrying round like human ants. Most of them, but fortunately not all, wore jackets like Kardosov's, red, blue or mustard. The few women, mostly young girls, wore mustard jackets or street clothes.

We separated and started looking for Kardosov. There were dozens, perhaps hundreds of red-jacketed men. In those days share options were an esoteric novelty and the Options Exchange was a new, speculative market; the brokers were quite different from their contemporaries in the City or on Wall Street, younger looking with fashionable shirts and hair. It should have made Kardosov easier to find but it didn't.

I wove through the babbling figures, ignoring their meaningless shouts.

'April one eighty.'

'Five eighths.'

'Jan. the twenty.'

'Quarter.'

'I'll split bid.'

Fingers flashed. Men clutched handfuls of little cards. Women, looking as if they should have been at school, pushed past.

I saw Julia ten yards away. And then, between us, Donnell, looking exactly like his photograph. He wore a blue jacket and was talking out of the side of his mouth to a man standing beside the IBM stand: Kardosov. Julia saw him at the same moment. We both stopped.

Donnell passed something to the Russian who pocketed it. Then Donnell reached towards Kardosov again, presumably to take something in return.

A mustard coat stepped in front of me, pushing a card towards a red coat. 'Take this for us.'

I shoved past. Kardosov was moving. And Donnell was falling, an odd look on his face: pain, shock.

Julia moved forward. I could only see Donnell's hand now, grasping at somebody's leg. I turned, pushing towards the door. Kardosov was leaving the floor. As I reached the door a few seconds later there was a clear shout of 'Ambulance' from behind. I glanced around. Julia was a few yards away. We met at the lifts. Kardosov had gone.

'He'll have to get out of that jacket,' Julia said. 'If he changes in the basement again we can catch him in the lobby.'

The lift was full and we descended in silence. Standing by the Visitors' Centre I asked the obvious question, 'What happened?'

'Donnell reached forward and Kardosov seemed to grab his wrist. He must have had a hypodermic or something. It's exactly the way they killed that Ukrainian émigré in Frankfurt last year.'

'But why?' I asked. 'Why attract attention? He could so easily have walked away.'

'I know. It's stupid. Perhaps that's the way the Russians think. No witnesses. No loose ends. Nobody who can give away the name Nils Olssen. To us it's madness but we didn't do it. Donnell may simply have asked for too much or was in too much of a hurry. Perhaps he panicked and insisted on a meeting right away. If Henning is bringing the payment Kardosov might have just decided to act rather than let Donnell go somewhere else.'

Before I could comment Kardosov emerged, without the red jacket. He marched to the doors without looking round, a satisfied smile streaked across his face. He pushed through the revolving doors and turned right.

'What's he doing?' Julia asked. He made no attempt to flag a taxi. Instead he looked up La Salle, as if to get his bearings, and then at his watch. Apparently satisfied, he turned left and walked along Jackson.

'We must call Nick Broadbent. Tell him what happened so he can grab Kardosov when he gets to the hotel,' said Julia.

'He's not going to the hotel. He didn't check in, he just picked up the jacket and badge. Now that he's got what he came for he'll be off. Why would he hang around?'

But he was hanging around. He walked off steadily: past the Telegraph Savings and Loan Association's electric sign informing the world it was forty-seven degrees. Under The Loop at Wells.

Julia took my hand. 'In case he stops and looks around. Looks less suspicious.'

Just then he stopped. I leaned towards Julia and kissed her. 'That looks less suspicious,' I said.

'At this time of the morning? I think not. We should separate.' A fleeting grin crossed her face.

Kardosov crossed the street and turned up Franklin.

'What do we do?' I asked. 'And don't suggest bopping him on the head.' It was my turn to grin.

Julia raised her eyebrows and shook her head.

As he approached the Sears Tower I realised what he was doing. 'He's playing tourist. His work's done. He's not going to risk going back to the hotel. He probably has time to spare before his flight. So what can he do? He climbs the world's tallest building, has a look at the city from a hundred storeys up.'

'It can't be. You can't kill someone and then go and casually admire a view. It's ridiculous.'

'So was attacking Donnell. And this isn't so stupid. Who's going to look for him up there?'

Sure enough, Kardosov strode into Sears Tower, past the reception desk and followed the arrows marked 'Skydeck'.

'Thomas, this could be our break. I'll tell Nick to drive down here as fast as possible and keep circling the block. You follow Kardosov.'

Julia was off and the Russian was entering one of the two lifts going up to the observation platform, the Skydeck. I joined the line buying tickets, plucking a brochure from the booth. I would need to remind Julia that she was supposed to be calling me Ashton, although I quite enjoyed the small breach of procedure. On the wall of the lift the number of the Skydeck's floor, 103, lay on its side, gradually colouring orange as we rocketed 350 feet in less than a minute.

The Skydeck was like similar vantage points all over the world, but higher. Grey carpets. A few bare wooden seats. Pay telescopes. Pay phones. Bars on front of the windows that sparked with static whenever I touched them. On the west side a souvenir shop.

People milled around or stared fixedly out of the windows; the piped music lost below the hum of voices. Men stole glances at the brochure and then authoritatively told their wives what they were looking at.

'That's the Chicago Board of Trade,' said a schoolteacher type pointing at the Museum of Art.

'That's Lake Michigan,' said another with unassailable accuracy.

Kardosov first stood staring towards the railroad yards and then moved methodically around the tower. I kept well away from him. He spent thirty minutes in the Skydeck, buying plenty of souvenirs.

He glanced at me as I followed him into the crowded lift. For a second I thought he'd recognised me, perhaps from the Board of Trade. But he did nothing. A cold wind whipped up the lift shaft until the doors closed and we started the ear-popping descent.

'Exit to your left,' someone shouted as the doors opened.

Without looking in my direction Kardosov strode past the ground floor souvenir shop towards the revolving doors. Only when he reached them did he seem to sense my presence behind him.

A black Dodge Tradesman van was parked outside next to a 'No Parking' sign, a tall man in tan overalls held the sliding side door open. Julia and another man were approaching the entrance. Kardosov hesitated a moment. I pushed him forward, into the revolving doors.

'Keep walking comrade.'

Julia had a raincoat over her arm. From the side it concealed the Colt .45 automatic in her hand but Kardosov could see it. Where the hell had the gun come from? Kardosov faltered for a second as he came out of the revolving door before walking slowly to the van. He probably thought we were the FBI and had a legion of gun-happy agents saturating the area. His eyes lingered on the U-Park multi-storey garage opposite and then he stepped into the van.

'Put your face on the seat and close your eyes,' I heard someone tell him.

Julia and I followed him into the van and the door was slammed behind us. Kardosov now lay on the floor and a woman in some kind of uniform knelt over him with a hypodermic syringe. As we moved off she inserted the syringe expertly into a vein at his ankle. Today was the day for needles, although the dose Kardosov had given poor Donnell was undoubtedly more dangerous than the sedative being pumped into him.

There were five of us in the back of the van: Julia, me, Kardosov, the woman I now realised was dressed as a nurse and a man I took to be Nick Broadbent. There was another man in the front alongside the driver.

It was over. So easy. Julia found the Interrogator in Kardosov's pocket. Exultation. Relief. Any worries I may have had disappeared. What was important was that we had succeeded. If there had been any doubts about my actions in Zandvoort I had redeemed myself.

'What now?' I asked.

'We drop you and Miss French near the hotel,' replied Broadbent. 'Go to room 544 and tell George "Pandora". He'll understand that means get the hell out of there and clear our tracks. You too.'

'And what will you be doing?'

'Losing this van as soon as possible and then going home.'

'How?'

Broadbent gave me the look Julia had given me earlier. 'You don't need to know that.'

'Presumably you're taking Kardosov back in an ambulance,' I suggested.

Broadbent ignored me and turned to Julia. 'We'll be home in six hours maximum. I'll expect to see you in Jarvis Street then. We'll keep Kardosov there overnight if necessary. You should maybe call London before you leave Chicago. And you can give me back that gun.'

He tapped the driver on the shoulder. 'Drop our friends here.'

And that was it. No farewells.

Back in my hotel room I booked a flight and phoned Watkins with the details. I expected him to want to know exactly what had happened but that, he said, could wait until I returned.

Julia knocked on the door and came in with the Griffin Interrogator. It seemed such a small thing to kill for. I wondered if the police had identified the dead man at the Options Exchange yet. It wouldn't take them long to discover that this was the man wanted for stealing the Griffin Interrogator and it probably wouldn't take them long to link his death to a couple with English accents dropped outside the Exchange a few minutes earlier.

The expressway out of town followed the railway tracks, past ornate churches, factories and crummy houses. Hoardings screamed

J&B Scotch, Budweiser and Walton Rugs. Trees pushed bare branches into the electric aura of the streetlights. 'BACK IN DROVERS COUNTRY' a sign told me. Streets passed with foreign-sounding names: Pulaski Road, Kostner Avenue. The moving panorama of the industrial Midwest. Montrose station sat in the middle of the road, a toy-like train pausing at the platform. And then, bearing right before the Illinois Tollway, O'Hare Field. Almost home.

Past the O'Hare International Tower Hotel, a couple of terminals sitting low and black, and then Trans World. Little more than half an hour from the hotel.

Julia had insisted that I be dropped first and when I left the taxi she gave me a peck on the cheek that I wanted to convince myself meant more than it did.

Inside, the clerk punched at his keyboard and asked a question unthinkable today. 'Smoker or non-smoker sir?'

'Non-smoker.'

'Window or aisle?'

'Window. Where's the duty-free shop?'

'There is none sir. Cigarettes and liquor on the plane.'

That was the worst blow since leaving London. The terminal was bleak. The gift shop had nothing I would give. The English Pub looked more like an English Launderette and I settled for the liquefied ice cream the drugstore called strawberry milkshake.

Most of the passengers were American. A group of sailors. A fat man with a lemon shirt and bootlace tie. A young boy and his father wearing identical jackets. Occasionally someone passed who looked foreign. Two Japanese businessmen. A tall, Germanic-looking man, the Varig tag on his bag identifying him as Hector Bunge. A family speaking Italian.

Time ticked by. Nearly 6.30. I stepped into the Gents opposite the doors leading to the Trans World gates, G1 to G12. It was empty. Someone came in behind me. Instinctively I turned to look at him, but too late. The blow caught me behind the right ear and I fell, the floor rising to catch me, a stinging pain filling my head. I passed out.

Coming to, my eyes flashed with glaring colours. Screaming pink, aquamarine, yellow, magenta. I screwed them shut but the colours were still there when I reopened them. Slowly things came into focus. I was looking at the world's most nauseous tie. I closed my eyes again.

A voice tried to penetrate my mushy eardrums. 'You all right buster?'

I nodded weakly. A hammer burst against the inside of my skull. I tried to rise, scrabbling at the floor, my legs feeling like sticks of chalk: weak, brittle, about to crack.

'Easy buster.'

'Take your time,' said a second voice.

With the help of the two men I groggily got up and leaned against the wall.

'What happened?' one of them asked.

I was asking myself the same question. I couldn't think properly. Should I say I had been mugged? That would mean the police.

'I slipped.' My voice sounded hoarse and unnatural.

'Probably wet floor. You oughta sue the guys who run this place, their insurance will pay.'

I didn't feel like suing anybody. Shakily I crossed to the washbasin and splashed water on my face, and then searched for a towel. The room was fitted with warm-air blowers. Finally I found paper towels near the door.

'You sure you're OK?' The man with the tie registered concern.

'I'll be fine. Just needed a minute or two. It was stupid of me.'

'Probably wet floor,' he repeated. 'Like I say, you oughta sue them.'

The other man nodded in agreement and left.

'Thanks,' I said to the tie, 'I'll be OK now.'

Outside there was no sign of anyone carrying a briefcase like mine. I wasn't surprised.

A board on the wall opposite showed that flight 77 had arrived from San Francisco and would continue to London at 7.10. Not long to go.

I walked around the terminal, skull still throbbing and eyes occasionally losing focus. At one point my head started spinning and I sat down for a few minutes before continuing the search. Nobody had a case that even approximated mine.

The Skycaps couldn't help. I thought of the police but not for long. Either they would not find the case or they would find it with the Griffin Interrogator gone. In the remote chance that they found the case intact, the FBI would surely have circulated Griffin's description and I could find myself in even more trouble.

'Be cautious,' Watkins had said, 'we can't afford another Lechlade.' If the police eventually found the case there was nothing in it to connect it with me, either in my real name or as Rupert Ashton. I had no leads of my own. The most sensible course was to go home, admit failure.

The signs to Gate G11 led me past an array of men's rooms I could have used. Passengers were already boarding. I let them get on with it. At the end of the room a huge red board bore the headline 'NOW PLAYING AT LONDON THEATRES'. I didn't want to know.

'We are boarding those passengers whose computer-generated boarding passes are colour-coded green,' boomed the loudspeakers. 'Only those passengers with the word "Green" printed on their pass at this moment.'

My pass was gold, the next to be called, and I trudged aboard. Outside, the terminal was busy. There were other planes, big and small, parked and moving, all normal. But something had changed. American Airlines, Eastern, United, they had all been there when I arrived. But yesterday I had been a bright young man with a glowing future. Tomorrow I could be out of a job. And I had no idea how it had happened.

The plane hurtled along the runway, hauling itself into the sky. The loudspeakers informed us it was 3 953 miles to London. I could have wished it was further. Chicago lay deceptively beautiful below, a jumble of coloured lights and roadways. Off to the right as we moved out over Lake Michigan the Sears Tower blinked farewell.

VII

Yesterday there had been gales in the North Atlantic and we had angled up to sixty-three degrees north to avoid them, passing over the mountains of Greenland, fangs of snow and rock, chilling in their beauty. Now there was just sea below, sea and more sea.

Failure. The word echoed round my mind. Mission failure. Personal failure. I hadn't expected to return the hero of the hour but at least I wanted to demonstrate that I belonged in this clandestine world. Instead I hadn't even been able to avoid a casual mugging, except that this had not been a casual, opportunistic mugging. I had been targeted.

Chicago had been a rollercoaster. I had left London suspicious that the whole mission was not what it seemed; a feeling confirmed when I met Julia French. The sheer amateurishness of everything we were doing brought back the doubts I had first experienced when Watkins told me we were off to Zandvoort to catch a spy. But when Kardosov almost literally fell into our hands and everything appeared to turn out so well those doubts disappeared. I had a feeling of what an old girlfriend used to describe as mild euphoria. We had found the Griffin Interrogator. We had caught Samovar. A picture flashed into my mind of Julia shepherding Kardosov from the Sears Tower with a gun in her hand: we were real secret agents. This was the life I had imagined when I travelled down from Durham to meet Mr Smith in Carlton Terrace. I had found my vocation.

But now?

Now I wasn't even sure I would stay as a junior civil servant. I had really ballsed things up.

Somewhere there had been a mistake. But where? I went over everything that had happened. Nobody had followed me from

London, or from Toronto. There was no sign that the hotel was being watched. And we hadn't noticed anything suspicious when we left the Options Exchange. So how had anybody got onto me?

By the time we reached London I had convinced myself that the answer lay with Julia French or Nick Broadbent and the Canadians. I knew nothing about French or Broadbent and nor had anybody else in London, except the DG. Nick Broadbent's name hadn't even been mentioned and Watkins at least had expected French to be a man. I realised that I had started thinking of Julia French as simply 'Julia' but something about her still jarred. She was too authentic. She knew too much about the Department.

The most likely scenario was that the Canadians had inadvertently done something to queer the pitch, but I had no idea what. And it brought me no nearer to discovering who attacked me. The Americans would have arrested me. The Russians wouldn't have let us grab Kardosov in the first place. Had Donnell also contacted somebody else, the Chinese perhaps? Possible, but surely extremely unlikely. The only people I didn't try to connect it with were the two men who attacked me in Zandvoort; I should have done.

I wanted to believe that I had simply been the victim of a mugging, that the thief had no idea what he was taking. But he had gone straight for the briefcase and only French and Broadbent knew I was going to put Griffin in the case.

And London knew of course. 'Where's the case?' Watkins greeted me at Heathrow.

'I lost it.'

'You what?'

I told him the whole story as Morgans whipped us through the morning traffic.

Watkins was at his best, showing why he was head of our section. No synthetic sympathy, just analysis, after he'd radioed the news to headquarters.

'Miss French has already reported. She's on her way here now with Kardosov, courtesy of the RAF. She's lucky to have arranged that so quickly.'

'She's RAF herself,' I explained. Watkins clearly didn't think that was a plausible explanation, as he himself had been unable to arrange for the RAF to fly him back from Nijmegen.

'So she is genuine,' he continued. 'The DG and the DO seem to have great faith in the Canadians, let's assume that they're also above suspicion. If none of them were working for the other side you must have been under surveillance. You and Miss French are fully trained, you would have noticed one man following you, therefore it was a team.'

In fact, as Watkins surely knew, I was not fully trained. I was not a secret agent, I was an analyst. And I was pretty sure Julia French was not fully trained either.

'I could have been followed, but I checked carefully on the way out to the airport.'

'They wouldn't need to follow you there, where else would you be going?'

'That's true, but how did they know that Griffin was in the briefcase?'

'Any professional would know. Subconsciously you were undoubtedly guarding that briefcase, gripping it particularly tightly. Watching it more closely. Look at it another way. It wouldn't be in your suitcase because you wouldn't let it out of your possession. And it would have been conspicuous in your pocket, like wearing a gun. It had to be in the briefcase.'

'And who has it now?'

'That's the mystery. As you said, the Americans wouldn't have attacked you. The Russians wouldn't have lost Kardosov. The Chinese couldn't get a team there that quickly. Of course it might be political, the Canadians could have taken it themselves.

Anything Watkins doesn't understand is political. I had one more question. 'What will happen to me?'

'I wondered if you'd ask that. You didn't really have much of a chance, not against a team. But you may have been off-guard, cocksure. Your first proper mission and you were returning a hero, making up for that unfortunate business in Zandvoort. It's happened before. Griffin's important to the DG, puts one over on the Americans and puts us in credit with the Navy. Don't worry about the future, concentrate on what happened. Are you sure nobody was following Kardosov? Nobody suspicious at the airport?'

I wanted to see somebody. A face seen once too often. The same face at the Sears Tower and at O'Hare. But no, it was wishful thinking. There must have been a tail but I'd missed it.

As we reached headquarters Morgans started whistling 'On the Sunny Side of the Street'. Not very appropriate.

The DG was waiting with Adam Joseff, a teleprinted message in his hand. Joseff's office looked exactly as it always did: chaotic.

'Bit of a mess,' the DG said and he wasn't talking about the DDG's office. 'Let's hear it all. Start with landing in Toronto.'

It took nearly an hour to recount the story, concluding with Watkins' theory that we'd been opposed by a team.

'You haven't answered two questions,' the DG said, stamping out his cigarette. 'Who has Griffin and how did they get on to you?'

'Not the Americans,' I started.

'No, we can be sure of that. They've just reported Donnell's death and asked us to keep watching for Griffin.'

'That leaves two possibilities. French and/or Broadbent are unreliable, or we were under surveillance.'

'No go,' the DG replied. 'Miss French is perfectly reliable. Broadbent too, although we'll check his team again. There's a possibility you forgot: *you* could be unreliable.'

He paused for a moment before continuing.

'Let's assume you're just incompetent. Still wet behind the ears. Now think. The Soviets sent Samovar. They wouldn't have risked that if they'd had time to mount a proper operation. So the time available was limited. That excludes the Chinese, freelancers and any third world agencies. They couldn't have got a team into Chicago faster than the Russians. The Eastern Europeans wouldn't do anything without Russian approval and they couldn't have got a team there either.'

'What about the East Germans?' Watkins asked. 'Koenig told us they've got a team in New York.'

'They're the one exception. We know some of them are not as fond of the Russians as they used to be but there's absolutely no possibility of them targeting a KGB operation. I suppose if the KGB ordered them to help Kardosov get from Holland to Copenhagen, they might just follow him to Chicago. Or suppose they notice our man Burton's arrival in Copenhagen and discover his interest in the plans of one Nils Olssen, they might well alert their men in New York to meet Olssen's plane and see why the British are so interested. If they saw Kardosov being abducted they might have followed you to the airport. Pretty remote but possibility one.

'Possibility two: the Israelis. One of their teams disappeared at least a month ago.'

I interrupted. 'At that US Embassy meeting I attended, the Company mentioned the Israelis sending an agent to New York six weeks ago without telling them. The FBI lost him but the Company seemed to think it may have been important, usually the Israelis inform them if they have a team operating in the US.'

'If the CIA representative mentioned this mysterious visit,' the DG replied, 'we can assume it has no importance. Possibility three has to be our friends across the Channel. The other Europeans either wouldn't risk anything in the US, like the Germans; haven't any inclination, like the Swedes; or haven't the capability. But the French at one stage had a team in Quebec. They could have got on to Kardosov in Toronto or on to our plans for bringing Kardosov home through Canada. They're my bet, unless anybody has any other ideas.'

'South Africa.' Joseff had a passionate loathing for all things South African. 'They have men in the States.'

'True. But Griffin is for nuclear submarines, which they don't have. They wouldn't risk American goodwill for something they don't need.'

'They could use it for bargaining.'

'How? The Americans don't want Griffin, they want to stop the reds getting it. If the South Africans threaten to give Griffin to the Russians, American favour will be gone for ever.'

Joseff tried again. 'They could sell it to the French, exchange it for jets or helicopters.'

'All right Adam, four possibilities: East Germany, Israel, France and South Africa. Let's deal with them one at a time.

'Six have nothing effective in East Germany since Koenig was blown. Our man in the Bonn Embassy is new. We'll tell the Americans that we've heard rumours that the East Germans have pulled off something really big in the US Midwest. Then if it turns out to be true we might get some credit even if we lose Griffin.

'Israel's a dead end. We can't penetrate them and they don't need anything we can offer. We can radio Philips but he won't find out anything. You can look through the files,' he said to me, 'and see if you can explain why an Israeli team would be in the US. Try the war crimes stuff, they could be Nazi-hunting again.

'South Africa I'll leave to you, Adam. I'm sure if they've got Griffin you'll soon know about it.

'That leaves France. There hasn't been a peep out of Paris about this. I suppose there's nothing to lose from a direct approach, we'll send Devereau over. We'll have to bid high to get a look-in.'

The meeting was over. 'You'd better see the medic about that knock on your head,' Watkins suggested on the way out, 'and then get a few hours' sleep in the dormitory. The files can wait.'

After I woke I went up to Watkins' office, hoping he would have something more interesting for me to do than looking through old files. I was under no illusion about why I had been sent to look at the war crimes files, it was the DIS equivalent of naughty schoolboys being put in detention. Watkins had gone home. On his secretary's desk was a photo of Julia French.

'Mr Watkins wanted you to confirm that this is the person you met in Chicago,' she explained. 'He tried getting her RAF files but they've been mislaid. It probably doesn't matter now. Miss French has arrived. The DG went off to meet her. Looks familiar doesn't she, in the photo, perhaps she's been here for training.'

I left her gazing at the photo and went down to Records. 'Mr Watkins has been looking for you,' Jenkins informed me, 'he's got a photo.'

'I know, thanks.'

The files were useless and their sheer volume left me bemused. I discovered that using the so-called 'ratlines' an estimated 9 000 Nazi war criminals had been smuggled to Latin America alone after the war, with hundreds more escaping to the Middle East, Australia and the United States. Where was I supposed to start looking and for what? The section on war criminals in the United States was meagre, the only recent addition being on Klaus Barbie, whom the CIA had spirited away to Bolivia despite his having been sentenced to death in absentia by a French court. The other files hadn't been added to or examined for nearly a year, since Roger Black had done a note on the latest Bormann theory. The index had disappeared, which didn't help, and I was more than glad when Joseff phoned.

'Pop up here a minute, will you, Thomas.'

Julia French was already there. We spent an hour going over our stories again but nothing new emerged. Joseff was keen to know if I had called anyone from the hotel.

'You didn't phone any friends? Nothing anyone could have overheard?'

I assured him that the only phone call had been the one from Watkins. I noticed he didn't ask Julia the same question. Eventually we were told to go home but remain on call over the weekend.

As we left the room I suggested to Julia that we might go for a drink but she declined.

'Another time perhaps.'

When we reached the lift she walked off in the direction of the DG's office.

Julia French remained an enigma. It was odd that her service files had been mislaid. In Chicago Julia had mentioned her school, Wycombe Abbey, and I vaguely recollected that a university friend, Jenny Merchant, had also attended a school in High Wycombe. Perhaps I could learn more about Julia French. Back in my apartment I found Jenny's phone number but her mother answered. Jenny had a temporary job with a tour company in Rio de Janeiro. Mrs Merchant insisted on giving me Jenny's phone number in case I ever found myself in that part of the world: an unlikely possibility.

By Sunday evening I was ready to face the office again. It seemed to be clear, if surprising, that nobody was blaming me for losing the Griffin. And if they weren't then why should I blame myself? But I was resigned to wading through more musty files. Watkins had other ideas.

'We need to move on,' he said. 'No good dwelling on past failures. My Directorate has better things to do than investigate historic war crimes.'

Instead he sent me off to compose an assessment of an assessment. The Foreign Office had produced an eighteen-page overview report on Angola where at least three different guerrilla groups were vying to take over from the departing Portuguese.

'Our ministers need an assessment of this today,' he told me. 'The FO don't seem to have taken air power into account at all.'

The FO's effort was a typical 'on the one hand this but on the other hand that' report. The guerrilla faction supported by the Americans would probably come out on top as their development programme was the most likely to be effective, but on the other hand the group backed by the South Africans had the support of the largest ethnic group and therefore might win out. A third group supported by the Russians was dismissed as militarily insignificant. I was no military expert but the DIS had quite a few and our conclusion seemed to be that none of the guerrilla groups were up to much militarily. The winner, I wrote, would be whoever could persuade their sponsors to commit their own troops. The Vietnam War was almost over and after that disaster the Americans certainly wouldn't be rushing to commit ground troops to war in Africa. The question to ask was not which guerrilla group was stronger but who was willing to commit the most of their own troops: South Africa or the Soviet Union?

I left it like that. I had become a proper civil servant I thought ruefully. On the one hand the South Africans might win, on the other hand the Russians. As it turned out the Russians surprised us all the following year by airlifting Cuban troops into Luanda and brushing everyone else away; I hadn't predicted that.

Watkins had told the typing pool to make my report top priority but when I went to pick it up it wasn't ready. The supervisor was clearly used to Watkins demanding priority for his section whether it was justified or not.

'Group Captain Watkins has already gone home,' I was told. 'Your report will be delivered to your office when it's ready.'

I wandered off to find a colleague who was trying to establish how many of the new Russian PSM pistols were coming out of the factory in the Urals. It was said the Russians were restricting their issue to the most senior KGB and Army officers only but I thought I had seen two this morning, in a photo taken in a guerrilla camp in Angola.

When I returned to my own office the Director Operations, Richard Mendale, was sitting behind my desk. He was reading the assessment I had just completed.

He made no attempt to get up. 'This is rather good,' he said. 'Perhaps you should stick to analysis in future rather than playing at being an action man.'

His warm smile did nothing to soften his words.

'You let yourself get jumped in Zandvoort and then just to prove you can do it again you lose Griffin in Chicago. Not very encouraging is it? What's your excuse?'

'I don't make excuses.'

'Good answer. As Oscar Wilde once said, it's better to offer no excuses than a bad one.'

It wasn't actually Oscar Wilde but I suspected that Mendale would not appreciate being corrected.

'Adam Joseff tells me you want to join Operations one day. Not a lot to recommend you so far is there?'

I wondered where the conversation was going. I had better things to do than stand in front of my own desk and let Mendale lob insults at me.

'When the bullets started flying in Zandvoort I thought I handled myself pretty well.'

'Perhaps you did but you shouldn't have let yourself be caught.'

'And we got hold of Samovar in Chicago.'

'That was pure luck,' responded Mendale. 'You and French hadn't planned to follow Kardosov. If his backup had arrived in time you would have been stuffed. And then again you let yourself get caught at the airport. Anyway, in my Directorate civilians make the tea, we don't have any civilians in the field. You would be the first.'

'I've always been happy to be first.'

Mendale nodded.

'I can believe that. Perhaps your day will come. Tell me: how did anyone get on to you at the airport in Chicago? And don't say Broadbent.'

'Why not Broadbent?'

'Because I've known him and his cowboys for years.'

'And have you known Julia French for years? By the way, is French an assumed name?'

'You don't need to know that.'

'Although she's allowed to have my real name. Why's that?'

Mendale just looked at me. 'Come on,' he said. 'The DG wants to see you.'

'What's it about?' I asked.

'I gather he wants to tell you himself. He's tied up at the House. We'll have to go there.'

As we set off on the short walk Mendale suddenly remarked, 'You're a clever bugger, aren't you? You knew that quote about no excuse being better than a bad one wasn't Oscar Wilde.'

'It's George Washington.'

'But you didn't try to correct me, you didn't point out it was Washington.'

'Perhaps I thought you didn't need to know.'

He didn't reply.

We crossed Parliament Square and went in through St Stephen's entrance, Mendale leading the way along the uneven corridors with their paintings and tapestries depicting scenes long forgotten elsewhere.

The Director General was in the Guest Room. As we approached a smartly dressed man in Savile Row suit and club tie who had been sitting with the DG stood up and walked past us. He glanced towards Mendale and nodded to acknowledge his presence. Neither man said anything. The DG rose to greet us.

'Dick, Thomas, good to see you. Some silly fool has put down a motion on badgers. I may have to go and vote at any minute.'

'What did Brasenose want?' Mendale asked.

'You know better than to ask about that,' the DG responded. 'We're here to discuss our plans for Thomas.'

A police launch cruised up and down the Thames outside. The DG relaxed into his red leather chair, obliterating the portcullis design which always reminds me of the old threepenny piece.

'The Griffin Interrogator's in Brazil,' he announced. 'Some freelancers have it, don't ask how. They're going to sell it to the highest bidder and we've been invited to the auction. They sent a message to the DO here via our man at the Embassy in Washington. We're to put the name of our representative in the *Telegraph*'s deaths column. We've arranged to put your name in. "Regret to announce the death of Thomas Dylan in Chicago." No time to produce another cover so you'll travel on your own passport.'

A waiter brought the glasses of exorbitantly priced, nasty white wine.

'Watkins thinks you're the man for the job; you know the area apparently and you speak the language.'

'I spent three months in São Paulo as part of my degree. And I've been back to Rio recently on holiday.'

'So you have contacts in Rio,' put in Mendale.

'Not really in Rio, although Jenny, an old university friend, happens to have just landed a job with a tour company there. I was in Rio for the sun.'

'On your own?'

'Yes.' I didn't think it was any of Mendale's business that I had intended to spend the holiday with a girl I had met in São Paulo. Unfortunately, it had soon become clear that absence makes the heart grow colder. I was not, after all, the man of her dreams.

Mendale nodded but said nothing.

'Dick here has your tickets,' continued the DG. 'And there are some background reports on the political situation down there.

Whoever is organising this auction will have booked you in at the Hotel Florianopolis, the address is with your ticket. You won't be on your own. We have a good man there, name of Vernon. He's on the case already. Try not to compromise him with the locals. You're the front man, if the auctioneers make contact they'll make it with you. But trust Vernon with any operational stuff. And report back on every step you take, that's very important. Watkins goes on leave on Wednesday but the DO here will make sure that anything you want gets top priority.'

'Just make sure you don't get into any fights this time,' said Mendale. 'You're there to take part in an auction. If you find out who else is bidding report back. In particular, if you discover a Russian presence let us know right away and keep close to them.'

Mendale and the DG made the assignment sound marginally more sensible than the decision to send me to Chicago, but only marginally so.

'Can I ask one question?'

The DG nodded. 'Of course.'

'Why us? Why the Defence Intelligence Staff? Isn't this sort of thing we have a Secret Intelligence Service to handle? Haven't they got people in Latin America?'

I thought I caught the hint of a smile on the DG's face but it was Mendale who answered.

'Six have washed their hands of this whole operation. We've given them Samovar and that's a big tick for them. That's what Six and Five wanted, although it won't do them any good. Kardosov's not going to say anything and we'll never prove he's done anything illegal here. In any case we could never admit we grabbed him off a street in Chicago. We'll have to discreetly hand him back. Perhaps Six could swap him for Koenig.'

The DG cut Mendale off. 'Kardosov is no longer our concern. Hopefully our colleagues will be able to learn something from him and his network will be disrupted. The relevant point is that Justin Brasenose feels that he cannot commit resources to this so-called auction.'

'Of course not,' said Mendale. 'Getting involved with anything connected to Griffin just risks upsetting the Americans and heaven forbid that happens again. We're on our own this time.'

As far as Six were concerned we were on our own in Chicago I thought, but I let that pass.

'The Griffin Interrogator is of prime importance to the Royal Navy,' put in the DG. 'The security of our submarine fleet is critical in the event of future hostilities.' He stood up. 'I need to get back to the chamber. Division could be at any minute.'

The DG seemed to belong here in the House of Lords much more than in his office; a slightly eccentric peer of the realm at home in front of the carved wooden bar and heavy wooden walls, the tapestry, the hideous brown and white ceiling, the vulgar red curtains.

'Just one thing for you to remember, my boy,' he said. 'It's for the sake of the Queen.' Squeezing my hand in farewell he repeated, 'For the sake of the Queen.'

I hadn't the slightest idea what he was talking about.

VIII

Looking down on the Atlantic below I kept coming back to one simple question. It was the question I had puzzled over on the flight to Toronto: why me? One minute I was doing what I had been hired to do, Analysis and Production, the next I was sitting on a plane going off to do something for which I had no training and no relevant experience. I didn't buy the explanation that I was being sent to Brazil because I spoke Portuguese. I might as well have been told it was because I drank coffee. DIS already had someone on the ground with far more experience of the country than I had and speaking Portuguese had certainly not been the reason for sending me to Zandvoort or Chicago.

And as Mendale had also pointed out, I had made a complete mess of things in Zandvoort and had done even worse Chicago. So why let me out of the office again?

Mendale had also made plain his opinion that I was not Operations material. My formal induction had included one day on self-defence and one day on surveillance and counter-surveillance. Both days were probably included just to persuade newcomers that the DIS was more exciting than it really was. Neither self-defence nor surveillance had any real relevance to my job as an analyst. The ten days in the Brecon Beacons that Joseff had arranged had been tough but not much preparation for the streets of Rio de Janeiro.

I fell briefly asleep convinced, not for the first time, that I was a pawn in somebody else's game and not enjoying the feeling. I awoke determined that whatever game was being played I was going to win. I might be being treated like a pawn but I wasn't going to act like one.

I needed to strip away the conjecture and concentrate just on the facts. I could forget all the idle speculation about the French,

East Germans and Israelis. The DG had said that freelancers had the Interrogator. But where did they pop up from? How had they come to hear about the Griffin Interrogator in the first place? Had Donnell somehow contacted them? If so, why didn't they take the Interrogator from him rather than let Kardosov grab it first? The question that worried me most was simple: how did they manage to identify me? And how did they know I was carrying the Interrogator? I had to trust that I would find the answers in Brazil.

God made the world in six days, a Brazilian friend once told me, and spent the seventh making Rio de Janeiro. Looking down from the plane I could believe her. Rio was strung out between the aquamarine ocean and deep green mountains, the jumble of the city accentuated by miles of pure white beaches.

The taxi from the Aeroporto Galeão hurled me into tumbling contrasts of a city where the world's richest live cheek by jowl with the world's poorest. Guanabara Bay with its ferryboats and steamers and islands. The white marble dome of the Candelária Church. The contrast between the Municipal Theatre, an almost exact copy of Garnier's Paris Opera, and one of Le Corbusier's modern masterpieces, the Ministry of Education building. Old and new. Luxury and poverty. Colour and noise.

And as a backdrop to it all the Sugarloaf, Pão de Açúcar, and, further south, the even more impressive Corcovado. I had been up there; the little electric train chugging slowly upwards through coconut palms and banana trees, past shacks tottering on rocky ledges, everything encased in creepers and bright scarlet flowers. And on top of the 2300 feet of rock the gigantic statue of Christ the Redeemer, arms outstretched, dominating the sky and dwarfing the city below.

The main part of the town lies north of Corcovado, originally clustered around the docks. To the south, over Lagoa Rodrigo de Freitas, lies Ipanema, where the girls come from. Between the docks and the small Aeroporto Santos Dumont lie the bathing beaches: Gloria, Flamengo, Botafogo and, above all, Copacabana and the Hotel Florianopolis.

The taxi rushed into the enormous Botafogo tunnel linking Rio with Copacabana. Twenty minutes from the town centre and we were on the Avenida Atlantica, beside the silver-sanded Praia de Copacabana. A few minutes later we turned off again and stopped before the Hotel Florianopolis.

The hotel, six storeys rising straight and smooth with no balconies, was jammed between two others, distinguished only by the electric sign over the entrance.

As I approached the swing doors they were pushed outwards and I found myself face-to-face with a tall, blond-haired man. As he pushed past me I realised there was something vaguely familiar about him. I'd seen his face before. He got into a parked Ford. America: I'd seen him in America. It must have been during my CIA course. So the 'Company' had arrived. And yet he hadn't looked like a typical Company man.

Another man left the hotel, again tall but this time dark, middle European perhaps. He rushed past, waving to the driver of a black Mercedes parked just up the street and jumping into it as the car cruised towards him. I caught a few words but could make nothing of them, they might have been Arabic, they certainly weren't English or Portuguese. The man was pointing at the vanishing Ford and the Mercedes set off sedately in its wake. The Americans and the Russians, it seemed, were already playing hide and seek around the town.

The hotel lobby was cramped, a bar on my left, a flight of stairs directly in front, the reception desk to the right of the stairs and, in front of it, a small lounge. The lift, on the right of the desk, faced the lobby and the bar rather than the lounge. Thus someone could sit in the lounge and see everybody entering and leaving the hotel without himself being seen except by the receptionist and those descending the stairs. I would have to remember to check the occupants of the lounge whenever I entered. At the moment it was empty.

The reception desk bore a small plaque inscribed 'Gerente Sr C. Cimate'. Behind the desk stood a small, underweight man in an ill-fitting suit, a stark contrast to The Drake only a few days before. Catching the direction of my gaze the receptionist confirmed that he was Cimate, the hotel's manager. He handed me the key to room 31.

'Who booked my room?' I asked.

'I do not know, Senhor.' He sounded like a Mexican bandit in a third-rate Italian Western. I tried offering him a handful of notes. He just widened his inane grin and passed me an envelope. 'There is a message for you, Senhor.'

A small boy appeared, looking like a Latin Oliver Twist. He carried my case the two or three yards to the lift which creakingly groaned its way up to the third floor. My room was exactly opposite the stairs, near the end of a short corridor leading from the lift.

When Oliver Twist had gone I ripped open the envelope.

'Welcome,' said the note inside in English. 'The auction will start tomorrow. Enjoy the city and get to know your companions, Mr Patrick Conniston, room 30; Mr Gary Stover, room 39; Mr Mamcouh Bitri, room 33, and Mr Mustafa Abdel Rassem, room 32.' That was all.

Gary Stover I knew was CIA. The Arabic names might really be Arabs or they could be Russians travelling on Syrian or Egyptian papers to avoid the attention the Brazilian regime would pay to visitors carrying Russian passports.

I sat on the bed looking at the piece of paper in my hand and thinking about what it meant. The auctioneers were telling me who the other bidders were. The operation had seemed unreal in London but this was unbelievable. Bringing potential bidders together in Brazil for an auction was bizarre in itself: why not simply ask them to send bids and then set up an exchange with the highest bidder in some neutral location? If bringing everyone to Rio was strange enough, putting them all in the same hotel was asking for trouble and then to put them in adjacent rooms was beyond belief. Conniston was in the room to my left, Stover almost opposite while Bitri and Abdel Rassem were to my right. Assuming that everyone received a similar list of room numbers the only possible explanation was that the auctioneers expected us to keep each other in line. If we were busy watching one another nobody could get up to anything untoward.

But the real world didn't work like that. If the Americans identified the two supposed Arabs as Russians a quick word from the American Ambassador and Messrs Bitri and Abdel Rassem would be on the next plane home.

There had to be something I was missing. I thought about the names again. One name had stood out. Gary Stover, with whom I'd shared Budweisers during my CIA 'Psyche' course at McLean. Gary was at least ten years older than me but retained a boyish enthusiasm. Before joining the Company he'd been with Spectre, the US Air Force group based at Ubon in south-eastern Thailand, shooting up the Ho Chi Minh trail in eastern Laos from transport planes converted into lumbering gunships. His grasp of the psychological rubbish we'd been there to learn had been impressive and his scores, when we'd spent an evening on the FBI's shooting ranges at Quantico, Virginia, had been perfect.

I was thinking about the Sampon nightclub in Ubon which Gary used to describe so vividly, when an odd coincidence struck me. I thought I'd recognised the man who'd left the hotel as I arrived and assumed he'd been on the CIA course with me. It wasn't Gary so presumably it was Conniston. But it was peculiar that out of the thousands of agents the CIA could have sent they should choose two I happened to have met. The name Conniston rang no bells. And then I realised.

The man at the hotel entrance was not Conniston. I'd seen him before certainly, and in America. But further west than Virginia, in Chicago. At the airport, just before he hit me.

I knew with a sickening certainty that I'd seen the man who stole Griffin and I had done nothing.

Even worse, the Russians were on to him. While he wandered around Rio waiting to be clobbered by a couple of Arabic Russians, I would have to sit in the hotel doing nothing. Not a very good start to the mission. Mendale would again be unimpressed.

I turned my attention back to the room. There was a bed with three chairs, dressing table, wardrobe, bedside table, phone, plastic wastepaper bin and no less than five ashtrays. It reminded me of Brazil's capital Brasilia with its air of neglect hinting at a grandeur which in truth had never been present. The carpet was worn bare beside the bed. The wardrobe contained a few hangers, only one inscribed 'Hotel Florianopolis'. The mattress was too small for the bed so that I soon scraped my skin on the extending wood surround. The chairs were comfortable but not matching.

A small bathroom led off to the left of the door. It occurred to me that I could stand inside the bathroom when opening the bedroom door to unknown guests, so that my body would be largely sheltered. I tried it but it didn't work, the bathroom door opened outwards making it impossible to open the bedroom door.

The walls were an off-white, matching the carpet. Bloodstains would be hard to hide. At least that was one thing I wouldn't have to worry about.

After unpacking I crossed to the two windows which stretched from ceiling to floor. They were locked by a simple handle in the centre which pushed long bolts down and up. A wooden rail crossed the window at waist height.

A taxi was stopping at the hotel opposite. Out climbed a man I had seen before. Captain Graham Mackenzie RN (Retd) was a marine engineer on business in Rio who had sat beside me on the flight out. I'd suggested sharing a taxi, hoping to confuse anyone watching my arrival, but he'd refused because he was being met at the airport. It appeared that his friends hadn't turned up; he evidently hadn't waited long.

The hotel's front was smooth: no balconies, no ledges and no drainpipes within easy reach. Nobody could enter the room through the window without using a ladder from the street below or descending from above by rope and then smashing the glass. And I couldn't escape that way either.

It didn't take long to convince myself that the room wasn't bugged. Mendale had given me a jamming device but I felt safer knowing that it wouldn't be needed. I went back downstairs.

'Have the other members of my party arrived?'

Cimate managed to keep his grin while looking totally perplexed. 'I do not understand, Senhor.'

'Have Mr Stover and Mr Conniston arrived? And Mr Bitri and Mr Abdel Rassem?'

'No, they are not here. They are still coming.'

That was a shock. If the Russians hadn't arrived, who were the two men in the black Mercedes who had followed the auctioneer away from the hotel?

I needed to visit Vernon, our man in Rio. But first I ordered a Brahma and sat down in the lounge. Almost immediately Oliver Twist arrived with my beer, ice cold. I gave thanks that most Brazilian brewers are German. I was tempted to stay at the hotel and wait for something to turn up. Perhaps Gary Stover would appear, or the auctioneer again.

In fact, it was the Russians. I hardly noticed them until they gave their names, Bitri and Abdel Rassem. They certainly weren't the men in the Mercedes and they looked a lot more like Russians than Arabs. They followed Oliver Twist into the lift and I knew they would soon discover my identity from the envelope Cimate had given them.

IX

I finished my beer and left.

The British Consulate is on the Praia do Flamengo, Flamingo Beach. I strolled to the Avenida Atlantica and got one of the little Volkswagen taxis. Praia do Flamengo is a continuation of the Avenida Beira Mar which once upon a time ran beside the sea from the city centre to Botafogo. Then much of the bay had been reclaimed and a new highway, the Avenida Infante Dom Henrique, built between the Praia do Flamengo and the sea.

The taxi dropped me outside number 248 and I climbed to the second floor. It was long after the 4.30 closing time but I was clearly expected.

Within minutes a man of indeterminate age, medium height, stocky build, military bearing, tanned face and with a mop of jet-black hair was pumping my hand and insisting that I call him Pedro.

'My name's Peter but everybody calls me Pedro.' There were hints of Lancashire in his voice. 'I would have met your plane but I had to stay here and collect some DIS stuff from a courier.' I didn't have time to wonder why anybody would send material out by courier when I could have brought it. He led me to his office and opened the unmarked door. 'Right handful you've been given old boy. Anything I can do and all that. The Department must have given you a briefing on me.'

'No, there wasn't time.'

His office was a large, apparently disorganised mess. The gigantic desk was cluttered with letters, memos and a stack of green files. This morning's *Diário de Noticias* hid the phone. A woman and a girl stared at Pedro from a coloured photo. The chairs were obviously his own, made for sitting in, not looking at. Covering the walls were photos and paintings of Copacabana Beach, Corcovado, the opera house at Manaus and the carnivals in Rio and Bahia. In one corner were grouped photos of Lisbon: the Tagus, the Avenida da Liberdade, the Hieronymites Monastery.

Beside his desk stood a combined bookcase and cocktail cabinet. The books were wide-ranging, many very technical. They included works that would undoubtedly be on the government's blacklist, like João Quartim's *Dictatorship and Armed Struggle in Brazil*. Pedro had the original French version. He caught the direction of my glance but assumed I was thinking about the cocktail cabinet.

'Sorry old boy, no booze in there. I use it for storing pamphlets and things the lefties churn out. It's a veritable library of subversive literature, wouldn't dare keep it at home.'

Pedro leaned back in his chair.

'Let's start by explaining what sort of animal I am. I'm responsible for the whole of Brazil and, since Andy Williams popped off in BA, for Argentina too. But Rio is what I know best. It's my city, although I've been away quite a time. I was here right through the sixties and made some really good contacts. Too good. When the Swiss Ambassador, Bucher, was kidnapped in December 1970, some of my sources were involved. The authorities went mad when they had to release seventy prisoners and somebody they got hold of dropped my name. I've no idea what they thought I was doing. Hints were directed to London and, after waiting a decent period to show we weren't going to do whatever the regime wanted, I was recalled home.'

'But they let you back.'

'Yes, a few months ago. Watkins wanted me at the Embassy in Brasilia but Mendale realised that was bloody ridiculous so here I am in Rio again. I also received a strict directive to keep my nose clean with the locals.'

Pedro looked directly at me. 'There is one other thing to say: we don't have any of London's silly office politics here. I work well with Six and I don't want that disrupted. In theory Six does all the real Intelligence work while DIS sticks to all things military but it doesn't work like that here. Since the 1964 coup the military and the government are the same thing. There's bound to be overlap between what I'm doing and what Harrison the local Six man is doing. And then of course there's the balls-up over the Embassy which complicates everything.'

I wasn't sure what he meant; fortunately, he was keen to explain.

'Officially the Embassy moved to Brasilia more than two years ago but it's still in temporary accommodation. London didn't really believe that anyone would be stupid enough to move the capital 600 miles into the interior. They simply didn't understand that in Brazil status and appearances are all important. Once the government announced it was moving nothing would be allowed to stop it. London have been catching up, they've only just established a team to design a new Embassy, and nobody knows how long it will take before building starts. I reckon they'll be scrabbling around in temporary offices in Brasilia for another ten years. And that's a problem for Harrison. The action is still in Rio but he is stuck up in Brasilia with ropey communications. That's why he is happy for me to spread my wings a bit, like I am doing now with you.'

'Do Six know I'm here?'

'Of course. Harrison will help when he can but he's off to London in a couple of days so if we want anything we need to ask quickly.'

'And he knows what I'm doing here? He knows we're trying to buy something that belongs to the Americans?'

'It seems so. He knew you were coming before I did.'

It was a sign of how much I had been influenced by Watkins and Mendale that I was pleasantly surprised to find Six and the DIS cooperating on the ground.

'Let's deal with a few operational details,' Pedro said. 'I'll get you a car, pay for it myself and claim from London.' He paused for a moment as if unsure how to proceed. 'I've been told to find you a weapon. It's not something visitors from London usually ask for but I understand there's already been at least one death so we should be prepared. The only thing I could get with a proper holster at this short notice is a Luger. If you want anything else tell me but there's bound to be a risk and I don't want the authorities discovering that I'm in the arms market.'

I wasn't expecting that.

Carrying a gun should have made me feel like a real spy but it just emphasised the unreality of the situation. The last time I was in Rio I had been carrying nothing more illicit than a student card that, strictly speaking, I was no longer entitled to use.

I liked guns and I was a good shot but I didn't know enough to be choosy. 'A Luger's fine.'

'Good. Now communications. You can contact me either here, at an apartment I've got or at home. My wife usually knows where to get hold of me.' He gave me the phone numbers.

'If for any reason you can't find me you're stuck. Most of the diplomatic people don't want to know about folk like us. They think we're a bit of a joke until somebody's kidnapped. Helping get those Tupamaros out of prison in Uruguay helped our position a lot, although strictly speaking that was Six not us. But that was a long time ago and memories are short.

'Anyway, back to communications. The phones in here are tapped of course, and so's my home. Just to confuse the buggers when you phone here ask for Jimmy Fitzwarren; there's a John Fitzwarren who's leaving next month so it won't matter if he's saddled with any embarrassing calls. I'll arrange with the switchboard that if you say "Jimmy" then the calls will come here. Identify yourself by reference to the Bluejay Marine Engineering Company. OK?'

'Fine. Funny you should mention marine engineering. There was a marine engineer on the plane out, name of Graham Mackenzie. He told me he was being met at the airport but he turned up alone at the hotel opposite mine just five or ten minutes after I did.'

'I can check him out.' Pedro removed the newspaper covering his phone and called someone named John, perhaps the real J. Fitzwarren.

'He'll call me back. Anything else?'

'A black Mercedes. Acting suspiciously, as they say, outside the hotel.'

It was a pity I hadn't noticed the number of the Ford which the men in the Mercedes seemed to be following.

He noted the Mercedes' number and then continued. 'Two more codes. If you think you're being listened in on use the phrase "about the Santos contract". And if you're in trouble use the word "compelling".

'The line from your hotel is bound to be tapped by the characters who set this thing up, the auctioneers. I've been over there. The manager is a shifty little bugger who's come into a lot of money lately. His name's Carlos Cimate. We can assume he's working for them although they won't have told him much. I don't think he's tape-recording the phone calls which means we can use a scrambler. I've got a simple clip-on one you can use. It wouldn't puzzle a professional but friend Cimate won't know what the devil's happening. I've got one fitted to this phone and at home.

'I've done a check on the hotel's owner. He has nothing to do with running the place and lives in Nova Friburgo. He has a few other hotels and restaurants, none in Copacabana. Nothing plush but it must keep the money coming in. I've got a report on him here if you want but it doesn't say anything. The same goes for Cimate. And I've got a list of everyone staying at the hotel.'

I was impressed. 'You got that together quickly.'

Pedro grinned. 'Actually I didn't. I know one of the secretaries working for Volmar, the CIA station chief, and she passed it on. Washington are sending two agents down here and they're booked into the Florianopolis. Volmar is checking all the other guests; he sent a list of names to Washington. You'll be on it.'

'The auctioneers kindly left me a note with the names of the two Americans and two others I assume are Russians. Presumably they think that if we're all watching each other we can't get up to any tricks.'

Pedro's eyebrows rose. 'That's a very odd thing to do. I can't imagine real professionals doing that.'

'The Russians are using the names Abdel Rassem and Bitri,' I continued.

This time Pedro nodded. 'They'll keep a very low profile; they won't want the Brazilians rumbling them. They may have local contacts. The old PCB disintegrated after the 1964 coup but there are odd Communist groups springing up and dying all the time. Most are pro-Chinese these days of course. I'll sniff around.'

He pushed back his chair, letting the sun stream on to his face. 'I used to have good contacts in groups like the VPR, VAR and ALN. If the Russians can find anyone to help them in Brazil that's where they'll have to go.'

He glanced out of the window and decided the weather was too good to be sitting in the office. As he stood up I reflected that there was something reassuringly good-natured about the man. Like Jacobs in Zandvoort, Pedro Vernon knew what he was doing. That made it all the more odd that I was to be what the DG had called the 'front man'.

'Let's go and have some coffee. Your problems can wait for half an hour and I don't want to use the phone to arrange your car. No need to worry about the locals seeing you with me,' Pedro added as we left, 'it's not my turn today.'

'Not your turn for what?'

'Surveillance. There's a little man from one of their secret service outfits who follows me around sometimes. One day with me, one day with the Dutch and so on. Poor old Harrison in Brasilia has a chap five days a week, he's lucky they assume we don't work at weekends. My day's Friday. Last week I had nothing to do so I led my man around the old city and finally bought a bra for my wife. He probably put me down as a pervert.'

'Who's he from?'

'I'm not sure. Probably the National Information Service, the SNI. They fancy themselves playing Gestapo. He actually used to wear a raincoat all the time. Could be one of the little army groups, they must know that my interests are military. God knows who they are. Things are getting worse here and I didn't think that was possible. Half my old sources have been spirited off and the rest are clamming up. Had quite a job getting your gun. Hope it gets cooler, you're going to feel pretty stupid wearing a jacket all the time just to cover it.'

We walked through the Parque do Flamengo, a beach and recreation area built on the reclaimed land on the other side of the highway. We bought ice creams from an enormous woman of pure African ancestry and watched the waves finish their journey from Africa against the shore. At a bar named O Mar Azul, the Blue Sea, Pedro stopped. It was full of people, mainly businessmen, drinking tiny cups of jet-black coffee. We sat down and sipped our *cafezinhos*.

'I'll go and arrange your car. Meant to do it this morning but I had to wade through the special briefing of yours.'

Before I could ask him about the 'special briefing' he was off to find a phone. '*Quero fazer uma ligação*' he shouted at the barman who pointed towards the rear. Pedro was gone only a few minutes and returned beaming. 'All fixed. Ford Corcel Sports Coupé, tuned a bit.'

On the way back to his office, Pedro briefed me on background trivia, not just the political stuff but how the local football teams Botafogo and Fluminense were doing, what the weather had been like and what films were pulling in the crowds. On the surface he was what my father would have called, somewhat disparagingly, a 'hail fellow well met' sort of man who should have been propping up the bar in a village pub in the Lake District rather than being one of the most senior representatives of British Intelligence in Latin America. Below his 'old boy' bonhomie he didn't miss much. I learned a lot about the minor intrigues within the regime that hadn't been in the situation reports back in London.

If I could come up with a name for the man who attacked me in Chicago I was sure Pedro Vernon would be able to dig up some information on him.

It was hard to keep secrets in Rio. Under the carefree mask were the realities of a police state. Since the military coup in March 1964 the knot of fear had tightened with each change in the political pattern. First President Castelo Branco, then Costa e Silva, then Garrastazu Medici. With each the imprisonments mounted, the tortures became more blatant, the reign of terror more oppressive.

As we walked along in the sweltering heat, Pedro laughing beside me, some poor unfortunate could well be screaming in agony out there on the Ilha Grande in Guanabara Bay. An illiterate peasant tortured to death because someone had accused him of saying governments should be elected; without trial, without any evidence.

A government minister named Passarinho once explained that torture was fine as long as it wasn't 'systematic'. But the truth was that in Brazil torture had become routine.

The drivers whizzing past had the same attitude to the sanctity of life. Nearly every car had a wing smashed, brake lights knocked off or bumper missing. There is only one rule of the road in Rio: the larger vehicle has the right of way. In a land where poverty is the dominant fact of life only the strong survive, on the road and in public life. Ruthlessness pays. That's the one thing life in Brazil had in common with the Chicago Board Options Exchange.

The Luger M1908 was still standard issue with the Portuguese army which, Pedro informed me, was the original source of the one he passed me when we returned to his office. I pocketed the nine millimetre Parabellum cartridges. Not a new weapon, but adequate. Standing up I strapped on the holster and slid in the gun. It was hardly noticeable beneath my jacket. I tried to look relaxed, as if wearing a gun was something I did every day. Pedro was not fooled.

'Ever worn one operationally before?'

'I've not really been operational before.'

'Well let's hope you won't need it. I've also got a few random number cipher pads in case we need to communicate in writing or on a non-scrambled tapped line.'

Pedro took four from his desk, ripped off the duplicate he would need and handed the top copies to me.

'Right, now we ought to talk about your assignment. The authorities here aren't fools. They may well know who you are and they'll certainly know that an American team is here without their being told why. They've got this town pretty well tied up and somebody fairly high up in their security apparatus should be asking himself what's happening. And yet you're not being followed and

I'm sure they've got nobody at the Florianopolis. They haven't even asked why you are all staying at a third-rate hotel in Copacabana. That's strange to put it mildly. Look at it another way: if you had this Griffin gadget where would you choose to trade it?'

'Not here.'

'Right. Brazil's crawling with police, informers, bugs, phone taps, mail intercepts, everything. You'd only choose Rio if you already had a secure base here. And there's only one way to be secure here, other than living in an Embassy, which we shouldn't rule out, and that's by being well in with the regime. Really well in. Contacts high enough to ensure that when three Western agents turn up at one hotel nobody asks any questions. Contacts that can ensure that when our friend banks his money he doesn't find a policeman knocking on his door to find out where it came from.

'Our auctioneers not only have police protection but political protection too. And that means military involvement. Think about that for a minute. We won't be able to outbid the others so we'll have to steal this Griffin thing. And you know what happens to people who play games with the authorities. They end up on Flower Island out there,' he pointed towards the bay, 'with their private parts being walloped about the countryside. I hope you know what you've been let in for.'

X

Pedro had lost his smile.

'Think about the hotel manager, Carlos Cimate. If someone in his position is offered money these days you take it and then call the police. If you don't, the policemen's benevolent association comes along in the middle of the night and you end up in the sea with your head missing.

'Crime doesn't pay in Brazil unless your business is supposed to be making the law or enforcing it. A weakling like Cimate would only work for someone with clout, a cop or a politician.'

He was right of course. It made my job look almost impossible. I knew enough about Brazil to know that even a diplomatic passport was no guarantee of immunity, and I didn't have a diplomatic passport.

'You mean that the whole thing could be organised from within the government? Or at least within their security forces?'

'I wouldn't go that far. Brazilian Intelligence abroad is a farce, certainly outside Latin America. They couldn't have got on to Griffin in the first place. And the generals are still very dependent on the US, they wouldn't be very pleased if one of their own people was found in the US trying to steal American military equipment.

'It's far more likely to be a freelancer with a long-established base here. But that doesn't make the situation any less dangerous. If somebody in power is getting his cut he's going to protect his own interests. Remember the regime have a lot more to gain from a dead British bureaucrat than a live one in prison. Deaths you can blame on the terrorists and turn round to London and say, "Give us replacements for our old Wasp helicopters and we'll destroy the terrorists." It's not so easy to explain the torture marks on someone you've been holding on no charge for a week.'

'That's really comforting.'

'Well it's not supposed to be.' The jovial Pedro had completely disappeared. 'I'll call Fitzwarren about that Mackenzie character on your plane.'

The conversation was very brief.

'Apparently Mackenzie is entirely above board. His trip has been planned for months and John's sure the man on the plane is the real Captain Mackenzie. I think we can forget about him.'

'Looks like it. I'm just naturally suspicious.'

'You should be.' He went off to fetch a set of car keys. 'Your car's arrived.'

It was a pale green Ford Corcel, mass produced in their thousands at a factory on Avenida Henry Ford in Sao Paulo. Full width radiator, slightly concave grill with horizontal bars, steep windscreen rising from the flat bonnet, large rear windows sloping down to the small tail and the wing line rising over the rear wheels accentuating the small passenger space inside. The normal top speed was over eighty miles per hour. This particular car, Pedro assured me, was much faster. Its twin exhausts were the only signs of modification.

'If you want to hide your gun,' Pedro informed me, 'the imitation leather stuff back here unstaples. I've hidden papers there. The police are not too good on subtle jobs like searching cars. But give them something easy, like beating up a child, and, if you'll forgive the pun, they can't be beaten.'

'I'll remember.' My stomach rumbled. 'How about something to eat?'

'No time sadly. My wife's due here in ten minutes. She's been off buying a birthday present for our daughter. Now Sonia wants me to replenish her money supply. In any case I'd better let London know you've arrived.

'One other thing,' he shouted as I started the car. 'If you like pirarucu there's a good restaurant opposite your hotel, Minha Mesa.'

Driving on the right again was no problem but the atrocious drivers almost persuaded me to stick to taxis.

I found a deserted side street near the hotel where I could transfer the Luger and its holster to the back. The hiding place was exactly as Pedro had described. There was no point in advertising my newfound mobility so I locked the anti-theft device and left the car there.

At the hotel I tried my Portuguese on Cimate, hoping to avoid his pidgin American. It was a wasted effort.

'*Existe alguma mensagem para mim?*'

'No, Senhor. There is only the message I give to you this morning when you arrived, Senhor.'

He dragged out the second syllable of 'arrived' like a real southern gentleman and then finished with the characteristically soft Portuguese 'd'. Why did every sentence have to contain 'Senhor'? While it's one of the commonest words in Brazil, if he was trying to speak English he might at least learn the term 'mister' or even 'sir'. He did it again.

'Is there anything other that you want, Senhor?'

'*Nao obrigado.*'

The Minha Mesa was next to Captain Mackenzie's hotel. It was nothing to write home about but the food was excellent. Palmitos, palm hearts in vinegar and olive oil, followed by pirarucu, a sort of well-cooked Amazonian codfish. The service was slow but there was no hurry. My table was right by the street, perfect for watching the Hotel Florianopolis.

The restaurant wasn't crowded. A noisy group from Sao Paulo left soon after I arrived. Only occasionally did the sound of voices reach me; the Carioca accents sounding harsh after the sweet sibilants of Sao Paulo.

Settling back with the coffee I kept an eye on the hotel, but nothing happened. A few beautiful girls walked by and served to occupy my mind, which was fortunate as I had nothing else to think about. I had no plan: just sit and wait and pray that something would turn up. Fatigue from the flight was starting to set in.

As I left the restaurant I noticed Captain Mackenzie entering his hotel. He walked with his hands clasped behind his straight back, his head slightly forward and his eyes looking directly ahead. How could have I suspected him of being anything other than he was? He might have stepped off the bridge of a cruiser just minutes before.

Cimate was perched on a stool behind the reception desk, munching a sandwich. He stopped eating for long enough to say 'no messages, Senhor' before returning to his attack on the sandwich.

I asked if Gary Stover had arrived. The answer was yes but both the Company men were out.

'Senhor Bitri is in his room,' Cimate added.

I didn't fancy a friendly chat with the KGB so I sat in the bar until eleven. Nothing happened and I went to bed after checking carefully that my room had not been disturbed.

My body clock was still on English time when I phoned Pedro next morning.

'Any news?'

'Nothing at all.'

'Nothing on that black thing?'

'No. My friends aren't being very talkative. I may not be able to get anything.'

If Pedro couldn't trace the black Mercedes I'd seen when I arrived there was nothing to do but sit around the hotel.

Downstairs Cimate came bounding up to tell me that Stover and Bitri had already gone out. My other two 'companions' were still in their rooms. There were no messages from the auctioneers.

After breakfast of croissants and coffee I sat in the lounge writing letters home on the free stationery and reading the *Jornal do Brasil*.

A man came down and glared suspiciously at me. He spoke to Cimate who merely shrugged his shoulders and pointed at the register. The man reached for it, copied something down and left.

'Senhor Conniston,' Cimate informed me. 'He wanted your name, Senhor.'

So that was what the CIA agent had put in his notebook. It didn't make sense. He would only have noted my name if he hadn't seen it before. And that meant that the auctioneers hadn't given it to him when he arrived. Then why had they given the Americans' names to me?

'Did you tell Senhor Conniston why I was here?'

'Of course not, Senhor.' Cimate retreated to his desk looking hurt.

I believed him and that again didn't fit in. Why keep me informed on the whereabouts of the Americans and the Russians but not help them in the same way?

My thoughts were interrupted by a voice asking Cimate for a room key.

'A chave do meu quarto por favor.'

The Portuguese was technically correct and precisely enunciated, but there was something wrong with the almost mechanical accent. The words were pronounced by a tongue that had been born to a much harsher language.

I looked up just in time to see Cimate taking a key from the board behind him and giving it to my auctioneer friend, the man who had attacked me in Chicago. He had entered almost silently which is more than could be said of the two people who followed him. He turned and glanced at them and then, with the bellboy I had christened Oliver Twist, entered the lift. It did not occur to me to wonder why the boy was needed because my attention was grabbed by the two caricatures of American tourists. The man, wearing Bermuda shorts and sunglasses and with a camera round his neck, was bellowing at Cimate that he wanted his suitcases taken to his room.

'The boy, he will be down in one moment, Senhor.'

'Then you'll have to take the bags. Your ad says prompt service and that's just what we want.'

Cimate started to explain that he could not leave his desk but thought better of it. He came round and summoned the lift back down. When it arrived he put the cases inside and followed the man and his wife into it. There must have been quite a squash. The woman was enormous.

Moving swiftly to the desk, I looked at the position on the key rack from which Cimate had removed the auctioneer's key; it was numbered 28. The register was still on the desk and it took only a few seconds to find the entry. Senhor Humberto Barcisa had been booked into room 28 on Saturday, the day after he had stolen Griffin in Chicago. I was back in my seat when Cimate, perspiring heavily, returned. I finished my letter, pocketed it and left. Oliver Twist had still not returned.

So now I had a name. Humberto Barcisa. I should pass that on to Pedro Vernon as soon as possible but first I wanted to see if I could spot the mysterious men in the black Mercedes who had been following Barcisa the last time I'd seen him. I now had no idea who they were: local police, Americans, Russians or somebody else entirely. It was unlikely that they were Americans or Pedro would have heard of it. And if they were Russians they would surely have acted by now.

I walked quite a way down the avenue and then crossed over and started walking back on the other side. I saw nothing suspicious.

It was lucky I hadn't gone further. Just emerging from the hotel was Barcisa. He looked carefully around him and I ducked quickly into a shop entrance. Then he walked to his car, the same battered Ford I had seen last time. I rushed across the street to my own car, nearly being knocked down in the process. I fumbled with the locks first of the door and then of the anti-theft gadget and by the time I'd started it seemed inevitable that he would have disappeared. I was lucky again. He was cruising along about ten cars in front of me.

I should have realised that he would hardly have returned to the hotel to stay at this hour. It was far more likely that he had come to leave a message. He couldn't just walk in and leave the message or messages at the desk, especially with me sitting there. So instead, he had gone up to his room with Oliver Twist and given a message to him. Then he had waited for me to go, Cimate had probably told him I had gone to post a letter, before leaving himself.

Now I had been handed a break from heaven, just as long as I could hold on to him and yet avoid being seen. He was driving away from the city centre towards Ipanema and he was driving slowly, letting the cars behind him pass. There were only two cars between us by the time we approached Leblon and the canal linking the sea and the lagoon. Somehow I had to let the distance between the two of us widen. I pulled in behind a row of parked cars and as I pulled out again the rain came with one gigantic rush. I cursed. The road directly in front of us was barely visible. I put my foot hard down, fighting to control the car as it surged forward on the slippery surface. After passing five or six cars, what I hoped was the silhouette of the Ford appeared ahead. I prayed that it was the right car and that he had not spotted my clumsy manoeuvre. It seemed impossible that he could have missed it.

I dropped back to let a Volkswagen Variant get between us. Driving in Rio has to be seen to be believed, it makes Rome look like a veteran car rally. Nobody obeys traffic regulations and intersections are habitually chaotic. Barcisa suddenly signalled right, away from the sea, and instinctively I did the same, but he shot off left across the oncoming traffic. A cacophony of horns erupted and the driver of the Variant slammed on his brakes. There was no way I could follow. I had lost my target.

The street Barcisa had taken ended at the ocean. I wondered which way he would have gone when he got there. He could either turn right, roughly the direction he had been going in before, or turn left and double back towards Copacabana and the city centre. If he was a professional he would have been leading me away from his real destination from the moment he left the hotel. In that case he might now conclude that there was nobody on his tail and be doubling back. If on the other hand his destination was somewhere like Gavea, further west along the coast, and he had only taken evasive action because he had spotted me, then the chances were that he would now be continuing in that direction.

In either event my only realistic option was to return to the hotel, contact Pedro and give him Barcisa's name and car number.

I turned back the way I had come and just three minutes later the gods smiled: I saw Barcisa again. He had evidently headed towards Copacabana but then, when he was sure he wasn't being followed turned again, inland towards the mountains. He flashed across in front of me. I pulled the wheel round sharply and turned after him, silently thanking Pedro for hiring such an inconspicuous car. It was soon obvious that Barcisa must be heading for the André Rebouças tunnel. The tunnel, opened less than ten years before, made it possible to reach Rio's northern suburbs without having to navigate the permanent traffic jams of the city centre.

As if by magic the rain had stopped when I emerged at the other end of the tunnel. I could see Barcisa's Ford some way ahead, now keeping up with the traffic around him. I had to decide quickly what to do. If I kept close it would surely be a matter of time before he realised there was someone on his tail. If I dropped back it would be easy to lose him. I decided to drop back. I had a name Pedro could work on and it was more than likely that I would lose Barcisa whichever option I chose. I had hoped he would stop not too far from the hotel but now it was clear that he could be going anywhere. The chances of successfully following him unobserved if he suddenly turned off again were tiny.

But he didn't turn off. He took the route north past the Aeroporto Galeao and continued towards Duque de Caxias. We passed the oddly shaped buildings that bore witness to the presence of the petrochemical industry, and out into the countryside. He was on the Petrópolis road now. There was still a fair amount of traffic and although there was little chance of my being spotted I dropped even further back. At times I thought I had lost him but he always came back into view.

He drove on steadily and we rose higher. The road twisted as it climbed the ridges across its path and descended into the valleys between, each one higher than the previous. The lush vegetation springing from the rich red soil reached the road. Occasionally a large house stood back from the road. The poor couldn't afford to live this far out.

I was watching the distance carefully. It was exactly twenty-six kilometres from Duque de Caxias when he turned off left. I'd been hoping he would stop somewhere along the main road. Now

I had to make a quick choice. I played safe and continued along the highway.

The road Barcisa had taken looked small, hopefully it didn't go far. If he was any kind of professional he would be stopped just along the road, waiting to make sure he wasn't being followed. I drove towards Petrópolis. Within a mile I found a small store beside the road. It was undoubtedly my lucky day for the store had a phone, something far from automatic in Brazil. I settled down to code a message for Pedro using the random number pads he had given me.

Perhaps nothing better illustrates the extent to which the world has changed than the cumbersome way we communicated in those days. The pads had thirty-six rows marked with the letters A to Z and numerals 0 to 9 and a series of columns containing two-digit numbers. To code a message I started with the number of the pad and the number of a column and simply read off the two-digit code for each letter I wanted. Every twenty or thirty letters I changed the column and carried on. It took less than five minutes to code the message and Pedro just had to choose the same pad and reverse the process.

Child's play but foolproof. Without the pads the cipher couldn't be broken even by a computer unless the message was much longer than the one I intended sending, which simply gave Barcisa's name, car number and the whereabouts of the road junction where he'd disappeared.

It took me some time to get through to the Consulate.

'*Posso falar com o Senhor Jimmy Fitzwarren, por favor.*'

Within seconds Pedro's voice boomed 'Hallo.'

'I'm calling on behalf of the Bluejay Marine Engineering Company. We have some specifications that you might care to note.'

I repeated the coded message interspersed with pieces of nonsense that hopefully sounded technical.

'No news here,' Pedro concluded.

After replacing the phone I thanked the uncomprehending man behind the counter. He remained impassive, as if strangers came in every day to babble away in English on his phone. The hotel manager in Zandvoort had behaved the same way when I'd emerged soaking wet from the mist and said I wanted to phone England.

I bought a Guarana, a carbonated fruit drink, and sipped it slowly, trying to guess what flavour it was supposed to be, but failing. There was no hurry. If I had made a mistake it was too late to correct it. I returned to the car and drove back to the junction where Barcisa had disappeared.

A weather-beaten sign indicated Barra do Pirai but if Barcisa had been heading in that direction he was taking a very long way round. It was more likely that he was making for a house or farm somewhere before that, at least that's what I wanted to believe. Even so that might mean forty miles of road to search and probably a lot more if there were turn-offs or crossroads.

The road was narrow. Almost single track. It seemed to travel one mile sideways for every two miles forward, twisting and turning like a tropical version of a Cornish lane. The countryside was deserted. It was two miles before there were any signs of human habitation: a collection of wooden huts. Two children played with the chickens. There was no Ford. I drove on, passing a few rudimentary dairy farms and two or three villas. These had garages and if Barcisa was in one of them, and it seemed more likely that he would live in a villa than a wooden shack, it would be quite a job finding him.

The road wound on through forests of liana-hung mango and silk cotton trees, the verges speckled with brightly coloured flowers: *Maria sem vergonha*, Maria without shame.

Nearly halfway to Barra do Pirai there was a fork in the road. I took the right-hand arm, the one farthest from Rio. The other seemed to curve back south. If nothing appeared in the first ten miles I would turn back and try the other.

I found what I was looking for almost immediately. It was a villa entirely enclosed by a twelve-foot wall. There was nothing suspicious about it and I drove past, but around the corner a car was parked half off the road. It was not Barcisa's Ford but it was enough to make me sure I had reached my goal. Parked against the trees was a black Mercedes. A quick glance at the yellow plates confirmed that it was the one that had been outside the hotel when I arrived.

So friend Barcisa was being watched, but who by? I needed to find out.

Nearly half a mile further on there was a gap in the trees on the left of the road, the same side as the villa. After driving on a little to ensure there was nobody nearby I reversed back and through the trees, leaving the car about ten yards off the road along what had once been a track. It was now overgrown and the car was visible from the road only if you knew where to look. Anyone driving casually along the road would miss it.

Strapping on the Luger nervously I walked back towards the villa.

XI

A pair of arms rose slowly from the front seat of the Mercedes, followed by a head and shoulders. I froze still twenty yards away. The man looked around but not in my direction and then slumped back out of view.

Turning away from the road I moved through the trees towards the villa. The undergrowth was thick, every step sounded like a rhinoceros.

If the other man hadn't moved, sending twigs cascading to the ground, I would have missed him. It hadn't occurred to me to look upwards but it should have done. Why, after all, would anybody sit in a car from which they could see nothing? Obviously he was waiting for somebody and that somebody was sitting thirty feet up a tree between me and the villa.

The man was sitting with his back against the trunk, his legs wrapped around a branch, staring in the opposite direction, towards the villa, through powerful binoculars. From his waist hung a two-way radio. He'd evidently used the tree before as there were a couple of spikes driven into the trunk to help ascent.

There were three options.

I could try working my way round the villa. The trouble with that was that however far away I tried to keep from the man in the tree, it would only need one branch cracking under my weight to alert him. Also the further I was from him, the further into the forest I would have to be, and I wasn't really equipped for hacking my way through a semi-tropical forest.

The second option was to stay where I was and concentrate on watching the two men rather than the villa. After all, I thought I knew what the occupants of the villa were doing, but I had no idea why these men were here. I decided against that not only because it smacked of doing nothing, but because I wanted to find Griffin and Griffin, I was fairly certain, was inside the villa.

I chose a third alternative and retreated the way I'd come. The road twisted to the right and as soon as the Mercedes was out of sight I crossed the road. Then I doubled back, through the trees to a point where I could see the villa through the gate, and, by moving a few yards, could also see the car. There was no reason why I shouldn't steal someone else's idea; I moved back until I found a tree that looked reasonably easy to climb. My effort at getting up wouldn't have injured the pride of a disabled monkey, but finally, after ripping open the seat of my trousers, I was in a position to see over the villa wall and watch the Mercedes at the same time.

The view wasn't first class. Large sections of the villa were obscured by trees. That had the virtue that I was also well hidden.

One feature was clearly visible. Beside the villa stood a metal tower bearing a giant aerial. The villa evidently housed a short-wave radio powerful enough to reach anywhere in the world.

For nearly an hour nothing moved. Then a man appeared from the villa and lumbered to the gate. As he did so, the driver of the Mercedes hurtled out of his car, whipped open the bonnet and stood staring at the engine. Obviously his companion in the tree had radioed a warning. Very professional.

Moments later a blue Alfa Romeo convertible came down the drive and roared off towards Rio.

From a distance the appearance of the woman driving it was striking. Jet-black hair cascading in gentle waves. An arrogant tilt to the head. A nonchalance in the parting wave to the gatekeeper. A controlled finesse in the surge of acceleration. Not young. Perhaps not happy. But beautiful.

Half an hour later a Volkswagen cruised past and stopped beside the Mercedes. Two men got out and I quickly descended from the tree. Drawing nearer I saw that they were the two men who had been following Barcisa when I arrived at the hotel. After a short conversation with the driver of the Mercedes they disappeared into the forest. Five minutes later one of them emerged with the original man in the tree, who climbed into the Mercedes. Then the two original watchers drove off. I had witnessed the changing of the guard.

I edged towards the gate of the villa for one last look.

The villa itself was fairly large, with nothing special about it other than its seclusion. I guessed at least six bedrooms. I would have to come out later and get right round to the back to get a good idea of the layout.

On the wall of the lodge beside the gate, there was a small plaque but it was too far away to read. I crept forward and could just distinguish the inscription, 'Villa Nhambiquaras'. Pedro should be able to uncover some background on Barcisa from that even if he had been unable to find anything from the Ford's number plate.

A few drops of rain fell as I turned away. Soon rainfall was spattering on to and through the trees, covering any noise I might make. I passed the Volkswagen unobserved and was thoroughly bedraggled by the time I reached my car.

To avoid passing the villa again, I drove back through Barra do Pirai.

By the time I reached Copacabana, I was dry but not for long. I parked the car a few hundred metres from the hotel and ran down the avenue with no raincoat and the seat of my trousers hanging in the air. The few pedestrians looked startled at my appearance but Cimate took it in his stride.

'The Senhor has been in the rain?'

'Yes, piranha fishing.'

He was momentarily silent before turning to the rack behind him.

'There is a message for you, Senhor.'

On reaching my room I realised I'd forgotten the key. I was in no mood to go down again. There was the sound of somebody moving in room 39 beside the stairs. I banged aggressively on the door.

'Who is it?'

'KGB. Come out with your hands above your head.'

The door was flung open.

'Thomas!' And then as Gary saw the condition I was in, 'What the hell have you been doing?'

Gary Stover hadn't changed: the hair was as short as ever and his face wearing the same, almost boyish, grin. Behind him, another man was perched on the edge of a chair.

'I'd like to introduce you to my chief, Pat Conniston.'

We shook hands and I turned to Gary. 'Could you phone that cretin at the desk and get him to bring my key up?'

'Sure. What are you doing here?'

'Presumably the same as you.'

We exchanged banalities, oddly inhibited by Conniston's presence, until Oliver Twist arrived with my key.

'See you later,' we both promised.

Back in my room the first priority was removing my wet clothes. The message had waited this long, it could wait five minutes more. After a quick shower I ripped open the envelope.

Like the first message, this one was brief and unsigned. 'We will require payment to be half in gold and half in West German marks, US or Canadian dollars or Swiss francs. All notes must be used and not numbered sequentially. Hand your bid to the hotel clerk who will post it for you. You are allowed one bid only and can expect a reply by Friday noon.'

Again I was left staring at a piece of paper from the auctioneers and thinking how amateur everything seemed. They wanted physical cash and gold rather than a simple transfer into a Swiss numbered account. What sort of people were we dealing with?

If the replies had to be handed in at once it was a safe bet that the winner would not have to wait until Friday to be contacted. That was purely a blind to keep the other two parties inactive. In any event there wasn't much time.

I drove to the Consulate.

Pedro seemed to have lost some of his bounce. 'Last time I was here I could have got you a vehicle's owner anywhere in the country in fifteen minutes. Now it's just not on. I could get the name if I spent a bit but not from somebody I know. We would probably soon find the car's owner being phoned to see if he would like to pay to find out who had been checking up on him. And there's nobody on that road called Barcisa or anything like that. I sent the name off to London but I doubt if they'll come up with anything. Pretty much of a blank. I have got a list of every landowner in the area if that's any use to you.'

'It could well be. Barcisa went into a place called Villa Nhambiquaras.'

'That should do it.' Pedro ran his finger down a list in front of him. 'Here we are. Villa Nhambiquaras owned by Senhor Adolpho da Costa Martines. Now that name rings a bell. I think I've met him, last time I was over here, but I can't think where. What does Barcisa look like?'

'Blond, not particularly young, middle or late forties perhaps. Tall, about six feet, and heavy. Wide face, pronounced chin and fairly big nose. No beard or moustache. Didn't notice his eyes. Strange walk, a sort of arrogant swing. I shouldn't think that he was born here because his accent isn't quite right, probably northern European, but he's learned the language well. He doesn't look like a real professional, more thug than James Bond.'

Pedro said nothing and I realised he would have a much better idea of what a real professional looked like than I did.

'I wouldn't be surprised if he's just a messenger boy,' I concluded lamely, 'perhaps for this Martines. If you want to get a look at him, he's got a room at the Florianopolis, number 28.'

'I can't place him. The thing to do now is to make a few phone calls, but not from here. I've got a room in an apartment block, ten minutes away. You can fill me in on what you've been up to on the way over.'

Pedro was especially interested in the four men watching the villa.

'They must be some police group. If Martines is the big man and he's got police protection, there's nothing more natural than that the cops will want to watch every step he makes. Nobody trusts anybody here. There's no honour amongst thieves.'

His room turned out to be a small apartment with a lounge, a very small kitchen, one bedroom and a bathroom.

113

'I have to have a place like this,' Pedro explained. 'We'd get nowhere if the locals could hear every call I make. I have to find a new apartment every couple of months to ensure that I'm not being tumbled. I've never been tailed to one but I only have to make one call to somebody who's being bugged and I can be blown.'

'How long are you likely to be here?' I asked.

'No idea. Are you in a hurry?'

'No, but I could do with a drink and a sandwich. Have you got anything?'

'Only coffee. There's a store down the street. I could use a beer myself. I'll start phoning round.' He handed me the key. 'You might as well have this in case you want to use this apartment. I've got a spare at the office.'

The rain had stopped but it was hot and sticky. The blocks of apartments contrasted sharply with the favelas on the hillside behind. Nowhere is the disparity between rich and poor as blatant as in the cities of Brazil. The people in the favelas, suburbs of cardboard 'houses' and wooden shacks, live in unbelievable poverty while within a hefty stone's throw the modern monuments of civilisation glisten around them.

Pedro was smiling when I returned. 'I've placed the owner of that villa, Adolpho Martines. You remember four or five years ago the Sudanese government found that the African guerrillas in southern Sudan were using American weapons?'

I had to admit that I didn't remember.

'Well anyway,' he continued, 'they did. There was a hell of a stink about the CIA playing around again but they swore blind that this time they weren't involved. In the end someone traced the actual weapons to a consignment sold to the Brazilian government and officially the trail stopped there. But the rumours at that time were that our friend Martines bought the guns from the military in Rio Grande do Sul and sold them at a huge profit to the rebels. And he's thought to be doing the same thing in a couple of other places.'

'So he's well in with the military. Did the Sudanese thing just blow over?'

'Seems so. I've remembered where I saw him now. It was at one of those receptions at some Embassy or other. We'll have the photos back at the Consulate. All I can remember is that he spent a lot of time talking to the locals and not much with the rest of us. He's certainly not the same person as Barcisa though. Martines must be into his seventies. I should be able to find out a fair bit about him, and, with a bit of luck, I might come up with his protector. Why don't you pour us both a beer while I get on with it?'

Time dragged. Pedro spent half his time cursing the inefficiencies of the phone system and the rest shouting Portuguese into the instrument at a fantastic rate. But he clearly wasn't getting anywhere. His informants were either ignorant of Senhor Martines, knew no more than we did or else were not very keen to tell Pedro what they knew. The afternoon ticked past. It was nearly four before Pedro's face lit up.

He had been swearing viciously at the phone as he dialled the same number for the third time but this contact obviously responded at once to the name Martines. Pedro fired rapid, staccato questions down the line. Then he hung up and turned to me.

'At last we might be getting somewhere. I need to find an ex-bodyguard called Persio, apparently he can tell us something about the Martines household.'

'Nobody's heard of Barcisa?'

'No, not a thing. Barcisa is obviously minor league or else that's not his real name or both. Fetch me another beer, will you. I think we're nearly home.'

He sipped at the beer and made call after call but the one-time bodyguard was being evasive. Pedro finally tracked him down to a bar in Ipanema.

'He won't tell me anything without seeing my money,' Pedro informed me. 'I'm meeting him at 6.30 at "Lord Jim's" pub in Ipanema, you know it?'

'British phone box outside and doorman dressed as a London bobby.'

'That's right. Persio thought it was appropriate. Let's get back to the Consulate.'

Pedro frowned as the car spluttered into life. 'Persio used to work for Cristiano Nebulo who is truly poisonous. If Martines' security is Nebulo that's bad news. Do you know anything about him?'

'No.'

'Well you ought to. Cristiano Nebulo is one of the most powerful civilians in the regime today. The fact that he's managed to keep influence while practically all the other civilians in the original coup have been pushed out, tells you what sort of a man he is. He was an aide to Lacerda in 1964 when the military took over. He helped organise the arrest of trade unionists by the Guanabara political police while the military mobilised their forces. And then when Lacerda fell out with the regime and took over the Frente Ampla, Nebulo stayed with Costa e Silva and he's picked the right side in every palace revolution since. He's very clever, totally ruthless and of course as bent as Al Capone.'

He was silent for a minute, concentrating on his driving, and then started again.

'Nebulo's a fixer. There are still parts of the upper classes who are too big for the military to shove around. Nebulo acts as intermediary. The big latifundists in the interior, the coffee people and so on come to Nebulo when they want some big concession from the government. And the generals use him the other way round when they want something. More importantly, he's a fixer for the multinational corporations. He gets them subsidies, permits, cheap labour, you know the sort of thing. It happens all over the third world. He's also close to Mark Volmar who's been the CIA's Chief of Station here for years.'

An idea of the auctioneers was forming in my mind.

I had imagined that Barcisa was the main force that we had to contend with. Now the picture had changed. Martines had appeared on the scene. An international arms smuggler. That was a tough and at the same time sophisticated world. To succeed Martines would have needed intelligence, ruthlessness, subtlety, decisiveness. Hearing about the Griffin Interrogator in the first place required the sort of contacts Martines would be bound to possess. The operation in Chicago must have been mounted quickly and I could almost feel his brain behind it.

But if Martines was the brains behind the operation, what about Nebulo? Cristiano Nebulo was no small fish being paid a few dollars a year for protection. Nebulo was a big star in the Brazilian firmament. What was the relationship between the two men? An old man, wise in the ways of the world, and the rising, grasping politician with his hands on the jugular vein of the largest country in Latin America. I could imagine Nebulo settling for nothing less than a full partnership. And yet Martines would not be the sort of man to take easily to sharing command. Providing that he was still fit and well. Pedro had said he was now in his seventies.

Then there was Barcisa. Where did he fit into the scheme of things? And how could the picture of a worldly-wise wheeler dealer and an equally experienced political grafter chime with the way the auction was being organised: gathering everyone together in the same hotel, giving me the Russian and American names, the last-minute demand for cash and gold? It was difficult to imagine Martines or Nebulo operating like that. Was Barcisa now pulling the strings or was there another player in the game?

The sun was burning down as we drove along the Praia do Flamengo past the statue of a Scout presented by the Republic of Chile.

'Two telexes for you, Mr Vernon,' Pedro was greeted at the Consulate. 'One from the West Indies.'

As Pedro read the first his expression darkened. 'Bloody cricket,' he said before putting that message down and quickly reading the other which he passed on to me:

'No information on party B. Will remain here until mission concluded. Inform me of all steps taken. Watkins.'

'What does he mean, "Will remain here"?' asked Pedro.

'He was going on leave. The DG must be on at him to get things sorted out. Let's see what we can find in your photo archives.'

'OK, they're next door.'

He led the way into a room lined with filing cabinets and went straight to one by the window.

'Now the Embassy reception pictures should be in here somewhere, unless I've got my dates completely mixed up.'

It took him five minutes to find the set of photos he was looking for. 'Here they are. It wasn't an Embassy do. It was a reception for some visiting Arabs on an oil delegation; can't remember exactly why I was invited, probably standing in for one of the commercial boys. Now here's Martines.' He pointed to an elderly man talking intently to a soldier in full dress uniform. 'And here's a better one.' I would have put Martines in his late sixties, and he would be older now, but he looked fit and tanned and held himself upright with military stiffness.

Pedro then produced a photo of Cristiano das Graças Nebulo. A long thin face with a crisp moustache and heavy eyebrows. He appeared to have no neck but apart from that was indistinguishable from a thousand others. It was difficult to judge his height precisely from one photo but Pedro soon found a host of pictures depicting him, usually in the background behind one of the leading figures in the regime or else in earnest conversation. He was around five foot six. Invariably he wore the synthetic smile of the politician. In one shot he stood behind Admiral Rademaker, then Vice-President, Nebulo's expression conveying instantly that here was a man in the know, somebody to be fawned upon in the hope of future rewards.

There was another photo in which he was talking to the archetypal businessman, and I could almost hear him saying, 'Ah, but it's not that easy, my friend. Now if I was on the board of your Brazilian subsidiary, I could perhaps be in a position to advise the Minister that…'

Back in his office Pedro produced a large-scale map. 'You ought to have this.'

'Thanks. There are a couple of other things I need which might be more difficult. I want to tap the phone at the villa. The line must go somewhere through here.' I pointed to the area behind the villa on the map.

I asked him for what was then the latest in 1970s technology: something I could attach to the lines at the top of a telegraph pole, a long lead from that down to the ground and then a tape recorder and headset.

'And before you smile,' I added, 'the tape recorder will have to be audio-controlled so that I can leave it there and it will switch itself on if there's a noise on the line. It would also be nice if you could get a couple of radio packs and best of all if we could install a radio tap.'

'You wouldn't like me to bug the villa as well while I'm at it? That's quite an order. I'll ask Six for help. The wiretapping stuff they'll have here at the Consulate and the headphones. And I can get the sort of tape recorder you need. I should be able to pick up a couple of radios without any trouble but as to linking them with the wiretap, I don't know. If we could get into the villa then we could bug their phone.'

'Quite, but that's just wishful thinking. At the moment we just need to get some idea of who's in the villa. It's a shame that wherever I attach the tap I won't be able to simultaneously listen in to it and keep the villa under observation.'

Pedro agreed to bring the tap out to the villa after he had seen Persio. 'I'll try to be there by eight-thirty, but remember I have a report to write for London. There's one thing you could do and that's take a camera. I've got a good one here and there are developing facilities downstairs. If it's not too dark, you could at least get a few shots of the men watching the villa which I could show some of my contacts tomorrow. I'll find some binoculars for you as well.'

'Right. Let's get on with it. Why don't you just send off a request for information on Martines and not bother telling them what we're doing tomorrow until we've done it. After all, Watkins did say "inform me of all steps taken". He didn't mention anything about steps about to be taken.'

Pedro grinned. 'That's not a bad idea. I'll just find the wiretapping equipment and the camera.'

He soon returned with a small holdall. 'Right. It's in here. The camera's not loaded but there are three rolls of film. I'll drive past the villa and try to spot your car and wait for you there.'

I left him to write his report. Pedro Vernon, I reflected, was a resourceful and well-informed man. He was also at least twenty years older than me and vastly more experienced. I had expected him to take charge of the operation while I remained the visible 'front man' at the Hotel Florianopolis. There was something unnatural about Pedro quietly assuming the role of my assistant.

XII

It was nearly 5.30 as I passed through the city centre and out on the Avenida Brasil towards Duque de Caxias. I continued as far as the turning marked Barra do Pirai, followed that road to the fork and this time went left. Five hundred yards further on I found somewhere to hide the car.

I strapped on the holster and marched into the trees, carrying Pedro's holdall.

There was thick undergrowth between the trees and it took almost twenty minutes to reach the line of telegraph poles stretching from the villa. The trees had been felled in a swathe twenty feet wide along the path of the poles but the space created had long since started to fill with new vegetation.

I followed the poles towards the villa but was about to turn back when I saw something I had half been looking for. Somebody had been here before me, with the same aim in mind. Screwed on to one of the poles was a small black box. Within a range of a few miles somebody was listening to every phone conversation that the residents of Villa Nhambiquaras had. And the people most likely to be doing that were the group watching the front of the villa. Like Pedro, I had assumed that these men were some kind of secret police, but suddenly that seemed unlikely. A government organisation would listen in at the exchange. There would be no need to put up this box. It was possible that Martines was known to have a spy at the local exchange or that this particular police department could not arrange a wiretap at the exchange without arousing somebody else's suspicions, but it seemed improbable.

I walked a few hundred yards away from the villa back towards the car before clambering up a wet pole and attaching the taps. I trailed the wire down the pole and about thirty feet into the trees and connected it to the headset.

With incredible luck within a few minutes someone began dialling. A woman's voice asked for Georgio di Roma, expressed herself pleased that he hadn't gone home and made an appointment for Friday at eleven for restyling and setting her hair. At least the tap worked.

I put the headset in the holdall, after first removing the camera and film, and zipped up the bag as far as possible with the wires to the tap coming out. After shoving the bag under a large bush, I returned to the car.

If I had read Pedro's map correctly I planned to turn right just ahead and after another six or seven miles turn right again. I did that and parked in the same spot as earlier after driving almost a full circle round the villa.

Leaving my car again I entered the trees and moved slowly through them. The first thing I saw was that the brown Volkswagen that had been there earlier had been replaced by a green one. It was starting to get dark but there was still enough light to take a few shots of the Volkswagen's solitary occupant. I hadn't seen him before. Nor had I seen his companion who emerged from the trees a few minutes later. The two men talked and changed places.

As I moved round to the front of the villa, a police car came down the drive. Before it sped off in the direction of Rio, I had time to snap the officer in the back seat.

The light was fading so it was safe to stay near the villa entrance rather than clamber up a tree.

In the next hour and a half only one car went past. Then the black Mercedes reappeared with three men inside. It drove past the villa and round the curve in the road. I moved quickly in that direction and found the Mercedes parked beside the Volkswagen with its lights off.

Four men stood talking beside the cars, silhouetted in the moonlight. A fifth emerged from the trees. Just then there was the sound of a car approaching; suddenly the road was becoming busy. Two of the men disappeared into the trees. The other three opened the bonnet of the Mercedes and when the new car came into view were peering at the engine.

The newcomer stopped and the driver climbed out. It was Pedro. I could see the three unknown men plainly in Pedro's headlights. One I'd never seen before. These three plus the two in the trees and two that I had seen before but who weren't here now meant that there were at least seven in the group. That was a big team if they weren't local.

Pedro walked towards them but evidently they didn't want any help. After a few words Pedro shrugged his shoulders and drove away.

Shortly after three of the watchers disappeared towards Rio in the Mercedes.

Pedro was standing by my car when I returned.

'You saw me stop?'

'Yes. Did you recognise them?'

'No, but one thing's for sure: they're not Brazilian. Only one of them spoke, the big bloke, and his Portuguese was terrible. He claimed they were Americans on their way from Duque de Caxias to Barra do Pirai for a meeting. I tried his English and he certainly had an American accent which may or may not prove anything. As you could see he was adamant that they didn't need any help and they made sure I didn't get to look at the actual engine. Not that I'd have been able to tell if there really was anything wrong.'

'So we didn't gain anything?'

'Wait a minute, old son, we did. The Mercedes had a sticker on the dashboard with the name of a car hire firm near the Praça Mauá on it; I'll follow that up. Whoever hired that car will have had to show his passport. Have you got the number of the Volkswagen?'

'Yes, I have and there are two of them; the one that's here now isn't the one that was here earlier. You think they may have hired them from the same firm but in different names?'

'Well we can always hope. If they've hired one car they may well have hired the others and from the same place. Any hire car firm is going to be suspicious of one man coming in and hiring three cars.'

I explained why there were at least seven in the group and Pedro's reaction was the same as mine. 'That's one hell of a team.

They have to be American or Russian but if they're American I'm sure the local CIA Station doesn't know about them.'

'But if the Russians have the capacity to get seven people here in a matter of hours why would they have sent Kardosov on his own to Chicago?'

'Maybe they just didn't want to make the same mistake again. But you're right. You can't just get seven KGB agents into Brazil without any preparation and with nobody here noticing. My money's on the Americans.'

Pedro was probably right.

'Have you got all the gear?' I asked.

'I've got the radios, binoculars and a tape recorder with an audio switch. We can attach that to the tap you've just set up. There's also a couple of spare cassettes and an ordinary cassette recorder to keep with you. I couldn't get a radio connection for the wiretap. We'll have to keep coming out here and running the tape through. And I have something else: a photograph of Hans Budermann.'

'Who the hell's Hans Budermann?'

'Budermann is Barcisa. But let's start at the beginning. I saw Persio, Nebulo's ex-bodyguard, and he filled me in on the details of the Martines household. There are seven people in the villa. Martines of course. Four servants, two local couples. A woman named Miranda Gonçalves who's a combination of mistress and nurse to Martines, and a general factotum called Hans Budermann who exactly fits your description of Barcisa.'

He handed me a photo. 'After you left I tried to find a recent photo of Nebulo and came across this.'

Nebulo was standing in the foreground, now without his moustache. Behind him sat Martines in a wheelchair. Holding the chair was a man in a white tuxedo.

'That's Barcisa,' I said. 'Not a doubt.'

'I showed the photo to Persio who identified him as Hans Budermann.'

'What else did Persio say?'

'Not much. Martines arrived here in the early fifties from Uruguay. He had a lot of money then and has made a lot since. He bought the Villa Nhambiquaras in 1962 and hired the two local couples.' Pedro consulted his notebook. 'The men are called Joao Moros and Paulo Pinteiro.

'The woman Gonçalves appeared eight or nine years ago. She's not Brazilian; Bolivian Persio thinks. Anyway, her native language is Spanish. She's got an Alfa Romeo, so that's who you saw this afternoon. Martines has apparently got an enormous pre-war Mercedes, a Mercedes 770, which he is very proud of. It's the only one in Brazil. And there are a couple of Fords and a Chevrolet van in the villa too, or at least there were when Persio was last there.'

'Did you get him to draw a plan?'

'Yes, but it's not too good. Just the ground floor.'

He passed it to me but it didn't help much.

'I think Persio put some of those little rooms at the back just to fill up space. He's probably never been in them. The servants sleep in two small huts behind the villa beside a big shed used as a garage. Martines, Budermann and Gonçalves sleep on the top floor, and Persio reckons there are at least four unused bedrooms up there.'

'Before we discuss anything else,' I suggested, 'let's get that tape recorder in place.'

We left the camera and binoculars in my car. Pedro stayed at the villa entrance with one of the walkie-talkies.

It took me nearly forty minutes to attach the recorder, put it in the holdall with the spare cassettes so that it wouldn't get wet, and return to Pedro.

'Anything happen?'

'Nothing. No traffic at all.'

'There never is, although before you arrived, a police car left the villa. I got a picture of the officer in it, although the light was fading. You'd better take the film out of the camera when you leave.'

'OK. But I can probably guess who it was. I should have told you about him earlier. His name's Jânio Gomes. You remember in 1971 the Archbishop of Sao Paulo claimed to have personally verified two cases of torture by the DOPS?'

The DOPS, the Department of Political and Social Order, was what the Brazilian regime then called the security police.

'I vaguely recall something like that. They were Italians weren't they, nuns or priests?'

'One priest and one woman social worker. They were treated pretty roughly to say the least. Of course priests getting tortured is nothing new here, but these two were foreign and one was a woman, and of course Archbishop Arns was creating quite a stink about it, so the regime promised to investigate.

'The actual course of investigation isn't important, but one thing that was beginning to come out was that one Tenente Jânio Gomes was up to his neck in the case. Then he suddenly appeared here in Rio, promoted to Capitão, and acting as bodyguard to Nebulo. Since then he's been doing an impersonation of Nebulo's shadow. He's a hatchet man and he's legal. If you can avoid tangling with him, my boy, you're going to stay a much healthier man.'

XIII

I put the walkie-talkies in the boot of my car and gave Pedro the film from my camera.

'I'll develop the film tonight,' he told me. 'I'd like to show those photos around and check on the car hire firm, so call me after eleven tomorrow.'

'OK. First thing tomorrow I'll give Cimate our bid and try to see what he does with it. I'll bid half a million.'

'Dollars?'

'Pounds.'

In those days the exchange rate was $2.40 to the pound so it made a big difference.

'You're joking. The DG can't have authorised that much.'

'So what? They'll probably assume we're bluffing. But if they don't it may keep us in the running. We probably can't win but we certainly can't lose.'

Once Pedro had gone there didn't seem much point in my staying. For one thing I was hungry. Nothing seemed to be happening in the villa and I had just decided to leave when the lights of a car appeared in front of the villa and came down the drive. The car stopped at the lodge and the driver opened the gates. Then it came out and turned left, away from Rio and towards the parked Volkswagen.

Stumbling through the trees I rounded the bend in the road and saw an old Ford with its lights on stopped behind the Volkswagen. There were two people in the Ford; Barcisa, or Budermann as I now had to think of him, got out and approached the other car whose driver was now fiddling with the Volkswagen's engine on his own. Budermann seemed to be asking what was wrong. The other man shook his head, slipped behind the driving seat and tried the engine. It started immediately.

Budermann rejoined his companion who had remained in the car, turned round and drove back towards the villa.

Budermann had come out of the villa just to check on the car parked outside: how had he known it was there?

I moved back to check that the Ford really had gone into the villa and saw its lights passing up the drive.

Then the Volkswagen appeared a minute or two later with two occupants, heading towards Rio. As I turned away there was a flash of movement in the moonlight. Somebody was walking up the drive from the gate. Evidently Budermann or his companion had stayed at the lodge, so they had seen that the Volkswagen now contained two men. What would they make of that?

With Budermann now inside the villa, I felt safe in driving past it and accelerating after the Volkswagen. I didn't catch it up until Avenida Brasil.

I dropped back but kept it in sight. They stopped at a petrol station and I drove on. There was another almost immediately. I filled up, then checked the tyre pressures, radiator, oil and battery. Plenty of Volkswagens passed but not the one I had been following. These men were professionals. I bought a Guarana and sipped it slowly but then gave up the wait and drove back, through the city centre, to Copacabana.

'There is one message for you, Senhor,' Cimate greeted me at the hotel.

'It says the bidding's delayed,' a voice informed me from behind.

Gary Stover was sitting in the lounge, grinning widely. I ripped open the envelope.

'One of the parties has asked for a delay. One day will be allowed. Bids must reach Senhor Cimate by midnight Thursday. Each bidder will receive a reply by Saturday noon.'

'It wasn't us,' Gary explained. 'You been requesting any delays?'

'Could be. You relaxing or on duty?'

'Both. Pat Conniston thinks you're up to something, so I'm supposed to keep an eye on you.'

'Well I'm going to have a shower. Then you can buy me a gin and tonic and we'll go and find a good restaurant.'

'Fine by me. I'll be in the bar.'

I turned back to Cimate and collected my key. He said nothing and retired to his room behind the desk. I counted his silence a distinct blessing: that was a mistake.

I was thinking about the delay in the bidding when I stepped out of the shower. It might be a ploy to make the losing bidders relax. More likely it meant the Russians needed time to get the gold into the country. Martines had made a mistake in not telling them earlier. I dried and reached for a clean shirt; its collar was bent back.

I was almost sure it hadn't been before. I'm obsessive about that sort of thing. But why would anybody search my room? What could they hope to find? The answer was quickly clear: nothing. The room had not been searched. The intruder had something else in mind.

The bottom of the drawer was lined with brown paper, one edge of which was now creased: somebody had lifted it up to put half a dozen pamphlets underneath. They were crudely duplicated sheets bearing slogans like 'Only the armed people will overthrow the dictatorship'. None of them were signed or contained the name of any organisation.

I made a quick search of the room. I only had time to look in the most obvious places. In the bottom of the bed were three more. This time one of them bore the signature 'MR-26'.

That confirmed what I had suspected from the slogans. The Movimiento Revolucionário 26, named after Castro's attack on the Moncada barracks on 26 July 1953, was now defunct and had been for some time. The pamphlets were years out of date. Obviously they were a plant, but what for? The three in the bed I had been bound to discover. Therefore either I was supposed to find them or else somebody was going to march in and discover them before I went to sleep. In any event they had to be disposed of. I couldn't burn them in my room or risk blocking the toilet so I stuffed them in my pocket.

I left the drawer slightly open at one end and a hair balanced on the handle so it should be obvious if it was searched again.

Gary was in the bar with my drink beside him and a whisky in his hand. The bar was not crowded and in the corner sat the person I least wanted to see, Jânio Gomes, the police captain I'd seen leaving the Villa Nhambiquaras.

'You've taken your time,' said Gary.

'Sorry about that. Let's drink up and go and eat.'

Gary's car was parked outside the hotel. He threw me the keys.

'You know this town. Take me to a good size steak and I'll do the rest.'

I chose the nearest good restaurant, the Ouro Verde on Avenida Atlantica. As we climbed out, I slipped the pamphlets under the front seat.

'What are you doing here, Tom?' Gary asked after we'd ordered. On the Langley course he had insisted on calling me Tom, a name nobody else ever used.

'Presumably I'm here for the same reason you are. To take part in an auction.'

'Really!' he exclaimed with affected disbelief. 'You must realise you haven't a hope of matching our bid. Your budget's way too small. And I just can't believe the English government will even let you bid for something stolen from us. We could get you kicked out, you know. A word from the State Department to your Foreign Office and you would be on the first plane home. Or a word to the locals here. After the Lechlade business in London DIS is not our favourite intelligence partner. Does your MI6 know you're here?'

I studied the menu and said nothing.

'Come on Tom, you're here because there's some sort of English connection in all this. Pat's sure of it and he's dealt with these people before. What do you know about an Englishman named Rupert Stanley Ashton? Arrived in Chicago last Thursday from Toronto. Flew out the next day, to London. Or Julia Louise French, arrived in Miami the same day, flew to Chicago and then on to Toronto, also English. And there's another name to play with, Nicholas Broadbent, Canadian, also in Chicago at the same time.'

'What have they done?' I asked innocently.

Gary looked at me with justified suspicion. 'Paul Donnell gets killed on the floor of the Chicago Options Exchange and we find a taxi driver who's taken two Brits from The Drake to the Options Exchange just a few minutes earlier, two Brits who had no idea where they were going, two Brits the hotel identifies as Ashton and French. Clearly they were following Donnell and they got him. But when we ask Brasenose for help, nothing.'

'Brasenose?' I interrupted, remembering the man Mendale and I had seen at the House of Lords.

'Justin Brasenose, our MI6 liaison. Don't you guys ever talk to each other over there? Anyway, we ask Brasenose for help and all he can tell us is that the names are phoney. This Rupert Ashton has landed in London using a phoney passport and then vanished into thin air. The way we figure it Donnell had a deal with these English guys. He would steal Griffin and sell it to them but what he didn't know is that they had no intention of paying him. They followed him around Chicago and when they had their opportunity killed him and stole the Interrogator thing themselves. Then they brought it here.'

From Gary's perspective the story made some sort of sense although it didn't explain how and why Donnell had gone on to the floor of the Options Exchange wearing an Options Exchange uniform. And it didn't make sense in another way. Gary had mentioned the names Ashton, French and Broadbent. Ashton and French I could understand. The taxi driver would certainly have remembered Julia and me jumping into his taxi at The Drake and it wouldn't have been difficult to identify us from the hotel records. But where did the name Broadbent come from? How had the Americans managed to connect Nick Broadbent with us?

I was soon to find out. 'How did the auctioneers contact you people?' Gary asked.

There didn't seem to be any reason not to tell him.

'They phoned our man at the Embassy in Washington. Told us to put a coded announcement in a London paper if we were interested.'

'And your man didn't ask for any proof they had the Griffin Interrogator?'

'Not that I know of. Why? Did you get proof?'

'Sort of. They phoned Rick Newell in Langley and said they had Griffin. I don't know this Newell guy, he's ONI liaison, but he's evidently smart and he starts asking them questions about how they got hold of it. Says he doesn't believe they really have it. They'd obviously expected something like that. They tell Newell they bought Griffin at The Drake in Chicago from two English intermediaries: Julia French and Nick Broadbent.'

It was easy to see what the auctioneers were doing. By providing the French and Broadbent names they had given the Americans something solid, something they could check, but at the same time something that would distract their attention and lead their investigation down a blind alley. But why hadn't they given them my name as well? Perhaps because they didn't want to draw attention to my misadventure at O'Hare airport. And the same question still remained: how had the auctioneers discovered Nick Broadbent?

'The English connection again,' Gary continued. 'Tom, let me tell you something. If the DIS were involved in anything that happened in Chicago you're making a big mistake. The top brass aren't going to like you poaching on our pitch. I'm amazed that Pat hasn't just insisted that you be called back home. He could do that. If Washington laid it on the line to London you would be on the first plane out.'

I tried to change the subject. 'Is Brazil your preserve too?'

'For our purposes, yes. It's Western Hemisphere, Monroe doctrine and all that.'

Even as we talked I realised that Gary was right. Of course we could not match an American bid, and not just because our budget was smaller. The Griffin Interrogator was American, stolen from an American research facility. The Americans were now trying to get it back and the idea that any British government would ever countenance us openly trying to stop them doing so was ridiculous. That's not how the 'special relationship' between the UK and US worked. It was one thing sending me surreptitiously to Chicago and not advising the Americans, it was quite another for me to be out in the open competing with the CIA.

Gary voiced just what I was thinking. 'This whole operation stinks. We're not getting any cooperation from the Brazilians after we've been helping them for years. Our Station down here is supposed to be right up the ass of the whole regime, military and civilian.'

'Perhaps they don't need your help any more. They've perfected their own torture techniques,' I reposted cynically.

'That's a bit too near the bone. No, it's our guess that the auctioneers are well in with the regime, or even part of it.'

'That's a pretty obvious guess,' I agreed.

We split a bottle of Dreher wine and lapsed into silence as the steaks arrived.

Somebody behind laughed loudly and instinctively I turned round. A Brazilian family were celebrating something, the father slightly inebriated. By the door a man was dining alone, Captain Mackenzie. It's a small world, although the restaurant was renowned for its steaks.

Gary returned to his theme. 'We've done a lot for this country, not just for their security apparatus. They rely on the US and now when it comes to us wanting something we get nowhere. The men at the top are helpful. There's a guy here called Nebulo that the local Station knows well. He's been scurrying all over the place, but he's just not producing anything. Hell, think of all the money we've poured in here. The government's pumped it in, and private firms. Everybody knocks us but just look around, every modern industry we've helped along, even the state oil monopoly.'

'That's a bit simple-minded,' I interrupted. 'Look at the profits American corporations are making here. You can't tell me General Motors is down here just to help the poor natives live a better life. Take a close look at those foreign aid programmes. Forget the military stuff. Remember Kennedy's "Alliance for Progress"? They shipped a rusty old synthetic rubber plant down here from Louisville, nearly fifty million dollars to produce five hundred new jobs. And what happens? It causes so much pollution that a thousand local fishermen are made unemployed.'

Gary grinned. 'Sometimes I forget which side you're supposed to be on. Let's change the subject before I ask to see your security clearance.'

We passed the time in desultory conversation about the state of the world. Gary had just been on another course at 'The Farm': the CIA's training school at Camp Perry near Williamsburg, Virginia. It sounded as useless as the one we'd been on together. It was late by the time we left, Captain Mackenzie had already gone, but neither of us were tired. I'd forgotten the pamphlets and decided to leave them in Gary's car. If anybody found them covered with my fingerprints that was unfortunate.

'Let's have a nightcap,' Gary suggested at the hotel.

Captain Gomes was still in the bar. 'I've got a better idea,' I offered. 'We'll get a bottle of Scotch and take it up to my room.' Gary smiled broadly, especially when I paid for the whisky. Again Cimate said nothing when he gave me the key.

In my room I checked the drawer I'd taken the leaflets from. It hadn't been touched.

The whisky was made locally from Scotch essence imported in bulk to avoid the prohibitive customs duties on real Scotch. I'd tasted better, but it went down well.

'Have you been watching Bitri and Abdel Rassem?' I asked.

'Off and on. You think they're Russians? We've had Nebulo's boys working on it for us and they haven't come up with much either way. We're waiting for a report from our Damascus Station. There is a Syrian trade group here and Bitri spent today with them.'

Clearly the Americans had not been sent the message that I was given when I arrived listing my competitors in the auction. Why not? Or more importantly why had I been given the names?

I tried to think of a way to ask Gary about the size of the American team down here. I was still toying with the idea that the men watching the villa might be American. Gary had other priorities and stood up.

'Just a second. That liquor wants to be let out. OK if I use your can?'

I nodded. They were his last words.

XIV

The doorknob of the wardrobe missed me by a matter of inches. It shot past my head and through the shattered window behind. The wardrobe itself fell forward on to the bed. My chair was knocked back and I fell heavily on my left arm, my head smashing down on to the glass fragments on the floor. The chair ended up on top of me.

The bomb must have been fitted inside the lavatory cistern and connected to the handle.

I pushed the chair off and made for the bathroom, picking my way past the twisted dressing table. A quarter of its mirror was still in place while the remainder lay scattered across the floor. The bathroom door hung drunkenly open on one hinge. The bomb had been quite small judging by the damage, which looked far worse than it actually was. It only needed to be small, exploding as it did just a foot away from the victim.

Conniston appeared in the doorway, gun in hand.

'Gary's in there.' I pointed to the shattered bathroom.

Gary was there all right, plastered over the room; I felt sick. This was the real thing. I turned and groped my way to the window, only half aware that a crowd was gathering in the avenue below. Vaguely I noticed Captain Mackenzie hurrying into the hotel. I looked down at my hand on the windowsill, it was shaking.

'Who did it?' Conniston broke in upon my thoughts.

'God knows,' I answered, not recognising my voice. All I could think was that it had never looked like this on television. I turned back into the room and there was Gary's foot poking out of the bathroom. It was not attached to an ankle.

'Why?' Conniston was asking. 'I don't understand why.'

Neither did I and now was not the time to start thinking about it, although I was beginning to grope towards an answer.

Another man with a gun rushed into the room, with Cimate on his heel. It was Captain Gomes.

'*O que é que você fez?*' Cimate screamed. At last something had happened to make him speak in Portuguese.

Gomes turned on him. 'Go and keep people away from this floor.'

He ignored Gary's mangled body and came straight over to me, paying no attention to Conniston. With a typical bureaucrat's sense of priorities he demanded to see my passport.

Conniston wasn't going to stand for that. 'There's a dead man here, aren't you going to send for an ambulance and cordon off the area?'

Gomes turned to stare at him. 'Your passport too, Senhor. If the man is dead an ambulance will be of no help.' He returned his attention to me. 'You work for the British government? What are you doing in Brazil? You are not attached to the Consulate.'

It was a ridiculous question. Somebody had just been killed. I had nearly been killed. I caught sight of myself in the remaining fragment of mirror, I was as pale as a ghost. My pulse was still racing. I babbled an inane reply to his inane question.

'I'm on secondment to the Civil Service Department.'

I was close to throwing up but had to fight that back. 'What are you going to do about this?' I demanded in as stern a voice as I could manage. 'My Ambassador will want it given top priority. What rank are you?'

'Capitão Gomes. You can be assured that the investigation will be thorough. Who is the dead man? Why was he in your room?' He looked at the passports. 'And why is Senhor Conniston here?'

Conniston answered. 'His name is – was – Gary Stover and why we're here is none of your business. I'm going to phone the American Embassy right this minute and I want some action. Somebody must have seen the bombers.'

'I'll tell you when you can leave,' Gomes fired at him.

136

At that moment a uniformed policeman arrived and blocked Conniston's way. Gomes was not a happy man and I was in no mood to improve his temper.

'Captain Gomes is used to dealing with foreigners,' I told Conniston, remembering Pedro's remarks about the tortured nuns. 'His speciality is Italians, last time it caused quite a furore.'

Gomes turned to Conniston and told him he could go. 'But do not leave this building.' I thought Conniston was going to protest but instead he rushed out of the room. Then Gomes turned to me. 'You have a good memory for propaganda but you should know that those slanderous accusations were completely disproved.

'Gilberto,' he shouted to the fat policeman, 'search this room. And you, Senhor, will tell me exactly what happened here.' He fired a barrage of questions at me without waiting for answers. 'When did you arrive? Did you notice anything suspicious? Can you explain why anybody would want to kill Senhor Stover? Why are you all in Brazil?'

I sat down shakily on the bed but my head was starting to clear. I explained what had happened, leaving out only the important bits, like finding the pamphlets and our reasons for being in Rio. I was convinced Gomes had planted the bomb but I had to pretend not only that I didn't know he'd murdered Gary but that I was unaware that he knew exactly why we were at the hotel.

'I don't understand your job here,' he said. 'What is the Civil Service Department?'

I wasn't quite sure myself; I'd never had any contact with it. 'It deals with recruitment and promotion of government employees. I'm here to perform job and personnel evaluations on Brazil-based staff. Surely you have the same thing in your own Civil Service.'

He looked at me blankly, obviously having even less idea of what I was talking about than I had myself, and turned to the man searching my belongings. Two areas were receiving particular attention: the bed and the drawers. The inspection of the bathroom was cursory. A doctor appeared and carried on with an air of bored efficiency, as if violent death was part of his everyday experience. It probably was.

Gilberto was obviously not finding what he was looking for. He shrugged his shoulders in response to the stare from Gomes.

'Where did you go this evening, Senhor?'

'We had a meal and a few drinks. First I went to the Consulate, I had some papers I wanted placing in the safe.' I hoped that would stop him looking for the leaflets. I didn't want him finding the pamphlets in Gary's car, covered with my prints.

'It is late. Why was the Consulate still open?'

'There's a guard. We're not getting far are we? It must be obvious even to you that I was the bomb's target and I can assure you I know nobody with a reason for killing me.'

'Terrorists do not need a reason, that is why they are terrorists,' he said with somewhat twisted logic. 'It is not obvious the bomb was meant for you, it is Senhor Stover that is dead.'

'But nobody knew he was going in there before me.'

'You knew. You are a rival of Senhor Stover perhaps. You were in the best position to plant the bomb. I must know why you are both here. You are not helping me and in Brazil it is wise to help the police. I think perhaps you are going home soon.'

'I don't know when I'm going home and I didn't plant the bomb. We both know how you operate here. Stop trying to throw your weight around and get on with finding the men who did this. You'll be able to play torture when you've caught them.'

'You are very knowledgeable concerning Communist propaganda, Senhor. There is no torture in Brazil.'

Torture in Brazil had been verified a thousand times, by the Catholic Church, Amnesty, the International Commission of Jurists, but there was no point arguing about it.

'Oh for God's sake don't give me that. We're getting absolutely nowhere. You've let a doctor in there. This man,' I pointed at Gilberto, 'has clambered all over the room and yet you haven't even taken fingerprints from the cistern. Don't you want to know who did it? My Ambassador is going to want a very full report of your actions.'

'You have already said that. I am conducting this investigation according to the correct procedures.'

Gilberto tapped him on the shoulder: he had found the scrambling device Pedro had given me. Gomes looked at it and handed it back without comment.

Conniston reappeared. 'Capitão Gomes,' he said, 'Senhor Nebulo wants you to phone him immediately. And get your men out of this room. I'm getting a proper forensics team down from Washington.'

Conniston was followed in by two white-coated men bearing a stretcher. I thought he was going to object to their presence but he let them put Gary on it, under the direction of the doctor, and almost piece by piece. Gomes instructed me to stay in the room and then disappeared. He left Gilberto standing impassively outside the door.

'Somebody's going to pay for this,' said Conniston fiercely.

'Who?'

'That's up to Gomes to find out. Nebulo will get him moving. The man doesn't seem to have grasped what's happened. You'd think he was dealing with a traffic citation.' He stopped to glance around but obviously saw nothing that he considered helpful.

'What were you and Gary talking about?'

'What do you think?'

He didn't answer. The crowd in the street below were dispersing, although there was still the occasional curious glance up at the shattered window.

'It doesn't make sense,' Conniston said. 'The only people with a motive for getting rid of you are the Russians but they would have a much stronger reason for getting at us, and I'll make damn sure they don't catch me now. They can't have thought we would allow you to be the highest bidder. Unless you've discovered something about the people behind all this. If you were on to them they might have a motive.'

I said nothing and he continued, 'I'm told that Vernon is quite good. Pedro you call him, don't you? An old hand down here. Perhaps he's discovered something.'

He seemed to expect me to be surprised that he knew about Pedro, as if everybody in the slightest way connected with our business in Rio didn't know what he was doing. I remained silent and Conniston left. 'Don't touch anything,' he instructed.

When the wardrobe toppled on to the bed my case had been thrown off. I picked it up and started to pack. It was all very well Conniston bringing in a forensics team but they wouldn't be here for hours and what could they tell us when they arrived? Gary's jacket was lying on the bed. I removed his car keys. Gilberto said nothing. I packed the jacket with my own things and fastened the case.

Gomes reappeared. 'The manager has arranged another room for you, he will take you to it.' In any other country if a bomb went off in a hotel the whole hotel would be cleared, but not here. The police weren't worried that there could be another bomb. It was clear, however, that most of the hotel guests weren't taking that risk.

'You are now free to leave this country and it is the advice of our government that you do so. You can rest assured that the terrorists responsible for this crime will be caught, but you will not be required for their trial. Before you leave you must sign a statement. I will bring it here tomorrow, there may be more questions then.'

Nebulo had obviously given Gomes a severe lecture. His old bluster had vanished. It was better not to aggravate him so I merely nodded.

Cimate was standing outside and led me to the top floor. He didn't speak. Perhaps he was trying to imagine how he would explain the explosion to the hotel's owner. He opened room 62 and gave me the key.

'I hope there will be no trouble here, Senhor.'

The room was an almost exact duplicate of my old one, or rather of how the old one had been. There was no point looking around, I didn't intend staying. It would be difficult to leave without being seen, especially carrying a suitcase. I left the case beside the bed and took the lift to the ground floor. The two Russians were checking out. When they had finished Cimate turned to me.

'You need something, Senhor?'

'Yes, a drink.'

'The bar is closed, Senhor, on the instructions of Capitão Gomes. I can bring a drink to your room.'

I could see the bar was closed and the last thing I wanted was him bringing something up.

'No thanks. I'll find a bar; I need some fresh air.'

Directly outside the hotel stood two policemen. One of them asked me for identification. When I produced my passport I was politely told I couldn't leave. I went back in and told Cimate I wanted to see Captain Gomes.

'He is still in your old room, Senhor.'

'Then get him for me.'

He tried the phone but evidently the bomb had cut the line. Cimate glanced at the two policemen standing outside, with their backs to us, and decided I could do no harm left there alone.

As the lift started to ascend I dodged around the desk and through the door behind it. I found myself in a room containing a few chairs, an electric kettle and a table bearing coffee cups that looked as if they hadn't been washed for months. I crossed the room to another door leading into a corridor. On one side was the kitchen, on the other a couple of small rooms, the staff's sleeping quarters perhaps. At the end of the corridor a door led on to a dark empty alley.

I crept cautiously out of the door. The alley ended in a dead end to my left, but on my right gave on to a street running at right angles to the Avenida Jaguariaíva. At the end of the alley I stopped and looked out cautiously along the street. The hotel was now on my right, my car on the left. The two policemen were still outside the hotel: Gomes and Cimate had obviously not come down to the desk yet.

Gary's car was almost directly opposite the hotel. There was no chance of retrieving the pamphlets.

I turned along the avenue towards my car, expecting to be challenged at any minute. But the shape of my back apparently wasn't distinctive; I reached the car without raising suspicions. As I drove away I saw, in the rear-view mirror, Gomes rushing out of the hotel, gesticulating at his men outside.

Now what? I ought to contact Pedro. But the first thing Gomes would do would be to check Pedro's phone and put his home under surveillance. The phone tap we'd put on the Villa Nhambiquaras might produce something interesting. But I couldn't sit out there and risk falling asleep with Budermann prowling around. Better to go later when everyone in the villa was asleep, retrieve the tape and leave.

I drove to Pedro's safe house apartment. The bed was just a bed frame and mattress but that was enough. There was an alarm clock in the lounge. I allowed myself two hours of sleep but I was still shaking. The image of Gary's foot lying on the floor was fixed in my mind. His death was real. The bomb was real. I had imagined I was a pawn in somebody else's game but this was no game. The two men in Zandvoort had tried to kill me because I happened to have stumbled across them. This was different. This time I was a target. Someone had decided that I had to die. Nothing had prepared me for that.

The alarm seemed to wake me before I had fallen asleep. I didn't want to go out again but I had to do something. It had been raining. Ghostly splashes of light reflected in pools of water. My imagination was in overdrive. I thought a red Ford was following me but it soon disappeared.

It was not yet dawn when I reached the villa and clouds still covered the moon. It took a long time to find my tap. Nobody had touched it and the tape was almost full. After dropping in a fresh cassette I followed the telephone line towards the villa.

Fortunately I'd counted the poles between my tap and the tap I'd found earlier. Even then I could barely distinguish it until a break in the clouds let the moonlight through. The other tap was still there but somebody had given it a hefty wallop with a hammer. It was pure chance that this tap was nearer the villa than mine and so had been the one discovered.

I continued towards the villa.

A cleared strip of land, fifteen yards wide, separated the forest from the wall surrounding the villa. It continued all the way round. There were no observation posts, windows or doors in the wall, except at the lodge, so there was no danger of being seen crossing the strip, but it stopped anyone entering the grounds by using an overhanging tree. The wall was twelve feet high and perfectly smooth. There was no way over unaided.

At the gate a figure was dimly distinguishable sitting by the lodge, a rifle cradled in his arms. He hadn't been there before.

The sun was stirring below the horizon, enhancing the natural redness of the soil. This was not the time to hang around the villa listening to tapes. I drove off.

I stopped at the Praia do Flamengo, near the statue of the Aztec chieftain Cuauhtémoc, and slipped the tape into the spare recorder Pedro had given me. On the beach the bass fishermen were starting their dawn routine casting into the surf.

The first call was brief. Someone asked for Martines and was told to wait. There was a pause and after three seconds the recorder had automatically clicked off. When it clicked back on another voice, presumably Martines, spoke.

'Who is it?'

'Cristiano.' That was one link confirmed, Cristiano Nebulo knew Martines well enough to be on first name terms. 'Jânio told you what had to be done?'

'I don't like it.'

'Well I do. If he traces Hans to you he might connect you with me. I can't risk getting involved.'

'But they'll send someone else.'

'We'll see about that. It's all arranged, I'll call you when it's over.'

Following this there was a long stretch containing only dialling tones and Martines repeatedly asking for Nebulo and being told he wasn't there.

Finally Nebulo called.

'Where have you been?' Martines asked. 'I've been trying to reach you. You must come here. We can't use the phone. It's been tapped.'

'What?'

'Hans found a bugging machine outside the villa, with a radio. He destroyed it, we're safe for now. And men have been watching me. Did you put them there?'

'Of course not. Why should I?'

'Hans thinks they're Americans. He chased them away.'

'Chased them away! Why didn't you call Jânio, arrest them?'

'And if they're diplomats! We have their car number, Niteroi AF 8108, it's a Volkswagen.'

'OK I've got that. I'm calling to tell you about our little present for the young Englishman. It didn't work. He didn't receive the gift. One of the Americans took it instead.'

Martines interrupted. 'What do you mean, an American took it? Is he dead?'

'It was an accident. He was in the Englishman's room.'

Martines interrupted again. 'I told you. I said I didn't like it. The Englishman shouldn't have been involved at all, it was too complicated.'

'We've been over all that, we didn't really have a choice, did we?'

'Why can't you have Dylan thrown out of the country? Plant those leaflets on him.'

'We've tried that but he found them. Now the Americans are involved, Adolpho, so the government wants everything settled and the Americans satisfied. If I try getting the Englishman expelled, they'll want to know exactly why. And there aren't good enough reasons. The pamphlets have vanished. Can't we bring the exchange forward?'

'No. They can't get the gold here before Saturday. Some ridiculous bureaucratic problem. They're waiting for the next diplomatic bag I think.'

'Then we'll just have to do nothing. I'm sending Jânio more men to watch our inquisitive young friend. I'll contact you if anything happens.'

The last call was again from Nebulo. Martines took a long time to answer.

'Dylan's gone,' Nebulo greeted him.

Martines sounded half asleep. 'Where's he gone?'

'We don't know. He slipped out the back. Gomes hadn't posted guards there. We'll find him. The Consulate's watched and so is every member of the staff, especially Vernon. Cimate will tell us

144

if he returns to the hotel. Jânio's finished there now. Do you know what car he's got?'

'Who?'

'The Englishman, Thomas Dylan. We must find him.'

'No. It's all collapsing, Cristiano, all our plans.'

'Nonsense. Everything's under control.'

Nebulo slammed down the receiver, leaving Martines whispering 'Cristiano, Cristiano' to nobody.

My mental picture of the auctioneers kept changing. I had pictured Martines as the smooth, experienced operator pulling the strings and perhaps he had once been like that. But the man I had just been listening to sounded like someone whose world was falling apart and who was searching for someone to cling on to. Nebulo seemed to be the man in charge.

There wasn't time to worry what the conversations meant. I drove back to Pedro's apartment. I wanted to retrieve the pamphlets from Gary's car but I was too exhausted.

After making sure the alarm wasn't set I lowered myself on to the bed. London would expect a report but that would have to wait. I fell into a fitful sleep, with the Luger under the pillow.

XV

My hand felt for the Luger as I awoke to the sound of somebody entering the apartment. The cold metal was comforting. I clicked off the safety catch while it was still muffled by the pillow. The clock read 11.35.

Footsteps approached the bedroom door.

'Thomas?' It was Pedro's voice.

'Come in.'

He entered, clearly disconcerted by the gun pointed at him. There was nobody behind him and I lowered the Luger.

'Sorry to wake you up at this unearthly hour,' Pedro said sarcastically. 'I would have got here earlier but I had to shake off a tail.'

'I've had a hectic night.'

'I know. I'll make some coffee while you get dressed. There's a lot to talk about.'

The coffee was black and invigorating.

'How did you know I was here?'

'Nowhere else you could have gone. I heard about the bomb at the hotel and that you'd disappeared. You had to be here.'

'You mean it's in the morning papers?'

'No, I heard it on the grapevine. The regime will have to let the press publish the story because Stover was American and the US press will be buzzing around soon. They're probably at the hotel now. It will be put down to terrorists of course. The CIA will be wetting themselves in case it comes out that Stover was one of them. Hopefully you won't be involved at all. What exactly happened?'

I recounted the whole story. Finding the leaflets, which Pedro confirmed were out of date. The conversation with Gary.

The explosion. My own narrowest of escapes. Gomes. Conniston contacting Nebulo.

Finally we played the tape I had retrieved from the villa. I offered no explanations: that's what I wanted from Pedro but he said nothing.

'I'm starting to suspect everything,' I concluded. 'This morning a Corcel, like mine but red, followed me towards Duque de Caxias. I thought I was being tailed but he turned off.'

'You seem a bit edgy,' Pedro agreed. 'People don't often point guns at me.'

'Well I have every right to be edgy. Somebody's just tried to kill me. But why?'

In my mind the only possible reason to kill me was that I had identified the auctioneers and they were worried about what I would do next. But how did they know I was on to them? Unless anyone from inside the Villa Nhambiquaras had seen me prowling around, which I was convinced could not have happened, somebody must have told them. And that meant Pedro or someone he had spoken to in London. That was not a chain of thought I wanted to explore with Pedro.

'Violence is the last resort of the incompetent,' I continued. 'The DG keeps saying that. It's from one of Isaac Asimov's books. I could see why Martines didn't want me around but the bomb was crude. London could have a replacement here in hours. The last resort of the incompetent. The Martines you described wasn't incompetent. I thought we were dealing with a veteran international arms dealer not someone who starts flailing out at the first sign of trouble. We saw Martines as the spider at the centre of the web, to mix metaphors he was the man pulling all the strings. But the Martines we heard on the phone taps was quite different. What's changed? Why is he so rattled he would risk killing me?'

'Perhaps it's just old age,' Pedro responded. 'It happens. You remember that photo of Martines in a wheelchair. Perhaps his mind has gone and Budermann has taken over. Or Nebulo. My conclusion from that tape is that you were on to Budermann and so Nebulo decided you had to go. Nebulo decided. Not Martines.'

Pedro then jumped to the question that had been troubling me earlier. 'What we need to work out is how they seem to have discovered that you had found out about Budermann. Did he spot you following him?'

'You tell me.'

I thought about the exact words Nebulo had used on the first phone call we heard. He was worried that the man he called Hans would lead me to Martines. So at that stage they hadn't known I had found the Villa Nhambiquaras. Budermann must have seen me following him but thought he had lost me. That prompted another question.

'Why couldn't Martines describe my car when Nebulo asked?'

'Perhaps Budermann just hadn't told him and he didn't think of asking.'

That sounded plausible but what about the men outside? Budermann had now chased them away but how did he find out they were there?

'Accident probably,' said Pedro. 'A neighbour drives past and sees the Volkswagens there each day. He gets suspicious and phones Martines, or phones the police and Captain Gomes tells Martines. I'm surprised anyone managed to observe the villa for any length of time without being spotted. I checked with the car hire firm. That Mercedes was hired five weeks ago. Someone called David Allenberg. He used a US passport for identification and gave an address in Upper Saddle River, New Jersey.'

'No local address?'

'Eighty-six Avenida Pasteur, which is a dead end. It's the South African Legation and they deny all knowledge of him.'

'You believe them? Adam Joseff thought the South Africans might be involved.'

'That's unlikely. Word would have got around if they had got anybody in our line here. And Allenberg doesn't have a South African passport. He probably looked for a confusing address and picked that. It's the sort of thing I'd have done. I've asked London to check the US address. Now we've got a name to go with the photos I'll put out a few feelers.'

'At least if he's been here five weeks he can't have anything to do with the Griffin Interrogator. Nobody had even heard of it five weeks ago.'

'There's another way Martines could have discovered you were on to him,' Pedro added slowly, following a chain of thought I had already explored. 'Through me. I've been asking around, discreetly, but word may have got back. Through Persio perhaps. I don't know him at all. He could have given me the plan of the villa and then phoned Martines.'

I half believed him. I was coming to believe that it was only through Pedro that the auctioneers could have got on to me. But he hadn't passed that information on through Persio. For one thing, if Persio had phoned the villa his call would be on the tape. And he couldn't have driven there because either I or Pedro had been watching the villa.

I changed the subject. 'How would you evaluate Conniston?'

'I'd say he's a thinker and not an action man. He's tightened up the Company security here, I haven't got a peep about what they're doing. He was here back in late 1969 when the CIA organised the killing of Carlos Marighella and the destruction of his revolutionary group. Like I said, if Allenberg and his group are Americans I'm sure the local Station didn't know they were here. But Conniston could have known.'

He paused, expecting me to supply a reason for the question.

'Gary Stover said something really weird, it was just an aside. We were talking about what Gary called an "English connection". Then for no reason he mentioned that Pat Conniston had dealt with these people before.'

'These people?'

'The auctioneers. Clearly Conniston doesn't know their names but the Company must have bought something from them and presumably they produced the goods. Now what would the CIA want from a gunrunner like Martines? Not guns: information. Our friend Adolpho Martines is no small-time gunrunner who's stumbled on to something big. Could it be that we are up against an efficient private intelligence service?'

I sounded melodramatic even to my own ears. Villa Nhambiquaras did not look like the hub of a global spy network. And it was plain from Martines' voice that he was far too old and infirm to organise anything like that.

'Let's not exaggerate,' Pedro said. 'Martines sells guns, he can guess what they're going to be used for. What could be more natural than making a little on the side by selling the information to Washington?'

I rose and walked to the window. There was a red Ford Corcel on the street below. Alarm bells rang until I noticed another red Corcel three cars away. It was, I reminded myself, a very popular model.

'OK,' I admitted, 'it's far-fetched but the auctioneers seem remarkably well informed. How did they get on to me in Chicago? Think about how they set this up. How did they get Richard Mendale's name to send a message to him? How did they get the right name at the CIA? How did they contact the Russians and persuade them they had Griffin? Perhaps they've also had previous dealings with Moscow.'

We were going round in circles and my mind was only half on the questions I had just asked. Part of it was framing another question which I didn't want to ask. If the auctioneers had been dealing with both the Russians and the Americans had they been dealing with anyone else. Had they been dealing with Six or even with us? Had Martines perhaps been selling DIS snippets of information over the years? And if so had it been via Pedro? When Pedro said nothing I changed the subject again. 'What news do you have?'

'By a circuitous but reliable route I've heard that Budermann has had at least two meetings with a member of a Syrian trade delegation here, a man named Khalid Attirmi. I've radioed London for information. It could be that we're on to the way that Martines is arranging the contacts with the Russians. The Russians' cover is Syrian. Unfortunately it's not as simple as it sounds. Not only has Budermann been seeing Attirmi, he's been doing so for some time: Attirmi has been in Brazil for nearly three weeks, long before Griffin was stolen.'

I shook my head. 'It doesn't make any kind of sense.' I had said that before.

I thought I knew why my room had been bombed and what I was up against but Allenberg and now Attirmi simply didn't fit in. As Pedro said, they had been in Brazil before anyone knew that Donnell was about to steal the Griffin Interrogator. There were only two possible explanations. One was that Allenberg and Attirmi had nothing to do with the Interrogator auction. The other was that Martines and Budermann had been in touch with Donnell long before the Interrogator was stolen and had developed plans for it which somehow involved Allenberg and Attirmi. If that was the case why had Donnell then apparently contacted the Russians?

'Talking of Arabs, one of the supposed Arabs at the Hotel Florianopolis has been active. It seems our Russian friends are trying to find friends of their own. Abdel Rassem has been asking after Alvaro Banteretti, one of the old guard from the Partido Comunista Brasileiro. Unfortunately for him Banteretti's now incarcerated on Flower Island, but Abdel Rassem had some other names. Looks like the Russians are trying to recruit local help.'

Pedro stood up. 'Watkins is demanding to know why we're not reporting fully so I'd better be off and send him something. And then I've got to go and meet a friend of yours. London are sending somebody else down, just in case Martines gets you next time.'

'That's cheerful. Do you know who it is?'

'Julia French.'

I should have been surprised, but I wasn't. She wasn't at all the right person to send: she had virtually no operational experience and no Portuguese. But London trusted her, they opened up to her. By her own admission she had not been with the DIS for long and yet she behaved like a complete insider. I admitted to myself that in other circumstances I would be looking forward to seeing her again. But right now my feelings were more wary than warm.

One simple question had lodged in the back of my mind on my flight to Rio: what was I doing here? Why had I been chosen? There must have been hundreds far more qualified than me. The same question applied to Julia. What was she doing here?

British Intelligence has long been populated by gentleman amateurs and while neither Julia nor I could be considered gentlemen we were certainly amateurs. The men at the top of the DIS, however, were not. Although the DG, Watkins had once told me disdainfully, had spent the years immediately before joining the Defence Intelligence Staff 'commanding a concrete battleship in Portsmouth Harbour' both Adam Joseff and Richard Mendale had been with the Department for years. They knew what they were doing and Watkins himself was no fool. Why would they – to use an expression they would doubtless have used themselves – send boys to do a man's job, or even worse send a boy and a girl?

Pedro had said they were sending her 'down' not 'over'. So she had gone back to North America after the debriefing in London. What for? And where exactly had she gone? I remembered Gary saying she'd reached Chicago via Miami, not the usual route from Winnipeg.

It was no good putting any of these questions to Pedro. Even if he knew the answers I was sure he wouldn't tell me. I stuck to practical matters.

'We'll need another handgun for Julia. And a rifle might not come amiss, and explosives.'

Pedro looked dubious. 'We're not the SAS old boy. Handguns I can manage, everyone needs that sort of protection in Brazil these days, but don't get carried away. We're not trying to start a war. I know someone who might sell me a rifle but I'm not about to announce that I'm in the market for explosives.'

He was right of course. I was getting carried away with myself. If he had suddenly produced a slab of Semtex I wouldn't have known what to do with it.

'I must run,' Pedro continued. 'If her plane's on time Julia French will be waiting at the airport and that won't help my popularity in London.'

'OK, I'll see you this afternoon. Then perhaps we can visit this Syrian friend of Budermann's, Khalid Attirmi. Make sure French knows the Americans are on to her, she can't stay at the Florianopolis.'

Pedro simply nodded. It occurred to me that he had spent his life in a world I still did not understand. He looked and sounded just as I imagined a DIS field man would look and sound but something grated. I looked at my watch. It was noon. Not much more than twelve hours from the explosion in my room and London had a replacement for me on the spot. That was quick, impossibly quick, even if they heard about the bomb the moment it exploded. Pedro must have a very efficient grapevine. And yet it was 11.30 before he'd bothered to come and check that I was alive and well. It wouldn't take him that long to shake off a tail. He was clearly in no hurry to hear my account of last night's events. He must have already known exactly what had happened and was sure I couldn't add anything.

The real question was: had he known it was going to happen?

XVI

Just as a ball left to its own devices will always roll downhill so, since the events in Chicago, my idle thoughts seemed always to roll one way: towards Julia French. I wanted to trust her. I was struggling to understand a new and unfamiliar world, surely she must be in a similar position. The culture of the DIS was in a time warp. It had been set by people who had come through the war and those who had joined in the twenty-five years or so after the war had absorbed that culture. Julia and I were a different generation, we were influenced by hippies more than Hitler, the Beatles more than the Blitz. In Chicago we had worked well together and without our initiative the mission would have been a total, not just partial, failure. But could she be trusted any more than Pedro?

On an impulse I looked out the phone number my friend Jenny's mother had given me back in London. I wasn't sure how I was going to explain to Jenny that although I was in the same city I probably wouldn't be able to meet up but I had a question about her schooldays I particularly wanted to ask. To my amazement she was half expecting me to call.

'I heard you might be coming to Rio,' she greeted me.

'How on earth did you hear that?'

'A nice man from the Consulate came to see us. He wanted to discuss tourist opportunities here and what our company could offer. We had a long chat. He asked me where I went to university and when I said Durham he said what an odd coincidence, the Consulate were expecting a visit from someone called Thomas Dylan who he thought might also be a recent Durham graduate. It's uncanny, such a small world. Peter asked what you were like.'

'Peter?'

'Peter Vernon, the man I'm talking about. I think he thought we might have been romantically involved. I told him you had a special friend in Sao Paulo so you certainly weren't coming out to see me.'

I let that remark pass. Jenny was more of an acquaintance than a friend and I didn't feel the need to discuss my disappointing love life with her. In any case my mind was racing. Within twenty-four hours of mentioning Jenny to Mendale and the DG, Pedro was sent to surreptitiously interview her about me. Why? What on earth had he been expected to discover?

Jenny was asking about my plans in Rio.

'It's a very full schedule. I couldn't visit Rio without calling you but I really don't think there will be time for even a quick drink, sorry. It's a shame because I could have asked about someone you might have known at school. I met her just before I came out here. Julia French, about your age.'

'What's her maiden name?'

'French.'

'Then she's not a Wycombe Abbey senior. Certainly not my year and we were supposed to know everyone above our year, even had tests on it.'

'Any Julias?'

'Let's think. Not many. Bordaberry, big fat girl, just married an old Etonian deb's delight, she was in Campbell, my house. Grimspound, my year, played lacrosse for England. Julia Richmond, three or four years above me, been in the papers lately.'

I didn't need to ask any more. Jenny had told me far more than I had expected. Grimspound was a name I knew well. I had a lot to think about.

I fell asleep again as the midday sun poured down.

Pedro and Julia's arrival woke me more than three hours later. Drawing the curtains I was momentarily dazzled by the brilliant sunshine. In the street below a red Ford Corcel moved off. My suspicions flared up but I consciously dampened them. I was in danger of getting a fixation about cars: black Mercedes, the green and brown Volkswagens, Budermann's Ford and now this Corcel Sports Coupé.

Julia French in blue and red was dressed perfectly for the Brazilian climate, her arms and face more heavily tanned than they had seemed in London. She bubbled over with enthusiasm.

'What a fantastic city,' she said. 'I can't get over the greenness of it all, the vividness of the plants. Everywhere you look the hills are matted with vegetation. And the vitality, the noise, the colour, the terrible traffic. You can sense that the town is going somewhere. We came past those hotels ringing the bay at Copacabana, midday and hundreds of people enjoying themselves on the beach. That's how life should be.'

'Your senses are letting you down. Those peaks and gullies that look so picturesque are the end of the line for Rio. There's just so little flat land and what there is very expensive. The place is hemmed in by Guanabara Bay, the ocean and the mountains. There's no more room. Add to that the regime's inability to organise electricity and water supplies and you see why industry is moving out, to Niteroi, Nova Friburgo, Petrópolis, even down to Sao Paulo.'

'You're just unromantic, Thomas. Beautiful weather, beaches, mountains and all you can talk about is industry. Just go and ask the people if they're happy, go down to the beach and ask the kids playing football.'

'True, but Copacabana's just the froth. Behind the nice modern hotels you'll find the rundown *praças*, the refuse in the gutters, the rows of decrepit cafés and shops and newspaper kiosks.'

She was grinning at me. We were talking about totally different things and we were both right. Brazil is a land of paradox. The land of the jet set and the favelas, of carnivals and World Cup football, and of a particularly brutal police state. It was good to see that grin again though.

'Pedro's briefed me on what's happened,' said Julia, 'but not on what sort of people we're dealing with.'

'That's because we don't know much about them.'

I waited until we had both sat down. 'Let's start with Adolpho Martines. He's an enigma. We've nothing on his background except that he's clearly not a native Brazilian. There are all sorts of immigrants here. Refugees from all over ended up in Brazil after the war: Germans, Croatians, Poles. From his accent I would say not Southern European. I had assumed he was the man in charge but having heard those phone calls I'm not so sure. He's old, infirm, still intelligent but overcautious. There have been mistakes: the bomb, the lack of foresight about the gold. And he's lacking decisiveness, there must have been a time when he wouldn't have been content just to scare off the men watching him. A Don Corleone perhaps wanting to remain the eternal Godfather but running scared as he feels his authority weakening.

'Then there's Hans Budermann, the man registered at my hotel under the name Barcisa. We know even less about him. Is he servant or partner? He's no fool. Conniston must have gone over every guest at the Florianopolis with a microscope but Budermann's kept his cover. He must know Martines is past it. What are his plans for the future? Can we offer him anything?

'Next Nebulo. You'd better describe him,' I said to Pedro as he entered with the coffee.

'He's easy. The archetypal third world politician. You know the picture. The heritage of slavery and serfdom is that work is somehow degrading, something to be avoided. So democracy becomes just a word and politics just a way to make money. Civil servants take bribes in order to live because the government's stashing all its money in foreign banks or paying for bloated armies.'

'The taxman syndrome,' Julia interjected. 'The tax collector takes bribes so the tax revenues are low so the government can't afford to pay the tax collector so the tax collector takes more bribes.'

'Right. And the population grows faster than production so standards of living fall and the incentive for corruption grows. The rich have more children, because they can afford better medical treatment. Nebulo is one of nine. But the size of the ruling clique can't grow so there's always a group born to riches but losing them, born to power but without it. People brought up with no thought of ever working but finding the regime has no room for them.

'So there are more coups, more violence, more palace revolutions. And each new regime knows how it will end so it tries desperately to grab all the money available.'

157

'And Brazil's as bad as that?'

'In some ways worse. Because it's a military regime. Soldiers with no wars to fight, but with a soldier's determination to ensure obedience. Where the answer to any opposition is the midnight knock on the door, torture, unexplained deaths. Anti-communist crusades with all the fervour of Stalin.

'And in the middle Cristiano das Graças Nebulo. Wheeling, dealing. Pulling this string, knifing that back. All the time making more money and therefore more power and so being able to make still more money. Obviously clever but crude. His world isn't the world of international espionage. That bomb was the idea of a thug, not a professional.'

'What about the relationship between Nebulo and Martines?'

Pedro thought about that for a moment. 'Nebulo probably feels superior to Martines; looks down on a man who only enjoys the security of his villa by having Nebulo's protection. But he is not fool enough to think he can handle the KGB and CIA himself. He's letting Martines make the actual arrangements. Nebulo is a big frog in the biggest pond in South America but Martines is from a larger and very different world. At the moment they need each other and Nebulo must know that.'

'As for Martines,' I suggested, 'to him Nebulo will be the upstart. The provincial. The muscle. Martines has been around for decades and dealt with hundreds of political animals like Nebulo. But he too must recognise that he and Nebulo are dependent on each other. However, now he's not sure of Nebulo. It showed in his voice on the phone: a hint of fear. The men outside the villa really rattled him. He wanted Nebulo's help but couldn't be sure they weren't Nebulo's men. There's not much to say about the other people involved. Captain Jânio Gomes is a thick, sadistic policeman and probably no more than Nebulo's bodyguard. He's not a partner in the enterprise.'

'What about the men watching the villa, Allenberg and company?' Julia asked.

I hoped Pedro would reply but he remained silent. He had come up with a name, Allenberg, but nothing else. I was surprised. Pedro's contacts in this town seemed second to none but apparently he could learn nothing more that might help us identify the men watching Martines. He had their car numbers and had actually spoken to some of them outside the villa but all he had been able to determine was that they were not local. Unless he had found out who they were but decided not to tell me. Perhaps he had always known. Perhaps he also knew more about my companion from the flight out, Captain Mackenzie, who seemed to pop up with surprising frequency. I decided to keep such thoughts to myself.

'We know virtually nothing about this Allenberg group,' I said, 'and the same applies to Khalid Attirmi, the man from the Syrian trade delegation who we know has been meeting Budermann. Attirmi may be one possible way into all this for us because we know where he is. The other possibility is Gonçalves.'

'Gonçalves? Martines' mistress?'

'Mistress or nurse. She could be a weak link. Budermann probably won't bite the hand that feeds him, but what about her?'

'Surely the same will apply,' Pedro said. 'She's doing pretty well; you noticed she drives an imported car. That must cost Martines quite a bit.'

'True, but she must be reasonably bright to have got where she is, so she'll be looking ahead. Martines is going to die, perhaps tomorrow, perhaps twenty years from now, but probably soon. What's she going to do then? A thirty-five-plus ex-mistress with expensive tastes. And we've got a chance to reach her – that hair appointment we heard her make. Don't you think Julia needs her hair done?'

'I can always find time for that,' said Julia, that ready smile again. 'What do I do?'

'You try to pump her. The appointment's tomorrow morning. If Pedro can get some bugs we might pay her to plant them.'

'That will be no problem,' Pedro assured us, 'much easier than getting hold of explosives.'

'Then that's settled. Now if Pedro can collect my clothes Julia and I will take a look at Mr Attirmi. We'll meet back here at seven-thirty.'

'I thought Richard Mendale wanted us to concentrate on the Russians,' said Pedro.

'He did but Attirmi's Syrian and the Russians are travelling on Syrian passports. Given that Attirmi was here long before the Interrogator was stolen that's probably a coincidence, but Attirmi's at a loose end we should try to tidy up.'

Pedro gave us the address of the Syrian's hotel and left. I had half considered asking him why he had gone to see Jenny Merchant but decided to postpone that discussion, he was hardly likely to give away anything useful.

Julia gathered the coffee cups and disappeared into the kitchen. I picked up her handbag. Inside was her passport. It looked genuine but then so did the Rupert Ashton one I had used to enter the US. It was in the name of Julia French although I was now almost certain that her real name was the one Jenny Merchant had inadvertently dropped: Julia Grimspound. There was a Canadian entry stamp dated six weeks before we met in Chicago. But after that she'd been to Argentina and Trinidad and Tobago. Gary had been right about how she had travelled to Chicago, the passport was stamped Miami, Florida. She had lied about being in Winnipeg. There was another Trinidad and Tobago stamp dated just two days ago, after turning down my offer of a drink in London she must have jetted off to the Caribbean almost immediately. All right for some.

I'd just replaced the passport when Julia returned.

We kept away from the gleaming crescent of hotels alongside Copacabana Beach, showing Julia the more typical parts of the city. It was too dangerous to venture into the heart of the favelas but we saw enough. The occasional stunted tree surrounded by refuse and mud. Everywhere the smell of decay. Groups of men standing idly on corners. Labour is cheap and used generously by Western standards but there is still high unemployment. And so people stand around doing nothing. Without work they are poor and the poor cannot afford to support the industries that would provide more work.

Julia had seen it before, not in Brazil perhaps, but it was the same picture in a hundred other countries. We drove for a while in silence.

Attirmi's hotel was near the centre of the city. There was little hope of finding anything there but we had to do something. All we knew about him was that he had been in Brazil for three weeks and he was attached to a Syrian trade delegation. I wondered idly if it was usual for a trade delegation to stay for that long. The only connection Khalid Attirmi had with the Griffin Interrogator was that he had met Budermann a couple of times; it was a pretty flimsy connection.

'Were you expecting to be sent down here?' I asked Julia as we drove through the Botafogo tunnel.

'I suppose it was a possibility. I was working on something else but London kept me in touch with what was happening and they wouldn't have done that unless they expected me to become involved.' She paused for a while. 'Pedro thinks Martines and Nebulo tried to kill you because you had discovered the Villa Nhambiquaras. Have you any idea how they found that out?'

'Your guess is as good as mine.'

Julia said nothing. Her guess would be as good as mine, but neither of us would be guessing. I was sure that we had both worked out that there had to be a leak in London, either that or Pedro was playing a very devious game. I still didn't understand why he had gone to see my old university acquaintance, Jenny Merchant. If I couldn't trust him I wanted to trust Julia, I needed someone who could tell me I wasn't completely out of my depth. Perhaps it was time for me to reveal that Jenny Merchant had inadvertently revealed the secret Julia was so keen to keep. I knew her real identity. But I wanted to confront her when I could see her reaction.

I concentrated on the driving. The man ahead of me, in a very battered Volkswagen, was apparently trying to commit suicide. I didn't want anybody swerving out of his path into mine.

Attirmi's hotel was old and majestic, the outside covered with little columns and ornamental foliage, the inside marble, wood and deep carpets. We decided to pretend Martines had sent us to arrange another meeting. It wasn't a very subtle plan and in any case was unnecessary. Attirmi wasn't there.

It looked like plan B, do nothing, but at the hotel, not Pedro's apartment. Julia arranged with the reception clerk to point Attirmi out if he came in. We tried buttonholing staff and showing them photos of the villa watchers. A waitress thought she recognised one as a man who'd eaten there on his own a week earlier. But it might have been somebody else.

We sat in the lounge. It looked like being a fruitless afternoon. We searched around for something to talk about that would cause no problems if it was overheard. Did that rule out what I had learned from Jenny Merchant?

'The chap at the desk wasn't impressed with my Portuguese,' Julia said. 'I picked some up on holiday in the Algarve but languages are not my strong point.'

'Portuguese and Brazilian are quite different,' I explained. 'More so than English and American. The Brazilians have thousands of words that you won't hear in Portugal, acquired from African slaves and Tupi Indians. And the pronunciation is a bit different. You have to articulate the unstressed vowels that are skipped in Portuguese. The nasal sounds are sometimes different and the language was softened by the Africans: Brazilian is more open mouthed.'

I was sounding more like a linguistics professor than a language teacher. Showing off perhaps. I wanted to impress.

As she spoke I warmed to her. She was an incredibly attractive woman whatever her real name and background. Her skirt crept up her legs with every move and her red blouse hung enticingly open as she leaned forward. I looked guiltily away but she must have noticed my glance, a moment later the blouse was buttoned up. Above all she bubbled with enthusiasm whether talking about school, life at Somerville, playing magic tricks with her young cousins, holidays in the West Indies or her officer training at Cranwell. To her life was to be relished. How would she react to seeing a friend blown apart like Gary? I kept coming back to the same question: could I trust her?

Could I trust anyone? I needed help. I had to take a gamble. There was no one within earshot.

'You need to tell me what's going on, Julia. I'm stumbling around in the dark. I could have been killed. You have to trust me, you and your father.'

XVII

'My father!'

'The DG, Lord Grimspound. Your real name is Julia Grimspound, isn't it?'

At first I was met with silence. I could see Julia's mind working. Finally she smiled.

'He's not my father. You should have checked *Burke's Peerage*. He's my uncle. But that's not the point is it?' She paused again. 'What do you think is going on?'

'I don't know. I can't believe that in this day and age the head of a major Intelligence agency is allowed to hire one of his own relations let alone then send her on a mission like this. It's mad.'

Again Julia said nothing. 'On top of that somebody in London is playing silly buggers. I'm sent on missions nobody in their right mind would send me on. The same appears to be happening to you except that you know exactly what's going on. I'm not only treated like an idiot but now it seems Pedro is checking up on me as if I'm on the other side. And I can't trust anyone in London because when I report back somebody tries to kill me. In any case London seems to be falling apart, one disaster after another. Six are apparently gunning for us after Mendale's operation in Warsaw collapsed. The Americans don't trust us following the Lechlade debacle. Then the operations in Zandvoort and Chicago went completely wrong. In both cases I messed up but I'm supposedly trusted enough to be sent down here. And your uncle, with the whole of the Department at his command, chooses to send his totally inexperienced niece on what is supposed to be a mission that's so important it's worth infuriating the Americans all over again. It's ludicrous.'

'Put like that it does sound unusual,' Julia admitted.

'Unusual!'

'Well all right, ludicrous.' Again she paused as if unsure how to continue. 'You're right of course. I'll tell you what I know, which is not everything. Perhaps you can make more sense of it, you know the people in London better than me.'

She sat for a moment looking across the lobby as if seeking inspiration or, more probably, deciding just how much of the truth I could be told.

'I was seconded to the DIS just a few months before you joined but I've been in the field the whole time; until I came back from Chicago I had never even been into the DIS headquarters. The DG, my Uncle Gordon, recruited me for something very specific: to help him catch a spy.'

'Samovar.'

'No. A spy in London. A spy inside the DIS.'

Yet again there was a moment's silence. I didn't believe her. Of course there could be a mole in the DIS but the idea that the DG would bring in a member of his family to trap the mole was utterly ridiculous.

'It all started with the MI6 operation in Warsaw,' Julia continued. 'Without any warning a Russian general slipped a note to our Military Attaché saying he wanted to defect but it had to happen right away, he would be going home in two weeks. Six knew they couldn't use anyone from their Warsaw Station, all their people were under observation. They had to find a team to fly in quickly and we had someone who knew Warsaw well: the Director Operations Richard Mendale. A joint MI6/DIS team was formed, headed by Mendale, but it all went wrong. The Russian disappeared, presumably spirited back to Moscow. Six were convinced somebody must have blown the operation and they decided that that somebody was Mendale.'

'Why?'

'As far as I can see just because he was not their own man. Six needed a scapegoat. They had made the mistake of telling the Americans they were about to haul in a Russian general and when it didn't happen they lost a lot of face. One of their senior people,

Justin Brasenose, had a stand-up row with my uncle's deputy Adam Joseff. Uncle Gordon had to do something. Mendale was suspended, unofficially of course, pending a full investigation into what had gone wrong in Warsaw. But the investigation got nowhere and eventually Six had to agree that Mendale should come back. But when he did he went to war with your boss Watkins. Mendale claimed Watkins had been empire building at his expense. Your department had taken over some of his operations and they had not gone well. An op in the Caribbean he had set up failed, an op in the Philippines went wrong and of course at the same time the Lechlade business blew up. Not only had we seriously upset the Americans by bribing one of their people but Six were apoplectic. We hadn't told them anything about it because Six were too near to the Americans. It looked as if there really might be a leak inside DIS and Mendale started to suggest that Watkins might be that leak.'

I was astonished. While Watkins was not the easiest man to work with, the idea of him being a Russian spy was absurd. 'One thing I can tell you about my boss is that he's no Communist. Was he even involved in the Warsaw operation?'

'No he wasn't. That op was all very last minute and there was no way Watkins could have known what was going on. If there was a leak in the DIS the finger pointed at Mendale and now he was right back in the centre of things. We had to find out if he could be trusted. But before we could do anything we lost control of events: Six's man in Berlin, Koenig, was blown, and the pressure to do something became unstoppable. Mendale was suspended again.'

'Hang on a minute. I remember Watkins telling me nobody in the DIS even knew Six had a mole in Berlin, let alone who it was. Mendale couldn't have leaked his name.'

'That's true. But we had access to material that came from Koenig. If that had been given to the Russians it wouldn't have taken them long to work out where it must have come from. Six were right, someone in the DIS could have blown their operation. Now put yourself in my uncle's position. He's not been with the DIS for long. He doesn't really know the people around him. His Deputy, Adam

Joseff, is telling him Mendale's loyalty is beyond doubt while at the same time Six are insisting Mendale be dismissed. What can he do?'

'Let me guess. To get to the bottom of it all the DG calls on his niece who's just graduated from the RAF staff college and presumably knows nothing at all about spies and spying. Find me the spy he tells her. Is that what you're saying?'

'There's no need to be facetious. I'm telling you far more than I should. Of course Uncle Gordon isn't expecting me to do anything of the sort. Let me carry on with the story. Mendale is suspended, people are throwing all sorts of allegations around, something seems to be seriously wrong in the DIS. Do we have a spy in our midst? My uncle had to agree to an independent inquiry. That's where the final complexity lies. Finding spies, counter-intelligence, is not our job, nor is it Six's.'

'It's MI5's.'

'Quite. It's Five's. We have a bureaucratic mess with three competing Services stepping on each other's toes. Eventually it's decided Five will lead but we and Six will be on the team. But who can we put on it? Not anyone from Mendale's department nor from Watkins'. Adam Joseff has already declared Mendale is in the clear so Six won't accept him. We don't need anyone with any expertise – all the real work, the surveillance, phone tapping and so on will be done by Five – the DG just needs someone he can trust who will keep him in the loop.'

'So that's where you came in.'

'That's right. I get seconded from the RAF to the DIS. My whole time with the DIS has been spent at a desk at Five's headquarters in Gower Street poring over interview transcripts, bank statements, surveillance reports or over at Curzon House listening in to Mendale's phone calls.'

'And what did you find?'

'Nothing. Absolutely nothing. The whole inquiry became a series of dead ends. Five pulled the plug a couple of weeks ago. They don't have the resources to carry on with round the clock surveillance so they convinced themselves Mendale was clean. Six wanted to go on, Justin Brasenose kicked up a devil of a fuss, but my uncle agreed with Five. The inquiry was over and it looked as though I would soon be back in uniform. Then the Griffin Interrogator was stolen, and suddenly it's all hands to the pump. If there is a mole in the DIS this might flush them out.'

It sounded plausible in a cockeyed sort of way. The DG, surrounded by people he can't trust, turns to a family member completely lacking any relevant skills, knowledge or experience but having the one quality he seeks above all – loyalty. Nepotism and amateurism, compounded by an English sense of fair play. Julia is telling me that there could be a spy right in the heart of Defence Intelligence. If that had happened in Russia all the suspects would have been shot just in case they were guilty. In America the best they could have hoped for would be transfers to the Embassy in Mogadishu. In Britain the Intelligence Establishment spends months considering what to do and then does nothing. I would have sent Mendale to the Ministry of Agriculture and let him count sheep in the Shetlands, but then I've never shared brandies with him at the In and Out Club. An English gentleman is innocent until proven guilty beyond even the remotest possible doubt.

Julia looked at me expectantly but I said nothing. Her story might explain why she was here but it did nothing at all to explain why I was here. If she was telling me the truth it was still a long way from the whole truth. Five had pulled the plug on the Mendale investigation a couple of weeks ago, she said, and before they did she spent all her time sitting at a desk in MI5. Odd then that the passport she was using seemed to show that she had been in Argentina four weeks ago.

Eventually Julia broke the silence. 'I suppose you discovered my real name from Jenny Merchant.'

I simply nodded. I still did not understand why Pedro had been to see Jenny. I had mentioned her name in passing to Richard Mendale and the DG at the House of Lords but why would they pass the name on to Pedro and why would Pedro immediately track her down and invent a flimsy excuse to question her about me? And how had Julia discovered that I knew Jenny? Presumably Pedro

167

must have told her when he picked her up at the airport, but again why had he thought it worth mentioning?

I tried to come to terms with the thought that Richard Mendale, the Director Operations, might be a spy. Could that really be true? Despite having chosen a career in Defence Intelligence I realised I was still so distant from the secret world of spies and espionage that I had no idea whether it was likely or not.

'Are you trying to tell me that now, because of what happened in Zandvoort and Chicago, the Mendale investigation is back on?'

'Well you said yourself that the bomb at the hotel can only have been because Budermann and Martines found out that you were on to them. How could they know that? Perhaps someone in London told them.'

'Oh I've suspected for a long time that there's a mole in London. Gary Stover confirmed it.'

'He did what!?'

'He didn't confirm it directly, of course, but something he said could only mean one thing. He told me that the auctioneers had given the Company the names French and Broadbent. How did they get those names? Did Budermann even see you in Chicago? How did he hear the name Julia French? Where could he have come across the name Broadbent? Unless you told him.'

'Me!'

'Yes you. You knew I would be carrying the Griffin Interrogator to the airport. You could easily have been working with Budermann. But if we assume it wasn't you and it wasn't one of the Canadians then the names must have come from London. Somebody in the DIS must have been feeding information to Martines and Budermann.'

'And who did you think that was?'

I didn't reply. She wanted me to say Mendale but I only had her word that the Director Operations was suspected of anything. For all I knew the DG himself might have been the leak. After all, the series of Intelligence failures being blamed on Mendale only started after Julia's uncle became Director General.

XVIII

We had arrived at the hotel just after four o'clock, by six we were more than a little restless.

'Let's do something,' Julia suggested.

'What? We could go back to the apartment. Perhaps Pedro has found something. Or else we could break into Attirmi's room. Or we sit here and keep on waiting.'

'I vote we search his room. One of us could stay here in case he comes in.'

'That's not a very good idea. At the moment Attirmi has no idea we're interested in him.'

'Well he soon will,' Julia pointed out. 'One of the hotel staff will no doubt tell him about the two foreigners flashing photographs around and asking after him, especially if he's had the sense to distribute money to the deserving needy amongst the staff.'

I still didn't want Attirmi knowing we'd given his room the once over. On the other hand, I was thoroughly tired of doing nothing.

'OK, I'll search his room. You wait here.'

'Why?'

'Why what?'

'Why should I wait here? If Attirmi comes back the clerk's going to be a bit dubious if I immediately ask to ring his room so that I can warn you. Do you know what room it is?'

'No, we'll find out.'

'It's room 27, second floor.' She saw my look of surprise. 'I noticed the clerk check to see if he had Attirmi's key. You'd better come with me.'

At my very first encounter with the DG, before he offered me the job, he had mentioned that his niece had just persuaded him to read *The Female Eunuch*. I had read it too but obviously the message had not sunk in. I followed her up the stairs.

Attirmi's door was locked but within seconds Julia had somehow clicked the bolt back and we slipped in. She seemed to have learned a few tricks from her time with MI5.

'Quite a suite.'

The room was massive. There was a large bathroom leading off it and a dressing room beside that. The furnishings were luxurious, though rather old-fashioned. The carpet sank beneath our feet like a cushion. A gilt-framed mirror threw our image across the room. In the centre an enormous double bed swept back regally to the wall. The Syrian government would be picking up a sizeable bill.

'What now?' asked Julia.

'I stay by the door in case we have visitors. You do the searching.'

Julia moved methodically, first through the dressing room and then around the bedroom. She looked everywhere, missed nothing and left everything exactly as she found it. She hadn't learned to do that by sitting at a desk in MI5 reading interview transcripts.

After half an hour she'd turned up nothing useful. Once or twice she handed me something: a one-way airline ticket from Rome to Rio, three weeks old; a sheaf of papers in Arabic in the bottom of a drawer, but judging from the tables they were concerned exclusively with trade and economics. On the bedside table were two photographs of Damascus, neither containing any people, and, obscurely, a book on mass psychology in French. The clothes all seemed to have been made, or at least purchased, in Syria. There were no weapons or false beards or coded letters.

'We're not getting anywhere,' I said as Julia completed her examination of the light fittings, glancing around to ensure there was nothing she'd missed in the bedroom.

'There's still the bathroom.'

Within a minute she had discovered Attirmi's hidden treasure. There was a row of tiles between the bath and the wall and Attirmi had evidently prised one of these up and discovered a three-inch gap between the actual bathtub and the wall. Julia removed four of the tiles and from the space that was revealed pulled a small, leather briefcase.

Attirmi was far more than the trade delegate he claimed to be: the first thing to fall from the case as Julia emptied it on to the bed was a Smith and Wesson revolver. Attirmi also had a box of special .38 ammunition that would enable him to kill a man through a very thick door with no trouble at all.

'I'll remember to steer clear of this chap,' I said.

'Me too, although I'd like to meet him when he's armed just with this.'

She tossed over a thick wad of American and Brazilian currency. Twenty thousand pounds' worth at least.

'Very nice. Not nearly enough to buy Griffin, but you could get a lot for this little package.'

'A lot of guns, for example.'

'Exactly.'

I threw the money on to the bed. Julia was thumbing through two passports, one Turkish and one Jordanian, both containing the same photograph, presumably Attirmi.

'Our man likes to travel.' The passports were covered with rubber stamps, mainly from Western European countries. Not that that proved anything: the stamps could be forged along with the passports themselves.

I made a note of the names used on the passports and turned to see what else the case contained. I was disappointed. There was just one piece of paper bearing a few lines in Arabic script.

'Do you read Arabic?'

Julia shook her head. 'None at all.' She copied the squiggles and dots into a notebook. Then she put the paper and the banknotes back into the case with the pistol and the passports.

'Not much help, is it?'

'There's one thing you've missed.'

'What's that?'

'You're slipping.' I emptied the case again, with the revolver falling silently on to the carpet next to my foot. Luckily it wasn't loaded.

I pulled open the case and pointed to the inscription inside. The letters were blurred, matching the case's battered appearance. Like the characters on the piece of paper, the words were not in Latin script, but they weren't Arabic either. We might not know what the words meant, although presumably they referred to the case's manufacturer or the shop where it was purchased, but we knew what language they were written in. Tracing the Cyrillic letters individually, Julia murmured 'Russian.'

'Yes Russian! But where does that get us? It's an old case. He may have just passed through Moscow or even picked it up elsewhere. Do we want to believe he's connected to the Russians just because it might tie him in nicely to what we already know about the Griffin auction?'

'But it doesn't even tie in nicely. Attirmi's been here for three weeks. If his presence in Rio is connected with Griffin, it means the Russians knew three weeks ago that Donnell was going to steal Griffin and that Budermann would get hold of it. That's just not possible. Attirmi's original reason for being here can't have anything to do with our assignment.'

She was right.

'So why is he here?' I asked.

'Search me. Maybe that Arabic note will tell us something.'

'Perhaps he came here for something else but has now been told by Moscow to assist Abdel Rassem and Bitri.'

'But he was in touch with Budermann before the Griffin thing came up.'

I'd forgotten Pedro had told us that. Nothing made sense.

'You'd better finish going over the bathroom.'

'OK. Perhaps Pedro can read Arabic, or somebody else at the Consulate. We'll have a hell of a job trying to radio these squiggles to London.'

Before Julia could continue her search, there was the clang of the lift door opening, followed by the sound of footsteps in the corridor outside. We'd been in Attirmi's room for far too long. I sprang to the door, pulling out the Luger and motioning to Julia to stand on the other side.

'If somebody comes in, wait until he's through the door and then I'll slug him. If there's more than one I'll just have to shout 'hands up' and play it from there. Be ready to push the door closed.'

We stood in silence. The footsteps approached the door and stopped. A key rattled in the lock and the door slowly swung open.

Then my tentative plans were destroyed. The door had opened about two feet when there was a sudden scuffle in the corridor outside and a sharp gasp of pain.

The door shot back on its hinges and a man rocketed into the room as if he'd been released from a catapult. He was closely followed by another, taller man wearing a deep blue jacket. The first figure staggered a few paces and the second man grabbed him by the shoulder and hit him on the neck; he collapsed gracefully in slow motion to the bed.

My attention was focussed on a third man who entered the room, gun in hand. Unlike the first two he noticed me as he came through the door and swung towards me. Julia pushed the door against him, knocking him on to me.

'Look out!' she shouted, but we were already entangled.

I grabbed for his neck with my free hand while jabbing up with the gun. The gun connected with nothing. My assailant had twisted aside. At the same time his blue-jacketed companion demonstrated instant reflexes by turning and jumping on to me. My gun fell to the floor. Out of the corner of my eye I saw Julia dart towards it. But I had more immediate concerns.

A heavy boot flashed towards my head and I rolled sideways. The kick landed on my left shoulder. I felt another kick on my leg. One of the attackers still had hold of my gun arm when suddenly it was released and the two men had gone.

Julia had grabbed the Luger and moved to follow the two men. But she stopped in the doorway. I hauled myself on to my feet, nursing my shoulder, and stepped to her side. Standing at the lift were our two visitors, with two guns aimed directly at us.

It was a farcical situation. For Julia or one of the men to have fired would have been to precipitate mutual suicide. The man in the blue jacket smiled mockingly as he and his companion stepped into the lift with the doors closing behind them.

Grabbing the Luger I raced towards the stairs. I reached the lobby, with the gun back in its holster, in time to see a black Mercedes driving sedately away. There were three men in the car, the two men from upstairs and the driver. I'd seen them all before, at different times, outside the Villa Nhambiquaras. There was no way of following them.

Julia was standing beside the bed when I returned, looking down at the unconscious figure draped over it. She'd lifted his legs on to the bed and he looked to be merely sleeping.

'It's Khalid Attirmi.'

Without looking up she continued in a cold, detached tone, 'There's nothing of interest in his pockets, just the Syrian passport he used to get into the country. The chap who hit him was a professional; he'll be out for a few more minutes yet. I've put the briefcase back where I found it and photographed him. Maybe London can produce an ID. Shall we go?'

I nodded. My shoulder throbbed painfully, and the kick in the leg caused me to limp slightly. They were both superficial wounds that would disappear by the next morning.

'Are you hurt?' Julia asked.

'Just a bruise here and there. How about you?'

'Nothing at all. I just stood and watched! As soon as one of them saw me picking up your gun, they left.'

'I'd have done the same thing at the sight of you pointing a Luger at me!'

'I don't know how to take that.'

I tossed her the car keys as we reached the lobby. 'You drive.'

'Back to Pedro's?'

'Where else?'

'We could stay here and see what Attirmi does now.'

'No. Let's see what Pedro's produced. We're late already.'

That was the wrong decision but we only realised that later. Julia weaved through the terrifying traffic with the ease of someone who'd been driving around Rio all their life. Not once did she ask me for directions and the car threaded its way back towards the apartment as if guided by radar.

'What do you think Attirmi will do now?' she asked.

'I don't even know who he is, let alone what he's going to do. He might go to the police. Or he might do nothing. He could even go home. If I was in his position, I'd try to disappear, at least change hotels. It depends whether he knows who his attackers were. If he does, he could try hitting back.'

'Who do you think they are?'

'I've no idea. We know they're part of a group of at least seven people, one of whom uses the name Allenberg. They aren't part of Martines' organisation and they don't seem to be connected with anybody else either. Other than that all we know is that one of them at least has been here for five weeks because that's when Allenberg hired the Mercedes.'

'So we can assume that they're nothing to do with Griffin,' Julia continued.

'I don't want to assume anything.' An odd thought struck me. The man in the blue jacket had smiled at me. A superior, almost condescending smile but a smile nevertheless. As if to say why are you amateurs playing in my world? I remembered the phrase I had just used to myself: a boy sent to do a man's job. Was Allenberg our A-team while I was just thrown in as a distraction? Before I had time to think the implications through Julia was offering her own thoughts.

'Surely the most likely explanation is that Attirmi's here to buy arms from Martines, nothing to do with the Griffin Interrogator. Suppose Attirmi is representing somebody, rebels somewhere, who intend to use the guns against somebody else – a government perhaps. There are always coups in the offing all over Latin America and the Middle East. If the government concerned found out that Attirmi is in Brazil buying weapons, what could be a more natural reaction than sending a group down here to stop him?'

'That group being Allenberg and company.'

'Right. Attirmi is here to buy guns. Allenberg is here to stop him. And we find them chasing each other all over Rio.'

'There's just one problem. Allenberg was here two weeks before Attirmi.'

'OK. So it's Allenberg who is buying the guns.'

'No go. Allenberg's the one watching Martines, while Attirmi has been negotiating with Budermann.'

'Perhaps Attirmi sent somebody to Brazil earlier to set up the meeting and Allenberg followed him. Or Allenberg intercepted the communications between Attirmi and Martines and came to Rio to wait for Attirmi to arrive.'

'It's no good Julia – we're just guessing and we can't base any action on that. We just don't know how they fit in.'

Julia relapsed into silence, but not for long. 'Did you actually see Attirmi's attackers leave the hotel?'

'Yes I did.'

'What car did they have?'

'A black Mercedes.'

'Like the one that's following us?'

My head swung around like a puppet's. Julia was right.

176

XIX

Four cars behind sat the familiar black Mercedes.

'Lose them.'

Julia turned at the first intersection. The Mercedes followed, closing the distance between us to two cars. At the next junction Julia darted into the right-hand lane. The Mercedes tried to follow but was blocked by a bus. When we turned right they were unable to follow. It was a simple textbook exercise, except that if we'd followed the book we'd have noticed the tail within moments of leaving the hotel. We'd been careless.

Julia weaved around the centre of Rio for fifteen minutes at high speed, or at least as high as the traffic would allow.

'As they say in Cairo – drive to kill, not to maim,' she murmured, the car almost rising on to two wheels as she whipped around a corner. We might be out of sight of the Mercedes, but she appeared to be making us very conspicuous to everyone else, even in the Ben-Hur atmosphere of Rio. Fortunately the police seemed to be on holiday.

Eventually she was satisfied that the tail had gone. We headed again towards Pedro's apartment.

'That was stupid. I should have spotted them much sooner.'

'Not to worry. At least they can't work out exactly where we were going. But they know the car now.'

'Right. I'll park well away from the apartment.'

When we reached the apartment Pedro was waiting. It was clear that he thought breaking into Attirmi's room had been a bad idea although 'impetuous' was his only comment. When we reported what happened after Attirmi arrived he was as mystified as we were.

We sipped the obligatory Brazilian coffee and Julia asked what he'd come up with.

'Practically nothing. London has confirmed that Captain Mackenzie's completely above board and that Allenberg's US address is phoney. I've shown various people the photos of the two villa watchers and may have a bite. One of my sources thinks he's seen them near the docks. I'll follow it up but don't pin any hopes on it, he's not too reliable. And I've retrieved your case Thomas, it's in the bedroom.'

He turned to Julia. 'This is for you. A nine millimetre Browning FN high power. Canadian. Not a lady's gun, but it stops people.'

Julia took the weapon, checking the thumb safety on the left-hand side. Then, pressing the button beside the trigger, she ejected the box magazine from the handle, balancing two pounds of lethal metal in one neatly manicured hand with thirteen double-lined staggered cartridges looking especially evil resting on the other. Then she clicked the magazine back and put the pistol in her handbag with two spare magazines.

'Any news on the opposition?' I asked. 'Mendale was keen that we kept our eye on the Russians.'

'Nothing. The Russians left the hotel right after the bomb and just disappeared. We need to find them. The Americans still don't seem to be on to them.'

'How do you know that?'

'From Harrison. Somehow Six has discovered the Company's Damascus Station reported to Washington that Bitri and Abdel Rassem are above board. There seem to be a couple of genuine Syrian businessmen called Bitri and Abdel Rassem who have been travelling in the Far East somewhere and the Station concluded they must have moved on to Brazil. What's more surprising is that the Americans don't seem to be on to Martines either.

'Conniston's now got their Station closed up tighter than a mouse's arse. I can't get a peep out of my contact there any more. But one thing I can tell you is that Volmar, their Chief of Station, is asking a lot of questions he wouldn't need to ask if he knew who they were dealing with. I'm surprised they haven't just got hold of that hotel manager Cimate and beaten Budermann's name out of him.'

'There's always one of Gomes' police there,' interrupted Julia.

'That wouldn't normally stop them. My guess is that they're using Nebulo as a link into the local police. Nebulo and Volmar have been close in the past, and he's convinced them that Cimate doesn't know anything. Perhaps they don't think Cimate matters any more. Since the bomb the auctioneers will be keeping well away from the Hotel Florianopolis, they'll need to find a new way of handling the bids.'

A new and more sensible way I thought. I stood up and crossed to the window with my back to Pedro and Julia. Someone had to voice the thought that had been in the back of my mind since I first arrived at the Hotel Florianopolis.

'You realise the whole set-up here is a farce. We're being played.'

I turned as I spoke and tried to judge their reaction. Neither looked surprised. Pedro's face gave nothing away. Julia, I thought, looked nervous, although why I had no idea.

'What do you mean?' Julia asked.

'Why are we going through this ridiculous auction process? Martines has been buying and selling guns for years. He knows how to negotiate deals with people all over the world. He knows how to move money around without leaving a trail. Why bring everyone here? Why insist on cash and gold? Why not just negotiate normally and then arrange an exchange somewhere on neutral ground? There is no need at all for any of us to be in Brazil.'

'Presumably we're here because Nebulo doesn't trust Martines and wants to be present when the money is handed over,' Julia responded.

'Perhaps. But if you were trying to sell something that both the Americans and Russians wanted wouldn't you make sure that they were kept well away from each other. Inviting both of them to Rio is crazy, putting them both in the same hotel is worse than crazy and putting them in adjacent rooms is farcical.'

Julia considered this for a minute. 'They must have thought that if everyone was watching everybody else there could be no funny business.'

'That's pretty flimsy and in any case I was the only one given the other parties' names. Think about it. The auctioneers gave me the names of the American and Russian bidders. Why would they want me to know that? The only answer is that they expected me to try to keep an eye on them. Why?'

'You tell us,' said Pedro.

'So that I would report back to London.'

'And why would they want you to do that?'

'Because the auctioneers had someone in the DIS in London, they knew that anything I reported to London would be relayed back to Martines here.'

'That's pretty fanciful,' responded Pedro. 'How would someone like Martines manage to plant a mole in the DIS?'

'Perhaps the mole came to him.'

Nobody said anything until Pedro broke the silence.

'Well that's quite a theory.' He sounded distinctly dubious. 'But before we start chasing moles through the corridors of Whitehall let's concentrate on the job in hand. Mendale told us to keep our eyes on the Russians. What are they doing?'

'They're probably not doing anything,' I said. 'I think they've already won the auction. Martines put the deadline back to allow someone to get their gold here. The Americans wouldn't have needed time so it must have been the Russians. And the Russians wouldn't risk bringing gold in unless they were sure they would need it and that they could trust whoever they're dealing with. And that means,' I added as another thought struck me, 'that as I suspected they've probably dealt with Martines before as well.'

'As well?' queried Julia.

'Thomas has a theory,' said Pedro 'that the Company have had dealings with Martines before, although obviously they don't have his name. The idea is that Martines has been running a private intelligence service flogging pieces of information to the Americans and the Russians.' He made my suggestion sound utterly far-fetched.

'But never to us,' I added and Julia flashed me a quizzical glance.

'That's not surprising,' said Pedro, 'we probably couldn't afford it.'

'Yet we've been invited to this Griffin auction.'

Julia changed the subject. 'Let's get back to what we're going to do now. I need to check in to my hotel and if I'm going to bribe Martines' mistress, Miranda Gonçalves, tomorrow I'm going to need cash, right there on the nail and a lot of it.'

'You'd better take my kitty,' Pedro replied. 'And you can take my car. I'll use my wife's. Let's sort that and then I'm going to the docks to see if I can get anything on Allenberg's group. Before that I'll set some balls in motion to find our Russian friends but in a city like this don't expect quick results.'

'We should start by phoning the big international hotels,' I suggested. 'After the Florianopolis I should think they would want somewhere a bit more comfortable.'

'And where they won't stand out,' agreed Julia. 'I'll do that while you head out to the villa and see if the taps are still working. When do we meet again?'

'I'll be outside the hairdressing salon tomorrow morning and we'll take it from there. If we need to get in touch we'll just have to phone around. There's one other question.'

I turned to Pedro. I was tired of beating around the bush.

'Why did you question Jenny Merchant about me?'

Pedro's face gave nothing away. 'Yes that was rather a coincidence. One of the commercial chaps asked me to check out tour companies for an event they're organising. Your name happened to come up.'

'Bollocks. You were sent Jenny's name. Why?'

'Don't bollocks me my son. We're on the same side. It was a coincidence.'

'Mendale asked you to check up on me.'

Pedro looked at me coldly then turned around and left. Julia followed without looking in my direction.

What game was Pedro playing? What game was anyone playing? I tried to grab a quick hour's sleep but my mind was whirring.

There seemed to be two separate sets of characters in two separate plays and the only time they were on stage together was when the scene moved to the Villa Nhambiquaras. One play involved actors I knew virtually nothing about: the Allenberg group and Attirmi. The actors in the other play I knew well but understood not at all. Mendale, the DG, Julia, Pedro, the whole of the Defence Intelligence Staff. I wanted to believe Julia's story about a Russian spy in the DIS but it just didn't ring true.

I cast my mind back to the meeting with the DG at the House of Lords. Mendale was not only there but he seemed to be in control of the operation. Would Julia's uncle really have allowed a suspected Russian spy to have full access to our plans for the Griffin Interrogator? What wasn't Julia telling me?

I was dreaming of Julia, rather exciting dreams, when the phone rang.

'Did I get you up?' she asked.

The double entendre immediately struck me but I didn't know her well enough to respond with more than a 'Yes.'

She gave me the details of the hotel she had found.

'You might as well hit the sack,' I told her. 'I'll drive out to the villa.'

'Why don't you pick me up first?'

An attractive invitation I had to ignore. I didn't want someone with me that I still couldn't completely trust.

'No. You sleep. We may be active tomorrow night.'

'Doing what?'

'Breaking into that villa. If we can't get anything from the Gonçalves woman and the phone tap is unproductive, that'll be the only option left.'

Wary after this afternoon's experience I kept an eye on the rear-view mirror. Nobody was following. It had rained earlier but when I arrived at the villa the night was clear. That might be helpful in finding the tap, but bad if anyone was waiting for me.

I wasn't looking forward to the night's business. Martines would have to be unusually incompetent not to have found my tap on his phone. I consoled myself with the thought that he should have discovered it when he found the tap placed by the Allenberg group and he hadn't.

Not much light penetrated through the branches and I crashed through the wet undergrowth. The forest was alive with the sounds of night. At one point there was the snap of a breaking branch behind me. I stood rigid for five minutes but heard nothing moving. I checked that the thumb safety on the upper left-hand side was down. Pedro had given me the standard model: on some Lugers the safety control has the exact opposite format. The German word '*Gesichert*' would now be showing above the thumb piece.

Occasional glimpses of the moon served as a guide. Hopefully, my sense of direction would do the rest. It did, almost too well.

The sudden flash of a torch was the real warning. The order to halt was submerged under the pandemonium of a submachine gun as I dived right. Bullets sprayed past, searing into the bushes and smashing into the fallen tree trunk which sheltered me.

The torch went out. To the left thirty degrees, ten o'clock. My silenced Luger gave a clearly discernible hiss. Another spray of bullets. Then silence.

Whispers. Again to the left. Ten, fifteen yards. Hard to tell at night. But close. I moved right, slowly, along the tree trunk. More shots, wide. The submachine gun, then two pistol shots: the flashes clear. Thirty-five degrees. Twenty yards or less. I fired.

Something fell. A gurgling noise, strangely loud, echoed through the night. Somebody had been hit.

It was anybody's guess how many were left.

They weren't professionals. Professionals would have waited until they couldn't miss, until I was practically on top. But it wasn't important. With their firepower it didn't matter how amateur they were.

I moved again. Further right. Towards the road.

A pistol opened up in front. Two shots. Close. Then more silence. No sound, no movement, just blackness.

Again I edged forward, slithering along the ground. More shots. Two pistols now, between me and the road. And the submachine gun behind. Again slither. Again bullets. I felt the air move that time.

I had to escape. The noise must have woken everyone in the villa. It was too dark to run so I crawled forward, inch by inch. Another shot. One of them was closer now.

Then I saw him and fired twice and he dropped on one knee and then fell forward.

But his companion was still shooting. How many bullets left in his magazine? He stopped firing. The submachine gun was getting closer. I had to run.

Ready, stand up. Run. And the man with the pistol jumped up too. Outlined in the moonlight. Amateur. Just like the shooting range. And he collapsed. Both shots in the heart. My last.

Keep running. The Luger's breach open, toggle points buckled up. Shove at the magazine release catch. Look where you're going. Too late.

I tripped, the Luger spinning from my hand. All hell broke loose. That bloody submachine gun. It was time to pray.

I could see him coming. A short little runt in an oversized police uniform. I registered that he was grasping a Heckler and Koch MP5 and then his head exploded.

Not like the shooting range in Durham. The sound: thirty or forty yards away. Two heavy shots, something like a .375 Magnum, something my time in the OTC had not prepared me for.

And only a gun like a Magnum could so thoroughly have smashed the face. Splinters of bone and red, spurting into the black of night.

The silence that followed was absolute. Even the insects were stilled.

Reflex actions took over. Grope for the Luger. Find it. Take the dismounting tool from the holster flap. Slot it over the magazine stud. Press down on the hook. Force the spent magazine out. Insert a new one.

The owner of the Magnum didn't appear. Who was it? I'd no time to find out, shouts were coming from the villa.

I ran.

XX

The road, when I reached it, seemed clear and I raced back to the car. Another car started up ahead of me and accelerated rapidly south towards Rio. Apparently the man, or woman, with the Magnum was also going home.

The tracks in the mud where he'd parked were caught by my headlights. I didn't stop to investigate. He'd parked by the road but I hadn't seen him when I arrived, so he'd come later. I drove at top speed but didn't recognise anybody in the few cars I passed on the way back to the city.

I noticed that my hands were steady on the steering wheel. After the bomb in my hotel room I had been shaken but something had changed. Back there when the shooting started instinct had taken over. Like Zandvoort. Both fight and flight but fight had won. I was suddenly in charge. I needed to take control of what was happening. But what *was* happening?

Possible identities for the mysterious benefactor were dismissed one by one. Pedro had a Luger and Julia the Browning. And in neither case was there any reason to disappear. The Americans we thought didn't know about the Villa Nhambiquaras. It could have been the Russians, but why would they want to save me? Perhaps I had a friend inside the villa, but my benefactor had disappeared towards Rio? Allenberg seemed the most likely answer. His group had been observing the villa. But why leave concealment to save me? That question couldn't be answered until I knew who Allenberg was.

Then I remembered the Syrian Khalid Attirmi, and especially his gun, a Mark Ten Smith and Wesson with ammunition that could have produced the same results as a Magnum. How much

185

difference is there between a .375 Magnum and a .38 Smith and Wesson? Enough difference for an expert to tell them apart but certainly not me, especially with my ears ringing from the noise of the submachine gun.

If it had been Attirmi, why had he done it? I stopped at the first phone and called his hotel.

'Senhor Khalid Attirmi, room 27.'

There was a brief silence. 'There is nobody of that name staying here, Senhor.'

'But I saw him this afternoon.'

There was a rustling of a book. 'Senhor Attirmi left the hotel earlier tonight.'

'Did he leave a forwarding address?'

'No Senhor.'

The call proved nothing.

I drove back to the apartment. I could have tried to reach Julia or Pedro but I was exhausted. More importantly I wanted a chance to think. Time and time again I kept coming back to the one overriding question: why was I here? I was completely unqualified for what my mission was supposed to be, beating the Russians and Americans to the Griffin Interrogator; therefore I had been sent for some other reason. Did British Intelligence really send a pawn like me on my own into situations where I could have my room bombed and be shot at by men with submachine guns? If not then I had not been sent on my own. London had sent somebody else to do the proper job; I was just supposed to stumble around and rattle cages.

But who would London have sent? Somebody professional. And that must surely mean somebody from Six, despite all the guff about Brasenose and Six being too close to the Americans. Six had a team here and I was their bait. It had to be Allenberg and crew. But they had been here for weeks, long before the Interrogator was stolen, so what were they here for? And if I was bait for some combined Six/DIS operation the DG must have sanctioned it, and that meant Julia knew all about it.

I collapsed on to the bed without even setting the alarm. When I awoke the day was half over.

I had an appointment at the hairdressing salon.

By anybody's standards Miranda Gonçalves was a beautiful woman, radiating a refined animal magnetism. Coming out of the hairdressing salon she seemed to command the whole street. Her bearing gave an appearance of height, although she was shorter than Julia who stood beside her. Well proportioned. Voluptuous but not Amazonian. Cascades of jet-black hair. Full lips which, from across the street, appeared as a sweep of deep red on the bronze of her complexion. Large brown eyes shimmered below heavy eyebrows, through artificially long lashes.

More than beautiful: elegant as only rich women of Latin nations are elegant. Casually swathed in pale lemon she could have stepped from a Mediterranean yacht or a Paris fashion show. But of course she hadn't. Instead she had chosen to live with an enfeebled gunrunner, isolated and surrounded by armed guards.

I'd parked behind her car and could see her more clearly as she approached in cheerful conversation with Julia.

Close up some of her magnetism had disappeared. Lines spread thinly from the corners of her eyes and the lipstick had been applied too thickly. The dress was exquisite and expensive, but her gold earrings were just a little too large and her ruby ring a little too ostentatious. Her statuesque figure was spoiled by an almost masculine walk.

Age had not been kind to her. She might have been thirty but could as easily have been well past forty. But despite all that men's eyes turned and stared.

'…another week or two,' I heard Julia say in passable Spanish.

'You must put it to good use. There is much to see.'

'It's all so beautiful.'

The conversation faded away as they both climbed into the Alfa Romeo.

I followed leisurely, the bright blue car made an easy target. Gonçalves drove directly to one of Rio's most expensive restaurants. I found one of the big orange shells that contain public phones and called the Consulate using the Jimmy Fitzwarren code. But John Fitzwarren answered.

'Jimmy's not here. He's disappeared.'

'What!?'

'His wife Sonia has called twice this morning. He didn't come home last night. She seems pretty upset.'

'It's not the sort of thing he sometimes does?'

'No. Apparently he's never been late before without warning her.'

'And you heard nothing at all?'

'Nothing. Don't you know where he is?'

'He said something about visiting the docks last night.'

'Well I don't know what you fellows are up to and we're not supposed to get involved, but Pedro's a friend of mine; if I can help let me know.'

'Thanks, but honestly I don't think there's anything to worry about. I'll keep in touch.'

I walked towards the restaurant. Pedro's disappearance made it, as the Americans say, a whole new ball game. He'd said he was going to follow up a lead on Allenberg's group. If that was true and they were responsible for his disappearance my theory that they were Six went out the window. Whoever they were they didn't look like amateurs.

A waiter led me to a table that, fortunately, was located where Julia could see me but Gonçalves couldn't. Julia seemed to be listening rather than talking, usually a good tactic. As the meal drew to a close Julia spoke more, almost arguing: chin jutting forward, forehead wrinkled in concentration.

Suddenly Gonçalves glanced anxiously round the room. I bent over my food. When I looked up again she was stuffing something into her voluminous handbag. She left soon after, without the smile she'd had when she entered. Her expression now was hard and cold: businesslike.

I approached Julia's table once Gonçalves had disappeared.

'Pedro's vanished,' I told her.

'What!'

'Nobody's seen him since we were at the apartment yesterday.'

'Nobody? You mean he didn't go home last night?'

'That's precisely what I mean. His wife phoned Fitzwarren this morning. Nobody knows what he did from the time he left the apartment.'

'We must get over there quickly,' Julia said, 'and see what we can find. He might be there and for some reason just hasn't spoken to anyone.'

'I don't think so. I slept there.'

We were both imagining the worst. I liked Pedro even though I knew I couldn't trust him completely.

We were interrupted by the waiter with two bills. 'Gonçalves was going to treat me,' Julia said, 'but she changed her mind.'

'How did it go with Gonçalves?' I asked when we reached my car. 'She didn't look happy when she left.'

'She ought to be; she's richer.'

'She took the money?'

'Without hesitation. The lady wants out. It was easy. I sat beside her in the salon and we just started talking, two foreigners together – she's Bolivian. It couldn't have happened more naturally. We talked about Rio, Europe, fashions, everything. Obviously it wasn't the place to tell her who I was. We just nattered like a couple of old women. She's clearly starved of conversation.'

'So you suggested lunch.'

'Not at all. That was her idea. Over the meal she started talking about the villa and the claustrophobia of the place. She described Martines as her uncle and moaned about him growing old.'

'Could he be her uncle?'

'No chance. She was his mistress, but now seems to be a nursemaid as much as anything. It seemed an opportune moment to let her know what I was after. She was obviously shocked, for a moment I thought we'd made a real mistake. But she didn't take long to work things out and ask for more money. In the end I gave her the lot.'

'And the bugs?'

'She took all four of them. They're small. Range about a mile, battery life of two weeks.'

'That's ideal, but can we be sure she'll plant them?'

189

'I think so. I said we'd remove her otherwise and she seemed to take that seriously. She asked if I'd been at the villa last night. Apparently two of the guards Gomes had posted there were killed and another injured, along with one of the servants, Pinteiro. Was that you?'

'Me and my guardian angel. I'll explain later. When will she place the bugs?'

'Right away.'

We continued our conversation in the car. 'What did she say about our friends in the villa?'

'Not much. She was pretty skimpy on information. Martines seems to be German but he never speaks about his background. Budermann is certainly German. His parents were killed in the war and somehow he ended up here with Martines in his teens. Their relationship used to be one of father and son but now it may be a bit strained. Budermann seems to be gaining control of the household while Martines relapses into senile paranoia. Just last night he woke up screaming that he was being chased by a black man; Budermann had to inject him with something. It's Budermann that does all the fixing of the arms deals.'

'She actually mentioned that?'

'Yes. She assumed I knew all about it. Martines left the business four years ago, but now Budermann is back in it. Gonçalves thinks their money is running out.'

'So Budermann is actually selling weapons at the moment. That could explain the meetings we know the Syrian, Attirmi, had with him.'

'It could. I mentioned Attirmi's name but it didn't strike any chords. Clearly Martines and Budermann have kept her away from their business affairs. She knows nothing about the Griffin Interrogator. All she could say was that everyone is incredibly tense at the moment. Martines keeps talking about one last deal and she confirmed that Budermann has been out of Brazil recently.'

'Did she mention Captain Gomes?'

'Only once. She obviously doesn't hold him in very high esteem. She called him an ill-mannered peasant. I expect he tried to bed her. His boss Nebulo, on the other hand, she'd probably love to get hold of. He's got Latin good looks and status. Apparently Martines has been paying him for protection for years, although Martines himself doesn't like the man.'

'Did she say why?'

'No. Just that Martines thinks he's crude. But there was no mistaking her views: Nebulo is a rising star and Martines a falling one.'

'And to mix metaphors,' I interrupted, 'she wants to desert a sinking ship. You don't think her feeling for Nebulo will stop her planting the bugs?'

'No. If anything, the reverse. She's probably tried to welcome him with open legs and been spurned. She'll see this as getting her own back.'

'The old combination of love and hate,' I commented tritely.

'I wouldn't say that. She's too hard to have ever loved anybody. And Martines has probably recognised that because he's kept her well out of the picture. But she did make a couple of interesting comments. One was that Martines is planning to leave Brazil. Apparently those men watching the villa really scared him. Budermann's started packing for a voyage.'

'Where are they going?'

'She'd no idea. Martines has a big ocean-going boat. She thinks they might just sail around until any commotion dies down. I got the impression she'd not been let in on the departure plans and that worries her. She also mentioned that she had overheard Budermann complaining that his share of their latest deal would be less than the other three.'

'Three? Who? Martines and Nebulo are two. Mendale?'

'Could be.'

Could be indeed but I was starting to think about other possible candidates. So I suspected was Julia but neither of us said anything.

Pedro's apartment was only a few minutes from the restaurant: it was empty. We checked all the rooms, there was no sign that Pedro had been there since I had left two hours before. Julia looked at my rumpled bed with a hint of disapproval; she was probably the sort of person who would always remake her bed before breakfast.

If Pedro's disappearance was involuntary somebody had him: dead or alive. And if they had him they could soon be on to us, on to the apartment, the car and on to our plans for Miranda Gonçalves. Pedro's absence could of course be voluntary. But why? If he was working for the other side – which other side? – why disappear now? If he was following a lead surely he could have phoned his wife or Fitzwarren.

'He's been gone for less than twenty-four hours,' Julia said. 'Perhaps it's too soon to worry. Tell me about your guardian angel at the villa last night, it obviously wasn't Pedro.'

'It could have been Pedro but I doubt it.'

I told her what had happened and about the mysterious man with the big gun. She offered no new solutions.

'A Magnum's an odd sort of weapon for this type of business,' I said. 'Big, heavy, and so powerful that the bullet could go right through someone, just leaving a neat little hole behind. I wouldn't have expected a professional to use one. More the sort of weapon for one of those dilettantes in Six.'

Julia looked up sharply. 'Well I wouldn't like to be on the receiving end of one.'

I agreed. The priority now was to try to find Pedro. 'Let's try Fitzwarren again,' suggested Julia.

'OK but not from here, they'll trace the call.'

We went out to a phone. 'Thank God you've called,' Fitzwarren greeted me. 'London has been showering us with demands for information. And right after you phoned earlier a message arrived for Pedro, by hand. Can you come over?'

'I'd rather not. There may be someone outside waiting for me.'

'It's like that is it? What should we do?'

'I'll send someone. She'll be there in twenty minutes.'

Julia dropped me near a *feira*, a street market. 'Don't eat too much,' she instructed.

'I wouldn't know where to start.'

I wandered through stalls of fruit, vegetables, eggs, fish, even live chickens. There are twenty-one varieties of banana in Brazil and they all seemed to be on sale alongside fruits that in those days were never seen in Europe: carambola and nespera, fruta doconde and jenipapo. One stall was piled high with caju, delicious when roasted but poisonous when unripe. There had to be a clever metaphor in that but it escaped me.

I bought some oranges from a smiling old woman wearing a crumpled linen dress.

The *feira* attracted all sorts of people. Middle-class women, with their maids pulling bulging trolleys, jostled peasants from the favelas buying the beans and rice on which they survived. Everywhere there was noise and colour. The *feira* was an example of Brazil at its best. Carefree. Harmonious. Prodigal. The antics of goons like Gomes seemed a million miles away.

Julia was away longer than I expected. 'Had to lose a tail,' she explained. 'And I needed to calm Fitzwarren down. He's had half of the DIS on the phone to him: Joseff, Mendale and Watkins all wanting to know if there was any news. There was another call from Watkins coming through as I left.'

'You didn't wait to see what it was?'

'I stayed long enough to learn it was Watkins and he had nothing to tell us. I decided to leave before Fitzwarren thought of passing him on to me. From what I've heard I'd have been there all day once he got going. And I had the message that arrived for Pedro. It was from somebody called Ferreira Maroja. Apparently Pedro saw him last night with some photos which he's now recognised. He wanted Pedro to visit him.'

'Where?'

'The note didn't say, but John Fitzwarren had found an address book on Pedro's desk. Maroja's address was given as Praça Escócia which is a small square near the docks.'

'You didn't discover anything else about him?'

'Nothing. Fitzwarren had asked London without results.'

'It could be a trap. Why should a night's sleep enable this man to remember faces he couldn't place when Pedro spoke to him? But I suppose we'll have to risk it.'

XXI

Julia forced the car through the densely packed traffic. After only twenty-four hours in Brazil she was driving like a native Carioca, which means like a raving lunatic. Finally we turned off the Avenida Rodriguez Alves into a maze of dingy side streets lined with warehouses, shipwrights, ship chandlers, grubby cafés, third-rate hotels and brothels masquerading as hotels. It took us twenty minutes to find the Rua Escócia which led into the Praça Escócia – Scotland Square or perhaps Scotland Yard.

We found ourselves in a small, grey square. In the centre amongst the refuse and the mud were a few stunted trees and ramshackle benches and a fountain that had long ceased to function. A church, devoid of any sign of life, occupied the whole of one side. A low, black warehouse occupied another. The remaining half of the square was flanked by a café with chairs and canopied tables straggling out from it, a few houses, a small hotel and two shops with an open space between them. One of these bore the name 'Maroja'.

'You stay in the car,' I told Julia, 'and toot on the horn at the first sign of trouble.'

'Yes boss,' she replied sarcastically.

I buttoned my jacket so that the Luger wouldn't be too conspicuous and walked towards the shop.

'Shop' was rather a grand word for the cluttered room that I entered. It could have been a hideaway used by a human squirrel to store randomly collected odds and ends. There was one dim electric light that cast a feeble glow on to a counter at the rear, but it illuminated even less than the sunlight coming in through the front entrance and grimy window. A door on the right opened on to the wasteland beside the building. It was difficult to say what Maroja sold. The only sign outside the shop was his surname. The shelves, table and floor were littered with a strange collection of goods, from kettles to carburettors, light bulbs to lubricating oil.

There was a bell on the counter but before I could ring a man came in through the side door. He was short, dishevelled and dirty with blue jeans and blue denim shirt. I put his age at around fifty. His sleeves were rolled to the elbow and his hands and arms, along with his jeans and shirt, were covered in oil and grease. He had apparently been working on the Volkswagen Kombi I could see through the door. He wiped his hands on a rag that seemed to be solid grease and stared in my direction.

'Senhor Maroja?'

He nodded but said nothing.

'I'm a friend of Pedro Vernon. You wanted to see him about some photographs.'

Again the man nodded silently.

'He's busy and asked me to see you.'

'I can wait until he has time for me,' Maroja said, pulling a chair from the counter and sitting down, as if he was prepared to start waiting immediately.

Obviously he was ready for a long bargaining session, the last thing I wanted. I took the only other chair and sat facing him.

'I'm sure I can do everything Senhor Vernon wants done. There's no real need to wait for him.'

'These are difficult days,' Maroja replied. 'Who can we trust? I know Senhor Vernon, but I don't know you. But still business is business. I am always ready to make new friends. New customers, I think, Senhor.'

'What can you sell?'

He looked around his shop as if trying to find something for me. 'Information, Senhor. Information that Senhor Vernon requested last night and which I now have. Information I think you want. We have to decide its value. I can tell you, Senhor, it has cost me a lot of time, a lot of trouble to find these things.'

He spoke with a muted Portuguese accent. Every nation has its traditional underdog, a convenient butt for jokes. For Brazilians it was

Portuguese immigrants. They are universally believed to be half-witted, grasping and crude. 'Why does the Portuguese Army patrol in threes?' I was once asked. 'One man to do the reading, one the writing and the third to keep an eye on the two intellectuals!' Maroja had probably heard many similar taunts. He looked a thoroughly disgruntled little man, affecting a phoney air of shrewdness. He wanted to believe he could better me. He would lead me on little by little, haggling over each snippet of information. But now I didn't have time.

'What have you got?' I asked bluntly.

'That depends, Senhor. What do you want?'

I took out a roll of new cruzeiros. 'Let's start with the photographs. Senhor Vernon came here last night and showed you some pictures. What do you know about them?' I put a good part of the banknotes on the counter.

Maroja said nothing but sat looking at the notes. I added a few more. 'I am not a rich man, Senhor. I must pay much taxes.'

I added another hundred new cruzeiros. 'That's my limit.' He pocketed the money. 'They are not Brazilians, Senhor. Americans I think. I do not know their names but I know where they are.'

'Go on.'

'They have an old warehouse with an office. It has been empty for a long time, but two weeks ago these men came. Four of them in a big, black car. They hired it for a month. It is by the docks. I'll show you.'

He furrowed under the counter and produced a tattered map. 'It is here.' He jabbed his finger on a spot half a mile away. 'It is near the moorings for some of the private boats, like Senhor Martines'.'

I looked up sharply. 'Why did you mention him?'

'Senhor Vernon asked if I knew him. He comes here sometimes with the German and with his woman. Nice one that,' he leered. 'You know her?'

I didn't answer his question. 'How will I recognise this warehouse?'

'Easy. It looks empty while the other ones around it will be full of people, it is in a busy area. And by the door is a wooden sign, much faded now, with the name "Lapatela".'

'Are the men there now?'

'I don't know, Senhor. Two of them were there this morning when I sent the message to Senhor Vernon.'

'Why didn't you tell Vernon all this last night?'

'I did not know these things. I asked people last night after Senhor Vernon left. I know many people in this area, they are all friends of Ferreira Maroja.'

'And your friends recognised these men just from the descriptions of photographs?'

He looked perplexed. 'Senhor Vernon gave me the photographs.' He dug into a leather satchel behind him, producing the photographs I had taken on Wednesday. 'You have spoken to Senhor Vernon today?' Maroja asked.

'No, I haven't. He's disappeared. You wouldn't know where he is?'

'Me? No, Senhor. I do not know. You think he has been kidnapped? In this area?'

'It's possible.'

'I could ask my friends.'

'We could make it worth your while. If you find anything contact Senhor Fitzwarren at the Consulate.'

He wrote the name down after I spelt it out.

'Did Senhor Vernon say where he was going when he left?'

'To the waterfront. He was going to see other people with his photos. He had lots of copies of them. "I have more friends to see tonight, Ferreira," he said. He went that way.' Maroja waved his hand towards the ocean.

'He said no more than that? No names?'

'No, Senhor, no names. Senhor Vernon is a careful man. He never tells people anything he does not have to tell them. Perhaps you have some names so that I know where to start looking for Senhor Vernon.'

'No, I have no names.'

I got up, but Maroja's face creased into a sly grin.

'You are a friend of the other man?'

'What other man?'

'The man who came this morning to ask about the photographs. Ah, Senhor, he would not be pleased that I had told you about him. He too gave me a gift. No, Senhor, I have told you all I agreed to. All that you paid for.'

I pushed two large banknotes towards him. Without asking for more he continued.

'He was foreign like you and came less than half an hour ago. Short hair and tanned skin, a sailor, I think, but distinguished. He drove a car just like yours but red. I have its number.' He passed me a scribbled sheet.

'Is that all?'

'What more, Senhor? He said he had heard that Senhor Vernon had seen me last night. What had I said to him?'

'And you told him?'

'Of course. He said he was a friend of Senhor Vernon. I think perhaps he has gone to the warehouse I showed you.'

That seemed to be all Maroja could offer. I asked a few more questions about his previous visitor, but learned little more. The man was definitely a foreigner. He wasn't American and he wasn't one of the men in the photographs. He could have been German or British. I bade farewell and he made no move to stop me again. If I'd had eyes in the back of my head I would probably have seen him grab a scrap of paper and a pencil to note my licence number in case he could sell that too.

Back in the car I recounted what had happened. When I mentioned the man who had been asking questions earlier Julia raised an eyebrow quizzically.

'The description that Maroja gave could fit hundreds of people,' she said.

'That's true. But it fits one man in particular, Mackenzie.'

'I thought Pedro had cleared him,' said Julia. 'Let's just see what happens. We must get to the warehouse.'

'It could be a trap; we might end up in whatever pickle Pedro got into. I wouldn't trust Maroja an inch. To be on the safe side we ought to let Fitzwarren know where we're going.'

'What about the tap on his line?'

'That's a risk we'll have to take. I'll try to make it sound as innocuous as possible. With a bit of luck anyone listening in will ignore the call. In any case they'd have to act fast to reach the warehouse before us.'

Fitzwarren was quick on the uptake. I introduced myself as Kim Philby and he immediately replied that it was nice to hear from me again.

'I'm just phoning to thank you for your help in finding my Company accommodation. I think we've found a suitable warehouse. It used to be owned by Lapatela.'

I gave him the address and then said goodbye. 'Just a minute Mr Philby, I believe you wanted to know about the car your colleague borrowed yesterday.'

I was momentarily confused until I remembered Julia had Pedro's car and he'd been driving his wife's. We should have obtained details of it before.

'I have the number here, a white Chevette, eighteen months old.'

Julia cursed when I gave her Fitzwarren's message. 'We should have been on to that ourselves. You didn't see a car like that in Praça Escócia?'

'No. Did you?'

'I don't think so. A Chevette's a Brazilian Opel Kadett isn't it? Perhaps we'll find it near the warehouse.'

We did. It was parked about 200 yards away and it was empty. So apparently was the warehouse. We drove past slowly and saw no sign of life. However, directly in front of it was a red Ford Corcel parked behind a brown Volkswagen like the one I'd seen outside the Villa Nhambiquaras.

'Wasn't that the Ford Maroja mentioned?' asked Julia.

I didn't need to check the number I'd written down: it was.

'Let's drive round to the back,' I said. There was a deserted cobbled roadway that led past the back of a row of warehouses. We parked nearby.

'Now what?' Julia asked.

'We both go in. Take your gun.'

We walked slowly to a wooden door set into the back wall of the warehouse. On the right-hand side of the door was a small window, while on the other side 'Lapatela' had long ago been painted on to the brick wall. I peered through the window which hadn't been cleaned for years. Through the gloom inside I was just in time to see a bright splash of sunlight disappear at the other end. Somebody had either entered or left through the front doors.

We waited a moment. No lights came. No sound emerged. I tried the door. It was locked but when I kicked it the ancient bolt on the inside fell off with a crash that echoed through the building. Then silence again. I pushed the door further open, it grated noisily. I stepped inside quickly, half expecting to feel the thud of bullets. Julia followed me, Browning in hand.

We stood unmoving and let our eyes become accustomed to the blackness that contrasted so sharply with the bright sunlight outside. The warehouse was practically empty. I ran to the other end. The front door contained a small glass panel. Looking through it I saw the Volkswagen; the Ford Corcel had gone. A flight of stairs led to a small office. The door at the top was open and we stepped into the only part of the building to show signs of human habitation. The sun shone in through a large window, illuminating a scene of disarray.

The only things in their proper places were a desk and a large new metal cabinet. Three chairs, a table and a wooden cupboard lay at crazy angles around the room. But our attention was immediately drawn to the corner beside the metal cabinet.

There, face down, lay the body of a man.

XXII

I rushed to turn the body over. We couldn't see the face, just a shock of black hair. My instinctive thought was Pedro. I was wrong.

'My God,' said Julia. 'It's the Syrian.'

We looked into the contorted face of Khalid Attirmi. He had been dead for quite a time but had not died quickly. Our rescue of him at his hotel had been a short-lived favour. His body was bent peculiarly, as if he'd been stuffed into a box before rigor mortis set in.

'We'd better search the place.'

Julia turned to the desk, which was standing, apparently untouched, beside the wall. She uttered an exclamation of surprise. I turned to see her holding a piece of paper.

'It's a note,' she said, 'for you.'

There were just a few lines. My name. An address in Gavea. And Pedro's signature. Nothing else.

'Is it Pedro's writing?'

'I've no idea.'

Why should Pedro leave a note like that? And if he'd gone to Gavea why was his car outside? It was possible he'd been the person who left as we arrived. But why would he do that and where had he been since last night?

I turned to examine the metal cabinet; it was locked. Julia tossed over the key which had been lying on the desk. As I unlocked it I felt something pushing against the door: it was another body, alive but unconscious. One of Allenberg's men fell on to the floor, bound but not gagged.

Julia was starting to check his pockets when we heard the wail of a police siren.

'Could they be coming here?'

'I've no idea. Let's sit in the car until they've passed.'

We ran down the stairs and out through the back. The siren drew nearer.

'Let's go.'

As we moved off, a police car stopped at the front. They must have paid attention to my call to Fitzwarren.

'Do we try that address?' Julia asked.

'I suppose so.'

'Where is Gavea?'

'It's out beyond Leblon on the ocean. Very expensive. Home to Rio's most exclusive golf club.'

We headed west. My reasoning said that the Gavea address was a wild goose chase at best, a trap at worst. Was the message really from Pedro? How would he have known I was going to visit the warehouse? If Pedro had been kidnapped he couldn't have left a message in full view and he wouldn't have known where he was going. If Pedro had gone voluntarily why hadn't he taken his car? And who was driving the red car that had been parked outside the warehouse when we arrived? Perhaps the message was really written by that man, not Pedro, and was intended to lure us into something we would be better to avoid.

We passed out of Leblon on the Avenida Niemeyer, named after Brazil's foremost architect and hacked out of the rock and jungle that descend into the ocean. To our left waves pounded on to fangs of rock a hundred feet below. We passed the huge favela of Rocinha, a sprawling slum of closely packed cardboard and wooden shacks clinging perilously to the hillside. Before us the Pedra da Gavea rose nearly 3 000 feet, a green jumble of stone against the skyline.

Fortunately our street map covered Gavea. We passed the twenty-seven storeyed, 600-roomed Sheraton Hotel.

'Strange shape,' Julia grimaced, glancing at the upside down L-shaped building beside the ocean. I agreed: when I was here on holiday I had arranged to meet someone in the lobby which turned out to be on the sixth floor.

We swung inland, climbing away from the sea but with occasional glimpsed panoramas over what had once been a peaceful village but was now dominated by hotels like the Sheraton and Oscar Niemeyer's twenty-six storey, round, black glass tower – the Rio Nacional.

We stopped on a gently sloping hillside and Julia pointed out our position on the map.

'The house is along this road, probably another 500 yards. There's a road behind it which must be just over the crest of the ridge. Perhaps we should go along there and approach the house from the rear.'

'Let's look at the front first. We don't want to go in the back while everyone escapes through the front.'

'Like the warehouse.'

'Right. We can always go round the back if the front gives no cover.'

We approached on foot. The house was set well back from the road: a modern two-storey building, square and squat. There were ornamental trees and bushes along the drive and dotted around the lawn. The hill behind the house was densely packed with vegetation. It was not an ideal hideout and instinctively I felt we'd been led up a blind alley.

I was wrong.

We were halfway up the drive, hopping from cover to cover, when a man emerged from the front door. We froze, thinking we'd been spotted. But without glancing in our direction he walked to a small garage standing beside the house. It was one of the Allenberg group.

He swung the garage door open. Moments later a green Volkswagen Beetle emerged and stopped in front of the house. The man went back inside, apparently leaving the keys in the ignition.

I was considering grabbing the keys to stop him leaving but Julia had read my thoughts.

'Let him go. The less people in the house when we go in the better.'

We moved forward, using every scrap of cover available. We knelt behind a large clump of feijoa bushes near the front of the house, hidden behind a mass of grey-green leaves. Soon the man reappeared, this time gun in hand. Another figure emerged from the house, someone I'd been half expecting: Captain Mackenzie. In his arms he was carrying Pedro – dead or drugged. He was followed by another man, also gun in hand.

'We've got to take them,' I whispered.

Mackenzie walked effortlessly to the car, as if carrying a sack of feathers, and put Pedro's lifeless form on the back seat. Mackenzie and the two other men were about twenty yards away, grouped around the car. None of them were looking in our direction.

I stepped out from behind the shrubs. Nobody saw me leaving cover but after I'd walked a few yards one of them swung towards me. He must have caught the flash of movement in the corner of his eye.

'Hold it right there,' I shouted. 'You're surrounded.'

'Drop those guns,' Julia echoed, running in a crouch along the wall of the house.

The men stopped in their tracks, then dropped their guns and slowly raised their hands. I told them to move away from the car and they sullenly obeyed.

Mackenzie stepped towards one of the others and suddenly gave him a violent push in my direction. The man lurched between us blocking my line of fire. Julia could see Mackenzie clearly, but she must have had her attention elsewhere for he was around the corner of the house before she reacted.

'He's mine!' she shouted, jumping after him.

I moved in front of the Volkswagen, motioning the men to stand against the wall. They were about ten yards away. As I stooped to pick up their weapons a flowerpot came hurtling towards me. It had evidently been resting on a window ledge one of the men was leaning against: I'd completely overlooked it. I jumped and, straightening up, levelled the Luger at the man who'd thrown the pot. He was standing perfectly still looking at the dent he'd made in the wing of the car. His companion had disappeared into the house. At that moment Julia returned.

'Get into the car,' I shouted, scooping up the guns and throwing them into the Volkswagen. I kept my own weapon aimed at our one remaining prisoner while Julia started up. As we spurted down the driveway the man rushed into the house to join his colleague. We expected a fusillade of shots: nothing came.

We were on to the road before I remembered the body in the back. I fumbled for Pedro's wrist. There was a pulse, but weak.

'He's alive, drugged. He could be out for hours.'

'Any injuries?'

'A bruise on the forehead. There don't seem to be any other marks.'

'Let's get off this road,' said Julia, when we reached my car. 'I'll try to find a secluded spot, and we can take a closer look at him. You follow.'

It took ten minutes to find a deserted stretch of road. I jammed my car in behind the Volkswagen. Julia was already examining Pedro's inert form.

'He's out cold all right. They've given him a massive dose of something. I don't think he needs urgent attention. We ought to get him to bed and then call a doctor. Although I don't suppose it will make much difference to him whether he's in bed or the back of a car. We might as well drive him home.

'Who were they?' Julia continued. 'We still don't know who those men were.'

'And we don't know what part Mackenzie is playing.'

'What do you mean?'

'Was he in with them?' I asked. 'Or did they have their guns out to stop him running away? They didn't look around very carefully when they came out of the house, yet they both carried weapons as if they expected something. And Mackenzie's first preoccupation seemed to be to escape himself. As far as I could see he made no attempt to help the others. Did you see which way he went, back into the house or into the trees?'

'I couldn't say. He vanished around the corner of the house but when I got there he'd gone. The trees were close, he could have reached them in the time it took me to run to the back.' She paused. 'What shall we do now? Shall I take Pedro home while you go back and take another look at that house?'

That was the last thing I felt like doing but it was a sensible suggestion. Allenberg's men were the major unknown we faced. They could wreck any plans we made. If I could only overhear a short conversation, or find something they'd written, I could discover their native language which might tell me who they were. At the moment I hadn't the slightest idea. But I decided against going back.

'They'll be on their guard now. And if they've deserted the house they won't be leaving anything useful behind.'

'You think they were planning to leave the house completely?'

'Don't you? They probably phoned the warehouse to find a policeman answering and immediately started a prearranged emergency procedure. Why else would they be moving Pedro?'

'That's reasonable. It's strange that a group as professional as they seem to be should have chosen such a bad hideout. We could have approached that house from almost any direction without being seen.'

'That's true. But house-hunting in Rio is awful. They were probably overconfident, they didn't expect to be tumbled.'

'Do you know where Pedro lives?' Julia asked. 'We ought to be getting him home now.'

'Leblon, a few miles back along the coast. I'll take him there. You go out to the villa. Those men we left back there may be watching Pedro's home, or alternatively Gomes may be. I'd prefer to keep you away from that.'

Julia looked at me with an expression I had come to recognise but not understand. A sort of fond irritation.

'Thomas that's very gentlemanly of you but we should get one thing clear. You don't outrank me. I'll let you take Pedro home because I do need to familiarise myself with the villa and the route out there.'

I could only nod my acquiescence.

'Have you got the radio receiver with you so you can tell if Gonçalves planted those bugs?' I asked.

'Of course.' Julia burrowed in her sack-like handbag and produced a transistorised receiver. She also produced the map. 'Show me how to get to the villa.'

'Right. It's about forty-five miles as the crow flies, but you won't be flying. You'll see what I meant about Rio running out of flat land. There are hills all across the city so go inland. Drive north through the tunnel. Keep going roughly north or north-west, parallel to the coast, and follow the signs to Duque de Caxias. From there it's easy. Take the Petrópolis road for twenty-six kilometres, then left towards Barra do Pirai. Keep going for ten miles until you reach a fork, the villa is just beyond that on the right-hand road.'

'I should be able to tune into the bugs near the fork then.'

'Perhaps even earlier. Don't risk going past the villa itself. Gomes may be checking the traffic.'

'What happens after that?'

'Phone me. There's a phone just off the Barra do Pirai turn-off on the Petrópolis road. It's just a shack with the owner sleeping at the back, he'll stay open late. We'd better set a definite time for the call.'

'I'll phone at eight,' Julia suggested.

'Make it eight-fifteen.'

'Right. You'll be at Pedro's house?'

'No. I want to get back into the city. You take my Ford and I'll stick with this Volkswagen. Where's the car you borrowed from Pedro?'

'At the hairdressing salon.'

'Let me have the keys. I'll drop Pedro off and perhaps wait to see what the doctor says, then exchange the Beetle for Pedro's car and go to the apartment. Call me there. If I have time I might do a little checking on Captain Mackenzie.'

'You're not going back to the house where we found Pedro?'

'There isn't time. Our top priority is the villa. Pedro put a couple of walkie-talkies in the boot of my Ford. I'll take one, you keep the other. If Gonçalves has planted the bugs you find a place to hide within radio range of the villa. Let me know where it is when you phone and I'll meet you there. We can use the walkie-talkies if there are problems when I get out there.'

'And if Gonçalves hasn't planted the bugs?'

'Let's cross that hurdle when we get to it.'

As we got out of the Volkswagen Julia had another thought. 'I'll put those two guns we took off Pedro's captors in the hiding place in the Ford.'

'That's not a bad idea, but I'll keep one of them.'

We'd been in such a hurry before that we hadn't examined the guns. That was a mistake. One was a nine millimetre Beretta which I slipped into my pocket. The other was quite different. Either the gods of coincidence were smiling deceptively or it was my friend from the night before. Dwarfing Julia's palm was a Colt Trooper Mark III Magnum, the six-inch barrel version weighing forty-two ounces. She flipped it open to reveal the .375 Remington 125 grain semi-jacketed hollow point ammunition. That was certainly capable of inflicting the damage I'd seen outside the villa.

But if Pedro's captors were on my side why would they kidnap Pedro who was also on my side – or supposed to be?

XXIII

Pedro's home was a rather luxurious apartment in a new four-storey block set back from the road. I drove past slowly, but saw no sign of surveillance. There were three cars nearby, all apparently empty. Returning I left the Volkswagen directly outside with Pedro still unconscious on the back seat.

The maid led me into a large *sala*, a combined dining room and drawing room overlooking the ocean.

Pedro's wife and ten-year-old daughter were seated on a green sofa.

Sonia Vernon exuded warmth. Her face lit up in welcome. She had been under considerable strain since Pedro had vanished; in the police state of Brazil any woman whose husband disappears must fear the worst. But she showed only a few signs of pressure. She sat on the edge of the chair, her hands whitely clasped together. Tiredness pervaded her deep brown eyes but her face was relaxed. A tanned, friendly face framed by jet-black hair, she was, I guessed, ten or fifteen years younger than her husband. Behind the sofa a print from one of Brazil's first 'modern' painters, Candido Portinari, seemed to reflect the essence of Pedro's wife: expressive, dynamic, emotional.

'I'm from the Embassy,' I said. 'Your husband is alive.'

She reacted slowly. The expression on her face softened. Her hands unclenched. She glanced at the maid.

'Yara, take Beth to her room.' She spoke in slightly accented Portuguese.

'Pedro was kidnapped and drugged. He's in my car outside, unconscious. Shall I bring him up?'

'Of course. Where else should he go? Why are you waiting?'

'Can you get a doctor here we can trust? The police mustn't know about this.'

'Of course. Of course.' She pushed me towards the lift. Quite naturally, she wasn't interested in my concern for secrecy, she just wanted to see Pedro. As we reached the ground floor she stepped past me and ran to the car which I'd left unlocked.

When I reached it she was already cradling Pedro in her arms. I carried him up to their apartment. He was heavy and I marvelled at the ease with which Mackenzie had carried him earlier. I laid him on a large double bed.

'Yara,' shouted Sonia, 'fetch Doctor Silva, quickly.'

'He lives just up the road,' she explained. 'A very fine man and a good friend of ours. He has looked after Elisabeth, our daughter, since we returned to Brazil. You can trust him.' Carefully she removed Pedro's crumpled jacket before continuing. 'What happened? Can you tell me?'

'I can tell you what I know, Mrs Vernon. But I can't explain it. Pedro was checking some information. Routine stuff. This afternoon I went to the places he was planning to visit and eventually found him. There were a couple of men there, but I don't know who they were.'

She said nothing.

'Could you phone John Fitzwarren?' I asked. 'Tell him I brought Pedro here and then left.'

'And who,' she asked with a smile, 'are you?'

I'd forgotten to give her my name and in the rush to get to Pedro she hadn't asked. When that omission had been rectified she called Fitzwarren.

The furnishings of the *sala* were modern, beautiful and above all comfortable. A large wooden dining table stood near a hatch to the kitchen, half a dozen chairs neatly arranged around it. Nearer to me were three easy chairs and a sofa. Three of the walls were covered with paintings and prints. There were modern paintings, most of which I didn't recognise, although two prints were clearly details from one of José Clemente Orozco's murals in Guadalajara. Full of passion and movement, they conveyed an empathy with the suffering of the world's oppressed. Similar feelings were stirred by a print of a linoleum cut by another Mexican, Leopoldo Méndez. It was his compellingly real 'Deportation to Death'. The despair of the Jews being herded into cattle trucks was overpowering, although it wasn't the sort of thing I would want hanging in my dining room.

However, it was not out of place here. It complemented rather than distracted from the incredible view seen through the glass that formed the whole of the fourth wall. Sand, sea and sky melted into a magnificent panorama. A gentle breeze whispered into the *sala* through the open glass door that led on to a wide balcony. Pedro had certainly chosen his home well. It contrasted glaringly with the mean apartment he'd rented on the other side of Rio where I'd spent the last two nights.

'Yes I've called a doctor,' I heard Sonia say. This was followed by a pause and she looked in my direction. 'No, he's gone.' Then another longer pause. 'Perhaps you should come out here, John.'

'He wants to see you,' she said, replacing the phone.

'Did he say why?'

'Just that a couple of messages had arrived for you.'

I decided to wait for him.

Sonia Vernon returned to the bedroom and sat beside Pedro. I sat in the *sala* with her daughter, Beth, who was sticking postcards into an album. She proudly showed me her collection, postcards sent by her father from all over Brazil along with a few from England, mainly London, and one from Lisbon. As she closed the album one card caught my eye. I didn't recognise the picture but the name of the city was clear: Warszawa.

What had Pedro been doing in Warsaw?

I didn't have time to think about it as Doctor Silva arrived with the maid, Yara. He was a small, bespectacled man in his late fifties. Grey hair clung tenaciously to the side of his head. He marched into the bedroom, clutching the black bag that serves as the ubiquitous badge of his profession.

'What happened?'

'I don't know,' I replied. 'He disappeared last night and I found him like this about an hour ago.'

211

'There doesn't appear to be anything organically wrong,' Doctor Silva concluded. 'He's been drugged obviously. Here.' He pointed at the left wrist. 'Two marks. Two injections.'

'What can we do?' Sonia asked.

'Nothing. I could try to bring him round but it would be better to let him sleep it off.'

'How long will that be?'

'I don't know. Hours. Just put him into bed properly and leave him. He'll feel awful when he wakes. He should be in hospital of course,' he added, looking in my direction, 'but I presume that is not possible.'

'It's not desirable.'

'Well Pedro's as strong as an ox. He'll be all right in the morning – although he'll have a feeling like an almighty hangover. I'll come back then.'

With that, and a warning not to try stuffing Pedro with food when he came round, Doctor Silva left.

Sonia turned to me. 'Perhaps you would help me get Pedro into bed. Then we can have some coffee.'

I did as she asked. When we returned to the *sala* we found that Beth had put away her album and was playing Ludo with the maid.

'Have you eaten?' Sonia asked me.

'No, but I had a big lunch.'

'That's no good. You must eat with us.' Her English had the same accent as her Portuguese: a lilting, soft blurring of words. 'It's no bother,' she added as I started to object.

Yara went into the kitchen to prepare the meal. Sonia and I were dragooned into playing Ludo. It quickly transpired that Ludo was not one of my strong points but Beth giggled happily as she rolled six after six.

After the meal Sonia and I sat drinking coffee and waiting for John Fitzwarren. The apartment occupied the whole of the top floor of the apartment block, and we were able to sit on the balcony entirely cut off from the rest of the world.

Sonia talked feely. I learned about Beth's school and the difficulties of finding somewhere to live in Rio, about the increase in food prices since they had been stationed here before and the state of Brazilian theatre. I could feel her mentally unwinding. She had obviously steeled herself to hearing the worst. How much, I wondered, had Pedro told her about his work. More than he was supposed to for certain.

She was a warm, intelligent person and time flew by as we relaxed in a cool evening breeze. John Fitzwarren arrived sooner than I had expected.

He burst into the *sala*. Standing over six feet tall with the rigidly straight back of the Army parade ground, he dominated the apartment. He was older than I had anticipated, around sixty. His hair slightly grey at the sides and appallingly short. When stationed in London he would live in Tunbridge Wells or Virginia Water. A mainstay of the local golf club or, I thought, noticing his MCC tie, the cricket club. But despite his physically imposing appearance, he lacked that aura of superiority that makes a natural leader. There was a hint of weakness in the perpetual nervous motion of his eyes. He was a born aide-de-camp. A perennial second in command. He would make an admirable club secretary but never become club chairman.

Sonia greeted him warmly. He shook my hand in his vice-like grip.

'Pleased to meet you at last,' he said perfunctorily. 'Where's Pedro?'

She showed him into the bedroom. I waited in the *sala*.

'I'll make you some coffee, John,' Sonia said when he returned, and bustled off to the kitchen.

'Kidnapped! In this day and age! I thought you cloak and dagger buggers had given all that up. Satellites and things these days isn't it? Who would want to kidnap Pedro? Marvellous chap. Not an enemy in Rio. Plays golf out at Gavea – but then you'll know that. You know he's a member of the yacht club in Botafogo Bay. Very exclusive.' I failed to see the relevance but Fitzwarren continued. 'Rum country this. Man like Pedro gets kidnapped and then you just walk in and find him. Now what I want to know is who grabbed him? Your DG, Hull or Grimsby, or whatever he's called, phoned the Ambassador and the Ambassador's tame spook, David Harrison, is flying down from Brasilia. London's been on at me all day. Someone called Mendale. And your man Watkins, blithering idiot! As if I knew what was happening. He wants you to contact him directly. I sent off Pedro's emergency number but they couldn't get you.'

'I'm not much wiser than you,' I said. 'It could have been anybody. Although not the locals.'

'Aha,' said Fitzwarren, who was obviously more interested in putting forward his own theories than listening to mine. 'Not the locals. What about the Communists? Have you thought about them? Are they involved in this escapade of yours?'

'They could be.'

He pounced on my words: 'Could be? No "could be" about it old boy. They're involved all right. That was one of the messages I had for you. Those Arab scribbles you found; Pedro showed them to me. I'm no Arabist you understand but I do know a chap down at the Monte Libano club. Frightfully nice fellow, banker, Lebanese of course. And naturally he speaks Arabic. Well I told Pedro this and he said go right ahead and show Hakeem the note.'

'And you did.'

'I certainly did. Right away. They're addresses. Three of them. In Syria. I sent them off to London this morning, first thing. And your people have been checking them.'

'And?'

'Well they've drawn a blank with two of them but the other's a corker. It's the Chinese Embassy in Damascus. Red Chinese of course.'

'Of course.' So Attirmi was carrying round the address of the Chinese Embassy in Syria. What on earth for? Could the Chinese be involved in the Griffin caper? It seemed highly unlikely as Attirmi had arrived in Brazil before Griffin was stolen. I was inclined to think that the new information was irrelevant, like the fact that Attirmi's leather case had been bought in Moscow. It was just another factor that complicated rather than clarified the situation.

Sonia brought in coffee for Fitzwarren and refilled my cup. 'I'll just go and see how Beth's getting on,' she said, tactfully leaving us alone.

'Thought that would make you think,' said Fitzwarren. 'Made me think too. I don't know what you're up to but I can tell you the Chinese are a nasty lot. Brazil's just recognised Peking, you know. Had to – everybody else was doing it. Détente, Kissinger and suchlike. Well, I've seen them here. Antisocial lot. Never let themselves go. Never unbutton. Wouldn't trust them an inch.'

I let him ramble on without really listening. But he soon changed his emphasis.

'Of course you can't tell me exactly what you're doing. I don't need to know. But you ought to watch your step with the Consulate, you know. We can't get too involved. Now this afternoon a package came for Pedro. Delivered by hand. Naturally I opened it, thought it might be a clue to his whereabouts, like that note from Maroja. You know what was in it?'

'No idea.'

'You'll see. I've got it outside. Of course I didn't tell anybody about it. If my Ambassador finds out Pedro's playing with guns in the Consulate, all hell will break loose.'

'Was there a message with the gun?'

'Nothing at all. Pedro will know where it came from. He must have asked for it. People aren't in the habit of dumping weapons on the Consulate steps, you know.'

'Quite.'

There was one more thing Fitzwarren might be able to help with. 'You checked on Captain Graham Mackenzie for Pedro. Has anything else come up on him?'

'No. Not a word. Like I told Pedro, nobody had ever heard of him. But of course lots of British businessmen come over here without telling us anything about their visit. I would have checked around a bit more, but Pedro told me to drop it. Do you want me to have another go?'

'No. It's too late now. You told Pedro you couldn't trace Mackenzie?'

'Yes, of course. I phoned him right back.'

I tried to take in what Fitzwarren had revealed: Mackenzie had never been cleared by him. But I'd been sitting in Pedro's office when Fitzwarren phoned. Pedro had definitely told me that John had given Mackenzie the all-clear. It wasn't the sort of thing Pedro could have made a mistake about. I remembered him saying Fitzwarren had reported that Mackenzie's trip had been planned for months.

Either Fitzwarren was lying, which seemed highly unlikely, or Pedro had lied to cover Mackenzie. But if Pedro and Mackenzie were working together, why had Mackenzie apparently been involved in Pedro's kidnapping? I had assumed that Pedro was abducted because he got too close to the Allenberg group when he was flashing their photographs around in the dock area. However, if he and Mackenzie were working together and Mackenzie and Allenberg were working together, where did that leave Pedro? Had he too been working with Allenberg's group but something went wrong and they turned on him? But that didn't make sense. If Pedro already knew Allenberg and company, he wouldn't have needed to show their photographs to Maroja.

Sonia returned looking tired. It was time to go. Fitzwarren had the same idea.

'We're in the way here, Sonia,' he said. 'If there's nothing I can do for you, I'll be going home. Jacquie will be wondering what's happened to me.'

'I know the feeling,' said Sonia wearily as Fitzwarren bit his tongue.

'I must be off too,' I said hurriedly. 'I'll be in touch in the morning.'

Fitzwarren looked in on Pedro, who was still unconscious, and then followed me out.

'Brave woman that,' he said. It was a comment that called for no answer.

He led me to his car and, after checking that there was nobody watching, unlocked the boot. The rifle was in a brown paper parcel, tied with string. He handed it to me like a hot potato.

'Your problem now,' he said. 'Glad to be rid of the damn thing. I hope you don't need to use it. It would cause an uproar if the locals found out.'

'I'll try and make sure they don't.'

The package was about four feet long and it seemed to me that nobody could mistake it for anything other than a rifle. I locked it in the boot at the front of the Volkswagen. Fitzwarren continued talking. 'It's a nice gun, you know. I hope you don't mind me having looked at it. Sniper's rifle. American. I wonder where Pedro gets hold of things like that. He never talks about his work, you know. Never.'

'He's not supposed to. Thanks for your help.'

'Glad to be of assistance. Makes a change from the usual stuff. Bit of excitement. If there's anything more I can do, let me know. I go home next month so I can afford to annoy the locals if necessary. As I say, this sort of thing can be quite fun. Especially now we know Pedro's all right.'

'I'll remember that, but we don't like involving regular people like you. It can be a dirty game. The people who grabbed Pedro also got hold of the chap who was carrying those Arabic addresses you had translated. What's left of him is now in the police mortuary.'

Fitzwarren blanched visibly. 'Yes, well it's war I suppose. What you're saying is "leave it to you professionals".'

'It's safer.'

'Yes. I'm a bit old to go chasing around with guns and things. Cheerio then. I expect I'll see you again before you leave Rio.'

I'd stayed at the Vernons' apartment far longer than I had expected and would have to rush to be in when Julia phoned. The traffic thickened as I drove east. I was thinking about the irony of Fitzwarren describing me as a 'professional' when a bus missed me by inches; the conductor seated at the back smashing his hand against the side as if urging the driver to go still faster. Brazil is the only country I know where traffic fatalities include drivers shot by other irate drivers who they happen to cross, often off-duty policemen. I found myself driving like the native Cariocas, one hand permanently on the horn.

Julia had parked Pedro's car directly outside the hairdressing salon. There was a crowded restaurant nearby and traffic passed incessantly. It was not the place to inconspicuously swap cars, with a rifle and walkie-talkie tucked under my arm. I found a quiet side street a few minutes away and parked the Volkswagen. It had the added advantage of making it less likely that the dumped car would be found quickly.

I walked back and returned with the other car. The street was completely deserted. As I didn't want to carry the rifle into Pedro's apartment, I took the opportunity to examine it there. I discovered a Second World War American Army rifle in apparently perfect condition. It was an M1903 Springfield. The A4 sniper's model with a powerful 2.5 Weaver scope which helped make it one of the world's most accurate military rifles. They couldn't have made more than twenty-five or thirty thousand of them, so Pedro had done exceptionally well to find one so quickly in a country like Brazil. There was also plenty of .30 calibre ammunition.

I locked the gun away again.

It was past eight o'clock as I approached the apartment. I assumed Captain Gomes would know what cars Pedro owned and I dared not risk drawing attention to the apartment so I left the car three blocks away.

Buttoning my jacket to hide the Luger and Beretta, I hurried towards the apartment.

There wasn't a soul to be seen on the street. Even the favela on the hillside above looked deserted. The apartment block itself seemed unnaturally silent. If I hadn't been in such a hurry I might have been more careful but as Julia was due to phone any second, I rushed to the lift.

As I put the key in the lock the silence was suddenly pierced by the jangling of the telephone. It was the only sound I could hear. Something was wrong. With the Luger in one hand I pushed open the door. Nothing happened. The apartment was enveloped in an unsettling darkness. Somebody had pulled the curtains shut. I tried to remember how I'd left them. I thought they'd been left open but I couldn't be sure. The phone kept ringing. I slammed on the lights but nothing happened. I was beginning to think my misgivings were purely nerves. Nothing in the lounge looked out of place, but the room contained practically no furniture that could have been moved – just a couple of chairs and a coffee table.

I bounded towards the bedroom from where the plaintive call of the telephone was echoing. Still with the Luger in my hand I opened the door and switched on the light. As I reached the phone the awful stillness of the room impinged on my senses. I spun around, phone in one hand, gun in the other, towards the bed.

The bare mattress on which I had been sleeping less than twelve hours earlier was a ghastly blur of red and white. Blood was splattered sickeningly over and around the sadistically knifed corpse of a naked woman that lay sprawled across it.

XXIV

A disembodied voice sounded my name: 'Thomas?' I looked around blankly and then remembered the phone in my hand.

'Thomas?'

'Yes.'

'Where have you been? What's happened?'

Relief swept over me. 'Julia. You're all right.'

'Of course I am. What's the matter?'

'There's a woman here, dead. I thought it was you. She's been hacked around.'

'Who is it?'

I moved unsteadily to the bed and looked into the twisted face of Miranda Gonçalves. The eyes were rolled up in petrified agony and the left cheek was ripped open.

'Miranda Gonçalves,' I mumbled into the phone. 'It's horrible, sadistic.'

Julia was silent for a moment. 'Somebody must have learned about our meeting this morning,' she said, trying to sound businesslike. 'She'd planted the bugs, I caught a snatch of Beethoven's Third as I approached the villa, and some conversation.'

'But why this? Why not a quick bullet and dump the body in the ocean? And how did the body get here? Somebody's on to us, who?'

'Nebulo,' Julia replied. 'Obviously he doesn't trust Martines so he kept the whole household under observation. He must have been watching Gonçalves and saw her talking to me.'

But nobody had been watching the hairdressing salon and nobody had followed us to the restaurant; I'd checked. Furthermore, if they'd seen Gonçalves collect the bugs they wouldn't have let her plant them. My thoughts were interrupted by a hammering at the door.

'I've got visitors. Keep listening.'

The banging continued. My mind suddenly cleared. Exits: none. Therefore one: prepare future escape route. Two: communicate the problem.

I put the Luger back into its holster and took the Beretta from my waistband. Then I placed the phone under the bed, the receiver still off. Julia should be able to hear most of what happened. There was nowhere to hide the Beretta in the bedroom or living room so I put it in the oven in the kitchen.

'Open this door immediately,' someone shouted.

'Who is it?'

'Open up.'

It was Gomes, appearing like a vulture as he had when Gary died. But vultures let others do their killing.

I had to let him in and try to bluff my way out.

Gomes stood outside, smiling broadly with a submachine gun pointing carelessly at me. Behind him were more armed police.

'Captain Gomes, thank God you've arrived. There's been a murder in here.'

I led him to the bedroom, gesturing towards Gonçalves' mutilated body. 'Do something.'

'I will,' he replied, letting the words hang in the air. 'I think, Senhor, you have a lot of questions to answer.'

A policeman entered carrying a flash camera. He looked sickened; obviously he hadn't been there when she was killed. Gomes led me back to the lounge where three of his men stood idly; pistols, handcuffs and truncheons at their waists. He sent one to stand guard outside.

'Tell me about it,' Gomes said.

'About what?'

'About the woman you've killed. What else?'

'I didn't kill her. I've just found her, like that. I don't even know her name.'

Gomes arched his eyebrows. 'You've returned to this apartment, obviously a love nest, and found a naked woman on the bed! Does such a fairy tale sound reasonable to you? Will any judge believe it?'

He was interrupted by the police photographer, who'd finished remarkably quickly. When he'd gone Gomes' attitude changed radically.

'Search him,' he barked.

One of his men rapidly obeyed, tossing my Luger to Gomes. When he'd finished he punched me sharply in the stomach. Instinctively I lashed out with my right foot, catching him on the shin. He fell back against his companion but I couldn't follow up: Gomes had his submachine gun cradled in one arm and my Luger in the other hand, both pointing directly at me.

'That will do Guerno,' he said to my assailant. 'There will be plenty of time for that. Remember the Senhor is a respectable visitor to our country, even though he carries a gun.'

'I need one with guardians of the law like you around.' I'd given up any hope of bluffing my way out.

'Come now, we're not going to have a silly conversation like that, are we?' Gomes scoffed. 'Let me explain your position, then perhaps you will cooperate. In fact, I'm sure you'll cooperate.'

He paused before adding 'Eventually' in a voice that was meant to be menacing. His theatrical tone made it more laughable than frightening.

He was a caricature of a tough man. The sort who uses a knife when others are using their fists. A sadist who'd watched too many gangster films. Dillinger became America's 'Public Enemy Number One' by vaulting over bank counters and brandishing his guns, he actually stole very little. Gomes was in the same mould. He stood waving his submachine gun, a Brazilian-made Model 953, in one hand like a toy. I remembered that the Model 953, unlike the Danish Madsen on which it was based, had a weird safety arrangement: to fire you had to grip the magazine housing and hold down a safety lever in front of the housing. The way Gomes was holding the gun he couldn't do that.

He saw me looking at the gun and evidently decided it didn't fit whatever image he was trying to project. He passed it to a goon he called Romeo and merely waved my Luger to illustrate his points.

'The position is very simple. I received a call from Senhorita Gonçalves saying she'd been lured to your apartment and you'd locked her in the bedroom. Obviously you forgot the phone is in there. Naturally I raced to her aid only to find her dead, viciously attacked, with you the only other occupant of the apartment. When I examine the murder weapon I feel sure I will find your fingerprints.'

He stopped as if expecting me to say something. When I said nothing he continued.

'If you say nothing I cannot help you. You will be tried and, I promise, convicted. Your government will disown you. Think of that: no help from London. And at best, years in a stinking prison. Or perhaps you will try to escape. Many try in Brazil but none make it.'

'You'll never make that story stand up in court. There are holes I could drive a tank through.'

'Such as?'

'Such as motive. Why should I kill her, a total stranger?'

Gomes smiled lasciviously. 'You're a man of the world. I need not spell out the motive. Why is a sex maniac a sex maniac? I don't know. No judge in Brazil will think twice about motive. It is well known that the British are a decadent people, very permissive. If that's your only objection, forget it.'

'Don't worry, it's not. You've forgotten the element of time. I'd been in the apartment only two or three minutes when you arrived. In that time I'm supposed to have locked this woman in the bedroom, let her phone you, stripped her and then hacked her around. That's pretty fast work, nearly as fast as your arrival here.'

Gomes was unmoved. 'Can you prove you weren't here half an hour ago? Perhaps one of my officers saw you arrive forty minutes ago.'

'That's strange. The two people who dropped me near here will swear I'd been with them for the last three hours. Right up until five minutes ago.'

'You're lying. You walked here. I saw you arrive.'

'I only walked a few blocks, to check I wasn't being followed.'

'And who are these two people? I can have a dozen people testify you've been here for the past hour.'

'They're diplomats,' I lied. 'Americans.'

'Western diplomats,' Gomes sneered. 'Once their government sees my evidence it won't dare let them testify. And as I said, you need not reach trial, you might try to escape.'

'And so what do you propose? I tell you whatever you want to know and then you carry on with your frame-up or shoot me.'

'Why would I shoot you? It would only be an embarrassment, to me and my government. No, I will release you if you cooperate. You have my word. Of course that will be after the auction is completed.'

It sounded plausible but I didn't believe a word of it.

'It is not so very much I want,' he continued. 'A little information. Who told you about us? When I met you, after Senhor Stover's tragic demise, you knew who I was. You mentioned slanders about me. How did you know about that?'

'You're famous, Gomes. There's a file on you in London. Naturally I read it; Brazil's my responsibility.'

'You flatter me, Senhor. But you're lying. You have been watching the Villa Nhambiquaras. Who told you about Senhor Martines?'

'You're wasting your time.'

'I think not. You will tell me what I want to know. The only question is when.'

Any minute he was going to say 'Vee haf vays of making you talk.' He nearly did. 'You are bound to talk eventually, but I want the information now.'

'Get lost.'

He nodded to the man I'd kicked. Guerno advanced towards me, swinging his truncheon.

'This is your last chance. We are not amateurs. You've heard of Operação Bandeirantes?'

I nodded wearily. It was an infamous training programme in torture techniques that included live demonstrations on political prisoners.

224

'Our specialists have lectured in military academies throughout Latin America. And Guerno knows it all. With the truncheon he will break every bone in your body.'

I told him exactly what Guerno could do with his truncheon.

Gomes kept the Luger pointing at my stomach while Guerno approached from the side. I could do nothing. Gomes only had to lower his aim, put a bullet in my knee and any chance of escape would be gone. I could only hope Guerno, or the other man, Romeo, would step into his line of fire.

I braced myself for a blow on the head. Instead Guerno swung at the back of my left hand. I whipped it into my mouth, convinced every bone was broken. As I did, the truncheon swung at my stomach. I turned, but not enough. The breath was shot out of my lungs. I doubled up, wanting to vomit but retching air. I put my right hand down for support but whipped it back as a boot stamped towards it.

Rolling on to my side Romeo kicked me in the ribs. I'd forgotten him and saw his lunging foot too late.

A hand grabbed my shoulder and as I was dragged up a pile-driving punch slammed my head back on to the thinly carpeted floor. For a fraction of a second I was dead to the world.

I forced myself to breathe deeply and steadily, waves of nausea crashing through me. I concentrated on Gomes' legs a couple of yards away. Slowly they stopped dancing around. Gomes had motioned his men back.

'You can see we mean business,' he said. I'd never doubted that. 'Start with Miranda Gonçalves. You knew her. You've spoken to her frequently. Perhaps she contacted you as soon as you arrived.'

'It's not true,' I croaked.

'How did you discover Martines? Through this woman? We know she spoke to the Americans; we saw her with Conniston this afternoon. When did she contact you?'

I said nothing and started levering myself up, using the wall as support. Romeo stepped forward and knocked my arm from the wall. I fell back. It wasn't worth struggling.

XXV

Gomes whipped the Luger across my face. Blood welled from my lips and nose. I spat it at him. He drew his foot back and aimed his steel-capped boot between my legs.

As his foot swung towards me I grabbed his ankle with both hands, pulling with all my remaining strength.

Gomes was carried forward by the momentum of his kick and that, as much as the little strength I could muster, made him lose his balance. I grabbed at his gun. We grappled on the floor. I had the advantage of already being on my knees. I pushed myself upright, launching a kick at his face. There was a gratifying crunch and his grip on the gun loosened.

Luger in hand I swung towards Guerno, who had jumped at me. I felt his hot breath on my face, an overpowering odour of onions and rotten eggs. He clasped me in what he imagined was a bear hug, grinning insanely through blackened teeth. My gun hand was jammed between us. Angling the Luger towards him I pulled the trigger. There was a muffled explosion, a burning on my stomach and his face creased in disbelief. The bullet had ripped through his heart, out through the armpit and into his shoulder.

I pushed the body towards Romeo, who seemed much slower. He was looking stupefied, the submachine gun pointing at the floor. He reached out to catch Guerno like a giant doll, staggering back under the weight.

Escape seemed possible, but I'd forgotten Gomes.

With blood streaming from his nose he lunged at me like a lunatic, apparently obsessed with retrieving the Luger. He jumped from behind, one arm encircling my neck, the other stretching for the gun. Fortunately he'd forgotten his own pistol still hanging in its holster at his waist.

I was unprepared and fell towards the floor under his weight. My breath came gulping out, my lungs still not recovered from the ravages of Guerno's truncheon. His grip tightened. Trying to distract his attention I flicked the gun into the centre of the room. It worked. He pushed me off and darted towards the gun.

Romeo was gently laying Guerno on the carpet, apparently oblivious of me. But the front door had opened and the third police guard was coming in. I jumped into the kitchen, slamming the door behind me.

The Beretta I'd hidden in the oven was the most beautiful gun I'd ever seen.

The kitchen was long and thin, stretching from the door to the window. On one side a plain wall. On the other a decrepit cooker, cupboard and, beside the door, a sink. I climbed into that, if Gomes started shooting through the door it was the only place I could avoid the bullets.

Nothing happened immediately. Then Gomes shouted, 'Come out you bastard, you can't get away.'

I remained silent.

'Come out now or we'll take you out in pieces.'

There was another brief silence. Then a burst of submachine gun fire ripped through the door at thigh level. The lower door panel disintegrated, as did the window. That should bring more police running. The door was kicked open and Romeo hurtled in, gun in hand, an expression of fierce determination on his face. He didn't stand a chance. As he entered, looking straight in front, I shot him in the side of his head. He spun against the wall, falling forward along the floor, one arm stretching towards the window.

Gomes appeared in the door, the colour draining from his face. He wasn't used to seeing someone crouching in a sink pointing a gun at his head. His own gun pointed uselessly at Romeo's body.

'Drop it,' I said, 'and tell your other goon to do the same.'

He complied with alacrity and I heard the thud of a pistol on the lounge carpet. Clambering from the sink I motioned Gomes back. He stood beside the sole survivor of his three thugs. The front door was open but there was no sign of life in the corridor; I shut it.

There were a lot of questions Gomes could answer, but no time to ask them. At any moment more police might arrive, drawn by the gunfire. But either Gomes had come with just three men and the photographer or the others had orders to stay downstairs. The sound of shots coming from a room where Gomes was 'interrogating' someone was not perhaps unusual. In any event nobody appeared.

I couldn't risk searching them, Gomes was mad enough to try jumping me. So I ordered the two men to strip to their underwear and handcuff their right ankles together, Gomes facing his subordinate's back. Then I marched them into the bedroom and handcuffed Gomes' wrist to the bedstead.

I had ordered them to kneel at the foot of the bed. As I bent to fasten the handcuffs Gomes grabbed at me. I'd hoped he would, it gave me an excuse to stamp hard on his hand.

'No more tricks now.'

He replied with some inaccurate remarks about my ancestry in general and my mother's in particular.

Before I could leave there was a knock on the door.

'Captain Gomes,' a voice said.

'Enter,' I barked in a weak imitation of Gomes.

Another policeman appeared, his gun in its holster. He looked around in bewilderment, his expression turning to disbelief as he saw the submachine gun I was pointing at him.

'Is there anybody else outside?'

Instinctively he shook his head. I shut the door.

'In there.' I motioned to the bedroom. He stared in horror at his handcuffed captain but paid no attention to the mutilated body of Miranda Gonçalves. I took his gun and fastened him to the bed with his own handcuffs.

Three or four minutes had passed since the shooting. There would certainly be more police around and they might be getting curious. They could be awaiting the return of the one who'd just arrived. I flushed the handcuff keys down the toilet and hid the five police pistols in the oven.

Then I remembered the phone in the bedroom. The line was dead. Julia had gone.

'Did you hear all that?' I asked the silent instrument in Portuguese. 'Most of it, good. You probably missed the fun in the kitchen.' I paused, grinning at Gomes who was staring venomously at me. 'You got the last bit on tape. Marvellous. Keep it at the Consulate, I'll be right over.'

After ensuring they had nothing to throw at the curtained windows to attract attention I collected my bag and the submachine gun and left.

The apartment block was long and thin with a corridor running the length of each floor between the two lifts. At each end there were two entrances, the main one and a smaller one at the rear. Pedro's apartment faced the back and I could see a police car outside the exit at this end, pointing away from the other entrance. Gomes undoubtedly had more men at the front.

The corridor outside was empty. At each end a staircase circled round the lift shaft. The windows on the staircase looked out from the front of the block. Far below two police cars and a jeep were parked outside the entrance.

I ran along the corridor to the other lift at the far end. Another police car stood outside the second entrance; I could only hope the back entrance wasn't guarded.

I slowly started down the concrete stairs. The lift opened on to the front lobby meaning it could be watched from the car outside, but the stairs finished at the back, in a corridor that kinked around the lift shaft. From their car Gomes' men therefore couldn't see the foot of the stairs but someone was standing below me. Unless he had his back to the stairs and was stone deaf, he must see me before I could grab him. I had to get him away from the staircase.

I ran back up to the lift and pushed the button. When the doors opened I signalled for the ground floor and jumped out. Racing downstairs I was just in time to hear the lift opening and boots shuffling towards the front of the block. I glanced warily round the bend in the stairs. There was nobody there. I descended quietly to the bottom step.

The corridor from the front lobby to the back entrance, forty feet away, was empty. I'd only got halfway to the back entrance when the lift clanged shut. Quickly I crouched between two of the rubbish bins lining the corridor.

I heard the guard return although I couldn't see him.

I was really in a mess, trapped halfway between the stairs and the back entrance. I had to go one way or the other but if I moved the man was bound to stop me. Every second delayed made the discovery of Gomes and the other two, trussed in Pedro's apartment, more likely. I'd decided to jump the guard and risk the consequences when he was joined by someone else.

'Anything happened?' the newcomer asked.

'Nothing. Only the lift came down empty just now.'

'Yeah. I saw that from the car.'

'What's been happening outside?'

'Sergeant dos Santos is getting nervous; you know what an old woman he is. The captain is still up with the Englishman. There was some shooting, dos Santos wants to know what happened.'

The other snorted. 'Nobody need worry about the captain. He's a tough bastard. Did you hear what he did to the woman? I'm glad I'm not in that Englishman's shoes.'

'I heard. I don't see why that was necessary.'

'It's an example. Nobody else will do what she did.'

'But what did she do?'

There was a silence before the new arrival continued. 'Anyway, dos Santos wants you out the back. He's sent a couple of others round already. And he's sent Valfordo up to see what's happening.'

There was no time for subtlety, the inquisitive sergeant would soon send more men up to Pedro's apartment.

I jumped out. 'Stand absolutely still.' Neither had been looking towards me, the surprise was complete. 'Drop your guns, quickly.' The guns clattered to the floor. 'OK back here carefully. Gomes can't reward dead heroes.'

Near the back entrance a large cupboard was let into the wall, a rusty key in the lock. Inside was a collection of brooms, mops and pans. There was enough room for my captives but it wouldn't be very secure. One of them had handcuffs so I ordered him to manacle their legs together and pushed them into the cupboard.

'Try escaping while I'm still here and you'll be dead,' I warned.

After dropping the keys and pistols in a rubbish bin I ran to the back door. Sauntering towards me were two policemen, both with submachine guns. I raced to the front lobby. Three yards away stood an empty police car, pointing up the street, away from the apartment block.

At the other end of the building sat the police cars and jeep I'd seen from upstairs. A lone policeman stood beside them.

I raced to the empty car, throwing my bag and gun in before me. The guard hadn't noticed me but as I accelerated away, rubber burning from the tyres, bullets whistled past. I turned left, out of sight.

The car had to be dumped. I doubled back, four blocks north of the apartment, and found my own car. Not until I'd transferred the bag and submachine gun and had left the police car behind did I start to relax.

There was only one worry now: to make sure that as I moved away from Gomes Julia wasn't closing in on him.

Julia should have stayed listening to the phone. She couldn't have helped and her priority ought to have been discovering exactly what was happening, exactly what information Gomes could get from me. But I wasn't displeased she'd ignored the textbook. Now I had to find her. That shouldn't be impossible if she kept to the direct route. She would still be half an hour away.

It occurred to me that she might have her walkie-talkie. So I stopped, took my set from the boot and tried to call her without success. I turned on the car radio, hoping that as she came within range she would pick up the music on her set and realise what was happening. She didn't but it wasn't important. We spotted each other almost simultaneously, with Julia slamming on her brakes and jumping out of her car.

'Thomas, you're all right.'

We crushed each other, and then lips fumbled together. I'm not sure which of us was more surprised.

We pulled apart in mutual embarrassment, in my case reinforced by the knowledge that, unless Gomes had struck lucky, there were only two ways he could have learned about Pedro's supposedly secret apartment. Directly or indirectly the information came from Pedro or from Julia.

XXVI

For once I was pleased to be followed. There was something reassuring about Julia's car behind me. 'I waited until they started hitting you,' she had told me, 'then I had to come.' I wasn't going to complain.

Now we retraced her steps back towards the Villa Nhambiquaras. The exchange of Griffin for the money could only be a few hours away and we were still no nearer to finding a way of getting our hands on Griffin. The very thought of hands made me wince, my left hand still throbbing from the blow of Guerno's truncheon.

We stopped for petrol and I phoned Sonia Vernon; Pedro was still unconscious.

The drive gave me time to work out what had happened back at the apartment. Miranda Gonçalves must have started prowling around the villa after her lunch with Julia and somehow she'd found out about the Americans. If we were willing to pay she must have reasoned that they would also. So she'd contacted Conniston who was obviously under observation. That had signed her death warrant and provided Gomes with a chance to remove me by framing me for her murder.

How much had Gonçalves told Conniston? The names of Martines and Nebulo alone would enable the Americans to ruin a lot of people's plans. If they believed her would they confront Nebulo or, perhaps more likely, go directly to one of the military junta? They were unlikely to storm the villa immediately; however gung-ho the Americans can be I was sure Conniston would want political cover before taking on someone as apparently powerful as Nebulo. That could give us a breathing space but we'd have to look out for anyone they might have watching the villa.

Fortunately I had no intention of getting near enough the villa to be seen by anybody. Julia had given me the radio receiver and as soon as we got within range of the villa I parked off the road. Julia joined me and we listened to the radio receiver. There wasn't much happening inside the villa. Somebody was playing Wagner. Now for the really serious business: Julia and I needed to talk. I took her hand gently.

'Don't you think you should really tell me what's going on. Not half a story like last time. The whole picture this time. What's happening here and what's really happening in London.'

'What do you mean what's happening in London?'

'I mean who in London is working with Martines and Nebulo? Who's the third man that Budermann complained was getting a bigger share than him? Someone in the DIS has helped set this whole thing up.'

'We don't know that. The bomb in your room could have been because someone saw you outside the villa.'

'No Julia, we are way beyond that. How did Budermann get on to me in Chicago? How did he know I would be the one with Griffin? How were they able to give the Americans Nick Broadbent's name? That all had to have come from Broadbent's team or from you or from someone in London. The Canadians aren't involved down here, that leaves you or London. Nebulo discovered I had found the Villa Nhambiquaras and you're right that could have been an accident, Budermann saw me following him perhaps, but unlikely. But now Gomes suddenly finds Pedro's apartment. How did that happen? Pedro was out of circulation. Perhaps you told him.'

'Don't be ridiculous,' Julia interrupted, not trying to keep the irritation out of her voice.

'Well it's either you or someone in London. Fitzwarren said he had sent Pedro's emergency number to London. That must have been the phone number for the apartment. Gomes could easily have found the address from the phone number. Tell me: what does Griffin stand for?'

'What?!'

'The Griffin Interrogator, the thing all this is supposed to be about. Griffin is an acronym, the letters stand for something, what?'

'How the hell would I know? And what's that got to do with anything?'

'You mean you didn't see the Company briefing, all the gobbledegook about garble recognition, interrogation friend or foe and so on.'

'No I didn't see it. What are you talking about?'

'Think back. How did the auctioneers get in touch with the DIS to invite us to the auction?'

'They sent a message to Richard Mendale.'

'Yes. An odd way to communicate perhaps but effective, as Director Operations his name is no doubt reasonably well known. But when they invited the Americans they phoned an obscure CIA case officer responsible for liaison with the ONI, the Office of Naval Intelligence. Why? Because he happened to be handling the Griffin Interrogator theft. How on earth did they know that? Of all the thousands of people in the CIA how did they discover he was the right man? I'll tell you: because he had sent a report on Griffin to the DIS and helpfully included not only his name but his phone number. You didn't know that, but someone in London did and they sent it to Martines or Budermann. And I think you know who that was. Was it Mendale?'

'You can't ask me that.'

'Why not? Because you promised your uncle? Because you signed the Official Secrets Act? Aren't we beyond all that?'

'Because I don't know, not for sure. It could have been someone else, I think it probably was. But it's all so complicated. Five think they've cleared Mendale. Adam Joseff has always supported him. My uncle is starting to believe them. Six are the only ones still pointing their fingers at our DO. They think he's been a Russian sleeper, a Soviet sympathiser worming his way into the intelligence establishment, waiting for the moment he can be really useful to Moscow. Waiting for something like the Warsaw mission, waiting until he can blow Koenig in Berlin. But now we're talking about something quite different. This isn't political. Martines isn't part of a Soviet spy ring, he never has been. Even if Six were right and Mendale is some sort of Russian master spy why would he be helping a Brazilian gunrunner? The Russians want to get hold of Griffin; they wouldn't be helping Martines.'

'You mean there could be two spies in the DIS. One betraying secrets to the Russians and one working hand in glove with Martines and Nebulo? That's a bit far-fetched, isn't it?'

When Julia said nothing I changed tack. 'What's happening here in Rio? What's Pedro's role in all this? Why did he lie to me about Mackenzie? He told me Fitzwarren had vouched for him, but Fitzwarren's just told me he's never heard of the man.'

Julia looked uncomfortable but did not reply.

'What was Pedro doing in Warsaw?' I asked.

Julia's head shot up. 'How did you know about that?'

'Does it matter?'

'I suppose not. Pedro was back in London when the Warsaw business came up. He had upset the authorities here and had to be pulled out for a while to let things calm down. Mendale wanted someone from the DIS with him in Poland and chose Pedro. It was an odd choice. Pedro had no experience in the region and didn't speak Polish or Russian, but Mendale had known him for years and said he felt sorry for him kicking his heels in Whitehall. Believe me after it all went wrong we crawled over everything Pedro did in Warsaw, indeed everything he's ever done. He's completely above board. Fitzwarren must have made a mistake about Mackenzie.'

'Nonsense. You're not telling me something. And why was Pedro checking up on me with Jenny Merchant? Mendale must have asked him to, but why?'

Suddenly I was interrupted by a strange, metallic voice. Someone inside the villa had moved within range of a radio bug.

'Looking for a drink. Don't suppose you have a bottle of Scotch?'

'Over there. You can take it to your room.'

Nothing more but it jolted me. Not only was the conversation in English, but one of the voices had a strong East London accent.

'Who was that?' Julia asked.

'God knows.' There were so many odd characters floating around that I couldn't keep track.

Julia was tense, fiddling with her hair.

'Thomas.'

'Yes.'

'There's something I want to tell you, but I'm not sure I should. Something that might help to explain things.'

'Something about that Londoner?'

'No. Well I don't think so. Something about you.'

She was interrupted by the barking of a dog. I felt her jump but it came from the radio. It was followed by someone saying in German 'He's arrived.'

There was the sound of greetings. Nebulo had arrived. But he'd lost some of his old self-confidence.

'It's all going wrong,' we heard him say. 'The Americans know I'm involved. They're going over my head. What did your woman tell them? How much did she know?'

'Nothing,' a strong, firm voice replied, Budermann not Martines. 'She knew nothing. Gomes interrogated her. What did she say?'

'She died before we learned anything. Gomes made a mess of it again.'

'Again?'

'He's let the Englishman escape.'

'How could he? From the apartment?'

Nebulo moved away from the microphone as he replied. 'Killed two of my men' was all we caught.

'We've got to go,' came another voice, 'leave the country.' It was Martines, barely audible.

'We will, after the exchange,' responded Budermann. 'Let's make sure we all know what's happening tomorrow. That's why Cristiano is here.'

Nebulo replied but we couldn't make out his words. I prayed that someone would say something that would tell us exactly where tomorrow's exchange with the Russians would take place. My prayers were heard. There was the scratching of furniture being moved before Budermann continued.

'Here on the map. Gomes follows the Russians from Petrópolis. They've been warned to expect a police car behind them. They'll continue towards Teresópolis. Then here they turn left. OK?'

'Yes, yes,' came Nebulo's voice, 'we've been all through this before. They follow the Rio Peixoto along here, three or four kilometres, and we'll be waiting at the junction.'

'Not quite. They turn right, over the bridge and then park, facing towards Santa Bárbara. But you won't be there. They're expecting one car following them. So you follow on after Gomes, just to make sure they're not trying any tricks.'

'How far behind?'

'Not far, a minute, two minutes. And keep in radio contact with Gomes.'

Nebulo replied, but he'd moved away from the microphone again.

'Why doesn't that bloody man stand still!' Julia whispered.

'He's nervous. And you don't have to whisper.'

She grinned sheepishly.

Budermann spoke again. 'No, no, we'll wait for you. At the bend in the road here, just before the junction. Gomes parks across the road to stop anyone who might interrupt things. The Russians will go on like I said and park on the other side of the bridge.' Somebody said something indistinguishable and Budermann replied impatiently, 'No when you arrive, park near Gomes and walk to the junction. That will be my signal. I'll join you there, then walk on to the bridge and we make the exchange. Easy.'

There was a sound of a chair scraping. Budermann and Nebulo seemed to have moved away. We could hear fragments of their conversation, but nothing useful. I thought I caught something about a boat.

'That's it,' said Julia. We had overheard enough to work out very roughly where the exchange would take place, but Budermann pointing out bends in the road on a map we couldn't see didn't guarantee that we could identify the exact spot.

Nebulo stayed for another few minutes. Martines said very little. Budermann had obviously taken complete control. At one point Nebulo asked him about 'Gadd'.

'He arrived this afternoon. We'll take him with us tomorrow.'

It was a safe guess that the English voice we'd heard earlier belonged to someone named Gadd. That didn't help much.

'I don't see why he had to come at all,' Nebulo said.

But Budermann interrupted him. 'Of course he had to come. The British had his name. It was only a matter of time before they caught him. Now that he's here he's disposable.'

'It all comes back to the English. We shouldn't have involved them at all,' Nebulo said, his voice rising. 'We tried to be too clever. You think Gonçalves was their source?'

'I suppose so. It doesn't matter now.'

'Nothing matters now,' said Martines. 'We're leaving, one way or another.'

'Don't start that,' Budermann told him. 'Nothing can go wrong.'

'But you've seen them, Hans. After all this time. Outside in their Volkswagens. Volkswagens. The people's car, Hans.' He spoke in German and repeated the name over and over.

'He's cracking up,' I said.

Julia nodded. 'And so's Nebulo.'

She was right. Nebulo's polish had worn off. What had seemed a simple game had turned sour. If Conniston did manage to appeal to the generals, Nebulo was as good as dead. Budermann had emerged in full control.

Budermann went out with Nebulo and we couldn't hear their conversation. 'Bed,' he said to Martines when he returned. 'You know what to do in the morning. Just be sure you're there at dawn.'

They both left the room and there was silence.

'What were you going to tell me,' I asked Julia, 'before Nebulo arrived? Something about me.'

Julia seemed to have had second thoughts.

'Later, let's talk later.' She laid her hand on my cheek and in an unexpectedly soft voice continued. 'There's a lot more to tell. We're on the same side, Thomas, I'm sure of that now. We have to trust each other. But right this minute we must go. If Budermann and Martines aren't travelling to the exchange together it probably

239

means that Budermann is going earlier to scout around. We must be in position by then. Let's hope we can find the place.'

I agreed. Now was not the time to grapple with my feelings or to ask questions. 'There's a walkie-talkie in the boot of your car,' I said. 'We can use that to stay in touch with each other.'

In fact she already had her set on the front seat. I should have wondered why, but I didn't. I was tired. The lack of sleep the previous night when I'd been avoiding bullets outside the villa and the treatment from Gomes' goons earlier had exhausted me.

'First stop Petrópolis,' Julia said as we moved off, the walkie-talkie seeming to exaggerate her upper-crust accent.

In the daytime the drive to Petrópolis, and on to Belo Horizonte, is spectacular. The road climbs 3 500 feet through tropical vegetation up to the city, now a weekend and summer resort, where Dom Pedro II had his summer court. But at night all we could see were the lights of the cars. The road was not busy but I didn't notice the car that I later discovered was following us. That wasn't surprising because it kept well back. There was no need to follow closely: he knew where we were going.

I drove mechanically, too weary to really work out what was happening. Julia had said she trusted me 'now'. What did the now imply? And did I trust her yet? I wanted to, I wanted to very much. And yet so much that the auctioneers seemed to know could have come from her. In fact, everything except the name of the CIA case officer who had sent the DIS the Griffin report. That had to have come from London. But that just meant Julia could not have acted alone, she needed to be working with someone else and there was one obvious candidate. Had the whole business been set up by Julia's uncle, the Director General himself?

When we reached Petrópolis we had no time to drive around looking at the beautiful old buildings, or the classical pink palace with its white pilasters. We wanted a road leading to Teresópolis. That wasn't too difficult, but somewhere we had to turn left and follow the Rio Peixoto. 'Three or four kilometres,' Nebulo had said, before turning right over a bridge on a road to Santa Bárbara. Budermann hadn't said anything about the road to Teresópolis so we chose the main one and drove as far as the river, before returning and taking the first road right.

We found nothing that fitted the description we had overheard. 'This is no good. Let's turn back,' Julia suggested after five kilometres. 'We'd best cross over the Peixoto and see if there's a road there.'

We retraced our steps to the Teresópolis road and almost immediately after the river a road turned off left. It followed the river's east bank for a few kilometres and then crossed to the other bank. Three kilometres further on it suddenly bore right again, towards the river. A small track kept on north while the road itself crossed the river.

'This has to be the bridge Budermann was describing,' I said into the radio.

We needed to get our cars off the road; in the dark that wasn't so easy. I wanted the cars on the Santa Bárbara side of the bridge but as near as possible. Eventually we found a track nearly a kilometre away and managed to hide the cars out of sight of the road, but it would be quite a hike from the bridge.

'Perhaps we could find somewhere on the other side of the river,' Julia suggested. Her voice sounded mechanical on the radio, like the station announcer's in Haarlem.

'No go. We've got to take Griffin off the Russians. We can't take it off Martines because we can't be absolutely sure that he'll be coming from Petrópolis. We know the Russians will be parked on this side of the bridge, so we wait there until after the exchange.'

'We could wait here with our cars and ambush them when they drive past.'

'If they go back this way,' I cut in. 'What happens if the Russians turn round after the exchange and follow the others back towards Petrópolis? The only place we can be sure of grabbing Griffin is this side of the bridge right after the exchange.'

Julia left her car and joined me without replying.

'Let's find some cover near the bridge,' I suggested. 'You keep this side of the road and try to hide near the Russians' parking spot. I'll cross the road with the rifle and try to find somewhere where I can cover both sides of the bridge.'

'So I jump the Russians when they've got Griffin, while you cover me,' Julia said. 'I suppose that's our best hope, we're assuming there are only two of them. They will be wary, looking out for a double-cross.'

'Right. We should wait as long as possible, preferably until Budermann and Nebulo are back in their cars. We'll play it by ear. Perhaps we should let the Russians get into their car and I'll pick off the driver as you jump them. Take the Magnum. The sight of you with that should scare them stiff.'

'Thanks. I'll stick to the Browning if you don't mind.'

The starlight was too weak to illuminate much and we stumbled to the bridge before splitting up. The land seemed clear of vegetation for twenty or thirty yards from the road and then the trees started. They provided excellent cover and we both settled down to wait for the dawn.

'Goodnight,' came Julia's voice over the walkie-talkie. 'I'll expect an early morning call and a nice cup of tea.'

Budermann arrived with the dawn.

'Who's that with him?' Julia radioed.

'I presume one of the servants. Pedro said there were two, Moros and Pinteiro. And Miranda Gonçalves told you that Pinteiro was wounded the other night so it must be Moros.'

Budermann drove slowly from the direction of Petrópolis. The first light of dawn clearly showed the lie of the land. The river flowed through a steep-sided valley, roughly north–south. Budermann was approaching from the south. The road turned sharply and crossed the bridge towards us, entering another, smaller valley at right angles to the first. Budermann stopped just before the bridge where the road turned. I could see now that it wasn't just a bend in the road, but a junction. The main road turned east but a smaller, unpaved track continued north along the left bank of the river.

Moros left the car and, clutching a submachine gun, marched off towards the trees on the far side of the road. Then Budermann drove over the bridge towards us. He passed slowly, but couldn't see us from the road.

'I just hope he doesn't decide to investigate the track where we parked,' I said into the radio. Neither of us could see the track but we heard the car drive off into the distance without stopping. Ten minutes later he was back and set off north along the unpaved road. Apparently satisfied that the area was clear he arrived back at the junction and manoeuvred his Ford so that it faced north again.

'They're going to leave along that track,' Julia said.

'Looks like it. It's not marked on the map; it could lead anywhere.'

We were interrupted by the arrival of Martines. He bowled down the road in his classic Mercedes. At the wheel was someone I'd seen before, at the wheel of a Ford Capri at Zandvoort Station in Holland.

XXVII

My mind reeled. How could that be? I had almost forgotten the episode in Holland, pushing it out of my mind as something I needed to forget. I had been more than happy to move on to pastures entirely new but now it was obvious that the auction of the Griffin Interrogator was in some way linked to the events in Zandvoort. Below me was one of the men who'd jumped me in the mist, the man whose companion I had killed.

We had all assumed that the men I encountered in Holland were Russians, some sort of Samovar backup. But that couldn't be. The man I was now looking at was without doubt the owner of the English accent we had heard the previous evening, the person Nebulo had referred to as Gadd.

Gadd parked in front of Budermann on the road north. Behind him came an old Chevrolet van which stopped diagonally across the road just north of the junction so that only Martines and Budermann could leave that way. From the van emerged a small, dark man with his arm in a sling, presumably the other servant, Pinteiro. He was joined by Budermann and Gadd. They stood staring south, leaving Martines alone in the back of the Mercedes.

I picked up the Springfield rifle and pushed five rounds, staggered, into the magazine and pulled out the empty cartridge clip. As an added extra I pushed the top cartridge down below the line of the bolt with my left thumb and, after pushing the bolt slightly over it, inserted a sixth cartridge directly into the firing chamber. Then I shoved the bolt right in, turned and locked it.

We didn't have long to wait. The Russians drove across the bridge and pulled up almost level with Julia, who was nearer the bridge than I was.

'There are three of them,' she said.

Through the Weaver scope I could see the car clearly. She was right. Bitri was at the wheel and stayed there. Abdel Rassem climbed out of the back seat clutching a case while a third man got out and stood balancing a submachine gun on the car roof. A police car had followed the Russians and now stood cutting the main road before the junction. Gomes and two others stood beside it. The scene was set. It just needed Nebulo to put everything into motion.

He arrived in an enormous limousine and pulled up beside Gomes before walking quickly to the junction where Budermann was standing. Budermann had a small box in one hand: Griffin at last. The two men exchanged a few words, then Budermann turned and walked slowly towards the bridge. At the same time Abdel Rassem left his two companions and strode purposefully towards him.

Nobody else moved. There was total silence.

The two men were ten yards apart when there came the sound of a car roaring up the road from the south. The trees blocked my view but suddenly a black Dodge smashed into the side of Gomes' police car.

'It's Conniston,' Julia shouted. 'They must have followed Nebulo.'

There was an absolute pandemonium as four CIA men tumbled out of the car, one of them blasting away with a .45 Thompson semi-automatic carbine, the others shooting handguns.

Gomes lay spreadeagled across his car, half his head smashed away. His men were firing back from behind the rocks that littered the side of the road. A burst of bullets came from the trees where Moros had hidden himself and Conniston clutched at his shoulder.

Nebulo was cowering behind one of the bridge parapets.

The Griffin exchange had stopped abruptly. Budermann, clutching the little box, was running towards his car. The Russian too had decided that discretion was the better part of valour.

He was right. 'Time to go,' I shouted into the radio.

'Too true,' Julia replied. 'The Army's arrived.'

I looked back towards the Petrópolis road and there stood an Army truck disgorging heavily armed soldiers. Obviously Conniston had been able to enlist the aid of one of the generals.

My last image of the scene was of Gadd, who'd been rooted beside the Chevrolet van, a pistol unused in his hand, suddenly turn and dart back to the Mercedes.

I ran through the trees, cursing that we hadn't parked nearer. In one hand I clutched the walkie-talkie, in the other the 43½ inch-long Springfield rifle. Behind me, the Russians' car started up and then shot along the road below.

Suddenly my walkie-talkie barked out a strange male voice, 'I'll get them', followed by an ear-splitting crash. The Russian car shrieked across the road, smashed into a large rock and rebounded into a red Ford Corcel that appeared from the opposite direction.

The two cars were a hundred yards away. I broke out of the trees and ran towards them, dropping the radio so I could handle the rifle properly.

The driver of the Russian car seemed to be injured but Abdel Rassem and another man jumped out, Makarov nine millimetre automatics in hand. At the same time the door of the other car burst open and Captain Mackenzie rolled out. Now I knew why Julia hadn't wanted the .357 Magnum: she hadn't had it. I didn't have time to wonder when she'd given it to him.

Mackenzie raised himself on to one knee and as he did so the nameless Russian took aim at him.

Instinctively I fired and the Russian dropped. Abdel Rassem spun round, saw me and stiffened. I waved the Springfield at him and he slowly raised his hands, his own weapon falling to the ground.

I also had Mackenzie covered. He rose, blood streaming from his nose and a gash on his forehead from his smashed windscreen.

'Hold it!' he shouted. 'I'm on your side. For the sake of the Queen, you understand?'

I understood. 'For the sake of the Queen.' I could hear the DG saying it, silhouetted against the Thames back in the Guest Room at the House of Lords. The stupid bastards. Why hadn't they trusted me? Why hadn't Julia told me?

'Griffin. Get Griffin,' Mackenzie shouted.

'They haven't got it. The exchange wasn't completed.'

Mackenzie ran to the car. Pausing to glance at Bitri's unconscious figure behind the steering wheel, then he grabbed one of the cases in the back. At least we had some of the money.

Behind us the shooting had stopped. 'Come on,' I urged as Julia emerged from the trees.

The two cars were hopelessly entangled, which would block any pursuit. We scooped up the Russians' guns and started running down the road, leaving Abdel Rassem beside the wreck of his car.

If the Brazilian Army had used a helicopter nobody would have escaped. But they didn't and we did.

'What happened to Martines?' Mackenzie asked when we reached the cars.

'I don't know. He may have got away, with Griffin.'

'Then he'll go to his boat. He must realise that the Army will be at the villa by now. You'd better follow me.'

He climbed into Julia's car and they roared off. I could do nothing but follow.

We drove to Santa Bárbara and then south again towards Rio and Baia Botafogo. It was a long journey which gave me plenty of time to think. It was a pity I'd left the walkie-talkie behind or I could have asked Julia and Mackenzie a few questions. Not that I needed many answers. I'd realised a long time ago that I was being used as just one more pawn. Somebody in London was playing games and part of that game was Mackenzie. He was probably MI6, sent out to keep an eye on me, see what I managed to stir up. I could now understand how he became involved in Pedro's disappearance. Pedro had gone to the warehouse being used by Allenberg's group and they had grabbed him. Mackenzie had tried to find him in the same way we had and got there just before us. Perhaps he had seen Pedro being driven away. In any event he had found one of Allenberg's men inside and somehow managed to get the Leblon address. He trussed the man up, left a message for me which he signed Pedro and set off for Leblon. But there, like Pedro before him, he had walked into a trap. Luckily for him we arrived and he was able to get away. That brought me to Julia.

Julia had known all about Mackenzie's role, just as she'd known everything in Chicago. In Leblon she had deliberately let him escape. And Pedro had known too: he'd covered up for Mackenzie and provided him with a car and the walkie-talkie I had just heard him using. He'd used it to monitor our conversation the previous evening. Mackenzie had probably followed us to Petrópolis, then gone on to Santa Bárbara and found the road from there back to the bridge.

I could see why they wouldn't trust me initially. I'd been the one who'd 'given' Budermann Griffin in Chicago. But later, after Gomes had interrogated me, surely Julia could have been allowed to tell me everything then.

But Julia didn't know everything as we discovered when we arrived at the docks. There were still parts of the story neither of us understood, characters still without identities.

Mackenzie jumped out of the car and rushed to the dockside. I don't know why. There was nothing there. He stood staring down at the gently lapping water and floating jetsam.

'They've gone,' he said, stating the obvious as Julia and I joined him.

Martines might have gone but not everyone had followed him. Almost silently the black Mercedes pulled up behind us. We turned to look into the barrel of an Uzi submachine gun.

XXVIII

'We're not going to try any heroics are we?' drawled a voice from the back of the Mercedes. 'Let's just have a quiet chat.'

The man who emerged from the car was tall, the same height as Mackenzie, and strong. He didn't need his companion with the gun to show that here was someone used to having his own way. Here stood the man who had kidnapped Pedro, murdered Attirmi and scared Martines half out of his mind just by putting Volkswagens outside his villa. And only now was I beginning to guess who he was, where he was from.

'Perhaps we can start by introducing ourselves,' he continued. 'Let's stick to first names then we won't have to tell any lies. Let's see, Captain Mackenzie we've met, ran away last time didn't you. Graham is the name I believe.'

Mackenzie nodded. 'Twice I've let myself get caught by you, not very professional.'

'And then there's Thomas Dylan, judging by your registration at the hotel.' He smiled. 'And finally the young lady. I'm afraid I don't know your name.'

'Julia.'

'Julia. Pleased to meet you. If only Pedro was here we'd have the whole set. How is Pedro by the way? I hope we didn't pump him too full of that stuff.'

'He'll live. You haven't mentioned your name.'

'I'm coming to that. You can call me David.'

'Allenberg?' I asked.

'Now how did you know that? I suppose you traced the car, but that wouldn't have got you very far. Not that it matters. Let's stick to first names like I said.'

He smiled at us as if inviting comment but nobody spoke. 'OK down to business. You represent British Intelligence.'

'And,' I interrupted, 'you represent the state of Israel.'

Only Julia looked surprised. Perhaps Mackenzie had realised who they were when they caught him trying to rescue Pedro. Or else, like me, he'd deduced that the most likely people to kill Arabs such as Attirmi and wave Israeli-made guns around were Israelis.

'Now again, how did you know that?' said Allenberg.

'London told us you had a team out here,' I lied. 'It wasn't hard to work out who they were.'

'Perhaps, perhaps. Anyway, it appears that we have business in common: the man calling himself Adolpho Martines. I'd like to know what business you have with him.'

Julia and Mackenzie looked at me. It seemed that for now I was nominated spokesman. I knew the least and therefore could give the least away.

'Presumably you're asking for an exchange of information.'

'You could put it like that.'

'And what do you tell us?'

Allenberg smiled. 'Don't beat around the bush, sonny. You tell us why you're after Martines and we'll tell you why we're here. Then maybe we can cooperate.'

There was nothing to lose by talking to him. 'Martines, or rather, his friend Budermann, stole something from us. We want it back. He intended selling it to the Russians and had arranged an exchange this morning, out near Petrópolis. Unfortunately the Americans learned about it and came charging in, along with half the Brazilian Army, at just the wrong moment.'

'I don't suppose you'd like to tell me what he stole.'

'You're right: I wouldn't.'

He paused. 'So that's what the CIA's doing here. When was the thing stolen?'

'Last week.'

'That figures. We've been here for weeks. Setting things up. Careful like. Too careful I guess. And then you show up with the Yanks and the KGB and Martines disappears. You think he got caught?'

'No idea. We didn't. He might have escaped. He's sure to have had at least one escape route planned.'

Allenberg didn't reply. He gazed unseeingly across the water to the moorings of the Rio de Janeiro Yacht Club.

'Now it's our turn to ask a few questions,' I continued. 'Why are you here?'

'We want Martines. We've wanted him for a long time. Since the war. Since the concentration camps.'

'War crimes!' Julia interjected. 'You're after him for that? After all this time?'

'That's right. It's not so long in the memory of a people. You're too young to remember, young lady. His real name wouldn't mean anything to you.'

'But it's not just war crimes,' I interrupted. 'If he was one of your most wanted targets we would have recognised him. You wouldn't risk an international incident in Brazil just for that.'

'Why shouldn't we? Brazil voted at the UN to equate us with the racists and Nazis. I don't give a damn for their reactions. We know there are hundreds of war criminals right here in Brazil.'

'But the Israeli government might feel differently.'

'Perhaps,' he replied. 'Anyway, you're right. We have a more direct interest. Martines and Budermann are arms smugglers: the Caribbean, Philippines, Ireland probably. And the Middle East. There are groups in the Middle East that even the Libyans won't arm. Lunatic groups in Syria that are as dangerous to the Syrian regime as they are to us. Trained in Russia or China but now on their own. One of them got hold of a lot of money in a bank raid during the Lebanese civil war and intended to buy weapons with it.'

'From Martines?'

'Right. We wanted to stop them.'

'So you hit Attirmi?'

'That's right. He was the courier. We knew Martines was in Brazil, we found a photo of him, but we didn't know where. And we knew Attirmi was going to contact him. So we came here and waited for Attirmi to appear, and followed him, via Budermann, to Martines. Then we stood around waiting for Martines to leave his villa. That was a mistake. We should have gone in and taken him out.'

'But you didn't. And now he's gone. Maybe we could cooperate on getting him back.'

'How?' Allenberg asked.

'You want Martines. We want our property back. There's no conflict there. You've been watching him for a month or so. You must have an idea where he might head. Presumably he's gone by sea or you wouldn't be here. We've got a Navy in the Atlantic, you haven't. You tell us where he's gone. We find him, retrieve what we want and hand him over.'

'There's one problem,' said Allenberg. 'We don't know where he's gone. The boat left last night; we couldn't stop it. Neither Martines nor Budermann was aboard. We went out to the villa first thing this morning and found the whole area cordoned off by the Army.'

'But you must have an idea where he's gone,' I insisted. 'You traced him to Brazil. You must know what contacts he has, where he got his papers, where his money is. He came from Uruguay didn't he? Could he be returning there?'

'Could be. We don't know. We traced him through his Arab contacts, not by following his escape route from Germany. He could be anywhere now.'

There was nothing he could add. And nothing I wanted to add. 'We'll just have to go home and hope we'll spot him if he contacts the Russians or Arabs again.'

Allenberg leaned back against the Mercedes, staring up at Christ the Redeemer atop Corcovado. He looked tired. I knew how he felt. Just as I'd felt back in Chicago when the Griffin had been snatched from my hands.

'If I asked you to let us know if you find him,' Allenberg said, 'I suppose there's no way I could hold you to a promise.'

'No. That's a policy decision London would have to make.'

'Even if we promise to hand over your stolen property if we get to Martines first?'

'Sorry. Like I said, London makes decisions like that. If they do agree we'll contact you through Mossad, normal channels.'

We stood in silence looking out over the water. A grimy tug chugged past.

'There's nothing more we can do then,' said Allenberg. He took a photo from his pocket. It was a shot of Martines in a wheelchair, with Budermann behind him. 'We thought we had the bastard. So near, so near.'

'You got him,' Julia said. 'He's cracked up. We heard him last night. He knew who you were and it scared him out of his mind.'

Allenberg said nothing. He walked to the edge of the jetty, ripped the photo into little pieces and dropped them one by one on to the oil-flecked water below. Then he turned, strode back to the car and got in without saying a word. His companion lowered his gun, climbed in beside the driver and the car moved off. At the end of the dock it was joined by a green Volkswagen and they disappeared into the traffic.

'We've lost the Griffin Interrogator,' Mackenzie said. 'Martines got away. The Americans will be furious.'

I stood staring after Allenberg, Mackenzie's words slowly registering. So even Mackenzie hadn't been told the whole story. Need to know again.

'You're MI6,' I said.

'That's right,' said Mackenzie. 'Sent out to make sure you didn't hurt yourself.'

I wasn't sure about that. Mackenzie wasn't here primarily to protect me; he was here for the Griffin Interrogator.

'We need to get to the Consulate,' said Mackenzie. 'I must talk to the Station Chief, David Harrison. Justin Brasenose will have a lot of explaining to do to the Americans.'

I remembered that John Fitzwarren had mentioned Harrison flying down from Brasilia.

'When did he arrive?' I asked.

'Last night. I was supposed to meet him at the airport but as you know I got delayed. I met him later and he followed me out to the exchange.'

'Harrison was at the exchange!' Julia exclaimed. 'Where?'

'He didn't stay there. Once I'd identified somewhere to hide he went back to Rio to update London on the situation. That's what I need to do now. Like I said, the Americans will be spitting blood.'

'Take my car,' said Julia. 'I'll go with Thomas.'

Mackenzie disappeared and I turned to Julia. 'Have we lost the Interrogator?' I asked.

'What do you mean?'

'I mean do you know where Martines and Budermann are going? Is it Trinidad?'

'How the hell did you know that?'

'I looked in your passport.'

'My passport! When did you look at that? And why?' Julia made no attempt to hide her irritation.

'The day you arrived in Brazil. Despite all that Germaine Greer stuff you're so keen on, when Pedro left the apartment you meekly went off to the kitchen to wash up the coffee cups. I looked in your handbag then.'

Julia just looked at me before a smile escaped. 'I must have forgotten that I outrank you.'

'Your passport showed you had arrived in the US from Trinidad and Tobago, not from Canada as you said. Why had you lied? What was so important about Trinidad? Why had you been there twice within a few weeks? And then I remembered my predecessor, Roger Black, drowning there and everything clicked. Even your trip to Argentina, it was to investigate Andy Williams' death wasn't it?'

'Yes,' Julia replied with a smile. 'And you're wrong about Trinidad, Martines' villa is in Tobago.'

I took her hand.

'You'd better tell me about the mole in London. We both know it's not Mendale.'

XXIX

Before we left Rio de Janeiro Julia finally told me everything she knew about our mission. I had pretty well worked it all out in any case. Without needing to say anything we both chose to avoid any further discussion of the mission on the flight to Caracas or later over dinner. We would no doubt be going over it all again when the Deputy Director General, Adam Joseff, arrived in the Venezuelan capital next morning.

Instead we stuck to safe subjects like our tastes in music and food and the latest films. Not surprisingly we had both loved *The Day of the Jackal*. We wanted to believe it reflected the world we had entered although the latest James Bond, *Live and Let Die*, seemed a lot more fun. When we moved on to more personal topics Julia was not so forthcoming. She was happy to apply amateur psychoanalysis to my decision to attend a university hundreds of miles from home but much less happy when I tried to do the same to her decision to join the RAF. We reverted to travel and food. We discovered that we both enjoyed a whisky nightcap and happily finished the only single malt the hotel had to offer. After lingering for too long in the bar we made our way to our separate bedrooms with, at least for me, a sense that had I been more assertive the night might have ended differently.

I wanted to believe that Julia's feelings were moving in the same direction as mine but she still seemed to be holding something back. It never occurred to me that she might believe that I was the one holding back a secret.

I was still upset that it had taken her so long to tell me the whole story.

'I nearly told you, Thomas,' she had insisted. 'I was near it several times, when Mackenzie told me he'd rescued you at the villa and again after we'd rescued Pedro. I started telling you when we were listening to the radio bugs; it seemed so stupid to keep you in the dark after that business with Capitão Gomes at the apartment, but each time something interrupted us.'

We spent the next morning in the Venezuelan capital, one of the most beautifully situated cities in the world. 'Like Vancouver without the Pacific,' Julia had said, staring down on the city nestling amidst the green mountains.

Like all good tourists we'd gone up the Teleferico, the cable car, and marvelled at the network of superhighways enmeshing the city. 'Makes London look medieval,' Julia commented, pointing at the Avenida Cota Mil snaking along the thousand yard contour, north of the city, better than any urban road in Britain. It was not a comment anyone would make forty years later when Venezuela collapsed into chaos.

We'd had time to take in the sleek American-style office buildings, the spacious houses of the wealthy and, perched precariously on the hillsides, the redbrick and cardboard barrios of the poor. Then we had surprised ourselves by strolling hand in hand through the Parque del Este, a tropical Kew Gardens with a monkey house, before returning to the airport to wait for Joseff.

Now Caracas lay behind us, through a range of tree-covered mountains. In front of us 'MILITARY AIRCRAFT COMMAND' was emblazoned in black letters along the fuselage of a Hercules transport. The little US Air Force insignia was hidden amongst the jungle camouflage paint which made the plane curiously conspicuous against the sandy soil and blue Caribbean on the far side of Maiquetia International Airport. Huge tankers lay at anchor just offshore.

'Let's sit down,' Joseff suggested after he'd taken a stack of telegrams from an Embassy courier. I wasn't surprised to find Richard Mendale with him. The lounge by the immigration area was crowded so we went up to the restaurant and found a table where we couldn't be overheard. As usual Mendale said

256

nothing. Once Joseff had read through his telegrams he turned to me.

'Well, Thomas, you start. When did you realise what we were up to?'

It wasn't the opener I'd expected. I took my time in replying.

'Right from the beginning nothing rang true. More like a *Boy's Own* adventure story than real life. There's a Russian master spy on the loose in Holland and you send one of your newest recruits to help catch him. A super-secret gadget that can change the rules of modern warfare is stolen and again boy wonder is sent off to Toronto to bring the treasure home. I make a mess of that and am told to go to Brazil on my own and try again. I was being played for a sucker by all of you.'

'I wouldn't put it like that,' remonstrated Joseff, but I ignored him.

'But it wasn't just that you were playing me, somebody was playing you. When Watkins and I turned up in Zandvoort the men who attacked me were ready. Budermann was waiting for me at the airport in Chicago. And the story was repeated in Brazil. Whenever I sent a message to London, Martines and Nebulo seemed to know about it. When I told Pedro I had identified one of the auctioneers my room was bombed. I told Pedro about the men watching the villa and Budermann suddenly appeared and chased them off. When Gomes discovered Pedro's apartment I couldn't see how until Fitzwarren mentioned he'd given London Pedro's emergency number. That was the apartment phone, wasn't it?'

'Yes it was,' Joseff agreed. 'We shouldn't have let it be relayed back to Martines. We should have stopped it all then. There was enough to hang him. In fact, we should have pulled the plug when they tried to kill you. It never occurred to us that they would be mad enough to do something like that.'

'But you didn't pull the plug.'

'We needed the insurance,' Mendale said. 'If everything fell through in Brazil we needed to be able to start again. And we were right. Do you think Martines would have gone to Tobago if we'd shown our hand in London?'

'Let's get back to Thomas' story,' Joseff suggested. 'You knew there was a leak but you didn't know who in London was passing information on to Martines and Budermann.'

'It took me a long time,' I admitted. 'I imagined all sorts of horrible things, that Julia was the leak for example.'

'Yes, and you took a long time to rule me out,' she put in.

'It had to be someone in London but I didn't rule you out completely. You could have been working with someone there, your uncle.'

'The DG!' It was Joseff who interrupted. 'You can't be serious!'

'Why not? It was possible. The leaks started under his reign. But no, I soon dismissed that idea. And I dismissed the possibility that the leaks could be coming from Pedro. In some ways he was the most likely person for Martines to have recruited because he was local. And of course he lied about Mackenzie. But Pedro would have needed to be working with someone in London to get the information about Zandvoort and Chicago. That seemed unlikely. Although,' I added looking directly at Mendale, 'I nearly revised that when I discovered Pedro was in Warsaw with you.'

For a moment neither Joseff nor Mendale spoke and I rushed on. 'I was pretty sure I knew what was happening until Julia suddenly came out with all that stuff about your suspension.'

'She shouldn't have done that,' Mendale responded angrily. 'There was never an ounce of truth in the allegations. Even that ass Brasenose admits that now.'

'I know. When I thought about it Six had to be wrong. Julia said they suspected you of being a Russian mole, lurking for years within the DIS. I just couldn't relate that to Martines sitting in a villa in Brazil. Why would a Soviet mole pass information to Martines?'

Joseff merely nodded in the direction of Richard Mendale. 'We'll come back to the bigger picture later. You were talking about Pedro Vernon.'

'If Pedro was involved he would have alerted Martines and Nebulo as soon as I found the Villa Nhambiquaras, but that clearly didn't happen. He told London, but because of the time difference the message wasn't passed back to Martines. I knew that Pedro was

258

on my side, and because he was clearly working with Mackenzie, it was plain he too was on my side. But I also knew that I couldn't tell Pedro everything because he would relay it to London.'

'Every way I turned I kept coming back to the same question: what was I doing in Brazil? Indeed what was anyone from British Intelligence doing there? Apparently the Griffin Interrogator is such a valuable piece of equipment that the Russians will pay a fortune to get it and the Americans will pay a fortune to stop that happening. So why involve us? We simply aren't in the same league. The only reason we were included was so that I could keep an eye on what was happening and report back to someone in London. To make it easy for me I was even given the names of the Russian and American agents. Why would anybody introduce that level of complexity? Why give the Americans two of the cover names we had used in Chicago? Somebody was trying to be too clever by half. They were introducing risks that didn't need to be there. The whole operation was ridiculous and that pointed me in one direction. There's only one person I know in London who has that sort of mind. Group Captain Watkins.'

One of the half dozen Avensa jet prop planes outside burst into life.

'You seem to have got it all,' said Joseff. 'I'll explain it from our angle.'

He pushed his tea away before continuing. 'You said the first operation to go wrong was Richard's in Warsaw. But there was a post-mortem on that op, everything was crawled over. We found nothing. So we moved on to the next occasion something went seriously wrong, the gunrunning in Trinidad. We hadn't really thought too much about young Black's death at first. It was odd. He drowned at Sans Souci which is well known to be dangerous for swimming. He must have passed safer beaches, Balandra Bay for example, and Mission. But we didn't do anything. Watkins and Williams were on the spot and both reported against foul play. And in any case shortly after Six's man Koenig was blown in Berlin and we had our hands full with that. We had no reason to connect the two events.

'Next,' continued Joseff, 'Six lost a man in the Far East. He just disappeared. A local who was selling them information about the Philippine insurgents' arms supplies, information Six had passed on to us. Again we didn't connect it with Black or Koenig. But then came the Lechlade business. You remember the American who approached us with reports the CIA had decided not to share with us. We agreed to buy them but the Company eventually tumbled him. It caused a hell of a stink not only with the Americans but with Six because we hadn't told them. We couldn't understand how the Company had found out what we were doing. Then at a meeting in Washington someone let slip that Mark Volmar had received a commendation for his part in unmasking Lechlade. Now why would the CIA Station Chief in Rio de Janeiro be involved in something that happened in London and had absolutely nothing to do with Latin America? Now we know the answer.'

'Martines had blown Lechlade to them,' Julia interposed. 'So Thomas was right. The Company had bought information from Martines before. That's why Conniston was willing to believe everything the auctioneers had told them about the events in Chicago.'

'Quite,' said Joseff. 'Now we started to realise what was happening. Somebody in the Department was leaking information. But there was nothing ideological; he was selling it to the Russians, Americans, Philippine guerrillas, whoever would buy it. So we went back over things again, including Black's death. Then Andy Williams, who'd been on the mission with Black, died in Buenos Aires in rather odd circumstances. And just before he was due to come home where we were going to question him about Black's death, as we'd just questioned Watkins. Williams was an old hand, former Naval Intelligence, and the DG had known him since they were at the Royal Naval College together. So he sent Julia down there to investigate.'

'As I told you yesterday Williams died in a tea shop, right in the middle of Buenos Aires,' Julia said. 'I discovered from his diary that he'd been going to meet somebody called Hector Bunge. And from a waiter we got a description we later discovered exactly fitted Budermann. I think we can be sure Williams was murdered, probably some hyoscine derivative.'

'Julia provided the crucial evidence that linked all this together,' Joseff explained. 'She discovered why Williams was going to meet Budermann. He was looking for information that Watkins had asked him to find.'

'But information for which,' Mendale interrupted impatiently, 'Watkins had absolutely no need.'

There was a moment's silence.

'So at last we arrived at Watkins,' Joseff said. 'But it was all circumstantial, just as it had been in Richard's case and we'd already wasted an enormous amount of time on that. In addition we couldn't pounce at once because we wanted more, accomplices perhaps. And we thought we might turn him round, use him to pump phoney information to the opposition. Julia went to Trinidad and soon realised that Watkins, Black and Williams had come a lot closer to finding the gunrunners they were after than Watkins had reported. In fact, of course, they found them. But instead of grabbing them Watkins swapped sides and started feeding them information which Martines sold to whoever would buy it. Black was presumably killed because he knew too much.'

'And they killed Williams for the same reason?'

'We presume so. He must have known something he didn't realise was important. Or perhaps Watkins was just being cautious.'

'I have a different theory about Roger Black,' I interrupted. 'Just a guess really, I think Black identified Martines.'

The others looked mystified and I barged on. 'Black's mother was a DP.'

Julia still looked confused. 'DP?'

'Displaced Person,' Joseff explained. 'After the war there were hundreds of thousands of people across Europe with nowhere to go. We set up DP camps for women and children whose towns and villages had been wiped off the map, East European refugees mainly, and of course concentration camp survivors.'

'Exactly, and I suspect Black's mother was one of those survivors. You remember when the DG suggested I try to find out what an

Israeli team might have been doing in America by going through the war crimes files. I noticed that the only person who seemed to have paid those files any attention was Roger Black. According to the library log he spent a lot of time combing through them, but I couldn't see why.'

'We'll never know,' said Joseff. 'But if he came across a photo of Martines and then saw him in Tobago he could have approached him and been killed as a result.'

'Or he might have told Watkins who might have spotted an opportunity. If Watkins tried to blackmail Martines that could have opened the door to something even more profitable, selling our secrets through Martines to anyone who would pay for them.'

'It all makes sense,' Julia said. 'Miranda Gonçalves said that Martines had been acting differently recently, he had lost his old confidence. She talked about him waking up screaming about a black man.'

'Roger Black?'

'Perhaps,' concluded Joseff, 'if he thought his past was catching up with him he might have started to crack. But like I said, we will probably never know.'

'So once you had identified Watkins you still let him organise the operation in Zandvoort,' I said. 'That doesn't make sense.'

'But we didn't set up the Zandvoort operation,' Joseff explained. 'That was always a Six enterprise. None of this has been a DIS op. We were allowed in on sufferance. For Six this wasn't about the Griffin Interrogator, it was about catching the Russian agent Samovar. And in normal circumstances that would have been purely a Six operation.'

'So why did they involve us?'

'Because the Russians were mounting an operation with Samovar which they called Project Ann Arbor, and Ann Arbor happened to be where the Americans had just lost their Griffin Interrogator. Getting intelligence on that was absolutely DIS territory. They were obliged to involve us. That's when everything started to get complicated and when things get complicated they go wrong.'

Mendale took over. 'The DG and Brasenose at Six had common objectives. The DG wanted Griffin, Six wanted Samovar and they both needed to establish the truth about Watkins. Even Brasenose had started to realise that if I wasn't their Russian mole it could have been Watkins who had blown their man Koenig.'

'But we still didn't realise someone like Martines was involved,' put in Joseff. 'We thought Watkins was dealing for himself. We looked at the things that had gone wrong. If you accept that Warsaw was an accident, nothing to do with Richard here, then like I said the first mishap within the DIS was the business in Trinidad and Tobago. We reasoned that if Watkins had been bought off there a line would have been crossed, from then on he would have no qualms about selling his country's secrets. There was a lot of money to be made by selling the Koenig material to the Russians, Lechlade to the Americans and who knows what else.

'So the DG and Brasenose concocted a plan. They would appear to put Watkins in charge of grabbing Samovar in Zandvoort and see if he tried to contact the Russians or perhaps try to warn Samovar directly. We put him under surveillance and tapped his phone as we thought that was the only way he could communicate with anyone in a hurry. But we were wrong. He visited a bar in Dean Street and we now know he slipped a note to Gadd. The tail we had on him simply missed it. Then we arrived in Zandvoort and things really went wrong.'

Joseff paused and asked if anyone wanted another tea or coffee. Without saying anything Julia stood and took our orders, giving me a wry smile as Joseff continued.

'The idea was that if we were wrong about Watkins, if he could be trusted, then you would all follow Samovar from the dead-letter drop and find out what he was up to. If on the other hand Watkins warned Kardosov off, Six had two backup teams in place. They would take over. But we had made the mistake of ignoring the weather forecast. The back-up team that was supposed to be watching you and Jacobs lost you in the mist. That wouldn't have mattered if your radio had been working. Six were listening in, except that they weren't because nobody could hear you. Kardosov got away.

'When he turned up in Toronto, Six were happy to let the RCMP Security Service take over. If The Cowboys managed to find Samovar, or Kardosov as we were now calling him, they would ship him back to London. But he gave them the slip and crossed over into the US. That generated what might be considered a little interdepartmental friction. The Canadians were all gungho, but, as you know, Six didn't want anything to do with poaching on US territory. Brasenose was very close to telling the Americans what Kardosov was doing in Chicago when you and Miss French retrieved the situation. Well done on that.'

Mendale nodded his grudging agreement before adding, 'But then you lost the bloody Interrogator.'

Joseff was not going to be interrupted. 'It never occurred to us that Watkins would be able to intercept you in Chicago. We thought you would give him the Griffin at Heathrow and then he would somehow contrive to lose it. Five had a team at the airport watching your arrival. But then you turned up without the Griffin.'

'And despite that failure you decided to send me to Brazil.'

'Not our idea,' put in Mendale. 'Only one person's been pushing you. Watkins. He insisted you accompany him to Zandvoort. Then when the DG decided not to risk letting Watkins himself go to Canada he pushed you forward again. And then of course the auction in Brazil comes up, a mission for which frankly you are entirely unsuitable, and Watkins wants you on it again.'

'So I could be his spy on the spot. Not only would I keep an eye on the Americans and Russians, but if Martines or Nebulo suddenly changed the arrangements for the auction without telling him he would learn about it from me. And he chose me precisely because I'm the new boy with no experience and no training.'

'That's right,' agreed Joseff. 'And we couldn't risk him thinking otherwise. That's why we couldn't tell you about our suspicions. I wanted your reports, your actions to be perfectly natural. You're an analyst, not what the Americans would call a spook, you've no tradecraft. That's one of the reasons Watkins was so keen to involve you, you've had no operational training. Watkins wanted you there just to observe, not to do anything, that's why he gave you those names. It never occurred to him that you might identify Martines or Budermann. Like you said he thought he was being clever and you're absolutely right: the whole idea was nonsensical.'

'But Watkins thought like that,' suggested Mendale. 'You remember his Vietnam project? Everything he touched was just too clever, one too many triple-agent, one extra twist.'

'No doubt as well,' said Joseff, 'he thought that Martines and Nebulo would be less likely to double-cross him if he had his man in Rio. He never trusted anyone.'

I was going to respond but Joseff was determined not to be distracted from his story.

'We had to put a lot of pieces together. Go back to the beginning. Forget that nonsense we told you about not telling the Dutch anything. They'd found the body in the canal near Zandvoort before you were back home. The photos you took of him at the station drop came out well incidentally. By the time Watkins returned we had the body identified as one Nicholas Peniter, recently released from Parkhurst. He'd been in for armed robbery and GBH.

'Remember at this stage Julia had finished in Argentina but Six still weren't convinced that Watkins was the leak. Or rather Brasenose didn't believe he was the only leak. We started to investigate Peniter's acquaintances and discovered that Peniter had been in Holland with another old lag by the name of Gadd. When Five followed up on Gadd's movements they worked out how he and Watkins had set up the operation in Zandvoort. But how had Watkins set up the attack on you in Chicago? That was way out of Gadd's league. How was Watkins communicating with whoever now had the Griffin Interrogator?

'We kept an eye on Watkins but we couldn't risk letting the surveillance get too close in case he spotted it. It turned up nothing. But what if Watkins had another accomplice, someone he could talk to every day without raising any suspicions? Someone who could then pass his messages on. Richard had one person in mind. It was a theory nobody else shared.'

'Yes,' said Mendale with no hint of a smile. 'I had one person in mind.'

He looked straight at me.

'You.'

I looked at Mendale in total disbelief.

'You suspected me of working with Watkins! After I'd just killed someone in Zandvoort!'

'What better cover? You said you'd killed him; the Dutch reckoned it could have been an accident. Anyway, Adam thought you were the one person in Watkins' section we could trust, I thought the opposite. So we decided to keep you under observation. If I was right you might incriminate yourself.'

'We couldn't pick up Gadd without warning Watkins,' said Joseff. 'We had to be cautious and rule nothing out. There was no need to bring you fully into the picture. It's standard.'

'Adam's putting a gloss on it,' put in Mendale unexpectedly. 'I ballsed up. Not my finest hour. Paranoia everywhere. You just smelled wrong. Your recruitment. No service background. You come to us courtesy of Six: when have they ever done us any favours? You follow Watkins round like a lapdog. He pushes you into missions you shouldn't be on. You take on two armed men in Holland and incredibly not only escape but kill one of them. Then you lose the Interrogator in Chicago. Finally, to cap it all, you turn out to have contacts in Brazil – Brazil of all places. Not only that but contacts we don't know anything about because you didn't mention either of the women in your initial vetting.'

What he meant by 'either of the women' I didn't know but I let that pass.

'I didn't trust you at all,' Mendale continued. 'And in Brazil it got worse. Your actions were more than bizarre. Somebody puts a bomb in your room so do you immediately contact Pedro, or even call London? No, you drive out to Martines' villa to check a phone tap. The next night you're nearly killed again and you just drive home and go to bed!'

'I was tired!'

Mendale looked at me as if I were mad. Perhaps I was, but I also remembered that at the time I was in no mood to trust anyone.

'Not even Julia really trusted me,' I said.

'She was under instructions. And of course, the less you knew the less you could tell if you were caught.'

There was nothing to say to that.

'Watkins did have an accomplice,' Mendale observed. 'We found out just before we left London. His secretary, Judy.'

'I don't believe it!'

'Not in the way you think. He gave her his coded messages and she'd go out and phone them to a retired Signals major named Newby in Tonbridge, a radio "ham", who'd forward them to Brazil. Watkins had told both Judy and Major Newby that they were helping a secret operation to uncover a leak in the Department. Incredibly they believed him.'

'Now Dick,' interjected Adam Joseff, 'don't be rude about Major Newby. He saved you.' Joseff turned to me. 'Watkins had given instructions that no copies were to be kept of his messages but the dear Major ignored him, apparently he thought it would be fun to try deciphering one of them himself. He failed but the boys and girls in Cheltenham succeeded. It contained intelligence from Six, intelligence that had come directly from Koenig. Watkins had passed it to Martines who sold it to the Russians.'

Mendale gave one of the very few smiles I ever saw on his face. 'Even Brasenose had to admit then that I wasn't the Russian mole he'd imagined. And now Brasenose is in a hole. He should never have promised the Americans access to our supposed Russian defector in Warsaw. When Six couldn't deliver they looked stupid. That was made worse when the material Six had been supplying from Koenig dried up. Six need to get back on to Washington's Christmas card list, they need a win, if necessary at our expense.'

Joseff looked as if he was going to disagree but decided to be diplomatic. 'There are some sensitivities here we all need to bear in mind. We must remember our primary objective is Watkins.'

'And the Griffin Interrogator,' I put in.

'No, Thomas. As I said our objective is Watkins. I know the DG was determined to ensure that the Royal Navy had access to the Interrogator but that is no longer our primary objective. There is a bigger picture here. As Richard has indicated, relations between Six and the Americans have been a little tense. It is in everyone's interest that good relations are restored. Quite correctly therefore Justin Brasenose wants to ensure that the Griffin Interrogator is returned to US custody. If we can find it the Interrogator will be immediately handed over to the Americans. Naturally this is to be effected in such a way that both Six and the DIS receive the maximum credit.'

Having nearly been killed trying to get hold of the Interrogator I was shocked. 'After everything that's happened we're just going to give it away?'

I looked at Julia for support but she merely smiled.

'You weren't in Rio to get the Interrogator,' said Joseff. 'Six wouldn't have allowed that. At first they didn't want you sent to Rio at all. It's American territory and Brasenose didn't want you queering their pitch. But for the DG the deaths of Black and Williams has become a matter of honour, he wants their killers caught. Brasenose and the DG met and reached an agreement. You would be sent to Rio but only because that might provide intelligence that Six could pass on to the CIA. Watkins wanted you to report back on what the Americans and Russians were up to. We were banking on the fact that to do that he would need to make sure you knew their names and perhaps how the exchange would be managed.'

'We wanted you to do exactly what I told you to do at the House of Lords,' interrupted Mendale. I wasn't sure whether he was angry or merely sarcastic. 'Stick close to the Russians. You were supposed to observe and report, that's all. Nobody expected you to try to steal the bloody thing. I thought we had left The Cowboys behind in Canada. Why the hell the DG told Pedro to give you a gun heaven knows.'

'If he hadn't done I'd have been dead,' I protested.

'Perhaps. Or if you weren't armed you might not have been tempted to go blundering around,' Mendale retorted.

Before I had a chance to respond Julia snapped back at him. 'You have a lot to learn about Thomas. Without him where would we be?'

Joseff waved us all to be quiet. 'It was on the basis that you, Thomas, would merely observe and report back that Brasenose agreed to your being sent to Brazil,' said Joseff more calmly. 'And that's why Conniston agreed to you being there. But then you identified the auctioneers and at your request Pedro even asked Six's man in Brazil, Harrison, for equipment to tap their phone. Nobody expected you to do that. Brasenose couldn't make up his mind what to do. Should he tell the Americans what you had discovered right away and let them go charging in or should he wait to see if we could get hold of the Griffin Interrogator ourselves and then present it to the Americans on a plate? As it turns out he waited too long. Somehow Conniston found out about the exchange himself.'

'Miranda Gonçalves must have told him,' I suggested.

'I don't think so,' said Julia. 'She didn't know anything about the exchange. Brasenose must have told him. No doubt Harrison found out where the exchange was taking place from Mackenzie and told London. But by the time the message got through to Brasenose, and Brasenose had decided he had to tell Conniston what was going on, it was too late to intercept Martines at the villa. So the American cavalry came charging in at the last minute.'

'Let's hope we can now retrieve the situation,' concluded Joseff.

Joseff then repeated what Julia had already told me. She had been in Trinidad when she was summoned to Chicago and had become convinced that whoever was working with Watkins had a bolthole there. But she couldn't find it. She had returned to the island again after the debriefing in London and found a lead that pointed towards Tobago. 'You know of course that the two islands form one republic,' Joseff added in his schoolmasterly way.

'We still don't know where on Tobago Martines has his retreat,' Julia said.

'We may now,' said Joseff. 'We hope Watkins will have led us to it.'

'Watkins is there now! You let him leave London?' I couldn't believe it.

'Of course. We want everything wrapped up before the Americans trace Martines to Tobago. Justin Brasenose is already there.'

'So Six are involved again?'

'Of course,' said Mendale bitterly. 'They're always involved.'

Joseff wasn't rising to that. 'We're not fighting old battles Richard. The Secret Intelligence Service has primary jurisdiction in matters such as this and that is entirely correct.'

Mendale was not going to back down. 'Two DIS officers have been murdered and there has been an attempt on the life of a third. But instead of helping us catch the men responsible Six have been pursuing a vendetta against me to hide their own foul-up in Warsaw.'

'We're all on the same side Richard, let's not forget that. Finish your coffees everyone. We leave in ten minutes: LAV Aeropostal, to Trinidad via Porlamar. We have a man in Tobago, he'll let us know if Martines has the airport there under observation. If he does we'll have to go over to Tobago by boat.'

'Martines is in Tobago already?' I asked.

'Yes. He, Budermann and Gadd arrived there yesterday evening. Apparently Martines arrived on a stretcher. I'm not surprised, the route they took to get here would have exhausted anyone. As far as we can tell they flew from Rio to the Iguazu Falls, crossed into Argentina, flew down to Buenos Aires and then back up here. They arrived at Maiquetia last night and chartered a plane to Trinidad. Pity we didn't get here a few hours earlier.'

'Christ, they had that well planned.'

'They certainly did. One of the telegrams I received just now was from Harrison in Rio. He reckons they were on a chartered plane leaving Belo Horizonte for Iguazu by the time you had your meeting with the Israelis.'

'What else did he say?' Julia asked. 'How's Pedro? When we left last night he still looked pretty groggy.'

'He seems to be recovering well,' Joseff replied. 'He and Harrison have been busy. They've spoken to Volmar, the CIA Chief of Station down there, and to somebody in the military. They both seem to have been surprisingly forthcoming. Apparently Martines' car, the Mercedes 770, was found in Nova Friburgo around noon. The army concentrated their search there and it wasn't until the early hours of this morning that they found Budermann's Ford near Belo Horizonte Airport and discovered their birds had literally flown away. The Americans are now searching Buenos Aires. It's only by working back from this end that we've managed to work out how Martines got here.'

'But the Americans will get on to them,' Mendale said. 'We can expect Conniston or some of his friends here at any time now.'

'What about Nebulo?'

'He was wounded. We don't know how badly. The Army have him and they probably won't treat him too gently. They owe the Americans a lot and this is one way they can show their good faith. I suspect that various generals have been itching to get rid of Nebulo for some time.'

'The next time we see his name,' said Mendale, 'will probably be on one of those lists of political prisoners that Amnesty International keep putting out.'

'It seems to have been a bloody affair,' Joseff continued. 'Gomes is dead, along with one of his men and one of Martines' servants. The other servant is seriously wounded. One soldier killed, two wounded, including an officer, and Conniston hit in the shoulder.'

'And the Russians,' Julia asked, 'Abdel Rassem, Bitri and the one Thomas shot?'

'Bitri was picked up unconscious, and Abdel Rassem was found half an hour later, he tried escaping on foot. They were immediately deported; it seems the Brazilians don't want an international incident. The other man has been identified as a Brazilian Communist named,' Joseff referred to a telegram, 'Luiz Colombo. Thomas killed him outright which is a lot better way to go than the way he'd have died if the military had caught him.'

'That about wraps it up,' said Mendale.

Joseff started to get up from the table but remembered something else. 'Here,' he said, 'we thought it better to use fresh

271

identities. You are Mr and Mrs Reed. In Tobago you will need to share a room, but,' he looked in Julia's direction, 'I am sure we can rely on Thomas's sense of propriety.'

'But can he rely on mine?' she responded.

Joseff looked mildly shocked, the swinging sixties had clearly passed him by. He checked that nobody was watching and passed over our new documents. Then I led the way to the Aeropostal desk.

'We'd better not stick together at the other end,' Mendale said, 'in case Martines has someone watching the airport.'

It seemed an unnecessary precaution but Julia and I had no objection to being left alone on the plane. We sat sipping at the little plastic cups of coffee that a hostess, chosen in those days primarily for her youth and beauty, brought round immediately after take-off.

In no time at all we descended again towards the island of Margarita and the city of Porlamar. A large red sign affirmed that we had landed at the 'Aeropuerto Internacional del Caribe'. The plane was emptier when we took off and headed once more over the Caribbean.

Piarco International Airport, Trinidad, looked surprised at the arrival of our plane and the stifling heat tried to push us back into the aircraft. We had to walk halfway round the airport terminal, something that took about one minute, before arriving in the small hall occupied by the Immigration and Health Authorities.

The formalities were brief, just an inspection of passports, smallpox certificates and immigration forms, but the waiting seemed endless in the overpowering heat. A group of identically dressed Venezuelan teenagers in front of us hadn't filled in the immigration forms we'd been given on the plane, so everybody else had to wait while they did so. It was too hot to be angry. We melted in silence, and once through with it all, stood in front of a huge fan to resolidify.

Justin Brasenose waved us over when we had passed customs. With him was another man introduced as Captain York. Brasenose shook hands without comment.

York led us to a small café near the Tobago departure gate and ordered six iced drinks. 'Right now all our birds are in one nest.

Watkins stayed at the Mount Irvine Hotel last night. This morning he went to the house that Martines has rented. We presume he'll go back to the hotel tonight. He's booked in for a fortnight's holiday at the end of which, presumably, he expects to return to London with nobody any the wiser.'

He sipped at his drink, a tall slim man in T-shirt and jeans. Only his very short hair made him stand out. 'We've got a house near the airport in Tobago. Here's the phone number.' He passed a card across to Joseff. 'We thought it best if you stayed in Trinidad, sir, in case anything goes wrong and we have to fix things with the local authorities. You're booked into the Hilton.'

'All right,' replied Joseff. 'I'm not a field man these days. What's the plan for the rest of you?'

'We'll go over to Tobago by air, the only surveillance at the airport is ours. The intention is to do nothing until just before first light tomorrow. The Navy had a ship, *Minerva*, in Bridgetown and it will be right off the coast opposite Martines' place at dawn. We must have Griffin and any prisoners we want ready. We'll have a couple of motorboats and there'll be time for one trip out to the ship. There's no way we can persuade the Navy to hang around. *Minerva* sails fifteen minutes after first light. It will be halfway to Grenada before the locals catch a scent of what's happening.'

'What about Watkins?' I asked. 'He may be at the hotel. How do we get him?'

York looked away uncertainly. 'I understand Major Mendale will be dealing with that.'

Mendale looked faintly embarrassed, but whether at York's remark or the unaccustomed use of his military rank I couldn't tell. 'We don't want Watkins back in London,' he said, 'it could be rather embarrassing. Something along the lines of young Black's misadventure will have to be arranged. It's my responsibility.'

York broke the silence that followed. 'Let's go, we'll discuss the details later. I've got tickets for us all, including you Mr Joseff, in case you thought it best to come along. My man Surl will meet us at the airport. Major Mendale and Mr Brasenose can stay at our house near Crown Point.' He looked at Julia and me. 'Mr and Mrs Reed

273

will be staying at the Turtle Beach Hotel; we'll visit you tonight. The road to the Turtle Beach passes by Martines' villa but too far away for anyone to recognise you in a taxi.'

Just to be on the safe side York furnished us with two appalling straw hats and told us to keep our sunglasses on. Then we bade farewell to Joseff. An old DC7 was waiting for us, an enormous hummingbird painted on its tail.

I glanced at my watch. Nine days ago to the minute I'd been standing on Haarlem Station waiting for a Russian homosexual who would set all this in motion.

The plane clanged into life. We could see the young, gum-chewing American pilot fiddling with the controls and then Miss Ramsingh smiled her stewardess smile, proffered sweets and we were off.

'This is a perfect place for Martines,' Julia said, 'sea and sun. Trinidad just seven miles from the Venezuelan coast and Tobago not much further but off the beaten track.'

'You're right. Perhaps we should stay on for a few days once this is all over.'

Julia smiled. 'I thought you would be wanting to get back to Brazil. To see your friend in São Paulo.'

Now it was my turn to smile. So Pedro had reported back on the gossip he had picked up from Jenny Merchant. That's what Mendale had meant when he referred to the two women in Brazil that I hadn't mentioned in my initial vetting, Jenny and a very old flame.

'That was all over a long time ago.'

'Really. Then I think perhaps we might stay on.'

XXX

We came in over the sea, smoothly on to the runway. To the right was a white house surrounded by coconut palms. Goats and a couple of herons were feeding beside an old steamroller in the garden. The plane clawed to a halt as the runway ended beside the sea; the pilot seemed to be taking us for a paddle to cool down. Then he turned left to the miniature terminal building, 'Crown Point' in white across its green corrugated roof, and the tiny control tower with its solitary radar bowl.

'We leave separately,' York whispered as he moved towards the door. 'Expect us at the Turtle Beach at nine o'clock. You're booked in for a week.'

We'd hardly left the plane when we were grabbed by a young Tobagonian who announced that his name was Bartholomew and that he had the finest taxi on the island. As he collected our luggage I noticed York introducing Mendale to a broad-shouldered West Indian in his early thirties. They glanced in our direction but showed no sign of recognition.

Bartholomew led us to the island's finest taxi. It was an amazing British-made Ford barely recognisable beneath a welter of extra chrome and plastic. An enormous chrome angel with orange plastic wings sat on the front while windmills, like children's toys or anemometers, whirled round the dumpy radio aerial. 'TOURISM BENEFITS ALL' proclaimed a faded sticker on the rear bumper.

'Newlyweds?' Bartholomew asked.

We tried to look sheepish as we confirmed his guess.

'You've come to the right place,' he told us.

'We're sure of that.'

York hadn't provided us with a map or told us exactly where Martines had his sanctuary so I tried to memorise the route from the airport to the hotel in case we needed it next morning. First out of the airport, right, away from the road to Pigeon Point. Past a National petrol station; Adina's Inn; prefabricated bungalows, 'Government housing,' Bartholomew told us; the Bon Accord Nutrition Unit; George Street; Robert Street; the 'Night Beat' restaurant and bar; St Cyr Street; an enormous advert proclaiming, 'GUINNESS, YOU KNOW IT'S GOOD'. Then left off the road to Scarborough, the island's capital, on to Shirvan Road, between the racecourse and a coconut plantation. A narrow road through houses past the Everyday Café. There were goats in the road and coconut palms everywhere. More government housing, little grey buildings too close together.

And then away from the sea past the Mount Irvine Golf Course. There was little chance that Watkins could be playing golf but Julia pulled down her hat and I could feel the pressure of her hand on my knee.

We passed French Turtlers Private Road and the Mount Irvine beach. Beside the road an old tractor rusted away, slowly being overgrown with vegetation. 'SLOW DEPRESSION 40 YARDS AHEAD' a sign said, the road bending beside the sea past a beautiful sandy beach. 'A BEER IS A CARIB' proclaimed another sign. Black Rock Government School was followed by the town of Black Rock itself. We wound downhill through the houses, many raised above the ground on stilts, then over a bridge, round a sharp bend and there before us lay the palm trees and tennis courts of the Turtle Beach Hotel.

The hotel was strung along the beach. The rooms, in white igloo-shaped clusters of four, stretched away from the thatched bar and the central administration complex. The dining area and bar opened on to a garden of colourful flowers and bright green grass.

Our room was superbly situated, away from the central block and looking out over the Caribbean through a fringe of palms.

'Twin beds,' commented Julia.

'Can't win them all,' I replied. 'The place is built for Americans; they don't believe in double beds.'

'Well I do.'

We managed to prove it didn't matter. When we emerged from our room the sunset was being blackened by hundreds of pelicans, diving Stuka-like at the sea, then lumbering back into the air. We watched them hanging on a wing, then spearing into the water as we strolled to the bar.

We'd finished our meal by the time York, Brasenose and Mendale arrived with the West Indian we'd seen at the airport.

'Sorry we're late,' Mendale boomed. 'Bloody Navy wanted every last detail approved by London.'

York interrupted quickly, as if afraid of being overheard. 'Let's go to your room, we can sort things out there.'

'You haven't met Clive Surl,' he added as we walked across the lawn, carefully avoiding the frogs.

'Don't be misled by appearances,' grinned the tall black man. 'I'm from Birmingham. Captain York brought me to add some local colour.'

Surl's handshake was strong and commanding. When we reached our room it was he who outlined the plan.

He jabbed his finger at the map York had unfolded. 'Martines has a house right here, under the "R" in Black Rock. The plan's simple. We've got two cars. I'll leave you mine tonight. Just before dawn you park here,' he pointed at the map again, 'out of sight, and walk along the beach. Major Mendale, Captain York and Mr Brasenose will park on the Crown Point side and we'll meet in front of the house. Our primary objective here is Griffin. I'll have two small motorboats and we'll use one to take Griffin out to the ship. Mr Brasenose will go with it. In no circumstances will the Navy land on the island.'

'Too bloody worried about creating an incident,' interjected Mendale.

'Right. If we can grab the men who stole Griffin as well we will do so and put them on the *Minerva*. Above all we don't want any bodies lying around for the locals to find so if there are any they go into the sea.'

'What's the opposition?'

277

'Gadd and Budermann as you know, and two or three local people. One, from his accent, is Jamaican. We haven't identified him but it probably doesn't matter because he went over to Trinidad tonight on the last plane. The other two are Trinidadians. Both with criminal records. They were mixed up with Black Power but apparently not for political reasons. They're used as guards. If they're awake they'll be armed with Colt Commando submachine guns, not much good for hand to hand combat. We should be able to get that close before they know we're around. There are no dogs. I've left a pair of silenced nine millimetre Brownings and knives in the boot of my car for you.'

'What about Martines himself?'

'We don't have to worry about him. He was carried off the plane looking like death warmed up. And Watkins should be safely in his hotel. We'll worry about him afterwards.'

We discussed the plan for another thirty minutes. Surl drew a sketch of our target. Martines had a fair-sized place with no other habitations within earshot. There was no wall surrounding it and there should be no difficulty getting into the house. The problem was that we didn't have long to find Griffin once we got in there. Brasenose insisted that we had to locate Griffin even if that meant staying in the house while HMS *Minerva* steamed away. He would take it home by air, he said, hoping to get out of the country before the local authorities discovered that anything was amiss. Providing the raid passed off quietly, that shouldn't be too difficult.

Surl gave me the keys to his car before leaving. Julia and I retired to bed, prepared for an early rise.

It was still dark next morning when we parked the car a few yards from the row of palm trees lining the beach. We made the rendezvous in front of the house with five minutes to spare after checking that there were no guards lurking in the grounds on our side of the house. Mendale and York were already there.

'All clear?'

'Yes. No sign of anybody.'

'Check the front,' Mendale ordered.

Cautiously I made my way round the house. Beside the front door there was a dim, very small, pinkish light that occasionally glowed bright red: the end of a cigarette. As I returned to the other three we were joined by Surl and Brasenose, rowing ashore, the noise of their oars completely lost in the sounds of the sea.

'There's a man at the front,' I reported.

'OK. You and Clive take him out. We'll go in through the back exactly two minutes from now.'

It took us less than a minute to move around to the front of the house, Surl moving ahead in total silence. We knelt about fifteen yards from the house, beneath a palm. There was no sign of the guard.

'Perhaps he's gone inside,' I whispered.

'No, I see him. To the left, sitting down.'

I strained my eyes but still couldn't see anything.

'Should be easy,' Surl continued. 'Keep along the wall of the house below window level. Just follow me. Leave it to the Marines as they say. OK, twenty-five seconds.'

He glanced at the dial of his luminous watch.

'Now.' He disappeared, without a sound. I prepared to follow and froze as a light flashed in front of me. But it was just the guard lighting another cigarette, exactly where Surl said he was. It was one of the two Trinidadians. We were almost on top of him before he noticed us. He suddenly swung around, rising from his chair, but too late. Two quick blows from Surl and he was out cold.

The front door was unlocked. Without a word we entered. There was no light, but Surl moved surefootedly towards the back of the house, with me at his heels clutching my Browning automatic. Julia, Mendale, Brasenose and York were standing by a doorway, York with a torch in his hand.

'Everything OK?' he asked.

'Yeah. The guard's unconscious.'

'So's the other one. He was asleep in there.' York pointed his torch into a small bedroom. 'Let's get upstairs. Julia, you stay in here in case one of these two wakes up or a neighbour drops in for a friendly chat.'

The rest of us followed Surl, me on his heels, Mendale and Brasenose behind, and York bringing up the rear, carefully screening the beam of his torch. The upstairs were arranged on an 'L' pattern, with the stairs in the apex. Surl pointed at the nearest door and tried the knob. It opened silently.

The shutters on the two windows hadn't been closed and the first, feint light of dawn crept over the horizon and stole into the room. Gadd lay on a huge double bed, shirtless but still wearing trousers and socks. He must have been half awake for as Surl reached him he lashed out wildly, knocking an almost empty whisky bottle and a lamp on to the marble floor. The sound of the crash seemed to echo through the house. Before he could do anything else Surl jabbed his knife towards Gadd's throat.

'Easy man. You ain't going anywhere.'

Gadd glared at him and said nothing. Surl pulled him up, not too gently. 'Now you just lead us to friend Budermann's room.'

Gadd staggered out of the room, pausing at the sight of the rest of us. Then he pushed past me into the other arm of the 'L' and stood outside the door nearest to the stairs.

'Go on in,' Surl commanded. As Gadd turned the door handle there was the sound of a door opening behind us. We all spun around. In the beam of York's torch stood Watkins, emerging from the room next to Gadd's. York was the more surprised. Before he could do anything the nine millimetre Steyr pistol in Watkins' hand spat flame and noise and lead and York's torch tumbled to the floor as he was whipped back against the stairs and fell headfirst towards Julia. Watkins ducked back but before I could register what was happening my eardrums were blasted again and Gadd rocketed into me, a stream of submachine gun fire continuing to smash into his inert body through Budermann's door.

Chest high, I registered. Budermann was firing chest high. And then Surl's feet were smashing against the door above the handle and I was into the room on my belly as the door opened.

Budermann was standing by the bed, naked except for his pants. Before he could lower his aim I fired and missed but Surl didn't and Budermann crumpled on to the bed.

Watkins had disappeared but Mendale was after him. 'Find Martines,' he shouted in my direction as he and Brasenose raced towards the end of the corridor.

Martines was in the first room I entered but he wasn't going to cause any problems. I didn't need to feel his ice-cold wrist to realise he was dead. He at least had died peacefully.

'Heart attack,' Julia said, joining me. 'Come on.'

Mendale had disappeared down the backstairs and out towards the beach. We raced after him. As we approached the sea a motorboat started up. We emerged through the palms to see Watkins dressed in his pyjamas standing at the boat's helm incongruously waving a briefcase. Mendale and Brasenose stood guns drawn about twenty-five or thirty feet away from him.

'No closer,' shouted Watkins, 'or Griffin's gone.'

I realised that with his free hand he was holding a hand grenade beside the briefcase. Where on earth had that come from?

Brasenose was clearly trying to reason with him.

'You'll never be able to hide. Give me Griffin and we'll come to an arrangement.'

Suddenly Watkins' shirt front erupted in red as Mendale pumped one, two, three shots into a three-inch circle centred on his heart. Almost instantaneously there was a shattering explosion and the briefcase disintegrated along with most of Watkins and the boat.

There was a moment of total silence. I noticed Surl carrying the wounded York towards the other boat. Nothing else moved.

Brasenose was the first to recover. 'You fool! We could have taken him. Griffin's gone.'

He gave Mendale an evil look, turned on his heel and marched off across the sand. Mendale slowly followed him. Nobody looked back.

When we returned to the house Mendale had revived one of the Trinidadians and was giving him a lesson in survival.

'You'd better hope nobody heard all the noise,' Mendale was saying. 'If the police find those bodies you're going to have a hard job explaining what happened. Now you and your friend dig a big pit and bury them. Or even better bundle them up into a fridge or something and dump it way out to sea. Got that?'

The man said nothing. Dropping his Colt automatic into its Hardy-Cooper spring shoulder holster Mendale announced that it was time for the Navy to take him home. 'We'll drop what's left of comrade Watkins en route, death in the line of duty and all that.' He turned to Surl. 'Clive, you clean up things at the house we rented and get off the island by the first plane.'

Mendale collected all the guns as casually as if he were out buying bread. We walked back to the remaining boat with him. A few pieces of wreckage were the only signs that another boat had been here moments earlier. York was lying in the boat and Mendale placed a surprisingly gentle hand on York's wrist. 'Not as bad as I'd feared,' he said, 'let's get him out to the ship. Thomas, you and Julia ditch the car and leave the keys inside. Stay at the hotel for the rest of the week and act like tourists. Keep an eye on what's happening here but don't arouse any suspicions. OK?'

We both nodded.

'What about Justin Brasenose?' Julia asked.

'Don't worry about him, he'll calm down. This is good news for the Americans. They don't want the physical Interrogator back, they've probably made another prototype already, they just wanted to make sure the Russians didn't get hold of it. I should imagine Justin is halfway to the airport and is already composing a report demonstrating that despite the DIS making a mess of everything, due to his own heroic efforts he was able to stop the Griffin Interrogator falling into Russian hands.'

Julia and I returned to the car as the little boat chugged out towards the Leander class frigate now visible to the west.

We left the car a good mile from the hotel and walked back along the beach, hand in hand, too shattered to talk.

The sea beat gently on to the sand. A copper-rumped hummingbird hung in front of a bush, bobbing its brilliant green head and curved beak at the dew-covered flowers. The sun cast palm tree-shaped shadows across our path.

The operation had been a success, but the patient died. We had lost the Griffin Interrogator.

It was as if Julia had been reading my thoughts. 'It's in Portland,' she said.

'What is?'

'The Griffin Interrogator. It's at the Admiralty Underwater Weapons Establishment, Portland. My uncle had the Navy mock up an imitation. I swapped it for the real one at The Drake after we grabbed Kardosov. That's what Budermann took off you in Chicago. I told Mendale before we went into the villa.'

'You could have told me.'

'Trust has to be earned. It takes time, like love.'

Julia was right. It took me nearly three years to convince her to marry me.

AFTERWORD

In May 1985 the FBI uncovered a spy ring that had been operating since 1967. Four Americans with between them access to an enormous range of US Naval secrets had been paid hundreds of thousands of dollars to spy for the Soviet Union. The Griffin Interrogator is fictional but based on real technology of the period, technology the US considered secret but which it transpired had been comprehensively betrayed to the Russians.

The character of the arms-dealing war criminal Adolpho da Costa Martines is fictional but in part I drew on the post-war story of the 'Butcher of Lyon' Klaus Barbie.

Barbie was in charge of the Gestapo in Lyon and responsible for the deaths of around 14000 in his cells or deported to concentration camps. He personally tortured hundreds to death in indescribably sadistic ways. He was arrested after the war by the British and passed on to the US Army Counterintelligence Corps. Despite being sentenced to death in absentia by a French court the US authorities refused to hand him over to France and instead arranged a new life for him in Bolivia as an arms dealer and spy for both the American CIA and West German BND.

In 1972 the French media discovered his whereabouts and France demanded his extradition. Due to Barbie's close connections with the Bolivian military these demands were rejected. In 1980 Barbie feared that a new government might accede to the French demands and in July allegedly participated in the so-called Cocaine Coup, a short-lived military coup by extreme right-wing officers supported by the CIA and funded by local drugs barons. In 1983 a newly elected democratic government finally arrested Barbie and he was extradited to France, where he was sentenced to life imprisonment. He died in prison in 1991.

Most of the Nazi war criminals who used the so-called 'ratlines', often travelling on identity papers provided by sympathisers in the Vatican, went to Argentina but up to 2 000 started new lives in Brazil. The most infamous was Doctor Josef Mengele, who had performed barbaric experiments on inmates at Auschwitz, and who drowned off a Brazilian beach in 1979.

Israeli agents actively pursued such men. Most famously Adolf Eichmann was kidnapped in Argentina in 1960 and subsequently tried and executed in Israel. In Brazil at the time of this novel the Israelis were hard on the trail of Gustav Wagner, one of the most sadistic of all the concentration camp commanders. He was eventually arrested in 1978 and subjected to extradition requests by Israel, Poland, West Germany and Austria. The Brazilian authorities rejected all the requests and Wagner was released. In October 1980 he was found dead in Sao Paulo with a knife in his chest.

ACKNOWLEDGEMENTS

Many years ago, when I was working for a former Director General of Defence Intelligence, I started writing a spy story, *The Griffin Interrogator*. I finished it in South America but couldn't find a publisher.

Thirty years and a lifetime of experience later I returned to that first manuscript and recoiled in horror at the shallow characters, casual sexism and improbable plot twists. I threw most of it away and started again. The result was the first draft of *Awakening of Spies*. My former Penguin colleague Mike Bryan cast a critical eye over it and suggested it needed rigorous editing. I was fortunate to be recommended to Bill Massey, who provided a very full and potentially dispiriting editorial review. For a second time chunks of manuscript were discarded, plot lines simplified and characters fleshed out or dumped altogether.

Then bookseller extraordinaire Peter Snell introduced me to Clare Christian at RedDoor. The team at RedDoor, Clare, Anna Burtt, Heather Boisseau and Lizzie Lewis have been fantastic. I owe them an enormous debt of gratitude.

My other even larger debt is due to my wife Liz. When Liz and I met at university and decided to get married her father had other ideas. We went our separate ways. It was only our meeting again, decades later, that prompted me to look out that very first manuscript. It is above all thanks to Liz's encouragement, guidance and unfailing optimism that Thomas and Julia Dylan have survived onto the printed page.

THE DYLAN SERIES

Families
of Spies

Brian
Landers

7th JULY 1977

Eveline 'Bunny' Sadeghi was smiling happily as she sailed to her death.

The sun had been rising behind them as they left the harbour at Sami yesterday. Now a glorious sunset was welcoming them to Syracuse, only an hour away. The winds had held steady and they had the sea to themselves. As they sailed westwards across the Ionian Sea there seemed to be more planes going their way than ships. Her brother-in-law's yacht, *Mahsheed*, was not as sturdy as her own beloved *Bunny Hopper*, which she had left safely moored at home on the Solent, but it was a lot more comfortable. As they approached their destination, her husband Davoud was down below fixing a welcome gin and tonic.

Bunny had enjoyed their few days in Kefalonia although Davoud's brother, Behzad, was not an easy man. His villa, some miles inland from Sami, enjoyed spectacular views but she was never able to completely relax there. The isolation was total. Despite the heat of the sun the villa always seemed cold, the accommodation whilst spacious was rough and masculine.

Behzad seemed to have no need for female company, he shared the villa only with his driver, and Shahryar whose role never seemed clear. Two women from the village came in to cook and clean but Bunny had never seen Behzad talk to them, hardly surprising as he seemed to have made no effort to learn Greek and they could certainly not speak Farsi.

On Sundays, which the two women had off, Shahryar would disappear somewhere and return with a parcel of books and letters and a mountain of kebabs and rice he had presumably picked up in the village taverna. Behzad certainly read voraciously and Bunny enjoyed their conversations about opera or Russian literature, but sooner or later Behzad always turned to politics and her heart would sink. It was not a subject that gripped her at the best of times and it brought out the worst in her brother-in-law. Behzad's paranoia would be comical if it were not so overpowering. Everyone was out to get him. Usually it was the Shah's secret police, the SAVAK. He insisted that when he was at home in Paris they kept him under constant surveillance. Here on the island SAVAK apparently had paid informants everywhere. And if it wasn't SAVAK it was the Israelis, and if not them the American CIA or even, heaven forbid, the British.

288

She had asked her brother, who was now something high up in Intelligence, whether there could be any truth in any of it. It had been just ten days ago at their niece's wedding. Gordon had just laughed and said that he could imagine all sorts of conspiracies in the feuding world of Iranian exiles but one thing he could guarantee was that the Shah did not maintain a nest of spies on an inconsequential Greek island in the Ionian Sea.

Bunny's thought drifted in a different direction. It had been a lovely wedding. Julia was her favourite niece and the last to marry. Her new husband was not at all what Bunny would have expected, a minor civil servant of undistinguished pedigree.

'Thomas has a First from Durham and is fluent in four languages,' Julia had indignantly proclaimed after deciding that Bunny was insufficiently welcoming.

Certainly his wedding speech had been surprisingly impressive and genuinely amusing. Whether he took after his pugnaciously argumentative father or rather dreary Westcountry mother, time would tell.

Julia had looked enchanted and enchanting. Bunny smiled broadly at the memory, tightening the mainsail as the wind had dropped.

Right ahead she spotted a small fishing boat seemingly becalmed. As she drew closer Bunny could see two men standing by the tiny wheelhouse, looking in her direction, and another man inside. She waved but there was no cheery response. As the boats came closer, perhaps eight or ten yards apart, the fishing boat's engine sprang into life. Bunny was startled and instinctively steered away. She looked up to see one of the men point his hand at her, but it was not just his hand. She saw the gun just as it fired and registered the thought 'Pirates' in the instant before the bullet struck her thigh.

The force of the bullet knocked her back against the tiller and the yacht slewed around directly towards the other boat. Davoud, emerging with two gin and tonics, was thrown on to his side. His first thought was that they had crashed into something. Then someone seemed to have thrown a cricket ball at him. He didn't have time to register that it was not a cricket ball: the grenade exploded with such force that yacht, crew and very nearly their attackers disappeared in a storm of splintered wood, metal and shredded sail.

ABOUT THE AUTHOR

After giving up on an academic career, and deciding not to join the government spy agency GCHQ, Brian Landers helped a former Director General of Defence Intelligence and a motley collection of ex-spooks set up a political intelligence unit in the City of London. Out of that experience sprang the character of Thomas Dylan, a novice who over the years progresses through the labyrinthine world of British Intelligence.

Brian Landers has lived in various parts of North and South America and Europe. He has worked in every corner of the globe from Beirut to Bali, Cape Town to Warsaw and points in between, and in industries as varied as insurance, family planning, retailing, manufacturing and management consultancy. He saw the inside of more prisons than most during three years as a director of HM Prison Service. He has a Politics Degree from the University of Exeter and an MBA from London Business School. In his spare time he helped set up the Financial Ombudsman Service, served on the boards of Amnesty UK and the Royal Armouries, and was Chairman of Companies House.

Landers subsidised his university bar bills by writing a column for the local paper and since then has written articles for various journals, newspapers and websites. As a director of Waterstones and later Penguin his passion for writing was rekindled. His first book, *Empires Apart*, published in the UK, US and India, was a history of the Russian and American Empires. His next book was going to be *Trump, Putin and the Lessons of History* but the subject was so depressing that he turned to fiction.

In 2018 Brian Landers was awarded an OBE in the Queen's Birthday Honours.

brianlanders.co.uk

Find out more about RedDoor
Press and sign up to our
newsletter to hear about our
latest releases, author events,
exciting **competitions**
and more at

reddoorpress.co.uk

YOU CAN ALSO FOLLOW US:

 @RedDoorBooks

 Facebook.com/RedDoorPress

 @RedDoorBooks